The es<del>tate</del> <del>…</del> ornate wrought iron ga<del>te</del> <del>…</del> bold eagles perched, four feet tall. On the gate, Winston viewed the centuries old Todd coat of arms which shone in gold-leaf splendor. He pulled up the reins, feeling a sense of pride and sorrow as he studied the symbol of family honor and loyalty.

Distant Darkness pranced in place, a prince of a horse, sopping wet, foaming at the mouth, and still eager to please his master's capricious moods.

"You're a grand horse," Winston whispered, patting him on the neck. "You deserve better than I'm giving you."

Distant Darkness, who had settled down with Winston's calming words, now perked his ears and turned around without being coaxed. Winston heard the sound of hooves and allowed Distant Darkness free rein.

The sun hit Winston directly in the eyes. Not until she was upon him did he realize the rider was a woman and was in command of one of the two most spirited horses at Windsor Royal. She had taken off her black riding hat and her waist-length honey blonde hair almost brushed against the back of her saddle.

"You must be Miss Darnley," he called out.

Winston Todd was the last person Diana Darnley wanted to see. But once he rode out onto the drive, her willful side dared her to continue her course. Winston looked like one who was coming out of a deep sleep. His eyes were glazed over, and the tension showed in the lines on his forehead. This was not lost on Diana as she walked Midnight up to within feet of Distant Darkness.

INHERIT THE STORM

Pamela Edwards

Tudor Publishing Company
New York and Los Angeles

Tudor Publishing Company

ISBN: 0-944276-14-8

Printed in the United States of America

First Tudor printing—August 1988

To Sam Weisbord—in loving memory.
To my mother and father, Marge and
John Edwards.

CHAPTER I

On the morning of June 7, 1914, Winston Jason Todd II yanked the reins from the stable boy, Jim. Mounting Distant Darkness, he raced the thoroughbred down the stable corridor nearly knocking down one of the grooms. Out the oaken stable door they flew, leaving dust and debris to hit Diana Darnley head-on. She gasped for breath and coughed.

'Someone needs to be taught some manners,' she thought irritably, brushing off her riding habit. Then she squinted against the blazing sun to see who the rider was heading over the great lawn.

Winston's six-foot-two-inch frame was lean and muscular, his face clean shaven, his black hair cut short. He was a fine figure in the English saddle, his body tense against the wind, his black boots shining as bright as the highly polished brass buttons that dotted the front of his navy blue riding coat.

Diana had never met Winston, but she had seen his picture on the society page. 'He looks like a gentleman,' she thought, 'but he isn't acting like one.'

In clear view of the hundreds of guests gathered on

Windsor Royal's veranda, Distant Darkness flew in a thunder of hooves over the great lawn as Winston repeatedly crashed his crop over the right flank of the fastest horse in Westchester County.

Diana heard the murmurs of disapproval coming from Windsor Royal's veranda. Apparently, she wasn't alone in thinking that the heir apparent to W.J. Todd's vast fortune was soiling his gentlemanly qualities and whatever graces he had inherited from his English aristocratic ancestors, who had crossed the Atlantic in 1701.

From what Diana had learned from her father, Sterling Darnley, the Todd Gala had opened the New York social season for twenty-five years. While W.J. was alive, the three days of festivities had begun with an equestrian show. Sterling Darnley had participated in the first show in 1889 and so impressed the grand patriarch with his riding, that W.J. had befriended him and eventually became Sterling's mentor.

Now one of America's foremost landbarons, Diana's father had taken Winston, W.J.'s great-great-grandson, under his wing. She supposed Sterling's partiality to Winston stemmed from nostalgia. But Winston's behavior contradicted the spirit of what had brought Sterling Darnley and W.J. together.

She shook her head in annoyance and entered the bowels of the stable. Blinded by the sun, she was unaware of the figure before her until they collided.

"Hey, why don't you watch where you're going!" the young boy, Jim, sputtered.

He sat on the cobblestones ready to elaborate until he raised his eyes to a woman's slender ankles and a skirt hovering at mid-calf. His eyes continued up her body to a handsome black coat buttoned at the waist, and the scarf to her white high-necked blouse which displayed a radiant emerald brooch. White silk cuffs peeked out from beneath black coatsleeves partially covering her gloved hands, one of which was extended out to help him up.

"I'm so sorry, Jim."

He hesitated, flushing, feeling foolish that a woman had knocked him down. Pride told him to get up on his own. Being polite, he extended his hand. She grasped it and pulled him to his feet.

She was surprisingly strong for one so thin, and she had the greenest eyes he had ever seen. Her hair was tucked beneath a black riding hat. The chignon pinned at the nape of her neck was a shiny golden blonde. Her skin was smooth as silk, and her generous lips opened in a smile that showed remarkably white teeth.

'She's a prize thoroughbred,' Jim thought in his own vernacular.

The gossip around Windsor Royal was that Robert Todd, Winston's father, was most impressed by seventeen-year-old Miss Darnley.

'This must be her!' Jim thought, and he looked at her anew, for the Darnleys bred some of the finest thorough-breds in the country at the Darnley Ranch in Kentucky.

The order had come from the main house to get the spirited Midnight ready for Diana. Winston Todd had recently bought the magnificent thoroughbred from Sterling Darnley. The sire was a prestigious addition to Windsor Royal's stables.

"Mr. Robert Todd thinks you're really something!" Jim blurted out. "So does my father. He's Harris Johnson, head of the household staff!"

Diana laughed softly. "They do, do they."

"Oh, yes, Miss Darnley! I'll get Midnight for you. Be right back!"

Diana watched young Jim run down the stable corridor. From their stalls, most of the horses stuck out their heads to watch him with keen interest. Jim halted at the side of his older brother, the stable foreman, who had opened Midnight's stall.

"I'll take him, Joseph!"

Jim led Midnight down the corridor past stable hands and grooms. The thoroughbred pranced rebelliously, nodding his head and skirting from side to side. The young boy talked to him gently, and the spirited Midnight calmed. It was obvious he favored Jim and few others.

'The boy's so much like Howard,' Diana thought. Her brother, Howard Darnley, was a writer and in her father's disfavor. Their conflict seemed accentuated now that Winston had become a favorite of Sterling's. Diana's heart swelled with anger.

Although only twenty-five, Winston had recently been

appointed President of Todd Enterprises. Never having met Winston, Diana imagined that he was a spoiled arrogant fop who had been handed position and power and had somehow manipulated his way into her father's life.

It was times like this that Diana wished her mother were still alive. Sara Darnley had understood her son's gentle ways and had a knack for keeping the peace between her husband and son.

"Here we are, Miss Darnley!" Jim beamed.

Diana shoved her private thoughts aside and ruffled the boy's hair. "You're a fine lad, Jim. Thank you."

Jim grinned from ear to ear like an endearing little fool while Midnight tugged at his arm. When he handed over Midnight's reins to Diana, the thoroughbred playfully nuzzled up against her neck. She patted him affectionately and winked at Jim.

"If you treat an animal nicely, he's easy to handle, don't you think?"

"Yeah," young Jim said in awe.

All the stable hands watched the beautiful blonde lady mount Midnight without assistance, walk the horse out of the stable door, and head west, in the opposite direction from Winston.

Two miles through the forest Winston approached Mayfair Road. Out on the land alone, riding among the red oak, white oak, and elm, Winston tried to calm down. This land was all he had to hold on to. Here, where his father seldom set foot, he had staked his territorial rights.

'Why didn't I stay in Manhattan at Todd Enterprises, the Todd Gala be damned?' he wondered. But then he would have missed Sterling Darnley. By now Sterling had probably heard about his escapades of this morning. The thought filled Winston with embarrassment.

"I met with Walter Kent last night," he had told his father just an hour ago. "His option is up. He's going to withdraw his offer!"

They were alone in the Renaissance Room and Robert had closed *The Call of the Wild*. "You know our funds at Todd Enterprises are limited. Our board has to approve the Kent Oil deal. It takes time—my hands are tied."

"You could demand their approval if you wanted to. I've

seen you go after what you want."

"And what do I want, Winston?"

"Isn't it obvious? With you at the helm, Todd Enterprises has staggered into the twentieth century. Now you're telling everyone in the business community about W.J.'s will and his wish that I marry and have a child before I become chairman. Walter Kent joked about it. No one will take me seriously after what you've done!"

On his way out the door, Winston had cursed his father loudly and wished W.J. had outlived yet another generation of Todds. Then he wouldn't be in this bind.

The estate of Windsor Royal was shielded by an ornate wrought iron gate. Atop massive stone pillars, bold eagles perched, four feet tall. On the gate, Winston viewed the centuries old Todd coat of arms which shone in gold-leaf splendor. He pulled up the reins, feeling a sense of pride and sorrow as he studied the symbol of family, honor, and loyalty.

Distant Darkness pranced in place, a prince of a horse, sopping wet, foaming at the mouth, and still eager to please his master's capricious moods.

"You're a grand horse," Winston whispered, patting him on the neck. "You deserve better than I'm giving you."

Distant Darkness, who had settled down with Winston's calming words, now perked his ears and turned around without being coaxed. Winston heard the sound of hooves and allowed Distant Darkness free rein.

The sun hit Winston directly in his eyes. Not until she was upon him did he realize the rider was a woman and was in command of one of the two most spirited horses at Windsor Royal. She had taken off her black riding hat and her waist-length honey blonde hair almost brushed against the back of her saddle. Startled as he was by her tailored black riding habit, complete with pants, which no woman at Windsor Royal had ever worn, he was impressed with her femininity.

"You must be Miss Darnley," he called out.

Winston Todd was the last person Diana Darnley wanted to see. But once he rode out onto the drive, her willful side dared her to continue her course. Winston looked like one who was coming out of a deep sleep. His eyes were glazed over, and the tension showed in the lines on his forehead. This was not lost on Diana as she walked Midnight up to within feet of Distant Darkness.

"Yes, Mr. Todd. I'm Diana Darnley."

"What are you doing out here by yourself?"

"Isn't it obvious?" she said pleasantly. "I'm riding."

Winston shook his head in exasperation. "You didn't have to do as he asked."

"What are you talking about?"

"My father. He asked you to come out here, didn't he?"

"No."

"Wait a minute. I thought . . ."

Diana laughed softly. "I'm happy I have this opportunity to dispel your fears."

"So, your father has talked to you as mine has to me?"

"Oh yes, but unlike your father, he is not looking for someone whom I may marry."

As soon as she said the words, she regretted them. Winston's grip tightened around the reins. His body stiffened, and the brooding glint in his eyes intensified beneath the shadow of his commanding eyebrows. Although she had her own reasons for being wary of Winston, she had not meant to be so blunt.

"But of course," she continued, "you would never be forced into such an important decision. If you married for the chairman's seat, you'd ultimately hate your wife for having that power over you."

"You're very good, Miss Darnley. No wonder your father likes you nearby."

"And you're very good, too, Mr. Todd."

"Why is that?"

"You're being so pleasant when I know what you really think of me. I heard you wanted to buy my land in Manhattan."

"You get right to the point. I like that. Sure, I was surprised you owned the land. First, you're a woman. Second, you're only seventeen. What would you know about business?"

"You are aware that we're living in the twentieth century?"

"I'm well aware of it. It's you who doesn't have a clue."

Diana laughed in spite of herself. "I've been told that countless times."

"Then you don't listen very well, do you."

"It depends to whom I'm listening," Diana said, holding

her temper.

He mulled this over as Diana calmed Midnight, who had sniffed the air once too often and showed his displeasure at Distant Darkness's close proximity. Winston noted that she had ridden Midnight hard. His reddish brown coat gleamed with sweat, although his mouth was not foaming like Distant Darkness. Winston felt a twinge of remorse. Where she had ridden Midnight with compassion, he had whipped his horse to exhaustion. What was this madness that possessed him?

"Do you listen to Walter Kent?" he asked at last.

'What does Walter Kent have to do with this?' Diana wondered silently.

Winston's eyes had taken on a faraway gaze. He seemed totally disoriented. Automatically, Diana softened her approach.

"Yes, Walter is a good friend."

"Is that all?" Winston demanded.

Diana bristled. Winston now seemed in total control. Was he a chameleon? She wanted to say, "It's really none of your business, Mr. Todd," but instead she thought it better to take her leave.

"I've interrupted you, Mr. Todd," she said, "and you've been very generous with your time. I'll just be on my way."

To Winston's surprise, Diana turned Midnight around. She was independent and headstrong, qualities Winston admired in a man and disliked in a woman—but she was Sterling's daughter.

"You weren't interrupting me," he said, guiding Distant Darkness alongside Midnight. They rode together up the drive shaded with red and white oak. "What have you been doing since you got here?" he asked.

Winston appeared confused and depressed again. His moods were unpredictable, with too many highs and lows to fathom. Why didn't he leave her alone?

"On my first day," she said, being polite, "your father showed me Windsor Royal. He also talked about you."

Winston gritted his teeth. Just imagining his father courting Diana for him filled him with embarrassment. "I'm surprised he didn't put an engagement ring on your finger on my behalf."

Diana laughed. "You're joking, of course."

Winston tried to smile, but failed. "You don't know my

father."

They had traveled up a quarter mile to the felled forest and pulled up their reins. Windsor Royal was in full view. Sitting majestically on a hill, the mansion was unobstructed by trees. Even from a mile and a half distance, the mansion's eight hundred and fifty foot façade, made of Indiana limestone with a gray slate roof, looked colossal. The four-thousand-acre Windsor Royal was complete with its own private railroad, general store, cemetery, stables, and reservoir.

"It will all be yours one day," W.J. had told Winston at this very spot when Winston was twelve. But every time Winston saw Windsor Royal he was reminded he still was not yet master of all that was rightfully his.

"Why isn't my father more like yours?" Winston asked, more to himself than to Diana. "Your father and W.J. earned their own fortunes on their own terms. I admire them for that. W.J. was a tough old guy who just hung on to life to find a successor. He outlived his two sons killed during the Civil War and his grandson who died of consumption in 1880. I think he was desperate by the time I was born. He insisted that my mother give birth here at Windsor Royal. Somehow he was convinced that I'd break the Todd curse and then he could die in peace. You see, every other generation of Todds was born weak and sickly. Those like my father were gentleman bred to read and write and reluctantly manage business affairs. None of them but W.J. had any initiative at all!"

Diana sighed in bewilderment. "Why don't you just accept your father the way he is?"

"Why should I if he isn't loyal to the Todd heritage?"

"Maybe he's loyal in his own way."

"But he has to contribute, by God! You know about W.J.'s will."

"Yes, I do and so do most of the guests. You saw to that when you argued with your father this morning. Everyone on the veranda heard you."

"So what. It's nothing new to them. Father's already made our personal problems a public curiosity. What's important is that he step down as chairman before our empire is ruined."

"Having met your father, I'm sure he'd probably love to

step down, but there's a reason why W.J. made up his will that way. Maybe your father understands why. Have you asked him?"

"Why would I ask him about anything so important!"

"You've never discussed any of this with your father?"

"He's an incompetent fool!" Winston said darkly.

Diana was taken back. "You don't mean that. You love him, don't you, Winston?"

Winston seldom heard the word love. That was what weak men felt. Love was for the weak—for men like his father and women like her!

"What is this, some feminine ploy? What does love have to do with business?"

"I don't like your tone or your insinuation, Mr. Todd," Diana said, unleashing an immediate anger. "We were talking about W.J.'s will and your father. One's value isn't justified only by success in business! Your father's a man, too, you know. Maybe you should think about that!"

"W.J. thought . . ." Winston started.

"I'm tired of hearing about W.J. He's dead. Why can't you live your own life and think for yourself?"

"I can't because my father's enforcing W.J.'s will!" Winston stormed. "Haven't you been listening, or are you just plain ignorant!"

'Why did I ever feel sorry for him?' she wondered. 'I must have been out of my mind!'

"It's obvious to me that W.J. wanted you to learn to accept responsibility for family. You don't know the first thing about love, women, or children. Why, you don't have any feelings at all except where you think it counts—in business. Besides that, you're an arrogant, rude ingrate!"

"Women!" Winston sputtered in absolute frustration. "I should have known better than to talk to you! I was right when I talked to your father. You won't do anything with that land. You might as well sell it!"

Spurring Distant Darkness into action, Winston galloped up the drive, leaving Diana to control Midnight who was eager to race.

'You're going to be sorry you said that,' Diana told Winston in her thoughts. 'Wait until you see what I do with that land. You'll be very sorry you said that!'

CHAPTER II

Winston marched through the wide halls of Windsor Royal. Eyes ablaze, hair tousled, he swung his riding crop in cadence with his step. His riding boots clicked against the marble floor leaving a trail of dust in his stead.

Passing the Billard Room, with the carved oak billiard table and paneled walls, he took a shortcut through the Renaissance Room without a glance at the thirty years of accumulated treasures of eighteen-century artists and stopped abruptly on the Garden Room threshold.

A few guests remained after lunch at round tables draped in damask linen. Beyond the wide round columns in a corner alcove, which looked out over a brook and the golf course, Winston spotted Sterling sitting alone reading the New York *Times*.

Few men commanded Sterling Darnley's respect. The perspicacious sexagenarian looked like everyone's loving grandfather. Impeccably dressed, usually in a navy blue suit, white shirt, and striped tie, Sterling had an aura of gentleness that set his few friends, "the solid people," as he liked to call them, at ease. Everyone else kept their distance. Sterling's reserve could be deadly.

He met Winston halfway across the room and guided him back out into the hall. "You look wildly out of sorts this morning, Winston. Don't you have enough trouble without showing everyone how upset you are? That stunt you pulled with Distant Darkness before breakfast wasn't very smart."

"I suppose not."

Sterling sighed. "What's the matter now?"

"I need to talk. It's personal."

For over a year, Sterling had been trying to cultivate Winston's trust. Whatever had prompted Winston to seek him out now? Fortunately, Sterling had already spoken to Robert Todd. Although Winston had solid objections against his father, Robert had his side of the story. With all the information before him, Sterling was better equipped to help W.J.'s great-great-grandson.

"Let's go to my suite," Sterling suggested.

While they walked through Windsor Royal, Sterling reflected on Robert's words to him.

"I blame myself," Robert had said. "Winston needed guidance. Since I didn't have his respect, I never had his attention. Winston knows you were a favorite of W.J.'s. You're my son's only confidant. If it wouldn't be an imposition, I'd like to enlist your help as our mediator. I love my son and want him to be happy."

Never before had Sterling heard a father talk so honestly and openly about his relationship with his son. He in turn confessed to Robert that he and his own son were not on the best of terms. Their hour-long conversation had benefitted them both.

Winston had reserved the largest of Windsor Royal's twenty guest suites for Sterling and Diana. It was decorated with antiques and an oriental rug of vivid red trimmed in gold and black braids. The oak-paneled parlor, complete with a fireplace and view of Windsor Royal's courtyard, was reminiscent of an English men's club.

"Are you comfortable here?" Winston asked, once they were inside.

"Yes, it's a handsome suite, Winston. Thank you for taking special care to make us comfortable," Sterling said, settling down on the leather tufted sofa. "Join me. I'm sure we can sort out your problems quickly. There's really a very simple solution."

"Simple?" Winston eagerly took a chair. "I'm ready for some quick answers . . . I . . ."

Diana entered the room and Winston stood.

Earlier, when riding Midnight, Diana's figure had been hidden beneath her coat. She seemed taller than he had imagined, her figure more voluptuous. The open coat fell away from an ample bosom, revealing a slender waist. Her honey-blonde hair flowed down behind her back and swayed gently over rounded hips as she closed the door. When again she faced him, he noticed her classic facial features and eyes so green they were almost hypnotic. Why hadn't he noticed her beauty earlier? Many women had traveled through his life, but Diana was the most beautiful he had ever seen.

"Winston," Sterling said, proudly, "this is my daughter . . ."

"Winston and I met earlier when we were riding, Father. Mr. Todd, it seems as though I'm continually interrupting you. When you're through, I'd like to talk to you, Father." Diana started across the room.

"I apologize for being rude earlier," Winston said, barring her access to the bedroom.

"That's very kind of you."

"You don't sound like you're accepting my apology."

"Maybe it's because I'm not."

Winston stared down at Diana's defiant expression and was so attracted to her that he wanted her nearby. "I know you deserve an explanation. Join us," he said, surprising himself.

"Don't just stand there, Diana," Sterling said from the couch. "Please, come over here. I want to hear more about your meeting."

Diana held Winston's eyes as she said, "I'd rather not." But when she finally glanced at Sterling and saw his displeasure, she said, "Very well, Father," and immediately crossed the room.

"Would you like to tell me why you're angry?" Sterling asked her when she was seated beside him.

Diana shook her head. Sterling readjusted himself on the couch to seek out Winston. The young man had his back to him and was facing the window.

"All right," he declared. "I'll let it be between the two of you. Why don't you continue, Winston. Or better yet, begin. Start with your father."

Winston walked over to them and looked down at Diana. "I'm going to tell your father just what I told you."

Diana took off her gloves without a glance in his direction. "Be my guest."

"Sterling, your daughter knows how to try my patience!"

"I can see that, Winston," Sterling said, amused. "I have to warn you, Diana's quite capable of taking care of herself when provoked. Now what about your father?"

Winston flopped into a chair, crossed his legs, and looked downright miserable. "My father," he said, "also makes me angry. When W.J. died in 1901, the Reconstruction and Industrial Eras had catapulted the United States into the position of the leading industrial power in the world. W.J. had left express instruction for my father to capitalize on all the new industries from transportation, to steel, to cars, to oil. I was only twelve, but I understood what W.J. wanted.

"By the time I went to Harvard, I was pleading with my father to expand W.J. Oil. He refused, professing he was inhibited from any innovation by W.J.'s will." Winston leaned forward, his arms on his knees. "Sterling, you and I know if W.J. had been in this bind, he would have been resourceful." He dropped back against the chair, flipping his hand disrespectfully. "But Father isn't W.J. and I'm ashamed he is my father."

Diana raised her eyes.

"Yes, I'm ashamed," Winston repeated. "My father isn't a man of initiative. He held on to W.J.'s tiny oil company, the railroad stock, the shipping line, the tool and chemical companies and maintained the status quo."

"As I said earlier, I'm sure your father has many fine qualities even if he isn't an industrial visionary," Diana said.

"I think your brother would get along better with him than I do."

"Maybe he would, and that would be a compliment to Howard, not to you. Howard's passion for the arts is equal to your obsession with business, I'll assure you of that."

"True enough, darling," Sterling interjected. "But your brother doesn't work hard at his art. He ponders the world instead of participating in it. That's why you're executor of my will."

"She's executor of your will?" Winston stammered.

Diana slapped her gloves on the table. "Father, I should know better than to take what he says personally, but it's difficult because he's so ignorant!"

"Diana," Sterling said, amused, "would you please behave." He noticed Winston's irritation. "She never lets me get away with anything, nor anyone else for that matter."

"Is that a compliment?" Winston asked.

"No," Diana piped up. "My father was insulting me."

Sterling laughed uproariously. "Diana, Diana, you have my disposition coated with your mother's sweetness." He shook his finger at her. "I thought I taught you better. Emotion, with a man like Winston, will get you nowhere. He's going to test your reasoning power and your patience. If you can deal with him, you can deal with any man. You need to develop that savvy we've talked about. Remember, you have big plans for that land in Manhattan."

"Yes, Father," Diana said, digesting every word.

"What plans?" Winston demanded. "I'd still like to buy the parcel. It's right next to my parcel, which is far larger. I want to build . . ."

"Don't talk to me," Sterling interrupted. "You made that mistake once before. It's Diana's land. But save that for later. Let's finish our conversation first."

Winston expected to see Diana smiling triumphantly. Instead he was met with a curious open stare. Sterling had tamed her right before his very eyes. Winston tried to figure out just how Sterling had done it, but Sterling asked him a question about his mother and the thought was forgotten.

"My mother? I never liked her, sir."

"Why? Because you never knew her?"

"Probably. She deserted my father when I was six."

"Yes, I know all about that. Your father says he made a mistake. He married a woman who didn't feel as he did about family. She tried to keep you away from W.J."

"I didn't know that."

"Your father should have told you."

"Why didn't he?"

"Would you have believed him?"

"Probably not."

"Maybe that's the reason. Why do you believe it now?"

"Possibly because you do."

"He thought you might say that. It says something for him, don't you think? I know you and your father disagreed conceptually about W.J.'s value of things, but let me try to clarify your father's position. I'll use my own life as an example."

Sterling left the couch and walked over to the fireplace and absently leaned an arm on the mantle, considering how to begin. "I loved my wife, Sara. She was my confidant, my partner." He glanced at Winston. "Yes, she was, Winston. Believe it or not, W.J. adored his wife, too. It's all in those journals of his where he set out the history of your family. Have you read them?"

"Of course I've read them."

Sterling rejoined them. "Then you should know—I see, you glossed over the family sections and got right down to business. Well, look again. You'll see what I mean. W.J. adored his wife. He worked for family, just like I do. Diana's my right hand. Yes, she is, Winston. Believe it or not— woman and all—Diana is an invaluable part of my life and my business. Grant you my son is in my disfavor, but I do love him, Winston. Family. That's what I work for. That's what W.J. worked for. To my mind, your father is right. Of course, a company doesn't talk back, but it doesn't hold and comfort you either."

"I still don't see what this has to do with business."

"It doesn't per se," Sterling said. "It has to do with the Todd name, the perpetuation of generations—maintaining an empire once you've built it."

Winston pondered the point and then said to Diana, "That's what you were telling me earlier."

Diana nodded.

"Go on," Winston said, groping to understand.

Sterling proceeded. "W.J. thought you were born with a streak of ambition so utterly obsessive that you would walk over anyone. He endorsed such behavior when warranted in business, but never with family members. Especially with one's wife and children."

Winston was totally baffled. "I don't understand."

"You choose a wife, you don't choose your children. Your wife should be a woman you respect and love. How you treat her will guide your children in their future relationships."

Winston shook his head. "I don't want to think about a wife and children. I want to think about Todd Enterprises!"

Sterling's pleasant disposition turned cold. "I thought you wanted to understand why W.J. put that stipulation in his will."

"I do. I do. Oh, all right, have it your way. But my mother and father didn't even have a happy marriage. Why would I want to follow in their footsteps!"

Sterling smiled easily now, his point worth repeating. "As I said, Winston, children can be influenced by their parents. If you don't do better than they did, the Todd line will die with you. If you have a strong relationship with your wife, it will influence your children to have strong relationships with their spouses and perpetuate the Todd line. That's why W.J. put the stipulation in his will. He wanted you to understand the true meaning of a family empire."

"Why should I have to carry all the responsibility? I have enough to do building up Todd Enterprises after all my father's blunders."

Sterling was amused by Winston's unusual but practical logic. "You were born a Todd. That's what comes along with your heritage—all that responsibility, and despite what you think of your father, he is a man worthy of your respect. He has high self-esteem. That's why W.J. was so adamant that your father be your teacher. Unfortunately, W.J. failed to understand that you would not respect a man who didn't share your passion for business. Your father didn't stand a chance. Think about it, Winston. Now it's time to get ready. We have a party to attend."

CHAPTER III

A t 7:00 P.M. the gatekeeper opened the massive wrought iron gates to Windsor Royal. The guests rode through and up the drive illuminated by a new electrical system. In the circular drive, footmen awaited the guests. At Windsor Royal's open door, Winston and Robert prepared to greet them.

"I talked to Sterling," Winston said quietly.

Robert, like Winston, wore a high starched collar with a white tie. His tailored tuxedo was accentuated with a diamond stickpin, diamond studs, and diamond cufflinks. His black hair was thick, white at the sideburns, his black eyebrows sprinkled with white strands. His expression was serene.

"I'm very happy you did. Sterling's a cultured gentleman."

'Cultured!' Winston thought, but for the first time in his life he held his tongue. 'I might find Sterling dynamic, but Father's allowed to have his own opinion.' They just thought differently, as Diana had said.

Robert exuded an inner peace that Winston had never understood and now perceived with curiosity. "I want to apologize, Father. I've given you a very difficult time. Sterling thinks I'm a cad for trying to oust you from the chairman's seat. I'll admit, I was underhanded."

"It's of no consequence as long as we understand one another," Robert said.

Winston was almost disbelieving. For over seven years, he and Raymond Baren, his Harvard chum, had wined and dined Todd executives at Delmonico's, The Stork Club, and Astor Roof. They had talked of Robert's lack of vision and his unwillingness to innovate at Todd Enterprises. The executives had gradually turned against Robert, making him totally ineffectual.

Secretly, Winston had even bought Todd Enterprises stock to pair with the stock he had inherited when W.J. died. Actually, it wasn't Robert who had told everyone about W.J.'s will. Rather, it stemmed from Winston.

When he attempted the takeover, Robert's lawyers told Winston that he had overlooked another stipulation in W.J.'s will. Winston would lose the remainder of W.J.'s inheritance if he proceeded with his plan.

When Winston backed down, everyone in the business community heard about it. Courageously, Robert held on, hoping that Winston would see the wisdom of the two stipulations. Instead, Winston had ignored the meaning of W.J.'s will, and this morning he had blamed Robert for embarrassing him.

"Is that all you want, Father?" Winston asked at last.

"That's all, Winston."

For the life of him, Winston would never understand his father. Yet, he believed Robert and told his father he would do whatever was necessary to make him happy.

"Don't try to make *me* happy, son. Make yourself happy. Then I will be too."

Robert had said that before, and Winston had never listened. "Why is it that your kindness makes me suspicious?"

Robert smiled. "Because you're perceiving my actions from your point of view. You aren't looking at who I am."

Winston's emotions, new as they were, got the best of him. He hugged his father. "That makes you a lot better man than I am."

"That depends on whose perspective you're looking from. Some people would admire you more. We shouldn't care about such things. As long as we love and respect each other, that's all that matters. I would like to see you become chairman as soon as possible, Winston. Truthfully, I'd rather spend my time at our Connecticut estate. Think about it, would you? I'm tired of the business world."

"Think about it!" Winston laughed. "That's all I think about, Father."

"But, hopefully, now with a new perspective?"

Winston nodded. "Yes."

Walter Kent walked up the marble steps. The sophisticated oil man of English descent noticed that Winston and Robert were on the best terms he'd ever seen. He shook each man's hand and graciously told them he was sorry about their deal.

"It's not important, Walter," Winston said grandly. "My father has other ideas."

Walter Kent cleared his throat and nodded, somewhat bewildered, while Winston laughed and Robert smiled. "We're going to have a good time, Father."

Winston enjoyed the following hour. Thinking of his father amiably and viewing the rest of the world with cunning had its advantages. He actually had the time to see the strength in his father's appeal. Robert had that sense of integrity that instilled trust in others. Winston's future business competitors walked through the receiving line, stopping to greet Robert, and divulged more than they should have while Winston eagerly listened.

The slender, tall, bespectacled Mel Christian owned Mel Christian's, an exclusive Manhattan line of specialty stores, which he told Robert he intended to expand. Winston had long received the cold shoulder from Mel, which made him so angry he had ordered Raymond Baren to find out everything about Mel's business and his personal life. As he shook Mel's hand, Winston wondered how Mel had time for business while delicately balancing a wife and four mistresses. One day

Winston intended to use that information against Mel. Winston never forgot a slight and intended to take over Mel's empire one day.

Sid Shore, an old friend of Robert's from Harvard, was in oil. Sid reminded Winston of a day laborer with his broad shoulders and strong square jaw. His company was overextended from mismanagement. Not many people suspected that Sid was an alcoholic. Winston was discreetly buying up shares of Shore Oil. Sid had refused to do business with him because of W.J.'s will.

Harold Dareel, a slight, thin, bald man, had inherited the largest fortune in the country. His grandfather built an empire from the railroad, oil, and steel. Winston shook his hand, knowing Howard was an epileptic. No hard feelings there. The Dareel line would end with Howard. He never planned to have children.

The thought gave Winston a start, and then he chuckled to himself. His newfound knowledge was helping him to reevaluate people.

Winston's friends also came through the receiving line. Raymond Baren, his Phi Beta Kappa henchman, entered. Winston quietly told him about Mel Christian and Sid Shore. Raymond headed off purposefully to find out more information about Mel's expansion and to befriend Sid Shore.

Senator Johnson and Congressman Bates followed Desiree Richards, a Washington socialite, and Winston's eyes and ears in Washington. Diplomats, members of the Cabinet, foreign dignitaries, and ambassadors rounded out the guest list and filed through the receiving line after top brass from the Defense Department dressed in full military uniform.

"I want to compliment you, Winston," Robert said, unaware of Winston's thoughts. "You've never been more charming than you were tonight. Thank you."

"You're very welcome, Father," Winston said, genuinely pleased. "I'm enjoying myself."

Robert looked over the crowd. "I see Sterling and Diana."

Winston placed an arm around his father. "You'll be pleased to hear that this time I don't need a push, Father."

Those guests staying at Windsor Royal had already

spread the gossip about Winston and Diana. The Todds were unique, feted and exaggerated as American royalty in the eyes of New York society. They only lacked a hostess.

Daughters of the Vanderbilts, Goelets, Zimmermans, Goulds, and Thaws had married European royalty. Diana had been courted by bachelors on both continents and had declined their proposals. Few believed the wild Winston and the independent Diana would be a good match.

Diana shocked the crowd with her Paris creation by Poiret. The startling green silk with elegant, dainty red flowers was designed with a slit hobble skirt, cummerbunded waist, and draped top. Her hair was pulled back tight, hardly visible beneath a green turban lined with red flowers. She wore her mother's emerald earrings, perfect stones in drop settings, an emerald bracelet of one hundred carats, and her mother's diamond and emerald ring set in a cluster.

"You're escorting the most beautiful woman here, Sterling," Winston said, joining the Darnleys.

"I'm sure she'd be delighted to hear that," Sterling said, his eyes twinkling.

"Right," Winston said, picking up on the hint. "You look lovely, Diana."

Diana noticed that Winston was sincere. Although she was guarded, she also remembered her father's words from this morning. If she could get along with Winston . . . "Thank you, Winston. I'm so happy you admire modern women."

'That's not what I meant at all,' Winston thought, but he saw her amusement. "This is probably just a natural way of thinking for you, but it's foreign to me."

"I'm sure that was very difficult for you to say. I'm impressed."

"I'll bet you are," Winston said. "Sterling, one day you'll have to tell me how to handle this daughter of yours."

Sterling viewed him in amusement. "Your first lesson: Stop making the same mistake. If you have something to say to Diana, tell her, not me. You know she's capable of giving you a straight answer."

"That's what I'm afraid of." Winston grinned, shaking his head. "Maybe you and I should dance, Diana."

As Winston twirled Diana around the ballroom, she said, "You actually look happy this evening, Winston."

"Business always brings a smile to my lips."

Diana recognized his humor and laughed in delight. "And what is that mind of yours plotting and planning?"

"I'd like to buy this lady's land," he said, holding her closer. "But I hear she plays pretty darn rough."

She spoke softly into his ear while they swayed to the music. "As you have your dreams, Winston, I have mine. The Darnleys have been patrons of the arts for centuries. I intend to build a Cultural Center in honor of my mother's memory and for my father to view with pride."

He looked down into her eyes in surprise. "It's my turn to be impressed."

Still, she saw his unspoken question. "I don't have a price. Money is not the issue. Of course, I intend to make a profit."

"But everyone has a price."

She leaned her head to the left a bit looking at him. "Then name your price for Windsor Royal and all your future Todd holdings."

Winston narrowed his eyes. "I think you've made your point. Come on."

He took her arm and guided her to the veranda and down the stairs out into the rose garden. There he confronted her.

"I don't know much about a woman like you."

"I know," Diana said.

"If I have to get married, at least I'd like to be able to talk to the woman—at least I think I would."

Diana laughed. "You could improve your approach."

"Maybe you're right," Winston conceded. "I was watching you and your father. You respond well to him."

"He's constructive, while you on the other hand are always trying to win a point."

"I see," Winston said thoughtfully. "What else?"

Diana reached out, tentatively at first, and then took his hand. He was startled, then aggressive; and he grabbed her by the arms and tried to kiss her. She pressed her hands to his chest.

"Please don't misunderstand . . ."

Gently, she pushed him away and noted his confusion. They stood apart looking intently at one another. She stepped forward, her heart pounding hard. She placed her arms around his neck and his arms automatically went around her waist. He understood that he was supposed to just hold her. He wondered why, but he complied.

What a peculiar sensation, he thought, just holding a woman. He noticed the weight of her head on his shoulder and the warmth and smell of her and the angle of her shape molded into his. A wondrous sensation came over him, a feeling of being protected and wishing to protect another. He was astounded when he realized that he was smiling.

"What are you doing?" he demanded, pushing her to arm's length.

"You just opened your heart for a moment in friendship."

Winston tried to grasp what she was saying. Then he laughed, helplessly. "You mean I have to be my wife's friend, too!"

"Yes, it would help if you were friends."

"And love her?"

"I know that's a lot to ask," Diana said, amused.

"Oh, no, you aren't asking much, are you, Diana. Friendship, love . . . when do I have time for business?"

"I'm sure you'll figure out a way."

"Would you like to be my guide?"

"Your guide?"

"You have to lead somewhere, Diana. You teach me about love and I'll teach you about business."

"Are you suggesting I don't know anything about business!"

"Hold on, Miss Darnley, I was merely saying . . ."

"I know what you were saying. And you are not the man for me."

"Come on," Winston coaxed. "Let's just hold hands."

"No, Winston. Stop it. I was only trying to help you."

"I need more help. Marry me."

"I'm not interested. Why, I'm not even sure I like you!"

Winston was smiling now, and he held her. She tried to push him away. "It's only friendship, just open your heart in friendship. Isn't that what you said?"

"You're impossible," Diana said, letting him hold her. "But don't think this is going to change my mind."

CHAPTER IV

"**D**iana! Come over here and look at this!"

Against all odds, they had been married for five years. They matched wits, found each other impossible, and loved every minute of it. She was pregnant with their second child, due any day. Yet, the sound of Winston's voice still excited her. How could it be, she thought, in her condition? She smiled mischievously and carefully crossed the veranda.

Her white lace dress fell over her blooming shape. A white ribbon tied in a bow held her shoulder-length hair back from her oval face. About her neck, a single strand of pearls blended with her creamy white skin. The diamond and emerald wedding ring sparkled in the sun as she shaded her eyes with her left hand. Looking beyond the colorful rose garden to the great lawn, she saw Winston and Winston Jason.

Winston rode Distant Darkness. Four-year-old Winston Jason III sat atop a blond, long-maned Shetland pony he had named Jim, after Jim Johnson, who had taken over as head of the stables at thirteen.

Jim's brother, Joseph, had been killed in World War I at Milestone along the Hindenburg Line. As the owner of a munitions company, Winston had earned a special status. He had tried to persuade Howard Darnley to work with him, but Diana's brother had declined and also had died in the Milestone battle. Fortunately, Sterling and Howard had made amends before Howard died. Sterling often told Diana that Robert Todd had done him an invaluable service. She and Sterling missed Howard terribly.

"Mommie, look!"

Diana set aside her painful private thoughts and looked at her son. Winston Jason was a handsome boy, with Winston's thick black hair and those glorious eyebrows. He had her green eyes and generous mouth. Yes, he was the best combination of them both. A fiercely determined, loving, little boy.

He looked like a jockey atop Jim, bouncing up and down, trotting alone down the lawn, decked out in beige jodhpurs and a navy blue coat just like his father's.

She clapped enthusiastically. "That's wonderful, Winston Jason!"

Robert, newly arrived from Connecticut, and Sterling, just in from Newport, joined her at the railing. Winston Jason twisted his curly head to seek Diana's approval. He lost his balance and tumbled to the ground. Within seconds, he sat atop Jim again smiling triumphantly and trotted back to his father.

"I want ten just like him!" Winston shouted.

Father and son returned to the stables, and Robert Todd guided Diana back to her chair. "Winston Jason's a prize."

"So is your son," Sterling added. "He's wonderful to Diana, a good father and an exceptional businessman. Did you see that announcement last week in *Fortune* Magazine? WJ Oil's the number one producer in the country. Winston's passed the Dareels."

"Before coming here, I had to wait in line to fill up my tank at a WJ Gas station," Robert said, sitting down beside Diana. "I should say everyone read the article."

"Winston put in a pump down at the general store," Diana said. "I'll mention to him to put one in at your home, too. I won't take no for an answer. Winston would love to do it."

Sterling glanced at his radiant daughter. Motherhood suited her. "I suppose you had something to do with Winston getting involved with John Stevens and Conrad Coleman."

"She certainly did."

Diana turned awkwardly in her chair. "John! I didn't expect to see you this soon!"

John Stevens, the tall, robust sportsman and Broadway writer-producer strode out onto the veranda with a cigarette between his teeth. Although he was clad in classic attire, his appearance was diverting. Whether his hair was untamable or he just refused to bother with it was unclear. The blondish-brown hair was long and wild and somehow suited him. Although arrogant, he had a potent, dry sense of humor. He and Diana were the closest of friends and unmercifully teased one another. He pulled her out of the chair and she kissed his cheek.

"You're always full of surprises, John," Diana said. "In their twenties, Conrad and John had lived in the same lower east side neighborhood, and still kept in close contact with each other despite Conrad's move to the West Coast.

"Not this trip. He's under a slave-labor contract with MGM. He wanted me to assure you, however, that he's still hounding me about writing a script for your husband."

"I suppose it will just have to wait," Diana said. "Although it seems to me between your novels and plays you should be able to squeeze in a script. Possibly it would be easier if you weren't so prejudiced about Hollywood." Diana playfully poked him in the shoulder. "If you didn't come bearing a script in arms, to what do we owe the honor of your company?"

"I came by to say hello to my godson."

"Your 'godson' is taking his time coming into this world. Either he is waiting for your arrival or she is insulted by your preference and refuses to budge until you've apologized."

"Lord help us all if it's a girl. One Diana Darnley Todd in the world is all it can handle!" John declared.

Diana took hold of John's arm. "You know you'd adore her."

John teased Diana by frowning as if unconvinced of her words, and everyone laughed.

Only John's closest friend, Howard Darnley, had known how devastated John had been by Diana's marriage to

Winston. Secretly, John had always loved her. Howard
Darnley had never trusted Winston, and John was still
inclined to agree, yet Sterling Darnley did approve of
Winston, and Diana loved him. Thus, John had decided, as
long as Diana was happy, he was happy. Looking at her
radiant expression, he had to admit maybe he and Howard
had been wrong.

Winston and Winston Jason bounced up the stairs to the
veranda.

"Uncle John!" Winston Jason screamed.

John Stevens picked up the handsome young boy who
ran into his arms. "My Lord, you're going to be a giant.
You've grown another inch!" John tickled the boy, who
laughed gleefully. "And what do you want?" John demanded. "A little brother or sister?"

Winston Jason sobered at once and placed his arm
around John's neck. "A brother."

"The boy has spoken, Diana," Winston said. "When is
Winston Jason's brother going to show himself?"

Diana looked calmly into her husband's eyes. "Call the
doctor."

The smile vanished from Winston's face. "What?"

"Call the doctor."

"Is it time?!"

"You and your son aren't patient men. Besides, the baby
is anxious to meet his godfather."

Their second son, Harrington Sterling Todd, was born
the following morning to the delight of all, especially the
boy's father and godfather. In the evening, three days after
the birth, Winston and John snuck a bottle of champagne
into Diana's suite. The men drank to motherhood, childhood, and life itself. Sterling, Robert, the nurse, and Harris
Johnson tried to coerce the men out of Diana's suite, but the
men put up a valiant fight. They sprawled in two chairs,
falling asleep while Diana lay awake with Harrington
suckling at her breast.

Diana's life with Winston was full of one celebration
after another. With the Armistice had come the 18th
Amendment and prohibition. On President Harding's inau-
guration eve, on their sixth anniversary, and on New Year's
Eve of 1922, they were frequenting the speakeasies. "Twenty-

one" Club and the Stork Club were their favorite haunts. In the fall of '22 with the opening of John's hit play, *Mary*, they invited an intimate crowd of fifty to celebrate and share in his success. Winston insisted on having small lavish parties for every occasion. Birthdays, anniversaries, and the acquisitions of Mel Christian's clothing stores and Sid Shore's oil company. Diana became so accustomed to preparing for an evening out that she was surprised, relieved, and delighted that Winston wanted to celebrate their eighth anniversary alone.

They had exchanged gifts that morning so that seven-year-old Winston Jason and three-year-old Harrington could share in the occasion. She presented Winston with a original oil painting of Winston Jason and Harrington, and he had given her a diamond locket containing pictures of the boys and himself photographed the Easter before. So she was surprised for a second time when Winston said he had a surprise for her in their bedroom suite.

"Not another gift!"

"Keep your eyes closed," Winston insisted as he led her into their bedroom suite and locked the door. "Just keep them closed, Diana. Don't peek!" He laughed as he led her across the room. "All right. You can look now."

Their parlor table was set with a beautiful dinner, and he held a gift extended out to her.

"This isn't fair. I don't have anything else for you," she protested.

"Open it," he said, looking mysterious. He watched her eyes widen in disbelief as she held up a scarlet-red flapper outfit. "Wear it just for me in the privacy of our room."

Diana went to change and returned to find the candles lit on the dining table.

"Do you know, Diana, that you are everything a woman can be to a man?"

Winston slipped off the straps of her dress and kissed the freshly perfumed creamy skin. Her breasts more than filled his large hands, and his lips took in the nipple of one as he lifted her into his arms.

What was it about this woman, his wife, his love, the mother of his children that aroused him so? He had gratified his desire with countless women, but he had never loved one. Diana was the most exciting woman he had ever known.

Possibly it was his love for her that drove him to such passion.

He placed her gently in the chair and replaced her straps. He had created this evening to tantalize them both, and Diana played into his plans so naturally that he lost himself in the moment. Trembling, he sat down.

They began their meal, sipping champagne. He watched her lips part, her graceful hand holding the glass, and his body ached with wanting. She crossed her legs and brushed up against his thigh. He touched her hand and she looked into his eyes and lowered the straps of her dress again by her own accord.

'Was there really softness like this?' he thought with her naked body in his arms. Her fragrance intoxicated him. He felt like a man who had a feast before him of everything delectable in the world. He appraised her body, trying to decide which part he should taste first and wished he could have all of her at once.

With every hour of their eight-year marriage, Diana had grown more passionate towards Winston. He set her free in their bed to touch, to explore, to feel. Lust, love, and passion, everything and anything they wanted, they did there.

She felt her way down his body, making him shiver. He encouraged her with his words and she responded to his pleasure until he could take no more, and he settled between her legs.

Afterwards, in the moonlight coming through the open windows, Winston saw the beads of perspiration on her brow. He brushed them away, then gently stroked her golden hair, which draped her like a cloak. Slowly her hair was edged away to reveal her smooth body, slightly rounded in the abdomen where their children had grown into life.

Possessively he placed his hand on her abdomen and squeezed gently. Sometimes he envied his sons that they had been more a part of her than he.

"What are you thinking about?" she asked.

He looked deep into her eyes, and his hands lowered between her legs.

"Don't ever betray me, Diana. I love you too much."

"Why would you say such a thing?" she asked.

He refused to let her go. "Do you love me?"

"With all my heart," she answered.

He lay on his back and lifted her on top of him. Dimly she thought he was telling her something. Why was he so afraid of losing her? Gently she cupped his face in her hands and kissed him. His face relaxed. He looked like a boy, lustful, loving, and innocent.

"We will be together always, Diana. I will never let you go."

It was 1924, another election year, with President Coolidge running against John William Davis. George Gershwin's *Rhapsody in Blue* was being played all over the city. Todd Enterprises was thriving. Diana was busy with the boys and with entertaining. Winston was happier than he had ever been. He felt it was due solely to Diana.

"Winston, you're going to spoil me. Not another surprise," Diana said as they entered "21."

At their usual corner table, John Stevens, Sterling, Robert, and Conrad Coleman awaited them. Diana greeted each man in turn and sat down beside Conrad.

At five feet, six inches, slightly built, with penetrating brown eyes, Conrad Coleman exuded power. His talent and passion for living had driven him from his humble beginnings on Hester Street to receive accolades from his contempories and critics. Conrad was MGM's most gifted director/producer. Some said he was the next D.W. Griffith.

"What is this all about?" she asked when Winston was seated.

Winston placed an arm around her and said in explanation, "I know how much the arts mean to you. I thought it appropriate that Howard's work finally be seen."

Conrad, sitting on Diana's left, presented her with a script written by Howard Darnley. "Your husband is financing the film. John is polishing up the script. I'll direct and produce. Mind you, John's and my schedules aren't free for a few months. So be patient."

This was Winston's first concession to her as a patron of the arts. Never mind that she had postponed building the Cultural Center to have their children. His support, in his own way, made it all worthwhile.

Proudly, Sterling Darnley read the title. "*The Rich In Spirit*. Howard would be very pleased."

* * *

Finally, in the spring of 1925, Diana decided it was time to resume the Todd Gala. City life had become trying, especially when she and Winston noticed that Harrington showed a propensity towards illness. Diana suggested they return to Windsor Royal where the boys would have fresh air and open space to play in. What better way to celebrate their homecoming than with the Todd Gala.

At once, Harris Johnson began interviewing employees, many of whom had returned from the war and wanted to resume their positions with the Todds. Diana packed up the Fifth Avenue house, which Winston planned to tear down and replace with a luxurious apartment building.

"We'll open the Gala with an equestrian show," Diana told Winston their first evening at Windsor Royal. "Just like W.J. used to do."

Winston laughed. "Remember our first meeting? I gave an equestrian show all of my own."

Diana smiled. "It seems like yesterday."

"Have I been that bad, Diana?"

"Winston, I was joking! Would you stop." She kissed him then, trying to be playful. He was so serious. "What's wrong, Winston?"

"Are you ready for bed?" he asked suddenly, smiling.

"Bed? It's dinnertime."

"Wouldn't you like to have another child, dearest?"

Over the last year, she had talked about building her Cultural Center. With Harrington in need of her care, those plans had been postponed. Diana had every confidence Harrington would overcome his weak constitution, but it might take time. Another child? Possibly Harrington needed to be a big brother. Taking care of someone else always made the weak strong. Diana reached out for Winston's hand. "Yes, Winston, I would."

The following morning Winston Jason ran into the Garden Room where Winston and Diana were talking about the Gala over breakfast.

Respectfully, Winston Jason waited while Winston finished talking. Diana watched her son out of the corner of her eye. Winston Jason had grown. Tall for his age and athletically built, he looked like a young man although only nine years old. It seemed as though he lived in his jodhpurs. He was waiting impatiently to ask permission to ride his new horse. Distant Darkness had been sired in Kentucky at Sterling's ranch and transported to Windsor Royal for Winston Jr.'s birthday.

"What is it, Winston Jason?" Diana finally asked.

"Mother, I want to ride now because Harrington's going to read a book to me before breakfast. I can't disappoint him. He's had such a bad time lately."

"That's very nice of you to keep your word to Harrington," Diana said approvingly. "How is your brother's reading coming along?"

"He hears the music," Winston Jason said proudly.

"What's this?" Winston asked.

"They're mother's words," Winston Jason explained distinctly. "When I do something well, she tells me 'Winston Jason,'" Diana chimed in with him in unison, "'you hear the music!'" Winston Jason laughed merrily, all full of himself.

Winston chuckled. "Your mother has quite a way with words. Now run along and ride, Winston Jason, but go directly to the stables. I'll call Jim to watch out for you."

Winston Jason dashed out of the room.

Winston kissed Diana. "Don't move. I'll call." He walked over to the phone and pressed the intercom. "Jim, Winston Jason's on his way over to see you. Ride with him, Jim. And only make it a half-hour." Winston returned to his chair. "Enough about the party. Tell me about Harrington."

"He still has a fever," Diana said carefully, not wishing to alarm Winston. "Dr. Smith visited yesterday. He thinks Harrington's condition might get worse."

Winston was more upset about the doctor's visit than about Harrington. He disliked any man so clearly attracted to Diana. His obsession with her had grown into possessiveness.

When she had talked about building the Cultural Center, he had secretly thought of ways to deter her. Harrington's illness somehow seemed more a blessing than a reminder of the Todd curse. Winston had capitalized on the tragedy, subtly suggesting they have another child. Diana was delighted. Winston was grateful. 'Better she never suspects I'm keeping her from building that damn Center,' he thought with guilt and relief mixed together in his mind.

He was plagued with this idea lately that he might lose

Diana. Maybe it was the way other men looked at her. Possibly he felt too vulnerable about opening his heart. He really didn't understand his feelings. He only knew he was fearful, and this disturbed him greatly.

Unconsciously, he took her hand in his and held it so tightly that he actually hurt her. Diana would have protested had Harris Johnson not interrupted them. Breathlessly, he rushed into the Garden Room.

"Mr. and Mrs. Todd, I don't wish to alarm you, but Jim says Winston Jason didn't come to the stables, so he went out looking for him with a few of the hands. Winston Jason isn't within eyesight of the house. I've instructed the household staff to look through the mansion."

Although Winston Jason never had been left unsupervised, he did have freedom within the confines of the estate. Diana, Winston, his nanny, Jim, Harris—someone was always privy to his whereabouts. Possibly he was just watching the horses out at the corral, or viewing the birds in a nearby tree. Better still, he might be visiting his younger brother in the nursery.

After the first hour's search, Diana and Winston returned to the mansion. "We need help," Diana said, knowing these were the last words Winston wanted to hear.

Winston telephoned the police, Sterling, Robert, and then Raymond Baren at Todd Enterprises. "My son has disappeared, Raymond! Call the head of our security. I want as many of our guards together as he can spare. Bring them out yourself, Raymond. We need them!"

Windsor Royal's twenty employees were summoned to the Garden Room. The gatekeeper stayed at his station. He had seen no one all morning near the entrance. Winston instructed him to lock the gates, keep an eye out for Winston Jason, and let in only those Winston had summoned to the estate.

The nanny brought Harrington to Diana. She sat at the table in the Garden Room's alcove trying to soothe her sickly son, who cried for his older brother.

The police questioned Winston privately. Yes, there were strangers about the estate. Harris Johnson had been interviewing prospective employees. The employee roster was called in to police headquarters while Winston and Diana anxiously awaited Sterling and Robert's arrival. At last Diana handed over her care of Harrington to them and rushed to change her clothes.

She and Winston rode Midnight and Distant Darkness over the estate in search of Winston Jason while, out front, one team of policemen used equipment to drag the bottom of the lake. Other teams of Todd security and police set out in cars and on foot to comb the four-thousand-acre estate. Everyone looked for clues—footprints, a broken twig, a scrap of clothing, tire marks along the road, eyewitnesses to anything unusual.

By nightfall, Diana was exhausted. She and Winston returned to Windsor Royal. Sterling found them by themselves in the cool dampness of the stables. Diana was crying softly into Winston's shoulder.

"There's no easy way to say this," Sterling told them. "The police captain has called in the FBI. He thinks Winston Jason has been kidnapped."

For two days they didn't sleep, and they jumped every time the telephone rang. They tried to console one another while they waited for the kidnapper's call.

Winston hired bodyguards. At once, construction was started on cottages for their lodging on the eastern grounds beyond the creek, and bricklayers began the arduous task of laying a foundation for a ten-foot wall, which would surround the inner sanctum of the estate. Anything to keep his family safe.

The FBI questioned employees, searched the grounds and found no clues. Winston Jason's photograph was circulated to their district offices throughout the country. Then Winston and Diana were told they would have to wait for further news.

Diana was beyond grief. She had lost so much weight that her eyes looked like huge, round, lackluster emeralds. Winston was equally distressed. His brow permanently furrowed, he rubbed his hands together as if he were scrubbing away his troubles. Sterling remembered to cancel the Todd Gala, and Robert took over Harrington's care.

"We have to try the news media," Diana said finally, after three weeks. "Winston Jason's photo must be seen and a handsome reward posted."

Winston didn't want anyone to think he was incapable of protecting his family. But now they had no choice. One month from the day of Winston Jason's disappearance, the news hit the newspapers and radio. Hundreds of calls flooded police headquarters and Todd Enterprises. Calls jammed Windsor Royal's lines. The reward for Winston Jason's safe return was $500,000. The FBI and the police investigated all new information.

The new year of 1926 brought more long and agonizing days. Each new development led to a dead end. Winston hired two detective agencies. Sterling confided to Diana that weeks ago he had done the same.

Charles Mancini was on retainer to Darnley Enterprises. Sterling used him for his business dealings when he felt a prospective investor or business partner was untrustworthy. Once Winston's detectives came up short, Sterling asked Charles to meet with Diana and Winston at Windsor Royal in the summer of '26.

"Mr. and Mrs. Todd," Charles Mancini said sadly. "Mr. Darnley's asked me to help. I'm trying. Do either of you have any enemies who know your home?"

"Hell, yes," Winston stormed. "I've got plenty!"

"Do you, Mrs. Todd?"

"I'm sure I do, Mr. Mancini."

"Give me names. I'll check them out."

For the first time in his life, Winston lacked purpose. Love and loss had somehow debilitated him. Solutions ceased to exist. He who had thought of himself as invincible was suddenly brought to his knees.

With Winston away from the helm for over a year, Todd Enterprises floundered. Normally Winston would have guffawed at Henry Ford's decision to implement a five-day week and an eight-hour work day. Many industrialists were outraged. When they tried to enlist his support, he listened without comment. He was so distressed about Winston Jason and so upset about Diana's despondency that work meant nothing to him.

Diana sensed his mood and summoned her courage. "We'll hear from Mr. Mancini soon. Maybe we should move into the city for awhile where you'll be closer to work."

"No! What if Winston Jason comes back and we're not

here? How could you propose such a thing!"

Winston never analyzed why Diana's comment was the turning point. He only remembered thinking that his love for Diana and his sons was destroying him. It was easier for him to deny pain than accept it. Using Diana's suggested move as a focal point, Winston redirected his hurt into anger—anger at Diana and Harrington.

He became more and more frustrated and dissipated and drained—all of which were tonics for intensifying his anger. By the time Charles Mancini returned to Windsor Royal in the late fall of 1926, Winston was ready to explode.

"I wish I had better news," Charles told them. "Everyone seems real sorry about your son's disappearance. My sources say most of the people on your lists are upset about seeing you both so down and out when you were so happy."

"That's big of them," Winston said darkly.

Charles Mancini paused in sympathy. "I have a son of my own, Mr. Todd. I think you're handling this better than I would."

Winston seemed to calm down. "What else did our 'friends' say?"

"Only that they are sorry for you. Todd Enterprises was doing so well. Now that you're . . ."

That brooding expression returned to Winston's face. "I understand now," he said quietly. "One of my competitors kidnapped my son and murdered him. He thinks that he has destroyed me, but he's wrong. He's laughing now, but he won't be for long. I want to get rid of that blasted horse, Darkness," he told Diana severely. "Everything related to Winston Jason must be destroyed. I'm moving to our Fifth Avenue apartment." He stormed out of the room, shouting, "By God! I'm going to make everyone pay!"

CHAPTER V

Just days before his seventy-fifth birthday, in the spring of 1927, Sterling Darnley suffered a heart attack. Diana visited him at Newport with Harrington and a nanny in tow.

"Did you hear about Lindbergh?" he asked her in greeting.

"Oh, Father! How can you talk of that at a time like this!"

She rushed across the room, which had windows facing the Atlantic, and sat in a white upholstered chair beside his bed. She was dressed in a pale lime dress trimmed in white and wore her emerald and diamond ring as her only jewelry.

"I think it's rather appropriate myself," he said. "The world continues on. What a marvel, a transatlantic flight. Diana doesn't it tell you something?"

She stared at him questioningly.

"You can't continue on this way, Diana."

Her brother was dead. Her father was ill. Her husband was obsessed with striking back at an unknown competitor whom he thought had kidnapped and murdered their son. Her younger son was sick. She was holding up. What did he mean? How was she supposed to live?

"For ten of your twelve years of marriage," Sterling continued, "you and Winston had a wonderful relationship. But he's reverted back to his old ways."

"Can't you talk to him, Father? He respects you. You are the only man he will listen to."

"You know I've tried, Diana. Countless times. But he refuses."

Diana sighed. "He'll come around, Father."

Sterling allowed his daughter hope and tried another tactic. "What have you been doing with your life?"

"I've been raising Harrington, running our homes, taking care of investments . . ."

"What about the Cultural Center?"

"I'm going to build it. I guess I've felt a bit tired lately."

That was not an answer worthy of Diana. 'Of course she wants to challenge her mind,' Sterling thought, 'to start to build again. But Winston has opposed it, and Diana has caved in.'

Unbeknownst to Diana, he had spoken to Winston the week before. Refusing to talk about himself, Winston felt free to discuss Diana. Sterling respected Diana's loyalty to her husband, but he thought her a damn fool for not sticking to her convictions.

"Before you married, Diana, the Center was the most important thing in your life. Do I know my daughter so little? Have her dreams changed, and her spirit?"

Diana had to admit she had gradually accepted her role in Winston's life. He had included her, but everything revolved around him: family, social events, business. She had enjoyed this, never thinking she was giving anything up, rather that she was gaining the love of a husband and children. But what had she really done? Why, she was only existing while Winston was living.

"Harrington is almost seven years old," Sterling continued. "He'll be fine. You build your Center. It's important."

"I know it is, Father, and I will."

"Why don't I believe you?" Sterling asked bluntly. "You're forcing me to be unkind, Diana, but someone has to shock you back to reality. I've changed my will. You will administer my estate as always, but the principal of the estate will be left to Harrington. Accept it, darling. Winston Jason is dead."

Tears streamed down Diana's cheeks. "I've told myself he's dead, but it is different hearing it out loud."

Sterling allowed her to grieve, comforting her in his arms. When she regained her composure, he continued.

"It's a peculiar phenomenon, Diana. The way a person meets tragedy shows his or her true colors. I supported, even instigated your relationship with Winston. Never did I suspect you'd be put through all of this. If he doesn't snap out of it soon, you have my blessing to divorce him."

"Father!"

"I won't stand by and see you waste away your life."

"But I'm his wife."

"He's taken on a mistress, Diana. Todd Enterprises has become his first love, above you, above his son, above all family, and I do believe it's forever. It's the only way he thinks he'll survive. He's going to end up alone and frightened and fearful of the world. I say that's his problem. I don't want it to be my daughter's. I've had it with your sitting at home feeling sorry for yourself. Build that Center! No, I don't want any argument. Go home. Think. I want you to leave right now!"

Once back at Windsor Royal, Diana blessed her father and reproached herself. She had been a fool. She ordered Harris Johnson to open the curtains and place bouquets in every room while she set up her home office in Windsor Royal's library. Then she went to visit Harrington.

He was propped up in bed, reading to his nanny and nurse. She studied the scene for a moment as if she were seeing it for the first time.

Because of his health, Harrington had occupied his time in the world of books. He had begun to read at age three. He was able to travel through his books, to meet people and to surround himself with a variety of fictional characters who became his comrades. He breathed life into the characters by reading out loud and became quite expressive as he assumed the personalities of those characters about whom he read.

Then, in his fifth year, she noticed a change. His reading became more than an amusement and an emotional outlet. He developed a mental agility and a keen concentration. Reading a scene in which many characters spoke, he began to assume the voice, mental attitude, and demeanor of each character, adroitly changing from one personality to the other as the various characters came forward in the narrative.

He was fascinated with this new development, and so was Diana. 'He's so very talented,' she thought while he read Mark Twain's *Tom Sawyer* aloud to his nurse and nanny. But that wasn't enough. Winston's relationship with Harrington had become nothing more than a mere formality. Because of this, Harrington had no male companionship except for infrequent visits from Jim.

She left the room without Harrington's knowledge and went to her own suite, where she picked up the phone and called the stables. Then she changed her clothes.

A half-hour later, she was riding out of Windsor Royal stables with Jim Johnson.

A young man now of twenty-one, Jim had developed a keen sense of observation. Mrs. Todd seemed to him like a wild filly who had been tamed, mistreated, and then set free. This was her first time riding Midnight since Winston Jason's kidnapping. He noted her resolve. Diana Darnley Todd was about to change the course of her life.

At the creek, Diana pulled up her reins and leveled her gaze on Jim. The stalwart, gentle young man returned her look openly.

"Harrington considers you his friend, Jim. He needs to get out of the house once a day. I'm hoping you can visit him on the veranda for lunch. He would be very pleased to have your company."

"I'll be there."

"You could listen to him read," Diana ventured.

"And just listen to him," Jim said.

Diana paused. "You understand, don't you, Jim?"

Jim nodded. "He needs to talk, man to man."

Tears rushed to Diana's eyes.

"I'm here, Mrs. Todd. I'll always be around for you and Harrington."

"Bless you, Jim."

Diana commuted to Manhattan daily, based her office there at Darnley Enterprises, and visited the Cultural Center site three times a day. When at Windsor Royal on the weekend, she used the library for her business.

The architect was under exclusive contract to Darnley Enterprises, the construction crew hand-picked from Darnley Enterprises's finest. The accountants gave Diana a daily summary of all expenses, and everyone eagerly worked on one of the most challenging projects of their careers.

Over the first six months of construction, Diana noticed a new face here or there at the site, but usually the same crew, familiar to her, worked at the Cultural Center.

By the spring of 1928, the unthinkable had begun to happen. Construction crews mysteriously stopped working. Permits for construction were challenged. Payroll checks were stolen. Accidents occurred. Then she received an urgent message from her father to visit him in Newport.

She was shocked by his white pallor.

"I've made an appointment for you tomorrow at noon at Franco's to meet with Charles Mancini," Sterling told her. "My driver will take you. Send yours home. You're staying here tonight."

"Why?"

"Just do as I say, Diana. I don't have enough strength or patience to argue."

Franco's was a familiar landmark in Little Italy. At its Bleecker Street entrance, Diana heard laughter through the open windows. Inside, the elegantly decorated room with small white tables and antique chairs was crowded with customers. She was at once caught up in the festive ambience.

Fred Franco, the small, jovial proprietor greeted her at the door. He took in her black Chanel suit, the pearls around her neck, and the pearl and diamond clustered earrings and said, "You must be Mr. Darnley's daughter, Mrs. Todd."

"And you are Mr. Franco. I've heard so much about you from John and Conrad."

Fred beamed. "My star pupils! I remember when John recited a monologue from one of his plays on top of the bar." Fred caught himself reminiscing and cleared his throat, a bit embarrassed. "That's for another time. Charles is waiting."

He guided her from the entry. As they passed the bar, someone whistled loudly. Fred Franco swiftly snapped at the bartender. "Mind your manners, Vincent."

Vincent respectfully took heed of Fred's words. The smattering of blue-collar workers who sat in front of Vincent on bar stools abruptly turned back to their drinks.

"I apologize, Mrs. Todd. It isn't often we have such a beautiful lady in our place," Fred said.

During the following hour, Diana heard the most astonishing news. The Cultural Center's construction crew confirmed that they had been paid to stay home from work. No, they did not know who or where the money came from. They received cash in their mailboxes. Those who continued to work watched a co-worker pushed off one of the girders. Fear set in at the site. The men stayed home.

City officials had also been bribed to prevent her from passing building inspections, hindering further construction. Sterling Darnley had called in his markers, however. Charles handed Diana all the necessary documents and permits to insure the building of her Center.

"Your father wants me to find out who's sabotaged your efforts. I'm doubling your security and checking all construction crews entering and leaving your premises. You've been through a lot, and I want to help."

Diana extended a white-gloved hand to press his. "Thank you, Mr. Mancini."

Charles knew that Diana's pain would be deep when she learned he suspected her husband. Sterling was already aware of his suspicions and had asked Mancini to personally protect Diana. Charles Mancini had enlisted his eighteen-year-old son, Marcus, to supervise security at the site so he could discretely look out for Sterling's daughter.

"Uncle Charles!"

Diana watched a little girl with blonde hair and large blue eyes scamper up to the booth. "She's so beautiful," Diana declared, watching the child hug Uncle Charles.

"My goddaughter, Cara Franco. You met her father when you came in. And I'd like you to meet my son sometime," Charles said, happily holding the child.

"His name is Marcus," Cara said with a brilliant smile. "What's your name?"

"This is Mrs. Todd, Cara."

"Vicent said you were beautiful, too."

"Vicent?" Diana asked. "Oh, yes, the bartender."

Charles shook his finger at Cara. "I've told you to keep away from Vincent." He glanced at Diana. "You steer clear of him, too. I have to go back to work, Cara, but I'll see you at dinner."

Cara looked at Diana. "Can you stay? I want you to meet Thomas."

"She'll be back to visit soon," Charles said, kissing Cara and placing her on the floor. "Don't pout."

"And who is Thomas?" Diana asked, enchanted by the little girl.

"Cara finds these street kids," Charles said of his goddaughter affectionately. "Thomas is a few years younger than my son. An orphan. Very smart. He adores Cara."

"What does he do?"

"He's a thief."

"Like Robin Hood," Cara said distinctly.

Diana smiled. "I'd like to meet your 'Robin Hood' soon. But your Uncle Charles is right. I must go now."

As Diana stood, the little girl looked up at her, wide-eyed. "I'm very pleased to have met you, Mrs. Todd."

"I'm sure we'll see each other again, Cara," Diana said gently, thinking Cara something special.

Diana waited for three weeks without word from Charles Mancini. Her spirits were low. The problems at the construction site continued. Then, the morning of May 25, 1928, Diana opened the paper to the news of Amelia Earhart taking off from Boston. 'The first woman,' she thought, 'to fly a plane across the Atlantic, and I'm not able to build a Cultural Center!' Her frustration mounted. She was about to reach for the telephone to call Charles Mancini when she saw his name in the newspaper. He had been found dead the day before, reportedly killed in an automobile accident.

Eighteen-year-old Marcus Mancini was the spitting image of his father only larger. Sicilian, distinctly so, with the accentuated bulbous nose, thick lips, and deep-set cold black eyes that Fred Franco had told Diana reminded him of the barrels of two .45's. Only a trace of his maternal Norwegian blood showed in his six-foot-four-inch frame. He was a rugged-looking young man whose massive head was covered with black hair.

Despite his appearance, Diana surmised at once that this young man far surpassed his eighteen years in wisdom. He had taken on responsibility while young and was quick-witted and intuitive. She made note of this for Harrington. Soon she had to find a way to develop the same traits in her son.

They sat in the corner booth where she had talked with his father just a few weeks before. "Is there anything I can do?"

"I know who murdered my father."

"Murdered?"

"Hello, Mrs. Todd."

Cara Franco stood shyly behind her. The little girl had obviously been crying.

"Come to me, Cara."

Cara wept in Diana's arms. The death of her godfather had wounded her deeply. Tears welled in Diana's eyes.

Fred Franco finally came over and picked up his daughter. "Now, now, *mia* Cara," he soothed as he took her into the kitchen.

"She lost her mother during childbirth," Marcus explained. "Since meeting you, she's talked of no one else. That's a compliment. Cara's a good judge of people."

"She loved your father very much."

Marcus's expression changed once again from sorrow to anger. "That's why I want Joe Field." He watched Diana's reaction. "I see you know the name. Yes, he's one of your husband's henchmen. Raymond Baren's been heading up the sabotaging of your construction." Diana turned white. "I think you need a drink," Marcus said. "I'll be right back."

Marcus had seen Joe Field at the site many times. After each visit, Marcus had tailed Joe to Todd Enterprises. When Marcus showed pictures of Field and Baren to two of Diana's workers, they had finally come clean. Both Baren and Field had approached the construction crew. Although Marcus found no witnesses to his father's murder, he was convinced Joe Field was behind it. Marcus told Diana he would get Joe, Raymond, and her husband one day.

Before returning to Windsor Royal that evening, Diana visited Winston at the Fifth Avenue apartment. It had been over two months since they had seen one another.

Winston was more arrogant than ever. Tall and brooding, yet feigning charm, Winston greeted her with polished civility.

"Hello, my dear. You look well."

"Do you know Charles Mancini, Winston?"

"Charles Mancini? Who is he?"

"You know nothing about his murder?"

"I don't even know who he is!"

Diana decided to try another tactic. "What about my Center. Do you know I've been having problems?"

"It should be 'my' Center. You think about it. No, I won't discuss it now. Not unless you want to sign over the deed."

"So you admit you had Raymond Baren and Joe Field bribe my workers."

"I won't discuss it! Go home and take care of your son!"

"You should come home and see *our* son, Winston. He needs his father."

"I'll make this short," Winston said. "Besides your Center, I'm unhappy about Harrington. I don't want to have anything to do with him until he's up and well." He pointed an accusing finger at her. "It's your fault. It's Darnley blood that has made him weak. You've never heard of a Todd bedridden! You better make him well. I'm leaving him in your hands. *Your* son, do you hear!"

Diana took off her gloves slowly, biding her time. 'He must be absolutely mad!' she thought. 'For years he's been paranoid about the Todd curse. Now he's denying it. And what is this about the Cultural Center? He's out of control.'

"What do you know about Charles Mancini's murder?" she asked finally.

"I've already told you—nothing."

"And I don't believe you," Diana said softly.

"Oh, I forgot," Winston said sarcastically. "You're the one with all the answers. You have all the morals, right? You can rely on yourself. You don't need anyone." He laughed, none too pleasantly.

He wasn't making any sense. Momentarily she pushed Charles Mancini out of her mind. She wanted to find the key to Winston. She had to understand whom she was up against.

She looked at him thoughtfully as she took a chair. "Why are you saying these things?"

"Your mere existence is unpleasant to me," Winston said. "You've never found one reason why Winston Jason was kidnapped. You don't even care that he's dead."

Winston was jumping from one subject to another. He was itching for a fight, but why? And why over accusations that were absolutely unfounded.

"You and W.J. asked too much," he continued. "You never did understand, Diana. You live in a world of dreams. It isn't the real world." He sat on the couch opposite her. "It isn't real at all."

"And what about W.J.? Did he live in a world of dreams, too?"

"No, he just lived in a different place in a different time and under different circumstances." Winston's face was void of feeling. "It's a man's world," he said. "W.J. would have called it the school of hard knocks."

He got up, sensing her pain and enjoying it. "Why I let you talk me into all that nonsense about 'feelings,' I'll never know. If I had done things my way, all of this never would have happened. Feelings make a man weak and vulnerable. That's what I get for listening to a woman! You rule men or they rule you, that's all I need to know."

Diana's heart pounded heavily. "Does that include murder?"

"I told you I'd get everyone who wished me ill."

"What about Charles Mancini?"

"Drop it, Diana. I told you I know nothing about him."

"You're going down a path more destructive than the one you were on before we married. Now you know what it is to love another and you're denying it."

"There you go again, Diana. I don't want to talk about feelings. I never loved *you*! Long ago you said I'd hate the woman I married for my inheritance. You were right."

"I want a divorce," she said quietly.

He felt his first surge of emotion in years. How dare she ask for a divorce. She would do as he wanted. She had no life except in relation to his.

He jerked her from the chair and crushed her to him. He kissed her roughly. His hands pressed her body, her bosom, her thighs. "You're very lovely, even now."

"Let me go."

When she fell into the chair, he stood above her menacingly. "You must raise your son. He is my only heir. You may not have a divorce."

She watched him sit down again on the couch. "Your rules? They apply to Harrington as well?"

"To him and to you."

"I told you long ago I didn't wish to be a possession. Nor do I wish that for our son."

"That was long ago," he said, smiling.

"You would try to take Harrington from me?"

"Of course."

She walked to within inches of him. He stood. She tilted her head back and gazed at him with determination equal to his. "What you're doing to Harrington and me is wrong."

"What a fool you are, a beautiful fool." He viewed her without an ounce of pity. He moved away, walking down the vast room to the window. "You will never survive out there," he said, pointing out as if to the world.

"Is that your answer? What does that have to do with me and Harrington and our relationship with you?"

"What I want is more important than either of you, and I will do what must be done. You're my wife," Winston said. "If I have to work and struggle, then you do, too."

"I won't go along with your madness."

"You'll do it," Winston said, "for Harrington."

"No, Winston, I won't. I'll make up my mind how to handle this, but I will live as I've always lived, I assure you of that."

CHAPTER VI

"I've had to reorganize since the stock market crash," Diana told Sterling in the spring of 1930. "I've cut back our employees, but Marcus Mancini is staying on our payroll."

"Good idea," Sterling Darnley said, weak, but happy that his daughter had regained her strength. He wished he had her resilience. For three years he had had difficulty staying on his feet. He sighed wearily.

Diana sat down beside him. He wanted her to "be safe," as he liked to say. When Winston came out to Newport a few weeks earlier, Sterling had refused him admittance.

Robert Todd had passed away shortly after the stock market crash. Winston had only been interested in discovering what could be salvaged from Robert's estate. Sterling had advised Robert on many investments. He had pleaded with Robert to get out of the stock market in 1928. Robert had not listened and had died in debt. Sterling had no intention of discussing Robert's shortcomings with Winston and had paid Robert's debts himself.

"What about the divorce?" he asked.

"I've decided to complete the Cultural Center and raise Harrington without Winston's interference. I need time—time for Harrington to grow up. I don't want Winston putting Harrington in the middle of our dispute. I'll battle with Winston later."

Sterling Darnley extended his hand, and Diana felt tears rushing to her eyes. 'He's so thin,' she thought sadly. 'So frustrated by his illness. Stuck in this room, unable to walk. Why he's only been holding on to make sure I'm all right. I have to give him some hope,' she thought frantically. She refused to waste a moment on tears when her father had so little time.

"Worry about yourself," Sterling said, reading her thoughts. "The Darnleys have never backed down from a good fight. I'm not sure you're taking the proper course, but then I know you're not in the best of health either. I suppose that has something to do with your decision. Why didn't you tell me you had a slight stroke after your last conversation with Winston?"

"How did you know?"

"Marcus Mancini told me Dr. Frazier came to see you at Windsor Royal. I called the doctor. How are you feeling?"

"So you've had Marcus protecting me all along."

"It's for your own good. Now answer my question."

"Fortunately, I take after my father," Diana said. "Remember what they told you long ago? 'Slow down.' 'Take it easy.' 'Don't place yourself in stressful situations; they will kill you.' But just look at you. At seventy-seven you've proved the doctors wrong, now haven't you." She raised her eyes to the ceiling. "Even though he denies it now, Winston truly believes that the Todds are the weak ones, not the Darnleys. Wouldn't he love to hear about my stroke! Never mind though," she said, focusing her emerald green eyes on her father. "I'll do the best I can under the circumstances."

John Stevens had visited Sterling just last week to enlist Sterling's support for Diana's decision. "I love her, Sterling," John had told him. "I would do anything to have Diana as my wife, except ask her to fight Winston and thereby jeopardize her health and her ability to raise Harrington."

John's admission had surprised and stung the usually perspicacious Sterling. Possibly Diana would have married the dynamic John had Sterling been less supportive of

Winston fifteen years ago. Sterling had promised to keep these thoughts to himself, but his heart was heavy.

"I know you'll do your best," Sterling finally said to Diana. "Now tell me about my grandson. I've missed seeing him these last few months. Is he still reading to Jim?"

"They've become fast friends," Diana said, then leaned forward in her chair. "Harrington is healthy and happy. Yes! Did you hear me? He's healthy! Just in these last few months since you've seen him, he's even put on some weight. And you know how you've always wondered whether you were getting through to Harrington? He's growing up, Father." Diana paused thoughtfully. "Harrington is an artist like Howard, but he has your drive and mine and actually the best of Winston in him."

Sterling smiled sardonically. "The poor boy!"

"Don't joke, Father. You really will be surprised." Diana leaned closer to Sterling, suddenly very excited. "Father, mind you, I'm trying to be impartial, but I think he's very talented."

"Bring him to me, Diana. I want to see my grandson."

Sterling Darnley appraised the tall thin boy dressed in a black suit who walked alone into his bedroom that Sunday afternoon. 'How he's grown! Do children usually change so drastically without your realizing it? He's extraordinarily handsome,' Sterling thought. Harrington crossed directly to his bed without a moment's hesitation, looking graceful as an athlete.

"Hello, Grandfather," Harrington said, sticking out his hand.

Harrington was ten years old and approaching five feet, two inches. He had a healthy complexion—stunning against his blond hair—and his body appeared to be strong. Sterling was struck by Harrington's maturity.

Startling blue eyes fixed on Sterling as Harrington took his grandfather's hand. The last time Sterling had seen the boy, their positions were reversed. Harrington had been in bed, and he held Harrington's hand. He wondered how he looked to Harrington in this reversed role.

"I'm happy to see you."

"Why is that?" Sterling asked, narrowing his own blue eyes.

"Because you're the only person I feel comfortable talking to about Mother."

Sterling tried to raise himself on the pillows. Harrington helped him before he could help himself. He felt more comfortable than he had in months.

"I've had some experience sitting in bed," Harrington said, smiling at his grandfather's surprise. "If you place the pillow this way in the middle of your back, and put another pillow under your head, it molds to your body better."

Sterling thanked Harrington, and then his thoughts drifted again. He had talked with Harrington many times. Their discussions centered around books, ideas, and family. Harrington had been a listener and only became animated when he read out loud. Sterling was surprised by Harrington's deep affection for him and was pleased that his visits had meant so much to his grandson.

"What about your mother?" he asked at last.

"I think she should stop worrying about me and be with Uncle John."

Sterling turned white and coughed. A glass of water was placed immediately in his hand.

"I'm sorry, Grandfather. I didn't mean to upset you."

Sterling sipped the water gratefully. As he lay back quietly, one thought was predominant in his mind. 'Harrington is sensitive, yet direct. He thinks things through and sets forth his ideas clearly. Reasoning power. That on top of his creative mind is a dynamic combination.'

For the first time in months, Sterling felt the color in his cheeks. "Why don't I spend some time with you at Windsor Royal, Harrington. There we'll have more time to talk."

"That would make me very happy, sir. I've missed you."

Diana was overjoyed by her father's renewed spirit. His doctors protested vigorously about his move to Windsor Royal. Sterling shooed them away and made the trip.

On this cool May evening, Diana and Harrington celebrated Sterling's first evening at Windsor Royal over dinner in the Grand Banquet Hall. Flags from all over the world hung in brackets attached to the molding on the walls just below the ceiling. A huge rock fireplace was ablazed with eucalyptus. Its scent intermingled with the fragrance of roses in a bouquet gracing the dining table.

"I have something important I want to talk about," Sterling told them, sitting tired but happy in his chair.

"What is it, Father?"

"It's about Winston Jason, Diana. Harrington has some questions about his brother."

Diana paled, but Harrington said, "I've wanted to talk about him for the longest time."

"I didn't know that, Harrington." Diana was astonished.

"I remember Winston Jason, Mother. He used to come and talk to me when I was sick. I didn't have much to give in return so I started reading—then we both had something to say. What really happened, Mother?"

Diana described the day of Winston Jason's disappearance, the months of hope thereafter that he would be found, and then the ultimate realization that he was dead.

Harrington was deeply affected. "I knew Father wished it had been me instead of Winston Jason, but . . ."

"That's not true!" Diana exclaimed.

"Mother, that is the truth. Don't worry. I'm all right."

"It isn't all right. I won't allow you to think that way without an explanation. Your father might appear to have that attitude, but it's only because he's in pain and doesn't know how to deal with it. Do you understand, Harrington?"

"That's a partial truth," Sterling interceded.

"Father! Why would you allow Harrington to live with such a burden. None of us really know how Winston feels."

"Because I do know, and I will never be untruthful to Harrington. He's strong enough to take whatever comes his way. Don't protect him, Diana. He doesn't appreciate it."

"That's pretty blunt, Grandfather," Harrington said.

Sterling laughed. "At my age, what's left? Now tell your mother what you told me."

Harrington turned to his mother. "I don't blame Father. He doesn't even know me. If he doesn't come around in the future, then I might not like him so much. But right now, I know it's his problem, not mine, and I understand. Also, I loved my brother. Winston Jason's with me every day. He helped me to hear the music, Mother. I'll never forget him."

Diana was delighted that Conrad Coleman was returning to New York in the fall of 1930, yet the circumstances were less than palatable. After the Winston Jason tragedy, Conrad had postponed the filming of *The Rich in Spirit*, Howard's script, in which he, John, and Winston were partners. With all their trouble, Conrad felt it inappropriate to bother Winston about the movie.

As the years had passed, Conrad confided to Diana that he hoped Winston would forget about the script. Unfortunately, Winston had called recently, insisting that Conrad and John honor their agreement. Contractually, if they reneged on the deal, the script would revert to Winston. Conrad and John decided to go ahead. How she wished she had never suggested that they all go into business together!

Over dinner at Windsor Royal, Diana looked around the table at the men who had stood by her over the years. Her father, dressed in traditional navy, looked healthy and happy. Turning over his business affairs to her had helped. She had suggested the merger between Darnley Enterprises and Walter Kent's, Kent Industries. Without the business pressures, Sterling was much more animated and relaxed.

Living under all that glorious California sunshine, Conrad was tanned to a rich brown. He, like Sterling, dressed traditionally. She had never seen Conrad in anything but a suit and tie. His reputation as a producer/director, MGM's finest, was recognized on both coasts. Recently, he had announced a bold move. He was leaving MGM and was using *The Rich in Spirit* to launch his first independently produced movie. Diana was somewhat apprehensive about Winston's involvement with Conrad's maiden voyage.

Then there was her beloved John. Artist, adventurer, hunter, sportsman, John had a sentimental heart beneath his intimidating exterior. He had become a legend on Broadway: a colorful and famous figure, Pulitzer Prize-winning playwright, director, and producer. And his novels sold in the millions. He was a towering figure with a healthy head of brownish-blond hair, graying at the temples.

Sometimes she wanted to walk out of her life as it existed and enter into a new life with John. How easy it would be to tour the world, patronize the arts, enjoy good conversation, and openly love John without the encumberance of an estranged husband. She seldom dwelled on this dream. It would only be possible after Harrington was on his own. She repeatedly told herself to be patient and live her life to the fullest now.

"This will be my first and last business with Winston," Conrad was saying.

"I couldn't have said it better," John grumbled, lighting another cigarette.

Sterling watched John and Diana together. They were so discreete about their true relationship that he would never have known about their affair had it not been for John's disclosure. Sterling never had mentioned it to Diana, nor would he. How had Harrington detected it? The boy was remarkable.

"But I had other reasons for coming to New York," Conrad was saying. "First, I wanted to see Harrington. He read for me this afternoon, Diana. He also showed me some of his writing. He insists he's going to work for John and me one day. He's a very talented young man. John says he's doing remarkably well in summer theater, too. I don't know how his father feels, but I think . . . well, I'll reserve my opinion. Let's see what Harrington decides to do. But warn him, Diana, I don't have any actors under contract, and I hope I never do. They're a pain. Encourage him to write. I know, I know, you don't want to influence him. All right, let's just all pray he decides to be a writer. Now, who's this little girl you want me to meet?"

"Her name is Cara Franco," Diana said. "She's Fred Franco's daughter, and she happens to be talented and only ten years old." Diana also told Conrad about Thomas Garvin, Cara's rebellious "Robin Hood."

"I've met them, Conrad," John said. "I'd like Cara to attend my summer theater with Harrington in June if you think she's as talented as I do."

"And don't forget Thomas," Diana reminded.

"I'll take care of Cara if you'll take care of Thomas," John said to Conrad as he winked at Diana. "Fair exchange, don't you think?"

"You might be surprised," Diana said, amused.

"Possibly you're right," John conceded.

"What about Thomas?" Conrad demanded to know.

"I think," John said, "that if he's away from New York and all the street influences for awhile, he could get into college—if he sets his mind to it."

"I'll see them tomorrow after work and let you know my

thoughts. Now about Howard's script. Winston's expecting me at noon tomorrow. I'm going to suggest we start production in a month. Let's get this business over with, John. The sooner the better."

Diana was amazed at how quickly two years passed. Conrad met Thomas Garvin and convinced the young man to return to California with him. With Conrad's endorsement, John had enrolled Cara in the summer theater group, and she and Harrington became fast friends. By the fall of 1931, Diana was delighted to hear that Thomas was entering his freshman year at USC in California. Marcus was working for Darnley Enterprises, and she was watching her Cultural Center become more of a familiar landmark in Manhattan by the day as the buildings began to dot the skyline.

Patiently, she had waited for Harrington to grow older before implementing the next stage of her plans. The time was rapidly approaching.

For many years, she had wondered just how she would expose Harrington to the obstacles in life without denying him the benefits of her and Sterling's guidance, which Harrington needed to become their heir. Granted, over the last two summers, John had been rough on Harrington in summer theater, possibly overly so. Harrington had to learn from his mistakes and also struggle to develop his potential. But basically, Harrington was not exposed to the reality of the word "survival."

Most of Harrington's friends were from his own class: those who had inherited wealth. Diana felt their influence was unrealistic, especially with times such as they were. Above all, she wanted Harrington to be street-wise like Thomas Garvin.

As Diana and John suspected, Thomas was bound and determined to succeed once given a chance. He had already decided that his forte was business, having learned the ins and outs of many an illegal business operation and having seen the inside of a juvenile hall a score of times before Conrad set him straight and financed Thomas's education at USC. Thomas thirsted for a better way of life and lived life hard, something which Diana finally decided Harrington had to learn.

Marcus had suggested that Harrington could have no

better teacher than Thomas Garvin, who was back in New York from college for the summer of 1932. Marcus arranged for the two young men to meet at 3 P.M., the first Wednesday in July. He suggested the hour because Franco's lunch crowd would be gone. Only the regulars stuck around to drink.

At 2:55 P.M., Diana's Bentley limousine drove down Houston Street, turned, and cut over to Bleecker. When they stopped alongside the curb, Harrington looked curiously out the back window at Franco's Restaurant with its wrought iron railing out front.

"I just ask for Fred Franco?" Harrington said.

Diana glanced at her twelve-year-old son. His attire alone would alienate him from the barroom crowd. "Yes, darling. Marcus will bring you, Cara, and Thomas over to the Cultural Center site around six o'clock. I have an appointment with the architect. You'll like Thomas. Have a good time."

Her heart beat rapidly as she watched Harrington enter Franco's. She told herself this was the only way, but unconsciously she had opened the car door.

"Are you going in too, Mrs. Todd?"

One of Marcus's detectives, Laster French, doubled as her chauffeur. Although it had been Diana's idea to have Harrington learn to take care of himself, Marcus had anticipated that Diana might have second thoughts.

Hastily, Diana closed the door. "No, no. I have to be at the Center site as planned."

The Center was a source of curiosity to the denizens of Manhattan. Museums, theaters, theatrical business offices, and rehearsal halls were all at various stages of development. Diana spent three hours talking to the architect and decorators. Her preoccupation with Harrington finally wore her down. She apologized to her co-workers for her behavior and rushed out to Fifth Avenue to wait.

At 6:45, when Harrington still had not arrived, Diana asked Laster to drive her back to pick him up.

Laster pointed down the street. "That won't be necessary, Mrs. Todd."

Diana was so blinded with worry that she didn't see Harrington until he was upon her. She unsuccessfully tried to cover up her shock.

"What happened?" she stammered.

Harrington had a black eye, torn clothes, and a huge grin on his face. He was so excited, his words spilled out in disjointed sentences.

"First thing is, I dressed all wrong. Shouldn't have worn a tie. Vincent hates rich people. He almost strangled me. I don't like him at all. Vincent gave me this," Harrington said, pointing at his shiner. "Thomas is going to teach me to box. Cara's invited me to stay with her at Christmas. I've invited Thomas and Cara to stay with us this summer. I . . ."

"Hold it, kid," Thomas said, joining them and throwing an arm around Harrington's shoulder. "Slow down. Your mother's gonna think you've cracked up."

Diana was horrified. Vincent Morello was a grown man! Harrington might have been severely hurt! Thomas was supposed to have been Harrington's teacher. She looked at eighteen-year-old Thomas, modestly dressed in slacks and a faded white shirt, tattered at the edges. Marcus had said Thomas and Harrington would be adversaries when they first met. But there was Thomas ruffling Harrington's hair just like a big brother. She was beside herself as to what to think.

Twelve-year-old Cara mixed into the group and took ahold of Harrington's hand. "He was so wonderful, Mrs. Todd! Vincent almost strangled him, but Harrington smashed Vincent's hand with a beer bottle!"

"A beer bottle," Diana said helplessly.

"Thomas was watching the whole thing!" Cara exclaimed. "He wouldn't have let Harrington get hurt . . . really hurt!"

"Yeah, that's true, sis," Thomas chimed in. "Harrington showed guts. I liked that. Vincent only grazed Harrington's eye. The shiner'll be gone in a few days. What I liked is that Harrington didn't give up. I stepped in when Harrington hit his head on the stool. Vincent's gonna be out of commission for a couple of weeks," Thomas said proudly.

"Yeah, you were good, Thomas. Really good. Mother? Are you all right? Aren't you going to say anything?"

Diana stood on Fifth Avenue looking from Harrington to Cara to Thomas, and then her eyes steadied on Marcus Mancini.

It was obvious to Marcus that she was in a fit of panic. He cautioned her with his eyes. Although Diana was beside herself, she said: "It looks to me like we've been leading too easy a life, Harrington. Both of us better toughen up a bit."

Harrington laughed. "That's the spirit, Mother. For a minute there, I thought you were going to faint!"

Marcus smiled a rare smile. "Not your mother. She understands these things. Right, Mrs. Todd?"

Diana flushed scarlet. "Please call me Diana."

CHAPTER VII

‎

"You see, Harrington," Sterling said, sitting beside Harrington on the veranda as they watched Cara Franco and Diana ride their horses in the summer of 1936, "your mother is happier than she would be wrangling with your father over a divorce. She has you, John, and now Cara. Maybe it's because she and Cara look so much alike, or maybe it's because they have so much in common, I don't know. But your mother thinks of Cara like a daughter. She has everything she wants, right here."

Harrington liked the way his grandfather talked to him as if he were a grown-up. At sixteen years old that made Harrington feel really good.

"You were right," Harrington said. "I'm glad I listened to you. I still remember the look on her face when she took Cara and me to the grand opening of the Cultural Center two years ago. I hope I'm that proud of something I do in my life."

"You and Cara have turned out to be good friends."

"She's a fine writer," Harrington said seriously.

Sterling smiled to himself. Harrington and Cara were

quite obviously infatuated with each other.

"Harrington!"

They heard Cara's voice before they saw her. Suddenly she was at Harrington's side. All flushed and radiant, clad in a riding habit, Cara reminded Sterling of an angel with her flowing blonde hair and sculptured features.

"Harrington," she said, pulling on his hand. "You promised to ride with us. Remember, we're seeing *The Rich in Spirit* later? This is the only time we have to ride with Diana."

Harrington grabbed her arm and gently pulled her into the chair beside him. "Pipe down, Franco. I want to ask Grandfather about Marcus first."

That caught Cara's attention. She straightened in the chair, eager to be a part of the conversation.

"What about Marcus?" Sterling asked.

"Sometimes he looks at me very hard. He seems to be searching for something."

"You're right. He wants to know how much of your father is in you," Sterling said bluntly.

"Why?"

"He doesn't get along with your father."

"He's not the only one, but I'm not very upset about it. I don't like Father much either."

Sterling shrugged. "That's your decision. Everyone's entitled to make up his own mind."

"Mother said the same thing," Harrington answered.

Cara nudged Harrington then, and he looked at her and shook his head.

"If you won't, I will," Cara said softly.

"Grandfather, I never said a word. Cara knows about Mother and John."

Sterling looked across Harrington to Cara. Her eyes were gentle. She loved Diana like her own mother.

"I wish they could be together," Cara said.

"They are together," Sterling said, pointing to his heart. "Where it counts. In here. Honor that. Don't ever let on you know. Otherwise they'll be inhibited and their joy cut to a minimum."

Sterling noticed the teenagers were holding hands as they solemnly promised to keep the secret.

"You'd better get to your riding," he urged. "I want a full report on *The Rich in Spirit* upon your return this evening."

Sterling overheard Harrington and Cara talking as they left the veranda.

"Did you know my Uncle Howard wrote the original script of *The Rich in Spirit*?"

"I know, I know," Cara said. "You've told me a million times, and Uncle John made the revisions."

Sterling smiled, looking out at the blue sky. "What do you think of that, Howard? Your nephew thinks you're a hero."

Windsor Royal was chock-full of history, and that summer, Diana utilized the most colorful of the Darnley and Todd ancestors, W.J. Todd, to captivate Harrington's and his friends' hearts and to teach them history and a sense of business, the main intent of her stories.

Cara, Harrington, and Thomas gathered around W.J.'s father's portrait as she told them that W.J. had proclaimed his own father to be a "kind old ignoramous." The three stared at the elderly gentleman's portrait, fascinated with his amazing twirling moustache. Much to Diana's amusement, Cara observed that "a speck of talent was necessary to grow such an auspicious facial adornment."

From the library shelves, Diana took down one of the volumes of W.J.'s journals. The trio's attention transferred to the portrait of W.J. as Diana read his words.

"The policies of government and the course of history must be anticipated and studied carefully before investing. It is essential when making money. Only a fool would have invested heavily in cotton and tobacco months before the Revolutionary War."

The English embargo and blockade had ruined W.J.'s father's trade and had caused the Todd family severe losses. W.J. had also invested in cotton and tobacco a hundred years later. Through his trading and shipping companies, he exported agricultural products and a myriad of American raw goods and imported manufactured goods from Europe to market in the States.

Upon Lincoln's nomination, he sold his interest in the southern farmland. During and after the Civil War, he joined with other businessmen to form a railroad company, but he concentrated mainly on his newly founded businesses—a bank, a tool company, and a chemical plant, all of which flourished during and after the Civil War. Later, he added real estate and a tiny oil company to his portfolio.

"W.J. learned from his father's mistakes," Diana told them. "Hopefully the future is not a carbon copy of the past, but the past is a reference point." She looked directly at Harrington. "You can learn one day from my mistakes as well."

"Oh, you've never made a mistake," Cara proclaimed adamantly.

"We all make mistakes," Diana replied. "That's how we learn. My father taught me that," Diana said, "and many other things." She looked at her watch. "He's out on the veranda now. Why don't you ask him about mistakes. I'm sure he'd be thrilled to tell you some stories."

Off the trio went with Harrington in the lead. Their afternoon discussions with Sterling about the world of finance and real estate were always a special treat.

Every day in June, before Harrington and Cara left for summer theater, Harrington and his chums played football on the great lawn behind the mansion.

Marcus Mancini showed up one afternoon and found himself enchanted with Diana's lessons. The morning had been monopolized with an intense football game. Diana over-heard the boys arguing about who had won, when Thomas marched up and asked Diana her opinion. She was reluctant to get involved, but Thomas insisted.

"Are you in competition with one another," she asked, "or are you a team?"

"We're a team," Thomas said, "but we also compete. You understand the competitive spirit, don't you?" Thomas queried.

"Of course, but I'm in competition with no one but myself."

"Yourself? What about with others?"

"I wish only for others to succeed."

"Someone has to lose."

"Do they?"

"There are winners and there are losers," Thomas answered. "Competition is everywhere."

Diana stared at him thoughtfully. "You've won all the games this summer. Possibly you don't know the true meaning of success."

"What do you mean?"

Diana smiled. "Consider that the true test of men and women is not to beat one another, but to stretch themselves—to expand, to gain knowledge, to test themselves. The competitive spirit makes our country great, but the focus of that competition is what's important. When one performs better than one did the day before, now that is a successful competition."

"What if we had done our best and lost?" Thomas asked.

"You still did your best."

"That's not good enough."

Diana smiled. "Then better your best."

Thomas turned to Marcus. "What do you think?"

The law of the street was different: survival. But in the world in which Marcus now lived, Diana's thoughts were the healthiest approach. Diana and he had talked many times, and he had grown to love her.

"Why don't you ask Harrington?" Marcus suggested. "He's one of us now."

Harrington glanced at Cara. She smiled, already knowing his answer. "If you want to stay on the streets, don't listen. If you want to make something of yourself, then do. Mother is right, as long as you keep your edge." Then Harrington laughed. "And I don't think you have to worry about that, Thomas."

Thomas tried to sneak an elbow into Harrington's gut, but Harrington was too quick for him.

"You taught him well, big brother," Cara laughed.

"Yes," Marcus said, staring right at Diana, "he's been taught well, as we all have."

Diana smiled. Her son had become a survivor.

There was magic in the air wherever Diana Darnley Todd traveled. Diana's love and support flowed into each of their lives and created a bond among them, which would never be broken.

All summer, Harrington and Cara secretly talked about Diana and John. When they returned from the Stevens Theater in late August, they sat in the cool damp shade of the hayloft at Windsor Royal stables, with the recurring question still predominant in their minds. What if they were in the same predicament?

"I'd leave," Harrington said angrily. "My father's a real bastard!"

"Harrington!"

"He abandoned me when I was five. And he's been a husband to Mother in name only for the past ten years."

"But you don't have a child, Todd. And there's a lot more that goes into your mother's decision."

"I know. But she's always told us we must live our own lives. She should live hers."

Cara had to admit this was true. "Let's think about something else for awhile."

Harrington agreed and opened Cara's most recent play. As he read, he spotted himself at once. Cara wrote about their first Christmas together, the summer months they had shared. She captured Thomas and Marcus, too, and the numerous scrapes they had gotten into. She described the people he had met: Depression casualties, out of work and hungry. She had captured his growth—the savvy he had picked up on the streets, the camaraderie between him and Thomas, and the feelings he had for her, as yet unspoken.

In the third act, he stopped in mid-sentence, then repeated her written words:

> I never knew there was a person who was like me, but you are. I feel so comfortable around you, as though I don't need to speak and you know my thoughts. Is it possible that we met before in another place or in another life, or is it that we're just in love?

"Is that how you feel about us, Franco?"

Her blush was answer enough for him. His fingers gently touched her chin as he tilted her head. Softly he kissed her generous lips.

It was there when they opened their eyes: the teenage infatuation known to them as love, unveiled between them, open and innocent. He took her into his arms. The beautiful long blonde hair he loved to stare at felt soft against his cheek. Her smell was delicious. It reminded him of lemons and apple blossoms all in one. The warmth of her body melted into his, as if a sculptor had carved their bodies for each other.

"I love you, Franco," he said passionately. "One day we'll marry, do you know that?"

All her life she had known love. Her father, Marcus, Thomas, Diana. But this was different. She had opened up to Harrington, and her body was reacting wondrously. Just cradling her head against Harrington's shoulder made her dizzy. The touch of his hands on her body clouded her thoughts. A sweet rhythm of physical pleasure crowded any form of reason out of her mind.

During the summer of '36, Harrington protected her against becoming pregnant as secretly, yet freely, they discovered the intimacy of man and woman. A new world opened up to them. They were lovers at last. The future was theirs. They made plans secretly, for what they had, they idealistically wanted for Diana and John, too.

Diana wished that she could focus her full attention on her life away from Winston, but it wasn't to be. She continually heard from him, and he liked nothing more than to boast about his success.

As Chairman of the Board of Todd Enterprises, Winston had renamed the company Todd Industries, thinking it a more imposing and all-encompassing name. From what Diana had heard from the Dareels, the Shores, and the Christians, whose fortunes Winston had virtually destroyed, he had been labeled by the business community as everything from the supreme capitalist to a corporate gangster while he hid behind the veneer of gentility. Rumor had it that he supported his own espionage network to guard his corporate secrets and to infiltrate competitors' businesses . . . a stolen idea here, a business forced to near bankruptcy there; then a discreet purchase of a company at a fraction of its true market value.

He used the formidable pairing of political and financial power as his sword and shield, creating fear and compliance, especially during these troubled times. His appetite for money and power was insatiable. Once a competitor was destroyed or a new business lured to the Todd banner, he readied himself for a new conquest, eager to show his invincibility to the world and to himself.

If power and money were drugs, Winston was an addict.

Winston bought land in California, Wyoming, and Texas and drilled for oil. He owned oil refineries, a chain of gasoline stations, cotton fields, and the tool company, and he continued the Todd Shipping Line. He acquired William Randolph Investment Brokerage Firm and many other private holdings, including a small aeronautical company in California.

While Diana built her Center, Winston used W.J.'s land in Manhattan, adjacent to her property, to build the Todd Business Center. Their combined efforts created the most prestigious, beautifully constructed business and cultural center in the world. Diana named her center the Todd Cultural Center, which she knew surprised Winston when he finally called her at the end of 1936.

"Congratulations for having the good sense to use your proper name, Diana. Have you heard much about me lately?"

Winston stamped his name on everything. Land in California, which was part of the Todd family's property for many years, was donated as a state park, and people from all over the world visited it and were told Winston Todd was the donor. There were Todd trucks and W.J. Todd gasoline stations and the Todd ships and Todd hotels. He was above all a glutton for notoriety.

"I know you've been conquering the world, Winston, but I'm more interested in your dealings with John and Conrad."

"Why would you care about that?" Winston demanded irritably. "Didn't you hear about my other investments in Hollywood?"

Winston had invested heavily in the new technology of sound for motion pictures, and had battled with Morgan and the Rockefellers for control of that industry and won. Through the first years of the Depression he more than quadrupled his fortune.

"You've made an enormous profit off *The Rich in Spirit*. Don't cheat Conrad and John out of their share."

"I have to go, Diana," Winston said angrily. "This conversation is boring me."

Winston's rudeness made Diana all the more determined. She traveled from Windsor Royal to Manhattan the following month and called on Winston unannounced at their Fifth Avenue apartment.

Winston knew that Sterling was living at Windsor Royal and that Cara Franco, Thomas Garvin, and Marcus Mancini visited the estate. He had no desire to visit Windsor Royal himself. Harris Johnson had reported to him that Diana and John were only friends. Harrington was getting the proper education, and Diana's life was routine. Until his son was older, he wanted to shut out thoughts of his family from his mind. He was unhappy to hear that Diana was downstairs waiting for him.

Dressed in a blue-gray suit with a white silk blouse, Diana looked like a sophisticated schoolgirl. She appeared younger somehow, almost happy. Maybe it was her blonde hair; she had cut it to just below her shoulders. Or had she lost more weight? She was already too thin for Winston's taste. But most of all he noticed she still wore her wedding ring. This pleased him.

"You've had your wish, Winston. I haven't filed for divorce, and I've raised our son. Now I want a promise from you that you'll stay away from Hollywood and Broadway or anything to do with the arts."

Seeking more power, he recently had focused most of his attention in Washington D.C. to obtain government contracts for W.J. Aeronautics. He didn't like to appear as though he were giving in to Diana, but what the hell, he had already decided to leave Hollywood. "All right, Diana," he said, smiling arrogantly. "Now you have *your* wish. How's John Stevens?"

Diana fielded the curve easily, expecting that Winston might one day try to take her by surprise. "He'll be much happier, hearing of your decision. So will Conrad."

"They sent you to do a man's job?"

"I heard recently that you called me a man. Didn't it have something to do with my Center? As I recall, you said that I was wearing pants the first day you met me and that you should have known then what I wanted to be."

Winston showed his displeasure openly. "I see, 'our friend' Walter Kent has been talking to you. I know about your business association."

"I didn't hear it from Walter. Did you tell him that,

too?"

"You're getting very good, Diana. Very good, indeed. By the way, how is Marcus Mancini? Isn't he in the army? You must feel fairly confident to let your protector trapse off for ports unknown."

Diana smiled. "Are you suggesting that someone might wish me ill?"

Winston laughed. "It is you who have given that impression over the last few years, having bodyguards and detectives on your payroll."

"Be careful, Winston. You're tipping your hand. No one knows who is on my payroll but my father and me. But let's continue that conversation another time. I would like to invite you to Windsor Royal for dinner. After all, you haven't seen Harrington for nearly eleven years. Did you know, he took his Harvard entrance exams and did so well they placed him in the sophomore class his first year?"

Winston flipped his hand in dismissal. "Thank you for dropping by."

"It isn't that easy, Winston. If you don't spend time with your son, you'll never have a relationship with him."

"It's your responsibility, Diana, to make sure I do."

"That might be possible if you and Harrington had shared any time together when he was younger. If he knew you cared. But you shunned him, Winston. I don't have a plausible explanation for your absence, at least not one he would accept."

"You'll think of something."

"It doesn't work like that. I can't cultivate his feelings for you. You have to do that yourself. You're telling our son that Todd Industries is more important than he is. Basically, he thinks you don't like him, and he doesn't care for you much, either."

"That's something he'll have to learn to live with."

CHAPTER VIII

S terling Darnley watched Harrington perform in *Hamlet,*
in summer theater of 1937. 'He's really very good,'
Sterling thought, and he heard confirmation of this opinion
from John's cohorts, who were always searching for new
talent.

Harrington had already been offered a contract in
Hollywood, which he had declined. He hoped one day to
work with Conrad Coleman. No one else would do for
him, or for Cara. And then there were the Broadway
contracts. Producers had offered Harrington minor parts
at first and then more substantial roles. On Broadway,
Harrington only wanted to work for John. He saved his
money from summer theater and he waited.

Sterling admired Harrington for his loyalty and for
finishing his schooling first. In December of 1937, he had
looked over his grandson's shoulder as Harrington studied
for his Harvard mid-terms. Determination, a keen
concentration, and a superb intellect, Harrington had it
all. Yet, he was kind and gentle. 'By God, the boy's like
me,' Sterling thought, very pleased. 'Diana's right. We're

just interested in different things.'

"You were right to guard him, Diana," Sterling told her in the spring of 1938. "He's more dedicated to his art—work —than any person I've ever seen. He and Cara are well suited. I believe they have a secret of some kind they're working towards. I've never seen two teenagers so driven!"

"Even I wasn't that determined," Diana said, feeling nothing but pride for her son and Cara.

"Almost, Diana," Sterling said, hugging her protectively. "And I want you to know I approve of you, your life, and your instincts. The Center is a magnificent accomplishment. I'm proud of you, Diana. I just wanted you to know."

Diana sensed this was a farewell speech. "Wait until you see what I have planned for Harrington in the next few years, Father. You're going to be so happy!"

Sterling was using a cane now, and his body had started to hunch over slightly. His white hair was still thick, but was turning a bit yellow on the back of his head. Awkwardly, he sat down and looked up at her with the blue eyes she loved so much, now rimmed in red. "All this excitement is wearing me out, Diana. Do you mind if I take the next few years sitting down?"

"Oh, Father!" Diana said, throwing her arms around him. "Of course not! You're a grand old man with the youngest heart I've ever had the fortune to know."

"And you, daughter, are too lavish in your compliments, but at my age, I'm beginning to appreciate the attention."

John came out onto the veranda waving a script. "It's ready, Diana!"

She smiled happily. "Let me find Harrington."

"I'm right here," Harrington said, following John with Cara at his side. "What's the mystery? Cara's been acting very strange today."

John winked at Sterling, who had wanted to be a part of the surprise. John thrust the script into Harrington's hands. "Read it."

Harrington stared at the title. *Remember When.* Watching Harrington, John had been inspired to write a play about his youth. Harrington knew this and looked at John questioningly.

"I want you to play the part of 'Ken' on Broadway."

Ken was actually John. "I appreciate your faith in me,

Uncle John, but . . ." Harrington looked back at the script.

John lit up a cigarette and placed it in the black holder, which was never far from his lips. "My granddaddy told me once," John said, "never to give money to a man who just asks for it because he won't know its worth. But, he also said that if a good plowman asks you to help him find work, you should. That man isn't asking for charity; he is simply seeking an opportunity to earn a living.

"Now, the only point my granddaddy left out was this: The good plowman who asks for work has to know he is good. Otherwise, no matter how good he actually is, he'll always think the farmer has done him a favor, and he'll never amount to anything." He paused. Then with an ever so slight smile he said, "As I recall, you asked me if you could audition one day for one of my plays. Are you a good plowman, Harrington?"

"Well, John, I don't think I'm a very good plowman, but I'm a pretty fair actor."

John threw back his head and laughed. "That's my boy!"

Harrington looked askance at Cara. "So you knew about the script all along, Franco. Why didn't you tell me?"

"You're so attractive when you're sweating, Todd. I couldn't resist keeping the secret."

Harrington glanced at his mother. "Did you think she'd turn into a smart aleck at eighteen?"

"But of course," Diana said. "You were meant for one another."

Harrington cracked a grin, which made his handsome face more rugged, almost sexy. "Are you sure you're not suggesting my guilt by association?"

"No, Harrington," Sterling smiled. "You'll have to take responsibility for that all by yourself."

In the winter of 1938 Harrington decided it was time to move to Manhattan. He counted up the money he had saved over the last eight summers at the Steven's Theater and set out with Cara to find an apartment. He rented the attic apartment in Cara's building with a view of Bleecker Street and A. Zito's Bakery.

A week later, he and Cara lunched in his room, which had one bed, set modestly in the corner with a brown

bedspread on it, one chair, and a dresser. They sat on the
floor, where Cara spread out a tablecloth, and ate A. Zito's
bread with slices of salami and mozzarella cheese and drank
wine.

"Everyone on both coasts talks about Conrad like he's a
god," Harrington was saying. "But he's your mentor, not
mine. And I'm not exactly in a position of power, you know.
He uses established actors in his films."

"If anyone can change his mind about actors, it's you."

The phone rang and Harrington answered it.

"Are you working or loafing?" John demanded of his
godson affectionately.

"Hello, John!" Harrington said as he played with Cara's
slender fingers, then pressed them to his lips. "Loafing."

"Glad to hear it. Broadway's tough, and I'm going to
work you hard. Better rest up. I want to see you for dinner
tonight. We have a few things to discuss. Okay?"

"Sure," Harrington said. "When are you leaving on
your hunting trip?"

"Changed my mind. Business. Now put Cara on the
phone. I've read her script."

"Which script?"

"Never you mind. Put Cara on the phone."

"Another script, eh?" he said, handing Cara the
receiver.

She nodded with a smug look that reminded Harrington
of her as a little girl. "And you aren't going to see it until it's
perfect." She took the phone and sat on the edge of the bed.

Cara never tried to drive him crazy, it just came
naturally. Hair golden and long, skin olive and smooth, nose
small and straight, lips generously full, Cara was striking in
her youth and beauty. The blue eyes that he knew so well
caught sight of his own. She tossed him a playful glance as she
laughed at something John said. Harrington watched her
brush a wisp of golden hair from her smooth skin. Her finger
lingered on her cheek, then fell to the corner of her pouting
mouth.

Harrington fixed his eyes on Cara's face. As she spoke,
her body shifted and straightened. Although she wore a black
business suit with a white blouse, the slender and sensuous
lines of her young womanhood were obvious. His eyes
traveled down her exquisite throat to the edge of her buttoned

blouse. She laughed again, making another abrupt move, and he caught a glimpse of her full, round breast. As she continued to talk, she reached out to touch his hand. He jerked his eyes away from her bosom, only to have his vision filled with a profile of sweet, moist, parted lips.

'My God!' he thought as she curled up like a kitten and brushed up against him. He grabbed the phone and told John they'd meet him tonight and slammed down the receiver.

"Harrington! What . . ." Cara stammered.

"You're going to marry me, Franco. I can't take this any more," he said, pushing her back on the bed.

At sunset, Harrington and Cara left their Bleecker Street apartment building to walk the few blocks to Franco's. Cara had put her business suit back on, which only reminded him of the sight of it lying on his apartment floor. The brim of her hat slanted over her left eye. She tilted her head to look up at him as they walked. "Get those thoughts under control, Todd. We have a long evening ahead."

Harrington laughed and held her more closely. They crossed the street and stopped in front of Franco's.

"You look very handsome tonight." She stood on her tippy toes to kiss him. "By the way, John said Conrad likes my movie script!"

"That's great news, Franco," Harrington said, hugging her.

"This doesn't change our plans, Todd. You establish your reputation. I start to work on my first play. Then, if Conrad gives you a contract: California. I think we're moving along right on schedule."

Fred Franco was at the reservations desk when they entered, and in his jovial style he clasped the tall Harrington affectionately and smothered his daughter with kisses.

"Now I will see you more often, eh?" he said happily. "You will live in the same building as Cara. I don't know why she moved out into her own apartment, but there it is. At least I can keep an eye on you two."

"Papa," Cara laughed. "You just saw us yesterday."

"Every minute is not enough!"

Arm in arm, Harrington and Cara chatted with Fred. "Business looks good, Papa."

"Oh, yes. Since Diana comes here, everyone joins her.

She is a grand lady. Did you know Marcus was here on leave?"

Marcus had decided the army was the best vehicle to finance his wish to travel. So far, he had been to Europe and the Far East. With recommendations from Diana, John, and Conrad he had become a lieutenant in Army Intelligence. Now he was stationed in Washington D.C.

Dressed in military uniform, he stood at the bar talking to Vincent Morello. They only saw Vincent's face, his pronounced broad nose, the large head covered with curly black hair. Vincent had a rugged almost handsome appearance, yet behind his burning black eyes, instability flickered.

"Marcus! Hello!" Cara exclaimed, coming up alongside him. When she saw his anger, she focused on Vincent. "What's going on here?"

Vincent jumped at the tone of her voice and the glass he was drying crashed to the floor. "You see! You see!" he said, startled. "He's threatening me!"

"What's this all about?" Harrington asked, looking at Marcus.

"None of your business, rich boy!"

Since their first encounter six years ago, Harrington had learned Vincent's history. This knowledge now restrained Harrington from jumping over the bar. "You're as cordial as ever, Vincent. Keep up the good work."

"That's enough, Harrington," Marcus said, donning a rare smile. "There's John! Let's join him."

Swiftly, he guided Harrington away before his young friend was goaded into another fight, which might have turned Franco's on its ear. By now, Marcus had no doubt Harrington was capable of going the distance with Vincent.

"You look a little flushed, Harrington," John said as they settled in a private booth away from the crowd.

"Vincent was being his usual obnoxious self," Cara said, "and Harrington sometimes forgets the advice he gave to Thomas and wants to turn into a street fighter."

"You have news for them," Marcus said, trying to change the subject.

Harrington ignored Marcus, the news, and everything— except Cara. "Listen, you little devil, I don't know why I have to be so patient with a maniac like Vincent Morello. After all, he's in love with you!"

"Would you please keep your voice down," Cara cautioned. "Honestly, Todd. Sometimes, I wonder about you."

As usual, they got so totally engrossed in each other that everyone else was forgotten.

"You've set your goals, I hear," John said, trying to intercede.

"You might wonder," Harrington said, ignoring John, "but I worry about you. The guy's crazy, Franco. I don't like the way he looks at you."

John and Marcus exchanged glances. Marcus had told John the same thing just this morning.

Vincent Morello and Fred Franco grew up together in Milocca, Sicily. Before the outbreak of World War I, Fred left Sicily for America. Vincent stayed behind with his brother, Carlos. No one, including Fred, knew Vincent's whole story, only that Vincent somehow got into trouble in 1926 and was tortured into submission by Perfect Mori. When he arrived in America in 1929, Vincent had the mentality of an angry child. Fred had helped Vincent, like he had helped many of his fellow Sicilians. Never had he expected that Vincent would one day fall in love with Cara. Everyone was worried about it.

"I'll take care of Vincent," Cara said. "You take care of our future."

"No, I'll take care of Vincent," Marcus interrupted. "And the two of you take care of your futures. Now listen . . ."

"No, I'll take care of Vincent," Harrington interrupted, his eyes on Marcus.

"You can try, but you won't as long as I am around to prevent it. You have a promising future, and I don't intend to let you spend it in prison. Maybe you'll feel better knowing that Fred is eventually going to fire Vincent. I just have to check out a few things first."

"What things?" Harrington demanded to know.

"All in good time, Harrington," John said. "Now will you listen to Marcus, or are you and I going to go a few rounds?"

The thought of fighting with John so amused Harrington that he was startled into laughter. "You've disarmed me, John. I'm all ears."

Marcus began abruptly, without any introduction. Sterling Darnley had suggested this strategy to shock Harrington and Cara into accepting the reality of their lives together.

Winston wanted an heir, and Harrington was his only son. In every way possible, Winston would try to take control of Harrington's life. For this reason, Sterling had asked Marcus to conduct a secret two year investigation with the help of his friend, Laster French, who had joined the FBI.

Marcus and Laster had poured over hundreds of unsolved crimes, finding numerous murders indirectly linked to Winston. Each case had something to do with the acquisition of a company—not always lured under the Todd banner, but often made available to one of Winston's allies as a payoff. Laster had tried, but had failed to catch Winston. Inevitably, he was cut off by one of Winston's powerful contacts or informants who ended up dead before they could testify. He and Marcus had concluded that, unless a unique opportunity presented itself, Winston would never be arrested.

"I'm not surprised," Harrington said. "I'd like to hear more."

"Talk to Sterling. He asked me to tell you about my findings," Marcus said.

Cara looked at the map of Sicily hanging over their booth. "Remember what Papa used to tell us?"

"I can tell you," Fred said, sliding into the booth beside Harrington. "See where Sicily sits," he said. "Right at the tip of the boot of Italy. We Sicilians have been kicked around by foreign invaders from the time of the Phoenicians and Greeks. We even kicked ourselves . . . the Mafiosi. . . . Some say they started honorably . . . I don't know. We Sicilians never could get it straight. I only know that any time someone criticizes the United States, I say it's worth dying for. Freedom. There is freedom here."

"That's right," Cara said. "Fear isn't a very productive stimulus."

"I hope being unafraid doesn't mean being unaware," John said.

"That's why Grandfather started the phrase, 'Be safe,' " Harrington said.

"It means," Cara explained, "always to be aware."

"Wonderful!" John boomed. "Let's eat! Oh, and by the way, Harrington, rehearsals start in June. You'd better begin researching your character."

Diana spent more time with Sterling Darnley during the following months as his health took a turn and he was again confined to his bed. When he passed away, in April of 1939, Diana was still unprepared for the news, although she had watched him slip away before her eyes.

Thomas and Conrad sent their condolences. Marcus came up from Washington D.C. for the funeral. Harrington and Cara took Sterling's death very hard. They solemnly watched him placed in the grave at Newport beside his beloved wife, Sara. Then they left for Manhattan, needing time alone together just like Diana and John.

Arm in arm, Diana and John strolled over the vast lawns of the Newport estate. They stopped at the Atlantic and looked out to the ocean. The biting air nipped at them, whirling around their bundled up bodies. John held Diana close.

"I mourn for him," Diana said. "I'm empty. Half a person. I expect him to come out onto the veranda any minute."

"If I die as he did, I'll be a happy man, Diana. He saw his daughter accomplish her goals. He watched his grandson grow up. He fulfilled his dreams and left his mark on the world through his work and his family. He will be remembered."

They went back inside and returned to the upstairs bedroom suite where they had rendezvoused many times over the years. John tried to think of something positive to say as he rekindled the fire and they sat down for tea.

He reminded Diana of Harrington and Cara. Between Harrington's researching his character for *Remember When* and Cara's writing schedule, the couple still found time for each other. Harrington had asked Cara to marry him, with Diana's blessing. They were an exceptionally talented duo and had a bright future.

"And what about Thomas?" John demanded of her, now that she had momentarily forgotten her troubles.

"He's a wonder, isn't he?" she said proudly.

Thomas had completed law school in two years. With

Conrad and Diana's help, he had established an impressive clientele, opened an East Coast office in New York, and become financially prosperous. Recently, he had even made the headlines, having negotiated one of the largest mergers in California.

"Now Conrad acts as though he discovered Thomas," John said almost indignantly. "Do you believe the gall?"

Diana laughed, kissing him. "No, I don't believe it."

"It wasn't long ago that Thomas didn't have a dime. He's done well. Conrad tells me he's thinking of buying a film studio. You wouldn't know anything about that, would you?"

Diana smiled. "Silent partners aren't allowed to."

"Diana!"

"Now, John, Thomas deserves it."

"Don't you understand, Diana? I'm just sorry I wasn't asked to be involved." He kissed her happily, grateful that he had distracted her. "And then there's Marcus. He's coming home in the fall, on leave, for the opening of *Remember When*. In the meantime we both have work to do. Or have you forgotten?"

Diana had been appointed chairwoman of the 1939 World's Fair. With the responsibility came an opportunity to set up the Fair's opening in conjunction with a milestone in communications. In April, New Yorkers would have a chance to watch and to listen to King George VI and Queen Elizabeth on closed circuit television in theaters all over the city. The Todd Cultural Center was already sold out for the event.

"Your father was very proud of that appointment, Diana, and impressed with how you were setting up the broadcast. I know you'll do a wonderful job; you already have. Never stop."

CHAPTER IX

D iana stared at the Manhattan skyline visible from her hospital bed on this evening of September 1939. As the full moon emerged from behind the clouds, the moonlight cut across her face and illuminated the entire city. The R.C.A. Building stood out like a rocket, a sparkling memorial to man's creativity. Its tower crowned the Todd Cultural Center, her own contribution to that creative drive.

'How stupid she had been,' she thought. How utterly naive! Her slender hand rested wearily above her head. Her second stroke! Her father's death had affected her more deeply than she had thought.

Winston had phone after her stroke, but she'd refused to take his call. He sent her a message through Harris Johnson, whom she had long known was Winston's dupe at Windsor Royal. "You don't have any protection now, Diana. You'd better hand over the Cultural Center." 'He's such a prince,' she thought angrily.

She knew she was changing. For the three weeks she had been here, she had thought of nothing but change. Her will was stronger than ever, a lesson from her father. Here in bed, during the long nights, she carefully considered her course. When she finally had discovered Winston's weakness, something so simple and right before her all these years, she realized she had unconsciously solved part of her problem long ago.

She sighed and looked out of the window again. The vision of the Cultural Center had kept her company these three weeks. At least, in one sense, her goals had been achieved with the Center's completion, but her true fulfillment would come through Harrington. He was her living memorial to freedom and creativity. She marveled that beauty so often sprang from tragedy.

The thought of Harrington's performance, in one week, turned her thoughts to John. He had been a part of her life for so long that sometimes she took him for granted. No longer would she do so. She was deeply in love with him. It was different than it had been with Winston, of course. Twenty-five years ago, Winston had been her first real love. Ten of those twenty-five years were happy with him; fifteen were happy without him. Now she loved her oldest and dearest friend.

Outside her private room, she heard muted voices, gurneys rolling by, the scurrying of footsteps, a cleaning crew buffing the floor. She had grown accustomed to these hospital noises, and none was more welcome than the crisp gait of Nurse Saunders.

"I thought you'd be awake," the plump, middle-aged woman said cheerfully. She stuck a thermometer in Diana's mouth, then took her blood pressure. While she recorded her findings on the chart, she reported them aloud. "Your temperature's down and your blood pressure's stabilized. The doctor will be very pleased."

"I'll be released from here by the end of the week," Diana said.

"Nothing you'd do would surprise me. I've never seen a more determined woman in my life. Your recovery is miraculous!"

Susan Saunders hung the chart at the end of the bed and noticed the New York *Times*, dated September 26, 1939, on the bedstand. The front page photograph of Winston Jason Todd II stared out at her. 'What a great man he is!' Susan thought. 'His wife's in the hospital a month and never a visit.

Such a dear lady with a husband like that!'

"Is something the matter, Susan?"

"Oh no, nothing! I do have a telegram for you."

"Why don't you open it?" Diana suggested, knowing Susan was always curious.

Susan turned on the overhead lamp. "My goodness, it's from King George and Queen Elizabeth, Mrs. Todd!"

Diana listened to the monarchs' wishes for her speedy recovery. They also included their thanks again for her help during their goodwill mission back in June.

"Was it you who got the King and Queen to speak at the Court of Peace at the World's Fair?" Susan asked in surprise.

"Yes. I thought it might be an omen for peace."

"Don't worry, Mrs. Todd. Americans aren't interested in war. Why, we have too many problems of our own with the Depression still going on." Susan patted her hand. "Get some rest. The doctor's making his nightly rounds. I'll be back soon."

'The eyes of the innocent are blessed,' Diana thought fondly. The promise of war often sped up the motors of progress. In the United States, progress ran with a dollar sign. War was a big business, and Winston knew just how to exploit such situations. He would deal with the English and with the Germans and profit from Europe's war if it came to that.

She closed her eyes to rest, weary of Winston's image in her mind. An ambulance siren wailed, its ululating cries reminding Diana of impending danger. She thought it curious that she had married Winston at the outbreak of the First World War and planned to divorce him on the brink of the Second. A violent world, a tumultuous marriage—the English and French had declared war on Germany, and soon she, too, would wage a war . . . against her husband.

'Can't you forget about him for a moment?' she asked herself angrily. She was so engrossed in her thoughts that it took a moment before she realized that someone was in her room. She opened her eyes, startled by the presence of the tall, immaculately dressed figure beside her bed.

"Good evening, Diana."

Diana slowly rose to her elbows and then sat up, waiting, her eyes curious.

"What's the matter, Diana? Aren't you happy to see

me?"

Susan pushed open the door. "Mrs. Todd!" she exclaimed. "What are you doing up?" Susan rushed to intervene, standing between Diana and the stranger. "I'll have to ask you to leave at once, sir! Visitors are absolutely forbidden at this hour. Mrs. Todd isn't well enough to see anyone except immediate family."

"If you're interested in keeping your job, nurse, I'd strongly suggest you leave me alone with my wife."

Susan's heart thumped in her chest as she gazed up at the six-foot-two figure. 'So, here you are at last,' she thought heatedly. "Will you be all right, Mrs. Todd?"

"Yes, Susan. Thank you."

"I'll be right outside," Susan told Diana. "And you, Mr. Todd," she said, taking her duties to heart, "have ten minutes to visit, no more."

Before the door had closed, Winston said, "Somehow you've always had a knack for enlisting the aid of commoners." His gaze was almost loving. Yet, when their eyes met, the aristocratic Todd cheekbones tensed and his lips pursed shut. 'Harrington has the same expression when angry,' Diana thought, struck again by the physical similarities between Winston and their son, despite the differences in their coloring.

"All right, Diana," he said, pulling a chair up to her bed. "Let's talk about Harrington."

Involuntarily, her hands tightened into fists and crumpled the sheet. "You haven't changed, Winston, but then I didn't expect you would. I'm afraid for you because you've never been understanding of others."

A slight smile flickered across his face. "Afraid for me or afraid for our son? The only thing I ever asked of you was that you raise Harrington properly. Although you have failed miserably, I'm going to give you one last chance. You either tell our son to forget about starring in *Remember When* and discourage his relationship with Cara Franco or I will. And if you force me to take such an action, I'll make sure John Stevens never gets another play produced on Broadway."

A reserved strength stirred in Diana, and once again she had her father to thank for his example. "If you wish something from our son, you'll have to ask him yourself."

"So you're refusing me again. I expected as much,"

Winston said darkly. "You've never done anything for me. I'll just have to take care of it myself, as I've always done."

"Yes, I guess that's true, Winston. You've had to do everything for yourself."

Winston missed her sarcasm and left his chair. "You never did understand that it's what I want that's important. Harrington's going to accept that even if you never have!" From the window, his own Todd Center, which now rivaled Wall Street as the business capital of New York, rose against the skyline, dwarfing Diana's nearby Cultural Center. He felt a sense of triumph and glanced over his shoulder. "I suppose you've drawn up your will?"

Winston wasn't usually so crude. Diana was astonished. "You come here with threats and ultimatums, and now you question me about my will? I have a few more years to live, Winston. Don't be so presumptuous."

He turned completely around. "Well, what about your will?"

"That, sir, is none of your business!"

Where he charmed others into submission, Diana inevitably saw through his façade. That he was transparent before her, irritated him, making him the more cruel.

"I won't allow my son to ruin his life nor to tarnish our name. If you leave him your money and the Cultural Center resources to finance his frivolity, I'll make him pay sooner or later."

"I've always admired your grace, although I've never respected your motives. Tonight you've given me reason to live, Winston."

She threw off her covers, and as she did so Winston registered surprise. But no more surprise than she experienced when Harrington barged into the room.

He looked from one parent to the other in astonishment. Then he brushed by Winston and hurried to his mother. "What are you doing out of bed?"

"I didn't know you were visiting tonight, darling."

"It was last minute, but I'm glad I did. I could hear your argument all the way down the hall." He glanced back at Winston and his anger showed on his handsome face. "What are you trying to do?"

"I don't answer to you or to anyone, Harrington," Winston said without a blink. "Actually, I'm happy to see you. I'd like to talk."

Harrington was astounded by his father's behavior. Without answering, he returned his attention to his mother. She had put on her robe. "Mother, please. Get back in bed."

"I second that," the doctor said, walking in with Nurse Saunders behind him.

Diana's purpose was clear. She thought best at home, at Windsor Royal. She considered it her sanctuary, more her home than Winston's.

Dr. Frazier's face was grave, filled with worry. He brushed by Winston and confronted Diana. "Mrs. Todd, please return to bed. You are in no condition to leave this hospital."

Dr. Frazier had overseen her progress for the last month and never had he perceived anything but the deepest compassion in her eyes. But something had happened to this delicate lady, and the change in her demeanor now made him pause.

"I am perfectly fine, doctor. I thank you for all you've done, but I must get home. It's time."

Harrington moved out of the way, and the doctor grabbed her wrist and listened to her pulse. He was absolutely astonished. He made her sit down while he took her blood pressure. Then he looked at the chart.

"You appear to have made a miraculous recovery. But surely, you can't be serious. You should stay here at least until the end of the week. Let's be sure you don't have a relapse."

"I'm afraid that's impossible," Diana said firmly. "Now, if you'll excuse me."

"Mr. Todd," the doctor said beseechingly. "Please tell your wife . . ."

"I stopped trying years ago, doctor. She will do what she wants no matter what you say."

The doctor was surprised to see a glimmer of respect in Winston's eyes and then he saw something else, something which he could not discern, but which Diana understood. Winston walked out of the room and Diana was left with the haunting reality that if Winston could not have her dead, he would live to watch her suffer.

Harrington also saw his father's expression. "If you get back into bed, Mother, I'll be by first thing in the morning to take you home."

Diana noticed that he was edging towards the door. Maybe it was time that Harrington spoke to his father. Normally she would have made her own arrangements, but she wanted Harrington to take his leave—so she sat down on the edge of the bed and gracefully fell against the pillows. "Go ahead, dear, I'll be fine, and I'll see you first thing in the morning."

Harrington caught up with Winston outside the hospital and spun him around right in front of his bodyguard, Joe Field.

"What the hell were you doing in there? If I didn't know better . . ."

"Lower your voice," Winston commanded.

"Take your own advice. The whole hospital heard you!"

Winston ushered Harrington to the limousine. During the ride to the Fifth Avenue home, Winston considered his son for the first time as a young man to be proud of. Just an hour before, when he had visited Diana, he had wanted to take control of Harrington on mere principal. Harrington was his son, his only heir. Diana had done her job and now he wanted to take over. After seeing how Harrington handled himself, Winston was more passionate about swinging Harrington over to his side.

Harrington was so angry, he was unaware of Winston staring at him. Once and for all, he would set his father straight, and Diana would be free of him. When the limousine stopped on Fifth Avenue, Harrington walked ahead of Winston into the apartment where he'd never been invited and turned on Winston with a vengeance.

"All right, Father," he said drawing out the name sarcastically. "I've got some things on my mind."

"You've never been here before, Harrington. Why don't you look around. Then we'll sit here in the drawing room."

"I'll stand."

Winston also stood. "You've made up your mind to be an actor."

"Long ago. Now about . . ."

"Goddamnit, Harrington, you were born into my world and that's where you belong. Why the hell do you want to kick around in godforsaken theaters? You're too young to realize what you'll be giving up when you turn your back on me. I can put the world at your fingertips. I want you to go on to Harvard Law School in the fall, and I don't want any arguments!"

"Let's get one thing straight. I don't give a damn what your expectations are."

"You're naive, Harrington. And I believe you're afraid —afraid to face the real world. Actors are cowards. They pretend to be someone else because they can't face themselves. They're weak and have to look to the strong for guidance and support. Is that the man you are? Have you hidden behind your mother's skirts so long that you don't know what it is to be a man?"

"I haven't been hiding behind anything. You have."

Winston smirked. "And what would that be?"

"Fear."

"I don't hide behind it!" Winston stormed, banging his fist on the table. "I use it. Maybe you need a lesson about the facts of life." Winston's tone became condescending and controlled.

"In the beginning of a man's business career, he has high aspirations and values himself above all other men . . ." Harrington started to interrupt. "By God, Harrington, you're going to listen to this! You'll have your say, but at least let me finish this thought!"

Harrington held his temper, gesturing with an impertinent shrug that he was indifferent to whatever Winston did.

"As I was saying," Winston said, ignoring his son's insolence, "over the years, a man shows his true value to others and to himself by the way he rises in his field and the way he protects his position. If he's inconsistent—if, for any reason, he strays from his personal convictions, then he shows his weakness. That spot, however slight, that makes him vulnerable. If his ideals are noble and he strays, guilt and self-hatred will haunt him. If his ideals are dishonorable and he strays, he'll be overcome by fear and self-doubt. No matter how strong or powerful a man becomes, if he displays weakness and inconsistency, his downfall is inevitable."

He paused to let the thought sink in. Harrington appeared not to have heard him, making him the more determined to get his point across.

"I'm the most consistent man you'll ever meet, Harrington. My greatest strength is that I seek out and exploit the contradictions in each man. When I find the inconsistency, a man is forever under my control. You're either a ruler or a slave, there's no in-between. I made a mistake one time in my life, and I learned. I became a ruler. Now I demand that everyone must live according to my standards. Refuse, and I'll find the means to change your mind . . . or I'll crush you. Take heed, son, before it's too late!"

"I've heard about this speech and I'm not impressed."

Winston had expected Harrington to think twice about being impudent again. His eyes narrowed as he considered the source of his son's bitterness. "I suppose your mother told you. She never could keep her place."

"A woman doesn't have a place any more than you or I!"

"That's where you're wrong, my boy. We all have our place, and yours is as a Todd, as your mother's should have been."

"Your love for her was conditional on her obeying your every command!"

"That's right. I tried it her way and it didn't work. We were almost destroyed. Don't you remember your brother? If I had done things my way, he would still be alive! I should never have listened to her."

"There was nothing you or she could have done, Father. Some things you just can't control."

"The hell I can't!"

"That's right, you can't. Now that you're in control, I don't see my brother back. He could still be alive. Why haven't you looked for him?"

Winston flipped his hand in dismissal. "You're talking after the fact. Nothing can be done now. He's dead, Harrington. My point is that Winston Jason never would have disappeared if things had been done my way . . ." He turned on Harrington then, seeing his son's surprise at his words. "That's right, don't contradict me. I know what I'm talking about. The Cultural Center is another example. By all rights it should have been mine. Instead, without my approval, she broke ground. She wasn't my wife anymore; she became a business competitor. I didn't want the Todd image tarnished by a woman's hand! Didn't she realize that Todd Industries was more important to me than life or marriage? She forced me to choose between her and my business. Todd Industries won!"

"You've missed the point, Father. She never asked you to make that choice. You're the one who turned on her! You thought you were the only important one in the relationship. You never stopped to consider that she and I grieved for my brother. You never thought of anyone but yourself! What you resented most was her decision to go on living, and I might add, to live very well without you. You wanted everyone devoted to you and you alone!"

"Call it what you like. Your mother was wrong and she suffered the penalty. Besides, she needed to be taught a lesson."

"A lesson? Why do you blame her for Winston Jason? Why are you punishing her?"

"That has nothing to do with this!"

"What does? That you were in pain? That you've been in pain? That you refused to love anyone again after Winston Jason was gone? You think it's manly to build a wall around your heart . . . to deny feelings . . . to deny me. Does she remind you of how much you really love her every time you see her? Do you hate her for it, Father? Is that the problem? Do you hate her, do you want to blame her for your own faults because it hurts too much to look at yourself?"

Winston astounded Harrington when he smiled. "I don't know what you're talking about, son. I can only tell you that no one betrays me. Your mother was and is a foolish woman. She deserves whatever life has done to her."

Harrington stood quietly, staring at his father. Winston showed neither remorse nor sadness. He seemed barely human. 'Is this man really my father?' Harrington wondered.

"Don't talk about her," Harrington said softly. "Don't say another word. You love her, Father, and so do I."

"Love! You love her? What play did you take that from, Oedipus? You know nothing of love and nothing about my relationship with my wife!"

"Your wife! That's a laugh! My mother was never your wife. She was your prize. She was a piece of art to hang over your mantel. A masterpiece to display your good taste. Your wife! You've never understood the meaning of the word." Harrington was inches from Winston now, his hands trembling. "I dislike you and everything you represent.

There's no point arguing with me. You can't buy me. You can't bribe me. Nothing you can do or say will ever make me think of you as a great man. And you need men around you who do. Forget about me. I intend to forget about you. You're not my father. *Her* blood runs through my veins, not yours. And if you ever think you can change my mind, forget it! I hold you personally responsible for her ill health, and if she has a relapse, I'll get you."

Winston formulated his words coldly and carefully. "You're going to fail, Harrington. You're going to fall flat on your face in public! You'll be nothing more than a whore, selling your body and my Todd name to every cheap tramp with a quarter. You don't care about the family. You don't even care that people will think you're worthless. What do you care about, Harrington? Whatever it is, I hope you don't mind if I don't join you in your grand undertaking. You see, I'm merely a humble businessman running a multimillion dollar empire. I'm quite sure your purpose in life is of greater importance than mine, but I just don't think I'll be able to tear myself away when you come crawling back, begging me to pick you up out of the gutter after you've tripped over your own feet!"

Winston paused to catch his breath. There was no point in continuing. His feelings for Harrington were dead. He would think about another heir. "One day you'll understand, Harrington, but it will be too late. Women have no place in business. I, for one, never want advice from a woman as long as I live. You'll learn, you'll learn. You're following in her footsteps all right. You'll never receive a cent of my money. Now get out of my sight!"

Harrington bowed slightly. "It will be a pleasure, and, sir, you can rot in hell."

Winston chuckled. "She's the one who will rot in hell, Harrington."

Harrington turned around. "You're such a fool, Father. You're living in hell; she's at peace."

CHAPTER X

Diana alighted from her limousine on the arm of Thomas Garvin. They both were well aware that the premiere of a John Stevens play was an event unto itself. With the added attraction of a scandal, the box office had been sold out months in advance.

Rumors about the conflict between Diana and Winston, and about Winston's behavior in Diana's hospital room, were fanned by Harrington's refusal to talk about his father in interviews. Would Diana be well enough to attend the opening? Would Winston come? The aura around the opening had the critics and theatergoers more curious than ever about Harrington and just how the illustrious Todd family would handle their private scandal in public.

Outside the 44th Street Theater was a madhouse. Diana and Thomas walked up the red carpet along with stars from Hollywood and New York as screaming fans rocked against the barricades.

Lawyer turned tycoon, Thomas looked like a wise old sage in a boy's body with his youthful wavy brown hair and his intent pale blue eyes. Lean yet athletic, he stood six feet tall and wore expensive clothes as if he had been born to wear them. He had recently bought World Studios where Conrad had his offices. Many stars and executives shook his hand, and he was delayed just outside the theater as Diana entered.

The hush of the crowd was like a gasp of astonishment when Diana appeared in the lobby. She paused in the doorway, commanding everyone's attention. She was forty-two years old, a woman of accomplishment who lived her private life in the public eye, and she guarded her secrets well.

Beneath the French crystal chandeliers that hung from the lobby ceiling, men stood in white tails with crisp starched shirts, white ties, and glossy shoes. Many still had on their overcoats, hats, and gloves. Women dressed in designer gowns, their wraps draped over their shoulders or arms.

Diana wore a white Schiaparelli evening gown and an ermine full-length fur. Emeralds and diamonds glistened from her neck and wrist. The diamond and emerald cluster earrings sparkled against her blonde hair, now touched with white and cut in the latest style. She looked as though she had just returned from a vacation instead of a prolonged hospitalization. Although weak, her iron will to protect her son filled her with courage. She stood alone momentarily, smiling at the crowd, just to let everyone see that she was quite well and interested only in enjoying her son's opening.

Graciously she walked through the crowd, with Thomas now at her side. Reporters tailed after them. Theatergoers shook her hand and his. Her powerful presence kept all from asking questions she didn't wish to answer. She was above reproach, and her grace and dignity set those apart from her whom she didn't wish to greet.

Just as the crowd had recovered from seeing Diana, they were filled with anticipation as Winston entered the lobby.

Winston was all charm and warmth. Diana privately seethed. 'And he wonders where his son has cultivated such an extraordinary talent!' His mere presence further strengthened Diana's will.

Why did a good fight spark her so? She who had always preached the positive side of life itched for this confrontation. Curiously, she and Winston were linked as no other two people on earth. Where once they had shared the same goals, where once they had fought the same battle, their courses had diverged. Winston had allowed his obsession and fear to control him, and in so doing, he had tried to destroy those he loved. As she considered this, she also heard Winston's words to the press.

"I don't want you boys being too rough on my son. *Remember When*'s his first real break . . ."

There was Winston, in front of all the most important theater people in New York, imploring the press to be kind to Harrington. Diana knew, unless something was done, Harrington would now have a hard time winning over the critics on his own. She had already prepared for such a dilemma, and her favorite critic from the New York *Times* bridged Winston's entourage to hers with a question from the outskirts of Winston's circle.

"Do you have a comment, Mrs. Todd?" Sol Chandelier asked.

Diana watched the press circles merge from two into one, and Winston was forced to stand directly opposite her. Then she made her move, so graciously that there was no loss of face. With a dignity that reflected her long life in the public eye, Diana nodded with a radiant smile to Thomas that she would be right back, for indeed she had something to say. In utter command of the entire group, she gracefully walked across the circle, extended a hand to Winston and a cheek, which he had to dutifully kiss unless he wished to appear an utter fool.

After these preliminaries were accomplished, she had the attention of the entire press corp, taking the limelight away from Winston.

"Gentlemen," she said so kindly they thought they would melt at her radiance, "my husband is so protective and of course proud of our son, but we both know Harrington would wish to speak for himself." She smiled, in just the right way, flushing a bit. "It's out of respect for his years of dedicated work, his many performances in summer theater, and his unusual talent that this thought must prevail."

The lights flashed and Diana was the first to leave, but not before she smiled up at Winston for the photographers and waved her good-bye to the reporters.

When Harrington learned of Winston's arrival, he was backstage in his dressing room, away from all the fanfare.

He tried to block his father from his mind and to

continue to recite the first act, but his concentration waned, and he groped for lines. At times, in past productions, he'd forgotten dialogue and had been forced to ad lib. Critics in summer stock had panned him when his timing was off. 'Not tonight,' he thought. 'Don't let that happen tonight!'

His hands shook; his nervousness infuriated him. As he jerked to his feet, he knocked over the chair. He picked it up and slammed it to the floor. The bang echoed in the room.

He scanned the dressing room, from the wardrobe that hung in the open closet to the dressing table where all his makeup was set. An hour before, he had checked all his props. Everything was in order. Now it was up to him.

He edged back into his chair and stared into the mirror. He noticed the perspiration on his forehead. He picked up the sponge and wiped it away.

'You're going to fail, Harrington. You're going to fall flat on your face in public! . . .' His hand froze as the memory jarred him. The words continued and he could not stop them. 'Actors are cowards. They pretend to be someone else because they can't face themselves. . . .'

He stared angrily into the mirror and demanded of himself out loud, "Are you going to let him get to you? Is that what this is all about?"

Sweeping her black organdy gown behind her, Cara stepped inside his door. Her golden hair fell to her shoulders. Many said she looked more like Harrington's sister than his future wife. She appeared in his mirror, flushed and radiant, a vision in black.

"You won't," she said firmly. "Is it really that bad, Todd?"

"It comes with the territory, Franco," he answered with their childhood salute.

They stared at each other, momentarily lost in thought.

"Just remember that tonight is for you," Cara said finally, breaking the silence.

"I know he's out there . . ."

"The night is still for you, and for your mother."

"Thanks, Franco, I'll remember. But it's also for us."

"Five minutes!" They heard the stage manager call out. Harrington sighed. "Here I go, Franco . . ."

Hastily he touched up his face, subtly smeared with makeup to give him a dirty, run-down mien. He wore a tattered shirt and pants. His hair was disheveled and dropped over his forehead. He had taken great pains to darken his hands and put dirt beneath his nails. He looked the part of a down-and-out writer, and that's how he felt, physically and mentally.

When he stood up, his eyes glazed over. He stretched once, then stooped over slightly, a pose he would use often during the performance. He squeezed Cara's hand, then strode awkwardly out the door, already in character.

He had prepared for this moment for nine years. 'Nine years!' he thought.

During those summers at the Stevens Theater, he had developed a special technique for researching characters. Part of that method was to wear the kind of garb and to frequent the kinds of places appropriate to the character he was portraying. He had ransacked second-hand stores on the Lower East Side in search of suitable clothing for this part. All winter he had worn tattered threads and hung out on Hester Street where John had lived when first in New York.

'All the long hours,' he thought as the curtain opened and he heard the applause.

For months he had rehearsed night and day, reading the part of 'Ken' countless ways, underlining words, marking sentences, developing mannerisms—throwing those out and developing others, until he began to feel comfortable with the character.

'After all that, you aren't going to let *him* win, are you?' he asked himself and then automatically said, as he did in every performance he'd been in since ten years old: 'Watch over me, Winston Jason. I need you.'

Was his voice carrying? He remembered a review from the previous summer. "With a look, a movement, with one single word, Harrington Todd filled the stage with his presence. He exuded a talent for the unexpected and stirred tremendous excitement in the audience." Was he doing that now?

'That's your cue! Get across the stage. Don't let him get to you, Todd!' He heard the applause again, just in the right place. Or was it? How was he really doing? Sweat, he felt sweat! He was supposed to be calm and he was sweating. He couldn't wipe it away. Christ!

'Listen. That's another cue. Pick it up!'

Time passed without his realizing. The second act began. He felt as though he was stumbling along, although he was saying all the right lines. The cast was reacting. No vacant eyes. No horrified expressions. He must be doing something right. Or was he?

He had no idea how he got back to his dressing room. He was alone. The door was locked. He wanted to run away, but he changed his clothes and dabbed at his makeup. His reflection looked like that of a stranger.

"Five minutes!!!"

Up again. The third act. When he tried to remember his first line, his mind went totally blank. He searched for the script.

"Harrington!!"

He was out there on the stage. The curtain opened. Applause. Was it polite or did they really mean it? 'Concentrate, Todd!'

Was he drunk with fatigue or was he playing the part? The fight scene. Awkwardly, he took off his ragged coat and dropped it on the barstool. Was he agile and powerful? He rolled up his sleeves with strong hands and imagined the rough hands of a laborer folding the sleeves in the same jerky fashion. He knew his manner and movements strongly contradicted his breeding and that everyone in the audience was aware of it. Winston came to mind. 'Take that, you bastard!' he thought as the choreographed fight began.

He heard applause. It crescendoed. Were those *oohs* and *aahs*, or was it his imagination? It couldn't be. The play's over. Yes, it is. You made it. Take your bow! He stared out into the audience, but saw only blinding lights. There were no faces. Then he was able to make out figures in the audience. They were standing and clapping.

He lifted his eyes to the ceiling, sweat pouring down his face. 'Did I hear the music, Winston Jason? Did I?'

When the cast of *Remember When* entered Sardi's, Winston started the applause. Stoically, Harrington listened to his congratulations as Winston's words echoed in his ears . . . 'You'll be nothing more than a whore, selling your body and my Todd name to every cheap tramp with a . . .'

Harrington reached into his pocket. "To reimburse you

for your trouble, Father," he said, disguising the bite to his words.

Winston chuckled and pocketed the quarter. "You should try comedy, Harrington. I think you'd be quite good at it."

Diana upstaged Winston when she entered with John and Thomas. Winston bowed out politely, telling everyone that it was his son's night.

Diana was fatigued, but insisted on waiting up for the reviews. In the hours that followed, Harrington and John got progressively more nervous. Finally, Marcus, home for the weekend, rounded up all the early morning editions.

They all sat parked outside the Bleecker Street apartment in Diana's limousine as Marcus handed out the reviews. Paper seemed to fill the backseat.

"Here's the New York *Times*," John said, peering at the print. "I'll skip to the part about you, Harrington . . ."

"Come on, John, I want to hear what they say about your play."

"Let me see," John said, ignoring him. "Ah, here it is . . . 'In spite of his wealth, Harrington Todd has a keen sense of the ghetto character, Ken . . .'" John cleared his throat. "'. . . with the support of his family, and friends such as Thomas Garvin, who proclaimed him "one of the finest talents he had ever seen," and with his father, Winston Jason Todd II, and mother, Diana Darnley Todd, to cheer him on, Harrington Todd proved himself to be a consummate professional.'" John stopped and looked over the paper.

Harrington's eyes had lost their life. "What? My father cheering me on! He really has everyone fooled, doesn't he? They should have just mentioned you, Mother, not him!"

"It isn't important, Harrington," Diana said. "The review is very good."

"You know better, Mother . . ."

"Cara, you have the New York *Post*," Diana suggested.

"Here it is," Cara said nervously. "Harrington Todd, son of supermagnate, Winston J. Todd II, and patron of the arts, Diana Darnley Todd, opened in a new play, *Remember When*, written by the illustrious John Stevens. Young Todd is superb as the ghetto character, Ken. Although one must wonder where such a priviledged young man, raised in Todd luxury, found the insight."

"What's the *Daily News* say, Thomas?" Harrington asked angrily.

"Here it is, let's see . . . 'The audience's reaction to Harrington Todd was astounding, although it was difficult to tell whether they were responding to Mr. Todd's talent or his celebrity status as the son of Mr. and Mrs. Winston Todd.'"

Harrington had thought that once the critics saw his performance they would judge him on his talent. He had been wrong. He was known more than ever as Winston Todd's son. The thought infuriated him.

"Any others? What about you, Marcus? It's your turn."

Marcus read the New York *Herald Tribune*, hoping for no further mention of Winston. " 'Harrington Todd was delightful as Ken. Word has it that he slummed around for three months researching the part. Seeing that his upbringing wouldn't have allowed him an inkling of insight into such a life . . .'" Marcus frowned.

"So that's the way the game is played, huh?" Harrington said, his jaw muscle twitching. "Maybe he *was* right. Maybe I *am* just a whore. The Todd name seems to sell newspapers."

Diana understood his disappointment and tolerated his mood. Still she said, "Why don't you sleep on it, Harrington. You might feel differently tomorrow."

John tossed the papers onto the floor. "Remember what I told you about my granddaddy and the plowman?"

"Well, John," Harrington answered irritably, "I don't think I'm a good plowman, or a good actor, so maybe I'd better not ask anyone for any more work. See you tomorrow, Mother. Good night, Thomas. Thanks for everything, Marcus. And, John, I'm sorry I can't even be generous enough to listen to the reviews." He grabbed Cara's arm and said, "Come on, Franco, I don't want to keep these people up all night."

Diana watched them leave the car, a bit irritated that her son had not been receptive to John's reminder. She hid it from Harrington and rolled down the window.

"Harrington, I want to see you and Cara at the Cultural Center tomorrow morning at eleven. We'll be waiting for you in the promenade. Good night, dears."

Marcus drove the limousine away, and Harrington confronted Cara outside the Bleecker Street apartment building. "I don't want to discuss this."

Cara was fuming. How could Harrington behave this
way! She had seen the calm on Diana's face, something she
wished she had the discipline to muster.

"You're being unreasonable, Todd."

"I know," he said simply.

Cara's eyes flashed in anger. "Why are you doing this to
yourself?" When he didn't answer, she walked away. "Are
you coming?" Harrington didn't move. "Well, good night
then!"

Harrington caught her arm and spun her around. The
blinding hate for his father consumed him. She saw this and
decided to speak her mind anyway.

"I've heard of many actors with self-destructive
streaks." He flinched and she tried to take the edge out of her
voice. "Don't let him destroy you, Todd."

She was right, of course, but he couldn't help himself.
He had the sense to enter the apartment building, although he
stormed ahead of her to her apartment. His thoughts were
running wild. He had been blocking out his feelings for
Winston. Now he wanted to barge into the Todd Center and
blow the bastard's brains out!

Cara touched his arm. "I love you," she whispered.

The tone of her voice touched his heart. She looked so
young, so vulnerable. Why was her expression affecting him
so profoundly? Had he hurt her? Had he taken out his anger
on her? Memories from the past collided with thoughts of the
present. Why had her expression stirred up memories? How
were they powerful enough to combat the pain inside him?

He stood there, his mind racing, his heart pounding.
Winston suddenly vanished from his mind, replaced with the
remembrance of a day in his sixteenth year with Cara in the
cool damp shade of the hayloft at the Todd Stables.

'How long ago that seems,' he thought, staring at her
now. "Franco, you're beautiful."

He led her into the bedroom and closed the door. There,
he unfastened the buttons of her dress with a touch so gentle
that she didn't feel the pressure of his fingertips against her
breast. She dared not move. His eyes were on fire. The hands
that removed her dress and slid the material from her
shoulders were as soft on her skin as the smoothest satin. Her
gown fell at her feet. The straps to her slip slid off her arms.

With himself, he was violent. He tore off his coat,

tugged at his tie, and ripped off his shirt. As they fell onto the
bed, he sought out her body with such power that Cara cried
out his name, and her thoughts filled with a wanting to mend
his wounds. She gave herself over totally to please him, yet
knowing that a part of his pleasure would come from his own
giving. She flowed with his movement, thinking of nothing
but the feel of his lips on her body. His hands told her of his
thoughts. His movements revealed the depth of his emotion.
And she drifted into a wonderful euphoria as they released
their love together.

"Harrington," she whispered, brushing his lips, when
they lay still and exhausted, "you did yourself proud tonight.
You were born to be an actor. No one can ever take that away
from you."

He picked up her hand and kissed her palm. "Thank
you, Franco. Thanks for everything."

"There's no need for thanks, Todd. You give so much."
They were content for a moment, and then she told him what
she knew he needed to hear. "When you were standing on the
stage, Todd, taking your bows, I saw you look up. I know
what you were asking Winston Jason. You did hear the
music, Todd. You did."

'My God,' he thought, choked up. 'How does she
always know what I need?' "What would I do without you,
Franco?" he asked, holding her close. "You're the most
precious person in my life."

CHAPTER XI

"Come on, Franco, we're supposed to be at the Center in a half an hour!"

Harrington, dressed in a gray suit and a Windsor knot tie, pulled Cara along Bleecker Street. She looked so pretty in her black suit, which showed her legs just below the knees, the black hat tilted on her blonde head partially covering her eyes. 'She's downright sexy,' Harrington thought, startling her with a kiss right in the middle of Bleecker Street.

"Todd!" she laughed, now leading him. "We're late!"

The noonday sun, directly overhead, drove back shadows to cower in the alleys. The street teemed—elderly men huddled in groups, arguing about Italy's possible involvement in the European War; women in black, holding rosaries, talked in front of the Lady of Pompeii Church; rambunctious children played tag, dodging in between parked cars. They skipped out of the children's way and hurried towards Washington Square and Fifth Avenue.

Dense traffic and hundreds of pedestrians congested the avenue. They walked along the sidewalk, heading towards Central Park. Before long, they saw the colorful assemblage of international flags flapping in front of the Todd Business Center.

They stopped at its entrance. In the distance, beyond the main promenade lined with skyscrapers, stood Todd Industries's headquarters. Above its glass doors, sparkling in the light like a solitary sun, the Todd Crest demanded attention.

Harrington stared at it, then lifted his eyes towards the penthouse suite. 'Goddamnit, Harrington, you were born into my world, and that's where you belong. Why the hell do you want to kick around in godforsaken theaters? . . .'

"Come on," Cara said, "let's see the real center."

"Just what I was thinking."

As they walked arm in arm down the sidewalk, a limousine pulled up and drove along with them. Raymond Baren opened the back window and called out. "I'd like to talk to you, Harrington. Thomas told me you were visiting the Center this morning." Harrington and Cara kept walking. The limousine moved with them. "Your father's upset about your relationship," Raymond continued, his voice strained. "He tried to warn you that the Todd name would be exploited. Come join me," Raymond suggested, motioning to the car. "I want to help. You and your father shouldn't be at odds."

'At odds? We're enemies!' Harrington thought as Winston's words rang in his ears: '. . . you're either a ruler or a slave, there's no in-between. I became a ruler. . . . everyone must live according to my standards. Refuse, and I'll find the means to change your mind . . . or I'll crush you. . . .' Harrington stopped. "You stay here, Franco."

In one swift motion, he strode to the car, swung open the door, and started to pull Raymond across the seat. Then he remembered his mother's words. 'Recognize the differences in men. Learn how to deal with them . . .' He released Raymond and started to back out of the car.

"Harrington! Watch out!" Cara warned.

Joe Field had him from behind and pinned his arms. Cara grabbed Joe's coat sleeve, but the material slipped from her hand. Harrington was boxed-in and shoved himself hard against the car, throwing his weight back into Joe's chest.

Diana and John were waiting for Harrington and Cara at the entrance to her Center. Diana saw a crowd gathering and saw Harrington's tall figure restrained by Joe Field. She hurriedly motioned to Marcus, who, upon seeing the scene, barreled up Fifth Avenue, scattering pedestrians.

Harrington had fought for advantage. Finally he was out from between the car and the gutter. He and Joe were on the sidewalk face to face. Harrington hit Joe with short chest jabs that backed the shorter man up the sidewalk.

"What the hell are ya doing, Joe?"

It was Joe's turn to be boxed-in. Harrington shoved him right into Marcus's huge arms. Joe squirmed.

"Get your filthy hands off me, Mancini!"

With one giant hand, Marcus picked him up. "If I ever see you around Harrington or Cara again, I won't be so polite. Now get the hell out of here!" He threw Joe against the limousine trunk.

Raymond Baren left the limousine just in time to see Joe reaching for his gun in a shoulder holster. Marcus shoved Harrington out of the way to shield him from taking a bullet.

"Do as he says, Joe!" Raymond barked.

Joe dodged out of Marcus's way, his eyes on Raymond. Humiliation mixed with rage permeated his features.

"Now!" Raymond commanded severely.

Joe rounded the limousine, his eyes fixed on Marcus. "Another time," he said, opening the driver's door.

"There won't be another time, Mr. Field," Diana said.

She had walked up the street and now stood before her husband's henchmen, her stature commanding their respect. Raymond sucked in his breath and started to apologize, but Diana interrupted him.

"Is Winston at his office?" she asked evenly, her eyes blindingly green and scrutinizing.

"Yes, yes, he's there," Raymond conceded. "I . . ."

"Please let him know I'll be up to see him after lunch, at 2:00."

"Diana . . ." Raymond pleaded.

She leveled her gaze at him with remarkable calm. "A complaint will be filed with the police commissioner this very afternoon. If either you or Mr. Field come near Harrington or Cara again, you'll face a contempt charge." She turned to Harrington and Cara and a smile curled her lips. "You're attracting a crowd, the two of you. Don't you think we should be going?"

Pedestrians had gathered, many recognizing the famous

matriarch of the Todd family. Others stared at Harrington who had been in the press a lot lately. John, of course, was a legendary figure, and no one could miss the towering man with the mass of whitish-brown hair and the ever-present cigarette.

As Harrington and Cara joined them, Diana said to John, "That was a wonderful experiment, John. You're right, Harrington did need some help with that fight scene in the third act. You staged this perfectly."

Harrington took Cara's arm and linked his free arm through Diana's. "You're a card, Mother, honestly."

When they reached the heart of Diana's Cultural Center, Diana looked up at her son. Harrington was staring at the theaters, museums, and office buildings, and she saw the depth of his feelings for her accomplishments. She had first brought him to this site when he was twelve years old. She reminded him of this and of the Center's opening in his fourteenth year.

"I remember, Mother. I admired your courage then, and even more now that I know him."

"Last night you allowed your father to irritate you. I asked you here today to remind you about the way in which you approach your work and your success. Like your career, Harrington, this Center took years to build. I found joy in the growth process—to me it's the essence of accomplishment."

"But Father doesn't want anyone to grow except under his conditions, in his way, and on his time schedule," Harrington said, his brow furrowing.

"And that is what you'll have to contend with as long as your father lives, Harrington."

"That's hard to accept."

"I know."

Harrington looked down at his mother. "How did you do it all these years? Tell me what to do, Mother."

"If you give in to conditions in which you don't believe, it will stifle your growth, inhibit your instincts, and limit your potential. The way you live is entirely up to you. I will not and cannot make that choice for you. I will not interfere in your relationship with him. It is your choice. Your life. I respect you, Harrington. I'm proud of you. As your mother, I will always be here for you as a counsel, but as of this moment

I'm volunteering my last advice. If you react as you did last night, you'll allow your father to destroy you."

Despite what she said, Harrington had this uncanny feeling she was still trying to protect him.

"It's time you lead your own life, Mother. In two years, Cara and I are moving to Los Angeles. We both want to work for Conrad." He purposely left out their wish that Diana and John finally be together, but added, "You've done so much for me, Mother. As I said, it's time you lived your own life."

Diana smiled up at her son, hiding her sadness. Did he really think a move to California would stop Winston?

"How long have you had these plans?"

"A few years."

That better explained his behavior after opening night. In his way, he wanted *Remember When* to gain him a reputation on his talent alone. Then, the move to Los Angeles. Thus, showing he and Cara could take care of themselves, leaving her free to divorce Winston.

"And what about your father?"

"Cara and I talked about it last night. Now that you and I have talked, I understand better. We'll have to learn to deal with him and keep to our plans despite him."

'California would put distance between them,' Diana thought. 'Maybe . . .' She would have to talk to John.

"I must admit, he put me to the test today," Harrington was saying. "But your courage is an example." Harrington squeezed his mother's arm. "That's why you were able to stay married to him, wasn't it, Mother? Your thoughts, this Center, they sustained you."

Diana reached up and brushed his cheek. "Partially, but my greatest hope is in you, Harrington. You were and are worth protecting. You are my greatest joy, my greatest hope. You can make a difference in the world."

He bent down and kissed her cheek. "Don't do anything foolish, Mother. You just said I was worth protecting. Earlier you said I was on my own. Don't change your mind. I know I said it before, but you must live your own life."

Diana smiled in amusement. "You're using my words against me, Harrington. Are the tables already turning?"

"I hope so, Mother. You raised me with the intention that I would one day take control of my own life. The time has come."

* * *

"Will you forgive me, John?"

"There's nothing to forgive, Diana. I feel as you do about Harrington. Now that I know his plans, I think it's a good idea. We'll monitor Winston for a couple of years. Then maybe we'll all move out West." He kissed her tenderly. "We've waited for years. It's not as though we won't see each other."

Although he said the right words, John was making an enormous concession. His optimism could have been labeled wishful thinking. If Winston acted as Diana suspected, her free time would be slowly gobbled up. But she had to direct Winston's attention away from Harrington and back to her. Her son needed his chance.

Her love for John was so overwhelming, it made her want to forget her plans. But she had come this far. "Two years," she said with determination. "Only two, John. I won't live without you longer than two years. I must have some of my own life."

John's power with the pen was so extraordinary that he had been sought out for years by men of power and political influence. Winston had at one time consulted him, too. But he was Diana's ally. Their relationship had been as well-guarded as the most delicate plot in his books and plays. He always had and would continue to guard this extraordinary woman who had been the well-disguised heroine of many of his novels.

"We've both made our decisions," he said, studying her grace. "We'll survive, Diana. But I'm warning you that Winston's going to play rough. I won't stand by and watch you flounder. If the pressure gets to be too much and you start to get sick, I'm coming for you, and that will be the end of it all."

Winston had heard from Raymond Baren and was expecting Diana at 2:00. She was escorted into his office. He marveled as he often had on how she made any room her own, just like her father had before her. This thought was even more vivid to him now, for this was her first time in his office.

"This is lovely, Winston, and suits a man of your

stature," she said as the secretary closed the door behind her.

The office graced the forty-fourth floor. On a cloudy day, it stood above the clouds. This afternoon, blue skies prevailed outside its windows, and the light shone brightly on the antique desk behind which Winston stood. He came around, bypassing two leather-bound chairs and guided her towards one of many sitting areas in the suite.

Winston had not missed her slight. He stopped her suddenly in the middle of the room near an elegant sideboard. "A man of my stature would have this office, but not me personally?"

Diana took off her black kid gloves, waiting to be invited to sit down. She had no intention of playing games about the decor of his office and made it quite clear.

"Please," Winston said, "sit down."

It was useless wasting time with niceties, so Diana got right to the point.

"Over the last year, I've contemplated a divorce," she said firmly. She didn't bother waiting for Winston's reaction. He was way too smart to show any. "Since, I knew you'd fight it, I wanted to wait until Harrington was on his own, which as you witnessed last night, he is."

"That, my dear, is a matter of opinion." Winston said, dryly.

"And you're entitled to your own opinion, although you're a minority of one."

He scrutinized her more closely. Her soft manner, the way in which she spoke, her idealistic way of treating all things, had vanished. He was dealing with a worthy adversary at last. Why did this please him?

"What is your point?" he commanded, more to see her reaction than from a desire to end the conversation.

"I already told you," she said mildly. "I want a divorce."

"You'll never get one. Never."

"Thomas Garvin disagrees. I have a file of your activities over the years. Any judge in the land would grant me my wish."

She knew this wasn't entirely true. Winston exerted great influence over many New York State judges. But he also knew the scandal would cost him great hardship and many favors. The latter he would hate to use for family matters, of this she was sure.

He was studying her carefully and knew the divorce was a bargaining tool for something dearer to her heart. He was a bit surprised at this stage of her life that Diana would resort to such tactics. He wondered again why he was pleased while waiting for her to reveal her true motives.

She surprised him again when she stood up, putting on her gloves. "I'm happy we had this conversation. Thank you for your time."

Winston smiled despite himself. They knew one another too well to play this game. He had no doubt she would walk out of the office and start divorce proceedings if he didn't ask her to sit down. He truly was having a good time. He asked her to remain. She sat down tentatively, on the edge of the chair putting on her gloves.

"Was there something else, Winston?"

"You've changed, my dear."

She noticed that he was pleased, and she wondered if he knew why. She did. "You have your wish, Winston."

"You're ready to do battle, my dear, how absolutely marvelous. What are the ground rules as you see them?" he said, unable to supress his delight.

Diana had seen him this happy only in the youth of their marriage. "Our conflict is between the two of us. If you have grievances with Harrington I will respect your right to have them, but you must play fair."

"What is fair, my dear?" he said.

"You can talk, but keep your henchmen away."

"And if I don't."

"I'll file for divorce and create a scandal that you'll never be able to live down."

Winston's good mood vanished. "I don't think you'd want to do that."

Diana was tempted to tell him her other plans. Not yet, she cautioned herself.

Winston weighed his options. She meant what she said, but he wanted her Cultural Center and his son. Joe Field was right. It had been a good idea to put Vincent Morello, the bartender at Franco's, on their payroll. Yet, his dear wife was making the game more enticing.

"All right, we'll try it your way, but I want you more at my side. Let's go out, be seen in public, act as husband and wife."

She had expected this. John had expected this. Still she didn't want to do it. Long ago, when he left Windsor Royal, Winston had asked the same of her, but he had not followed through. She weighed her options. Although she had told John she would say yes, she still wasn't sure of her answer now that she was in Winston's company.

He took her by the arms and helped her stand. "I've been with the most beautiful women in the world, Diana, and none of them match your beauty or strength."

Before she had a chance to speak, he kissed her with such longing that it took her breath away. "Winston." She pushed him hard, which was a mistake. He only held her tighter.

"Maybe my love for you will change me, Diana. And I do so enjoy having you near."

She wanted to laugh. "Do you have so little regard for the female race that you are going to try and flatter me into submission? Do you really think I'll stand for that?"

Winston carefully took her glove off her left hand and stared at her wedding ring. When he knew he had her undivided attention, he turned her hand over and kissed her palm. As he did so, he looked up at her with such amusement she had to laugh, although in the pit of her stomach she was repulsed.

"You do!" she exclaimed.

"I'll pick you up for dinner at 8:00, and I plan to spend the night."

"I decline both invitations. You and I will be civil, that's all I will promise."

"As you wish," he conceded. He intended to get back into her good graces. Tonight, tomorrow night, a week, a month, a year . . . it didn't matter. He had a new challenge.

During the fall and into the winter, Diana saw Winston at one social event or another. She was polite, even gracious, never wishing him to know how much his presence bothered her. Often she wondered if he really had committed murder, extortion, and blackmail. Then she would remind herself that he was a seducer, the quintessential chameleon. Winston's life was one big grandstand performance. She had to admit he was the best she'd ever seen.

The last place she thought she would see him, however, was at Walter Kent's Park Avenue apartment on a cold brittle evening in February 1940.

"He invited himself in," Walter told her in confidence at the door. "I decided it best not to make a scene."

"Thank you, Walter," Diana said without further comment.

Walter had just become Chairman of the Board of Darnley Enterprises. Tonight he had invited captains of industry and politicians to his home to discuss the world situation. Many American companies were interested in expanding into the European market. He was cautious about extending Darnley Enterprises into that arena.

Within minutes of arriving at Walter's elegant apartment, she found herself drawn into a crowd of friends. Winston barged into the discussion, ignoring the polite but disapproving expressions of the group.

"I just returned from Washington," he said.

Diana wondered what response he expected. There was an awkward silence. Walter was too gracious a host, even with a party crasher, to allow his feelings for Winston to color his gentlemanly duties.

"You must have met with the President and the British Ambassador."

Winston seemed unaware of the tension surrounding him. He smiled affably. "That's right, Walter. You're quite the expert on International politics. Don't you have your eye on the English Ambassadorship? I'd support your appointment, you know."

Walter brushed aside the remark in good humor and winked at Diana. "You're not going to get rid of a competitor that easily. Wait a few years, then try me again. Now, tell us Winston, what did the Ambassador have to say about our relationship with Britain?"

"There's not much support here with American anti-war sentiment as strong as it is." Winston sighed as the others shook their heads in concern. "The masses are so difficult to sway. I'm surprised we men of business get anything accomplished. How do you stand, Diana?"

Winston used to ask her opinion when he wasn't sure of a group's reaction. This evening, they were surrounded by her friends. She would speak her own mind this time.

"I grant you, it's a sensitive issue. The first war is still fresh in many people's memories, and the scars from the

Depression are deep. There's some pro-German feeling in this country. And most important, the isolationists would prefer not to become involved on the continent. But I don't think that anything will stop Hitler."

Everyone nodded and Winston jumped on the bandwagon. "I told the President that very thing yesterday. Let's begin preparation now for manufacturing planes, munitions, and tanks. It will be many months before we can convert our industries. With mine, at least a year. These isolationists are naive. They don't understand that there isn't enough water in the world to keep the Japs and Germans away. It's imperative we sway popular opinion as soon as possible. Otherwise, we might all find ashes between our toes before we get our boots on."

"Well said," Walter Kent replied, "but I hear you're doing business with the Germans now."

Diana had never heard anyone but her father speak to Winston in that tone. She could easily have smoothed over this awkward moment with something like, "As you were talking, Walter, something came to mind . . ." Then, capturing all the men's attention, she would have subtly changed the subject to protect Winston from making a spectacle of himself.

'I'm going to let him sink this time, Father,' she told Sterling Darnley in her thoughts.

Winston stared inscrutably at Walter. "I happen to know that a few others of our friends in this crowd are also indiscriminating in their business associations. Shall we include them in this discussion? What do you think, Diana?"

Diana looked around at the men standing awkwardly in silence. Obviously some of them wished to remain anonymous. Winston had placed her in the position of either smoothing over the pending argument after all or having her friends embarrassed.

"All of you men have influence," she said gently, capturing everyone's attention. "To various degrees, you must become desensitized—you must forget about the individual in order to make sound business decisions for your companies. I don't have to make excuses for any of you. Of course, you are experts in that area." She noticed the men looked relieved that the danger of an argument was over and then amused by what she said. "But whatever your politics, whatever your business, the reality is that we all have sons. The reality is, we'd like them to live. The reality is, they might not. Should we be drawn into the European conflict?"

Walter Kent, like many of Diana's friends, wondered why she didn't divorce Winston, but was too polite to ask. He admired her, as he had many times before, for shifting the emphasis of the conversation to smolder flaming opinions. "You're right, Diana. It's difficult to always have a social conscience when running a company."

She smiled in agreement without looking at Winston. He was out for himself at everyone's expense just as Walter had suggested.

When she prepared to leave she found Winston waiting outside. Right in front of the other departing guests, he grabbed her arm and tried to usher her into his limousine.

"Let go of my arm," she whispered.

"All right, if you won't ride with me, let's walk a block. Our limousines will follow."

They walked down Fifth Avenue to a deserted portion of the sidewalk before Diana turned to him. "Don't ever do that again."

"What? Try to talk? I so enjoy your company, Diana."

"You know perfectly well what I mean. What do you want?"

Winston stared at her, his commanding eyebrows shading his gray eyes. Over the years he had grown to consider Diana as another of his beautiful possessions. Sterling Darnley had told him Todd Industries would never provide him with love. Sterling had been wrong. Todd Industries bought him companionship and many mistresses, including Desiree Richards, his favorite. Still, he did love Diana and allowed his feelings to surface.

"You've pointed out already tonight that I think in large concepts and not of the individual, but I do love you, Diana. I do."

She realized now why she loved John so deeply. He placed things in their proper perspective—he was more like Sterling Darnley—like Walter Kent, who was as important and powerful as Winston. These men had the capacity to build mighty empires and at the same time, as Kipling said, "To walk among Kings, but never lose the common touch." Winston acted as though he had been raised on a corner in "hell's kitchen." He acted more like Thomas Garvin could have, and Thomas Garvin behaved more like Winston Jason Todd II should have.

"Tomorrow you will deny you love me, Winston. Tomorrow on your desk you will have a government contract. Tomorrow you will want to expand your aeronautics company. Tomorrow you will find something new, and you will tell yourself that there's no room for your wife and son in that world.

"If we obeyed your orders, possibly. If we helped you with those government contracts, possibly. Otherwise, there would be no room for us in your life except during a moment when you took a breath and you realized you were lonely. You are married to Todd Industries—she comes first, even above yourself, because you will pay any price to protect her."

CHAPTER XII

Conrad Coleman was back in Manhattan to film *The Eastsider.* At five minutes to ten on September 2, 1940, he walked into his Madison Avenue office. He respected time and was inevitably punctual, usually early. Actors were notoriously late. Seeing Harrington in the reception area, he felt, but did not show, his approval.

He had every intention of helping Harrington, but Diana had cautioned him. Harrington must be treated like everyone else. 'So be it,' Conrad thought.

"Good morning, Harrington," he said, extending his hand. "I was sorry I didn't see your performance of *Remember When* in Los Angeles this summer. My schedule's been hectic lately."

Harrington stood immediately and shook hands. "I understand, sir."

Conrad's suite was spacious, with large windows opening onto the dreary morning. Sitting down in a chair before the desk, Harrington felt as though Conrad's gaze was penetrating his soul and reading his every thought. 'You'd better get your wits about you,' he cautioned himself.

"Harrington," Conrad said firmly, "if you hope to be in films, you'll have to display a better posture. Just look at you. You're slouching terribly."

Harrington slowly tightened his muscles in his legs and arms. In gradual, barely noticeable stages, he altered the appearance of his entire body. His face took on the look of maturity and elegance. At last he straightened fully in the chair, completing the pose.

Conrad laughed in appreciation. "That was quite a transition."

"Thank you, sir. Conrad, I . . ."

"Yes?"

"I want you to understand that I'm going to try to change your mind about actors, just as I told you years ago. You don't have any actors under contract. I want to be your first. I know you've been getting pressure from some people close to us both, but this is between you and me, O.K.?"

Conrad smiled slightly, thinking of John, Thomas, and even Cara's calls. "Delicately put, Harrington. I'm happy you clarified your position. You have a deal. This is between us." Conrad leaned back in his chair and propped his elbows on the arms, interlacing his facing in front of him. "There's a script over there on the table. The monologue is marked. Read it."

Filled with apprehension, Harrington went to the table and picked up the script. 'My God, how am I going to read this without knowing anything about the character?' he thought.

"I don't want you to know anything specific about the material. It's a cold reading. Just read the words; feel them. Do what you feel."

Was that traffic he heard outside the windows down on Madison Avenue? Every little noise penetrated his ears: the phone rang outside the door; he heard voices from the reception room. 'Concentrate, Harrington, concentrate,' he thought to himself, 'and damn the distractions!'

He was pacing the floor, concentrating on the foreign words, feeling the writer's style and groping for the right emotions to bring the character to life. When he completed his first reading, he started again. He sat on the windowsill. The hazy light filtered through the window against his broad shoulders. This time he forgot about the words and concentrated on the emotion. Then he was reading a third and a fourth time, standing, sitting, pacing; he varied his intonation, delivery, and interpretation.

The monologue detailed the sad plight of an American soldier in London. He learns of his sister's death. She was his only relative and she had worked to put him through school.

As Harrington read it over and over, he thought of Winston Jason, and he felt driven to anger at her death. He was bringing a part of himself to the character: the anger and helplessness he had felt when Winston Jason disappeared from his young life forever. It was painful. He read it again. This time he found himself quieter and more cynical. He felt tears beneath the surface, but repressed them. Bitterness crept into his voice. He became so intensely involved in the scene that, when he finished fifteen minutes later, he dropped exhausted into the chair.

"I want you to begin again," Conrad said quietly. "Shift the meaning of the words. Make them comical, light, even gay."

Again on his feet, Harrington read the scene as if the soldier's tragedy was the funniest thing in the world. And a most peculiar transformation took place. The funnier he thought the situation, the more tragic it became. Tears slid down his face as he wept through his laughter. By the time he completed the last reading, he was totally spent. He sat down and wiped his eyes.

Conrad stared reflectively out the window. Days like this had stirred his imagination and sparked his hunger to leave Hester Street. Thirty-two years ago, when he was a boy of eight, he became fascinated with the wind. He still vividly remembered standing on Madison Avenue, the home of what was then the tallest building in New York, the Metropolitan Life Insurance Building, watching the effects of the wind as sedulously as he would have watched Buffalo Bill's Wild West Show at the Winter Garden, had he had the money.

He was fascinated by that which he couldn't see. Unlike the rain, the snow, and the land, the wind was invisible, making its presence known only by its sound, feel, and effects. Just like the wind, Harrington's talent sent chills through his body, twisting his emotions and leaving him breathless. Harrington had a charisma—a quality which he could feel, but could not touch.

Suddenly on his feet, Conrad said, "I have some thinking to do. I'll call you this afternoon. That's all you're going to get out of me, Harrington, so don't ask."

Harrington was tongue-tied. He felt the deep tormenting pain of rejection. He had given everything he could, but it hadn't been enough. He shook Conrad's hand, maintaining his quiet reserve expression. "Thank you for seeing me, sir."

Once alone, Conrad sank back in his chair. Finally, he shook his head and picked up the phone. "Reschedule my afternoon appointments," he told his secretary, "with my apologies, and set up a meeting for me with Diana Todd and John Stevens."

"Cara wrote the play that I was reading for Conrad? You're joking. I would recognize Cara's writing anywhere, Mother."

"I guess you were a little nervous, Todd," Cara said.

"Come on, Franco. Don't kid around. You don't like this any more than I do."

Diana and John had invited them to dinner at Diana's Waldorf suite. Harrington refused to eat until they explained themselves.

"You're being a temperamental artist," John said. "Snap out of it, Harrington. It doesn't become you."

"Maybe he is," Cara said. "But I agree with Harrington. Why should you close *Remember When*. You've had a year's run and it's still a hit. You should play it out. We don't want you hurting yourself to help us."

"It's my play. I'll do as I please," John said.

"Now look who's being temperamental," Diana laughed.

John lit a cigarette and shrugged as the smoke curled up around his bushy white hair. "Maybe I am. I just thought they could handle it."

"It is a sound business proposition," Diana finally said. "Conrad promises to consider giving Harrington a contract if John produces and directs Cara's play and Harrington stars in it. *Remember When* can reopen any time. But you two won't have another opportunity like *My Sister, Kierston*. Conrad's available now. Who knows when he'll be back again."

"Either you're professionals or you're not," John

added. "That's what we want to know. Besides, if you two want a chance in Hollywood, you need this credit under your belt."

While Harrington and Cara mulled this over, Diana was reminded of this morning's paper. Winston was in the New York *Times*. A reporter had asked him to comment on the presidential candidates, Roosevelt and Wilkie:

> "Who am I for? I'm for the man who gives Americans incentive to work, not to dally. I'm for the man who gives corporations incentive to create job opportunities, not to close up shop. I'm for the man who gives increased incentive to each individual to protect this fine country of ours. Now you tell me which man fits that description? Neither of them!"

Staring at Winston's picture, Diana had felt a quiet desperation. He would never leave Harrington and Cara alone. Laster French, still with the FBI, had found out that Vincent Morello was on Winston's payroll.

"It's time you two were informed of some new developments," Diana said quietly.

"Not now, Diana," John said, putting his arm around her. "You look a little pale. Maybe some rest first."

Diana saw the immediate concern on Harrington's face. Cara sat down beside her and held her hand.

Diana mustered her strength. Head high, she smiled at them all. "I know I promised not to interfere in your life, Harrington. I'm breaking my promise, however. Over dinner you're going to hear me out. Don't look at me like that John. I'm just faminished!"

After the New Year of 1941, John closed down *Remember When* and began preparations for rehearsal of *My Sister, Kierston*. While Harrington and Cara worked, Diana made plans of her own. Winston was busy lobbying for the Lend Lease Act, which, if it passed through Congress, would insure Winston millions of dollars with his munitions company and WJ Aeronautics. Diana took this interum of peace to plan out the future.

"Diana," Thomas said, extending his arms. He knew

she was tired the moment she came into his arms. She's so frail! He pushed her to an arm's length. Feelings from the street swept over him. He would protect this lady as long as he lived. He had rushed East after her phone call. Whatever Diana wanted, she would always get from him.

"Will you draw up my will, Thomas?"

His heart sank. Draw up her will! "Are you ill?"

She did look pale, but she flushed now with worry and said. "No, I'm just being careful. It's important, Thomas, that I have everything in order. I know you don't practice law anymore, but you have an East Coast office and . . ."

"Diana, you know I'll take care of the will. Don't give it another thought. I am worried about you, however."

"Please, Thomas, this is a complicated business, and I want it started. Once the will is completed, I'll feel better. Also, you'll understand everything by the time the will is drafted. That's important, Thomas, because we now have to have a plan."

The will was finally drafted, typed, and signed by the end of March. Diana was relieved and more composed. Speaking to Thomas about all of her assets and property and how she wished her will to read clarified her course. She turned her attention to dealing with her husband in the present, now that the future was secured and locked away in Thomas's safe.

She set up a meeting with Thomas, Marcus, John, Harrington, and Cara. If they agreed to her plan, she would call Winston. For years, she had refused to dine with Winston. She wanted to throw him off, just for awhile.

CHAPTER XIII

The following weekend, Winston escorted Diana to Franco's for dinner. Diana remembered her first visit to Franco's back in 1928. Then, the restaurant had consisted of one room, small and quaint. She had sat in a corner booth with Charles Mancini, discussing the problems with her Cultural Center. Afterwards, she had met the beautiful little girl, Cara Franco.

Over the years, the restaurant had been transformed from a modest income-producing café, to a Depression casualty, then into a thriving restaurant business. Charles Mancini no longer conducted his business in the private booth in the back corner, but his son, Marcus, did, now that he had returned from active Army duty. Cara Franco had grown into a talented professional, having sold two movie scripts and *My Sister, Kierston*. And Fred Franco? Fred looked the same. Dressed in his black tuxedo with the red rose in the lapel, the slight, small, jovial proprietor still greeted guests politely, although maybe a bit more proudly.

"Diana!" Fred Franco exclaimed joyously, meeting her at the door.

"Hello, Fred," Diana said, smiling warmly. "Fred, I would like you to meet Harrington's father, Winston Todd. Winston, this is Fred Franco, Cara's father."

"It's a pleasure, Mr. Todd," Fred said, extending his hand.

Winston reluctantly shook Fred's hand, wondering why Diana had insisted they dine here. Admittedly, Franco's had an impressive clientele. He noticed Walter Kent at a corner table with a couple of senators. In June 1940, Paris had fallen. With the invasion of Greece and Yugoslavia last weekend, Germany and Italy controlled most of Europe. Still many Americans called it the "phony war." Winston knew better, and by snatches of political conversations around the restaurant, others agreed with him. Probably the same was being discussed at Walter's table.

Thomas Garvin and Conrad Coleman sat in the center of the main room. Several industrial leaders were leaning in Thomas's direction, obviously interested in the motion-picture business.

Without looking behind the bar, Winston felt Vincent Morello's presence. To Winston's amusement, he also recognized a couple of well-known gangsters. He had heard they frequented the restaurant. Cohorts of his had expressed curiosity about Franco's. After dining here, they'd had some pretty colorful stories to tell.

"I've heard about your restaurant, Fred, and its excellent cuisine," Winston said, trying to be heard over the festive crowd.

'I'm sure you have,' Fred thought angrily, 'and probably from Vincent! Why has my old friend betrayed me?' Fred wondered.

The more Vincent had seen Harrington and Cara together, the more strangely he acted about Cara, as if she was his. Marcus was keeping them apart. Fred knew Vincent was totally irrational. Why had Vincent become so possessive of Cara?

Fred finally issued an ultimatum. Cara was Harrington's fiancée. If Vincent didn't like it, he would have to find another place of employment. Although Marcus was against it now, Fred Franco wished he had fired Vincent a year ago.

Fred was skeptical of the evening's plans. Winston's mere presence threatened his daughter's happiness. If Diana were not Harrington's mother, Fred might have forbidden Cara to marry Harrington.

Diana smiled to herself, noting Fred's reaction. He had seen Winston before, in other men who had tried to intimidate him. From what she had heard, Fred was quite a fighter in his younger days. Marcus had seen him pummel a man twice his size and shoot a hitman for killing a patron. Fred had friends and paid protection money, and even now he kept a gun in a secret drawer at the reservation's desk.

"Good evening, Diana."

Marcus had entered behind them, and Joe Field followed him. Winston's henchman was taking no chances. Winston shooed him out the door. Diana suspected Winston didn't want Vincent Morello to see Joe. Winston had never met Vincent. Joe Field was the go-between.

She greeted Marcus with her usual warmth, then said, "Marcus, do you know Winston Todd?"

"Yes."

"You're a rather substantial looking man, Mr. Mancini. I think I'd remember if we'd met."

"You're right, Mr. Todd. You've never seen me. Excuse me, will you please? Hello, Fred."

Fred greeted Marcus, then followed him with his eyes.

At the bar, Vincent saw Marcus coming. The bastard had poisoned Cara's feelings for him. Joe Field had said so. Right away, he and Marcus were in a heated argument.

"Are we supposed to stand here all night, Diana, or does Mr. Franco have a table?" Winston demanded, tiring of the scene they had been watching.

Once they were seated, Winston gave Diana his full attention. "You keep interesting company, my dear. When did your Mr. Mancini return from the service?"

Diana waved to Walter Kent at one table, Thomas and Conrad at another. "You know perfectly well Marcus was discharged a week ago. Why must you pretend otherwise?"

'So she knows I've been aware of their movements, and she knows Vincent is on my payroll,' Winston thought. Marcus's behavior tonight was Diana's message. If Vincent or Joe Field came near Harrington or Cara, Marcus would interfere.

"I appreciate your move. I'll consider your message."

Diana held his eyes, refusing to show how surprised she

was. She cautioned herself to be careful as the captain took their order.

Winston continued as they dined on veal scaloppini. "At least have him live in a decent part of the city."

"Harrington's on his own now. I told him after opening night, I wouldn't interfere in his life."

Winston raised a commanding brow. "Really? And what would you call tonight? Never mind, Diana, I understand. But back to my thought. He lives on Bleecker Street in an attic. Is that really what he wants?"

"He wants to earn his own way."

"But he doesn't have to live in poverty."

"You wonder if your son has a price, don't you, Winston?"

Winston responded honestly. Why not? She would know if he weren't. "You're damn right. What is his price?"

Here Diana didn't need to be careful. "He doesn't have one."

"Don't be ridiculous. He's just secure in the knowledge that he'll have your inheritance one day."

Diana conceded the point, for who could deny this gave Harrington security. But more importantly, Harrington was confident of his own abilities.

Like W.J. had done before him, Harrington intended to break with tradition and blaze new trails for the Todd family. Harrington didn't want to buy his way into the motion-picture industry. He wanted to earn his way, to build a reputation on merit. Production was a part of the future, but his interests at present were more in the acting area.

"How are you, darling?" Winston said, stirring her out of her reverie. "You look a little pale. I'm worried about your health."

"I'm quite well, Winston."

"Good, good," he said, patting her hand. "I might just buy Harrington a studio if that's what he wants. I've toyed with the idea for years anyway. Besides, you're investing in *My Sister, Kierston*. What kind of deal did you make with John? You aren't investing your own money on an unknown playwright are you?"

Only when her will was read would Winston know the details of her involvement with *My Sister, Kierston* and World Studios as Thomas's silent partner. 'And,' she thought, 'he has a while to wait.'

"After your run-in with John and Conrad in *The Rich in Spirit* you promised me you wouldn't invest in Hollywood."

"Yes, but we're talking about our son's future here. As you've reminded me so often, I have to think of Harrington. If Harrington wants a career in Hollywood, I'd like to help him."

Diana's attention was diverted to the door. "If Harrington wants your help, I have no objection. He and Cara just came in. Why don't you ask him?"

"All right, I will. Any suggestions on how to handle it?"

Diana stood up. "You're on your own, Winston, just as he is."

"Where are you going?"

"I'll just visit with Thomas and Conrad for awhile so you can talk to our son and to Cara."

Harrington was worried about Cara and wondered if this evening was the best time to confront Winston. The pressure from the play was on and, oh, how they had sweated. The cast of *My Sister, Kierston* had returned from the New Haven try-out last week with a trunk-load of mixed reviews. Cara had been working on rewrites ever since.

"Come on, Todd, let's get this over with. It's not just for our future, don't forget. It's Diana and John's."

Winston stood up as Cara and Harrington approached the booth. He was taken with Cara's appearance. Her suit coat and slacks and white cashmere turtleneck did not cover up her sensuality.

'She doesn't look Italian at all,' he thought, amazed.

The tired blue eyes in her lovely sculptured face made her all the more sensual. And her blonde hair was almost the same tone as Diana's. Cara and Harrington looked as though they were brother and sister. Obviously, they were very much in love. Harrington held her arm possessively, reminding Winston of his early courtship of Diana. Cara walked proudly like her father, but she brushed against Harrington's body while she did. Only a woman intimate with a man behaved thus.

"Good evening," Harrington said. "I'd like you to meet Cara Franco, my fiancée."

Winston took her small soft hand in his. "I'm delighted to meet you, Cara."

Cara's tired eyes sparkled with curiosity. "I'm very happy to hear that Mr. Todd, because someone told me you might wish this to be our first and last meeting."

Winston smiled, so amused that he glanced over at Diana, shaking his head, allowing her the honor of knowing she had won another round.

"Shall we sit down?" Winston said. "Would you like to have dinner? You look famished." Winston signaled to the captain as Harrington and Cara settled into the booth.

"We won't be staying for dinner," Harrington said.

Winston ordered for them anyway.

Once the waiter was gone, Harrington reopened the conversation. "We know you've hired Vincent Morello. We can't imagine why you would, except that you want Vincent to somehow take Cara away."

"Or possibly you've hired Vincent to teach your henchmen the art of intimidation," Cara offered.

Winston laughed loudly. The patrons at the nearby tables looked over curiously.

"Listen, Franco," Harrington said, "we're never going to solve anything unless you cut out the wisecracks."

"I'm too tired to swoon from fright, Todd. If your father doesn't want us to marry, he'll tell us."

"We aren't here to ask his permission."

"I know, Todd, but why else would he have hired Vincent?"

Winston was fascinated by the repartee and momentarily forgot about the true intent of this meeting. Cara had such warmth and love for his son that Winston was almost overcome with tenderness for her. This irritated him.

"I don't want you to marry Harrington, Cara, but it appears that I've been outvoted."

"You don't have the right to even comment on our relationship," Harrington said evenly.

"Why do you dislike me so much, Harrington?" Winston asked.

"How do you want me to feel about you when you have Vincent Morello on your payroll?"

Never before had Winston been confronted by such directness. Their youthful glowing faces, tired as they were, looked at him expectantly, as if he could lift a weight from their shoulders. He resented the position Diana had placed him in. Yet he wanted to remain, to talk to his son and, yes, even to Cara. This thought irritated him, too. The Todd empire was more important than either of them.

Although he feigned sincerity, he would never keep his word. "If it bothers you, I'll get rid of Vincent. Would that make you happy?"

Harrington and Cara exchanged glances. "Yes," they said in unison.

"Good. Now, eat in good health. Here comes your dinner."

Cara scrutinized the food served by her father's waiter, then looked at Winston with a bedeviled expression. "You mean I don't need a taster or a life insurance policy?"

Winston shook with laughter. "You have a remarkable mind, Cara. That I will say for you. I'm going to look forward to seeing *My Sister, Kierston*. I hear you have some very influential people backing you two. Too bad you didn't ask me."

Winston was looking at Cara as he spoke. Harrington had that rare opportunity to observe his father without Winston noticing. Although Winston had spoken the words, Harrington knew his father would never fire Vincent, bless their marriage, or stop interfering in their lives.

By exposing their knowledge of Winston's association with Vincent, they were only gaining time. Winston would have to come up with another plan. That would get them through opening night. Then Diana would use her secret weapon. A mighty sword it was, too. Hopefully that would take them into the New Year of 1942 when they would marry and move to California.

"Remember what Thomas told you on the phone," Diana said the following week as she and Cara sat with Conrad Coleman and Fred Franco in the last row of the Todd Cultural Center Theater.

It was an opening night sellout crowd. Cara was chock-full of nerves. Nothing anyone had said thus far lessened her opening-night jitters. She squeezed Diana's hand and tried to remember what Thomas had said. The theater buzzed with activity.

"Be positive," Thomas had told her. "Especially when you're waiting for the first act to begin." 'What should I think about?' Cara wondered. And then the thought of last night filled her thoughts, and she remembered what Harrington had said and how tender he had been.

She could almost feel his hands on her, strong, gentle hands, artist's hands. "You've given me so many beautiful gifts, Cara . . ." She tried to ask him to explain, but he had kissed her lips, turning her question into a lingering thought for later. As he caressed her body and they lay in each others arms, he told her: "Your play is your most recent gift." He had kissed her eyes closed, and it felt as if he'd touched her mind. "Tomorrow night, I don't want to see you before the performance. You spent hours alone creating something for me, and I, in turn, want to give you a gift. My performance tomorrow night will be dedicated to you." Cara glowed, remembering. Then the lights dimmed, and she grabbed Conrad's hand as well as Fred's for moral support, and squeezed tightly.

The audience hushed as the theater turned dark; the curtain lifted, and the play began.

A spotlight centered on the set as Harrington, in a soldier's uniform, entered stage right. He took Cara's breath away. She anticipated each word and movement and was captivated more than once by Harrington's dramatics. What subtle undercurrents he brought to the part! The other actors seemed to live only in relation to him.

Even Conrad had to admit he was more than intrigued with Harrington. Secretly, he had slipped in to watch an occasional rehearsal. Whether Harrington was reciting lines, taking John's direction, or just standing by while other actors received direction, he was consistently a professional.

Harrington seemed to understand that the better the production, the better he appeared. When John had taken his lines away in order to highlight the characters of other actors, Harrington had listened, analyzed John's reasons, and helped make the scene work. With that kind of confidence, he maximized every situation without trying to upstage his fellow actors.

'Of course, with such talent, Harrington can afford to be generous,' Conrad thought wryly.

Harrington had such a talent for varying emotion. One minute up and joking. Then, as suddenly, serious. He could change course, alter mannerisms more quickly than Merlin.

Excitement surrounded Harrington even when he stood still. Conrad's instincts stirred. Harrington's talent, his charisma, was like the wind, indefinable, unseen, yet a prevalent, powerful force.

When the curtain fell for intermission, the audience applauded enthusiastically. So far so good, Cara thought, but the third act had been the roughest one for her to write.

When the curtain was finally raised again, Cara awaited Harrington's monologue, the one which he had recited in Conrad's office. She was so keyed up that she sat forward with her hands gripping the back of the seat in front of her. When the moment came, and the tension of the drama built to a climax, the theater was still with anticipation.

The setting was a London barracks. Harrington stood center stage, surrounded by his RAF buddies, holding a letter that notified him of his sister Kierston's death. The audience detected no emotion on Harrington's face, but they saw the slight trembling of the letter in his hand. Within seconds, gasps sounded in the audience. Cara heard Conrad blowing his nose. She felt tears on her cheeks.

The play ended on a positive note with Harrington's character falling in love with a girl he'd met in England. When the curtain fell, the audience stood cheering and applauding. They had seen a young artist and future star at work, and they knew it. By the sixth curtain call, Harrington returned from off-stage with two dozen red roses.

When the house lights came on and the audience stopped their applause, Harrington extended the bouquet.

"Miss Franco, would you please step forward . . ."

The audience turned to Cara and again began to applaud. Flushed with excitement and more than a touch of shyness, Cara walked down the aisle to the stage. Harrington helped her up, and when the bouquet was in her hands, the cast applauded. John, too, was pulled out onto the stage.

Fred Franco clapped wildly, cheering "Bravo!" Conrad joined in and so did Diana. Winston applauded without the bravissimo.

Sardi's was jammed. Harrington had to push through a crowd that spilled out the door onto 44th Street. He lost Cara once and had to retrace his steps.

"Hold on, Franco. I don't want to lose you now."

"Fancy chance of that, Todd. Lead on."

They slid past the drawings of celebrities that covered the walls and sidestepped the waiters carrying large dinner trays. When they joined the cast of *My Sister, Kierston*, already seated in the main room of the restaurant, the entire crowd gave them a standing ovation.

A strange woman with a huge floppy hat and bejeweled fingers suddenly pushed her way up to John and Conrad, and fluttered all over them.

Conrad introduced Harrington and Cara to Arlene Habor, one of the most powerful gossip columnists from Hollywood.

"Aren't you beautiful, my dear. A wonderful play," she told Cara casually as she nudged her aside to confront Harrington. Not a bit phased by Harrington's cool expression, Arlene began lecturing him on his career.

"Franco, I told you to hold on."

"You'd do well to listen to me, young man," Arlene said indignantly as Cara slipped her arm through his.

"Please continue, Miss Habor," Cara said, egging her on. "We're all ears." Harrington pinched Cara's arm. She didn't even flinch, her dark-circled eyes suddenly quite alert and humorously interested in Miss Habor.

Within minutes, Arlene had given Harrington advice on the "right people to know" in Hollywood, the way to act, the type of press coverage he should solicit, and the proper attire for a movie star. "Oh, and Harrington dear, you should change your name. It's too-oo long. You'd better remember who I am when you come to Hollywood," she said arrogantly. "And where is your father. He and I are old and dear friends. Oh, there he is!" She left as she came, in a whirl of theatrics.

John and Diana had been listening to Arlene. "It's only beginning, Harrington," John chortled.

'Yes, it's the beginning,' Harrington thought.

Cara squeezed his arm. "Don't, Todd."

Ever since that evening at Franco's with Winston, Harrington had been on edge. The performance had something to do with it, of course. But Winston was the true key. Harrington hated his father, despised the man who was making everyone readjust their lives and plans.

"It looks like the show will have its run, Cara," he said,

"then I'll go on tour through the summer. We'll be out in California within a year and Mother and . . ."

"And Mother what?" Diana asked.

'You'll be with John,' Harrington thought, 'and you can tell that son-of-a-bitch to go to hell!'

Cara covered for him. Harrington was so angry again that not even her gentle touch snapped him out of it. "And you'll come and see us. So will John! We're going to have a wonderful time. Right, Todd?" Cara said, nudging him.

Harrington was too angry to speak. The sight of his mother in the same room with Winston turned his stomach. He took Cara and Diana in his arms and hugged them. Only John saw at whom his eyes were directed. Harrington's expression made him shudder.

CHAPTER XIV

"They aren't getting married, Diana. Not yet!" Winston said, viewing his wife across her Waldorf suite.

She wore black gabardine slacks and a black cashmere sweater. Her blonde hair fell softly around her shoulders. She sat the dining table looking at the morning paper, eating breakfast. The rumors of FDR's secret meeting with Churchill and Stalin were finally verified in this morning's newspapers.

"As soon as Harrington returns from California," Diana answered. "They've set a January 10th wedding date."

Before leaving on summer tour three months ago, Harrington had bought a duplex apartment in Washington Mews. Cara was only using it for work. Fred Franco had fired Vincent. "I don't like you any more," Vincent had screamed. "Marcus is keeping Cara and me apart and you don't care! But I'll be back. You'll see! Cara does love me!" Joe Field had so poisoned Vincent's mind that Vincent truly believed Cara loved him. Cara was staying with Diana at the Waldorf while Harrington finished the remaining three months of his six-month tour. Marcus was monitoring Cara's activities. As of yet, Winston had not fired Vincent Morello.

"I don't believe this!" Winston said irritably. "You've read this morning's papers."

"Yes, but I don't see what that has to do with their marriage."

"We're going to war, Diana. What if Harrington is drafted? Cara could be a widow before her honeymoon."

"Harrington will not be drafted."

Winston raised an eyebrow. "Why? Did you buy someone off?"

"Nothing so ingenious. I inquired about qualifications. It's the Darnley history, rheumatic fever, heart ailments—not the 'Todd Curse,' as you like to call it—which Harrington has inherited. Harrington will always have to watch himself."

"Why are you telling me this?"

"Because once you get something in your mind, no one can change it—even if you're wrong. You were wrong about Harrington. He should be angry at you, not the other way around, Winston. You wronged our son."

"I don't look at it that way."

"Our son is a fighter, Winston. If you hurt anyone he loves, he'll come after you. And then, if you retaliate and harm him and he's gone and I'm gone, you'll be all alone. You'll have to find someone else to blame for your mistakes. Your motives for success have been contrived. You've always used your family as a negative catalyst. We tried for many years to love you despite your abuse. Now it's going to end. I want you to fire Vincent Morello."

"Who?"

"Stop it, Winston. I don't have time for your games. Pay off Vincent Morello. Get him out of our lives. Mr. Field can't handle him."

"All right, Diana, what's the deal?"

"There is no deal. If you don't do as I ask, I will file for divorce and place my family's crest over the Cultural Center."

She had played her trump card. Winston's eyes turned so dark that the steel gray irises looked like hot burning coals.

Winston remembered back to 1936 when he had called Diana, congratulating her on using the Todd name on her Center. She had played him for a fool. The Cultural Center was too important to him. He had to have it for the Todd image. The Todd Business Center and the Todd Cultural Center together created that powerful symbol of the Todd family.

"You've been saving that, haven't you. I don't think you would want to do it though."

"I will and I shall. Fire Vincent Morello and don't replace him."

"And if I do, what will you do in terms of your will?"

She had expected him to ask. 'Lord forgive me,' she thought. "I will seriously consider leaving the Cultural Center to you."

Winston scrutinized her. "I want that in writing."

"No."

"Then no deal."

Diana shrugged indifferently.

"You would embarrass me and my family heritage by letting everyone know the Center is yours!"

"That isn't my problem, Winston. You're the one who lied and pretended that you had built the Center. That you're in a fix is your own doing, no one else's."

"It's your fault. If you had done what I wanted . . ."

"Do we have a 'deal' as you say, or don't we?"

"One day, you'll pay for this, Diana."

"No more than you will, Winston, if you don't do as I ask."

Winston fired Vincent Morello. Word on the street in Little Italy was that Vincent was throwing money around. He drank at every bar on Mulberry Street and talked to anyone who would listen about that bastard, Joe Field. Marcus still insisted on watching Cara. He and Diana suspected that Winston would retaliate.

Harrington had been gone four months while Cara worked on *My Immigrant Father*, dedicated to Fred, a surprise she wished to present to her father for his fifty-fifth birthday. She worked long hours at Washington Mews. Marcus set up his operation so he knew Cara's whereabouts at all times. Cara had religiously followed the schedule through the summer and into the fall of 1941. Her first draft of *My Immigrant Father* was finally completed on the first Sunday in November. She placed a call to Harrington in Seattle, Washington.

"I wanted to give you the good news before you boarded the train. I completed my first draft!"

"That's great news, Franco! I wish I could talk to you longer, but we're ready to leave and I'll be on the train for two days. We're heading right through to L.A. I miss you!"

"It's only a little longer, Todd. I'll talk to you in two days! I love you!"

"Follow Marcus's rules. Don't forget, Franco! And keep away from Vincent. I love you, too!"

Their separation had been so difficult that Cara planned to surprise Harrington. She hung up and rushed off to tell her father and Diana that she intended to leave for Los Angeles in the morning.

Every Sunday, Franco's was closed, and Fred experimented in the kitchen. Lately, he'd prepared one dish on Sunday to take over to the Waldorf for Diana to sample before it was placed on Franco's menu. Although she was a little early on her schedule, Cara knew Marcus wouldn't mind. She ran the entire way to Franco's.

As soon as she unlocked the front door, Cara smelled the aroma of red sauce and meat. Dutifully she locked the door behind her. Marcus's order.

"Papa! Get out of the kitchen. I'm taking you and Diana out to dinner. We're celebrating tonight."

She skipped across the restaurant and through the kitchen door and crashed right into Vincent Morello. Stumbling backwards, she broke her fall, landing against a table.

"Vincent! What are you doing here?"

"I wanna talk."

Blood soaked his clothes. She backed up, turned, and then rushed into the restaurant for the telephone. Vincent beat her to it and yanked the cord out of the wall. She screamed. Vincent cupped his hand over her mouth.

"You're safe now, my Cara. Marcus can't hold you prisoner anymore. Don't you see? You're free. We can be together."

She threw off his arm. "Prisoner?! What're you talking about? I haven't been a prisoner. Vincent, what's that blood from?"

"I saved you," he said.

She had to talk, anything to keep him away. She edged

towards the front door, her heart pounding. "Vincent, where is my papa?"

He ignored her question and blocked her path, his face flushed with uncontrollable excitement. "I love you." He took a roll of money from his pocket and held it out. "See, I can take care of you better than Harrington."

"They fooled you, Vincent! I love Harrington!"

Vincent watched her edge towards the front door, and he put the money back in his pocket. "Dont' leave me, my Cara. Your papa . . ."

She was almost there. No hasty moves, otherwise he'd be right on top of her. "What about Papa?"

"Never mind!"

She reached slowly for the secret drawer at the reservations desk. Vincent stood opposite her. "I'm very flattered that you like me, but . . ." She yanked the drawer.

"No! No gun!" Vincent yelled. He grabbed her wrist, yanked the pistol from her hand, and tossed it back in the drawer, slamming it shut.

He caught her at the door. She struggled, but he overpowered her and dragged her towards the kitchen. She squirmed and fought, knocking over chairs and tables, trying to get free.

"You do love me!" he said angrily. The bastard, Joe, had said she did. He had train tickets to Connecticut, a cottage for them to live in, and cash, lots of cash. When he tried to kiss Cara, she bit his lip. He jerked away. He was so enraged that he shook her until her teeth clattered.

"You bastard!" she cried, trying to knee him.

'After all I've done for her!' he thought. Cara had to be taught some respect.

He slapped her so hard that she reeled back and crashed into a table only for him to yank her brutally around and back into his arms. She fought with all her might, but he pinned her arms behind her. Then he lifted her up and threw her to the floor. He was on top of her before she caught her breath.

"Don't do this, Vincent! You don't want to do this!" she cried as he ripped at her clothes. "Help!"

He tried to stifle her cries. When she bit him again, he pulled a cloth napkin from a nearby table and stuffed it into her mouth. She strained under his weight, screaming against the cloth. His rough hands spread her legs. Never before had she felt so helpless.

Hatred spread through her body. She fought with all her might. Then something in Vincent's expression caught her attention. In some perverted way, he appeared to enjoy her struggle. Her instincts warned her not to fight. She shut her eyes tightly as he rammed himself into her body. Grimacing in agony, she repeated over and over: "Be calm . . . Be calm . . . Be calm." She wasn't a body. She wasn't being assaulted. She was far away. Alone.

When he lay exhausted on top of her, she kept her eyes closed, her body as limp as if she were a corpse. He moved off of her. Then she heard him kick tables and chairs and hurl a lantern over the bar, breaking the glass behind it. She thought for a moment he was going to take her again. Then she heard his footsteps, and the kitchen door slammed shut.

She lay still for what seemed like hours. Finally, she sat up and painfully pulled the gag from her mouth. Then the trembling began. She crawled along the floor and struggled to her feet.

In that instant, a jet of rage streamed through her veins. Harrington's image came to her, but she shoved it from her mind's eye and with it the woman she had been. Unconsciously, she built a wall around her heart and soul, protecting those precious possessions from her own scrutiny.

Her mind blocked out everything. She didn't think of Vincent's reference to her father or wonder where Marcus was. She was possessed by her emotions, emotions that had crystallized into a hard line of hatred.

Fred Franco's words came to her: "See where Sicily sits at the boot of Italy. We've been kicked around for generations!"

She threw back her head and went to the secret drawer and took out her father's handgun, which she had tried to use earlier. She felt chilled and utterly filthy. She would take a bath and clean her body. Then she would hunt him down. No police, no scandal, she would just hunt Vincent down!

A sound from the kitchen caught her attention. She took the safety off the gun and crept over to the kitchen. Only then did she realize something was rattling in the utility closet. She trembled violently as she took aim with the gun and swung open the door.

Her father was bound and bloody on the floor, seemingly barely alive. She opened her eyes in terror. She had almost pulled the trigger! The gun dropped from her hand. She bent down, ungagged him, and frantically untied his hands.

"I thought I heard you scream! Cara, what has happened?" Fred cried out, horrified by her appearance.

Cara had forgotten about her clothing, which was ripped and soiled. So many thoughts were jumbled in her head that she didn't even hear her father's voice. She only saw visions of Vincent, intermingled with visions of the gun she had almost shot at her father. It was too much for her. She was beyond hysteria. She blocked it all out in order to cope, in order to unbind her beloved father who had been brutally beaten.

Marcus Mancini entered through the Franco's kitchen door. "What in the hell's happened here!"

Fred jabbered about Vincent, but he shrugged helplessly when he looked at Cara who was still busily untying him. Marcus tried to help, but Cara threw his hands away, mumbling incoherently. Marcus didn't want the police in on this. Protection was needed, and medical attention for Fred and Cara. He picked up the kitchen phone.

After calling Laster French, he dialed Diana. "I'm not sure what happened, Diana. Cara's in shock. Fred's unable to get her to talk. They're both pretty badly beaten up. Yes, once Laster arrives we'll come directly there . . . wait a minute, Diana." Marcus heard a car approaching at full speed. He dropped the phone, pulled out his gun, and flipped off the light switch. "Get Cara into the main room, Fred!"

Fred couldn't move fast enough. Bullets shattered the windows, spraying glass all over the room. Fred hurled himself onto Cara and twisted his body so he could land first, cushioning her fall to the floor. The car sped away. Fred groaned. Pieces of glass had sprayed all over them. Cara lay limp on top of him, unable to grasp what had just happened.

Marcus carefully helped Cara up and then Fred. "He's got a machine gun," Marcus said quietly to Fred. "We'll have to hold him off until Laster gets here. Be careful of the glass." He glanced at Cara. She seemed like she was in a different world.

Marcus's eyes had adjusted to the dark. Quickly, he

picked up his gun as the car approached again. Fred grabbed Cara's arm, pulled her into the restaurant and closed the kitchen door.

Marcus was off, crawling across the room. At the window he adjusted his position, straining to hear. He edged up to the window when the room exploded in a thundering round of bullets.

"Marcus!" Fred yelled.

Marcus twisted around just in time to see Fred burst into the room. "Get down, Fred!"

Fred stumbled through the dark and crashed hard against the kitchen floor. Marcus tried to reach him, but the round of bullets continued. Then there was silence.

Marcus crawled along the floor, forgetting about the glass that punctured his skin. He knocked over a stool, and a large pot of spaghetti fell on the floor, splattering all over his right hand. He recoiled from the burning food as the car screeched away.

"Papa, oh Papa! We were supposed to 'be safe'!"

Marcus would never forget that cry. He looked up to see Cara, eyes dull in the shadows, rocking her father's mutilated body in her arms.

When Diana and John arrived at Franco's, the restaurant was swarming with police. Laster French talked to a burly police captain near the corner booth. A coroner's wagon was seen outside the kitchen door. Police cars crowded the alley. Their lights whirled brightly. Marcus spoke to a police lieutenant while other policemen examined the scene in the kitchen. Cara was huddled in a corner. Her eyes were dead.

"Oh John!" Diana exclaimed, tears rushing to her eyes.

Cara's face, hands, and clothes were covered with dried blood.

"Be careful, darling," he warned. "She's in shock."

Diana moved carefully around the upset tables, chairs, and broken glass. Marcus stopped talking to the lieutenant. Diana glanced from him to Cara.

"Cara?" Diana asked gently.

She tried to help Cara up, but Cara withdrew. Silently, Diana extended her hand. Cara stared from it to Diana. A moment passed before Cara was in Diana's arms.

"Excuse me, Mrs. Todd," a cocky police officer said at the door. "Where do you think you're taking Miss Franco?"

John held on to Diana as Diana held on to Cara. "Let us pass," John ordered.

No one tried to stop Marcus as he barreled across the room. The young cop hastily stepped out of his way. Marcus opened the door. The restaurant was quiet as all eyes watched Diana, Cara, and John walk out with Marcus.

Two hours later, Diana came out of the bedroom suite, looking drained. Cara's grief for her father and her physical beating had left her wishing nothing but sleep. Diana had given her a sedative.

Marcus's rugged face was shaded with vulnerability, softened by the slight parting of his lips. It brought back memories to Diana of the day she met him, after his own father's death. He was angry, yet almost vulnerable in his love, he cared so deeply.

Although numb herself, Diana couldn't let him grieve alone. Very softly she embraced him and kissed his forehead. He clung to her and cried.

"We'll face this together," she soothed. "We'll make her get well, you'll see."

"She'll never be the same, Diana. My little sister's never going to be the same!"

"Please, Marcus, please, don't cry!" Diana said, gazing at John across the room.

Then John was with them, holding them; and they all broke down.

An hour later, they were drinking tea. Diana had checked on Cara every few minutes.

"She's restless. I think I should stay in her room tonight, John," Diana said.

"Good idea," Marcus mumbled.

The phone rang. Diana picked it up at once, not wishing to awaken Cara.

"Diana, is there anything I can do?" Winston asked on the other end of the phone.

"You must be joking! You are joking, aren't you, Winston! I have lost all respect for you. You are and will be for eternity my mortal enemy. You have bastardized the meaning of the word 'father.' You are a traitor to your family. You have no decency. Never call me again!" She slammed down the phone; her face was scarlet red.

John held her closely. "This is it, Diana. I'm going to take care of you from now on."

Marcus stayed in one of the four guest bedrooms in Diana's suite. Cara told him over and over that she had left the Washington Mews apartment early. If she had stuck to the schedule, her father would be alive. She should have been more careful!

Marcus tried to console her. If she had arrived on time, Vincent would have killed Fred anyway. She was blameless. He hoped she believed him. It was the only way Cara would survive this tragedy.

Diana, with John's help, made arrangements for Fred's funeral, took care of Cara, canceled wedding plans, and decided how best to break the news to Harrington. He was on the road between Seattle and Los Angeles. John talked to Thomas Garvin and Conrad. They agreed to tell Harrington after his opening night performance in Los Angeles the following evening.

Although the police had questioned the local shop-keepers that evening, not a single witness came forward. No one dared to aid the police in their investigation. Marcus knew it was the way of the old Italians. Nobody wanted to get involved. They thought like Vincent: Since government officials were untrustworthy, they only confided in their own people.

The police put out an all points bulletin on Vincent. Joe Field had an alibi. He had attended a party at Raymond Baren's eastside penthouse suite honoring the Washington socialite, Desiree Richards.

"I want to come home now, Mother. Cara needs me," Harrington said the following evening.

Diana handed the phone to her future daughter-in-law.

"Harrington?" Cara said softly.

"Oh, Cara. I wish I could hold you!"

Cara nodded, tears glistening on her lashes, her head bowed. "Me too. We've already buried Papa." She raised her eyes to the ceiling and gulped in a deep breath. "With the war going on . . . uh, he can't be buried next to Mama in Florence. We'll have to wait for later and ship his body. Your mother made special arrangements. He's at Windsor Royal out at Meadow Hill for awhile." She was almost whispering now. "So, you see, I want you to stay in California and I'll come out there, Todd. I want to leave here. Understand?"

"Yes, of course, Cara, but . . ."

Cara glanced at Diana and a resolve lit her features. "I want to come there, Todd. I want you to find us a beautiful little house somewhere quiet and have it ready when I arrive in a couple of weeks . . ."

"A couple of weeks?"

"I have to pack all of our things, and I have some business to do for Papa. We'll get married in Los Angeles. O.K.?"

"Yes, but two weeks!"

"Your mother and John and Marcus are coming, too. Please, Harrington," she pleaded. "Get our new life ready out there . . . please. Please."

"Don't get upset. Of course, I'll do as you ask, Cara. Tomorrow. I'll start tomorrow, looking for a home. Will that make you happy?"

"Oh, yes!"

Diana kissed Cara's forehead and left the room quietly and closed the door. She told John what Cara had decided. "I'm worried about her, John. Besides her father's death, she went through an awful ordeal on her own. I've seen bruises. Cara isn't telling us everything."

"What do you mean?" John asked.

"I don't know, maybe I'm imagining things. Oh, John! I could . . ."

"Hush, Diana," John said, knowing her thoughts on Winston. "Give her time, Diana. Now back to bed with you. Those are Dr. Frazier's orders. I'll stay up for a while and make sure she's all right. We'll all be out in California before you know it."

Cara walked through life in another world, calling on all her years of self-discipline to control her emotions and protect her from private thoughts too excruciating to face. She arranged for the move to California, met with lawyers to organize Fred's estate, and had Franco's repaired to reopen for business.

As though she were two people, she stepped outside herself and pretended to be cheerful. She cared for Harrington more than for herself. His future depended on the next few weeks with Conrad. He could do nothing for her in New York; besides, she would be coming out to California soon and they would have a home and she would forget . . . everything. She loved Harrington dearly, but all feelings of passion and desire were wiped from her mind. If she caressed his image with memories, and thought of how she truly felt, she would break down and beg him to return home. And what would there be for him to return to? She wasn't sure. She had missed her period. Was it shock or something else?

Harrington combed the Los Angeles real estate market. He had every intention of quickly buying the most beautiful home available and then returning to New York to accompany Cara back to Los Angeles. But it took longer than he thought. By the second week, he showed Thomas and Conrad the two-story red-brick home on Rexford Drive near Conrad's Lexington Drive estate. They thought it perfect for Cara and Harrington's needs.

"I found it, Cara! Conrad's having a set designer help with the furnishings. Thomas is preparing the contracts with Conrad. One for you and one for me! Everything should be in order by the end of the week. When are you coming?"

Cara was so preoccupied with controlling herself that she didn't detect the concern in Harrington's voice or realize that he phoned more than usual. She never considered that Harrington knew something was wrong. When she said she would be delayed for a couple more days, she thought Harrington took her at her word. Three and a half weeks after Fred's murder, Harrington could take it no more.

"Mother," Harrington said to Diana by phone the last day of November, "I'm chartering a plane to New York."

Diana's heart fell, but she knew Harrington was right. John and she had been packed and ready to travel for the last seven days. For some reason Cara was delaying their departure.

"Don't tell her I'm coming, Mother . . ."

"Why not, darling? I think it would please her."

"I know what I'm doing. Please. Just don't tell her."

CHAPTER XV

'**P**regnant!' Cara thought wildly, leaving Dr. Smith's office. She hadn't seen Harrington in months! He didn't even know about the rape!

'It can't be,' she cried inside. She ran and ran, as if the motion would wipe away the thought. She fought her way through the pedestrians, running again, torn between anger and despair, hoping that the infant would be drummed out of her body by the thundering rage in her heart.

She stumbled along until she could run no more, forgetting that she had slipped out of Diana's suite and Marcus would be looking for her. She sat down on a bench on the Lower East Side and thought of the life within her. She could not blame it for being alive. Still, she considered an abortion.

Feelings of guilt washed over her, and she cursed her Catholic upbringing. During those hours on the park bench, she decided not to take the child's life, although she considered taking her own. The irony that this, too, was considered a sin escaped her.

Hours ceased to exist. By the time she wandered into

Washington Mews, it was dark.

"Cara!"

Harrington was home, standing in the doorway. Diana was frantic. Marcus was out looking for her. Harrington was overwhelmed with relief that Cara was safe. He reached out to embrace her. She cowered against the door.

"Cara . . .?"

The bruises on her face had disappeared, but the scars inside appeared vividly in her expression. Her hair was dirty and unkempt. Her clothes were wrinkled, her blouse halfway out of her skirt. Her mouth etched a thin tight line into her sculptured face, making her eyes seem the wider and accentuating the dark circles beneath them.

She placed her hand against his chest. 'Why had he come home tonight!' "Please, don't touch me, Harrington. No, please, I don't want to talk now. Don't say anything. Leave me alone. We'll talk tomorrow. Please, Harrington."

'Please, don't touch me,' Harrington repeated in his thoughts. Cara had never said those words. His mind's eye flashed on her appearance. What had really happened?

Without a word, Cara unlocked their door and tried to disappear inside. His hand blocked its closing. "I'm coming in, Cara." He rushed after her up the stairs into the living room, again trying to hold her in his arms. "I'm so sorry about your father, Cara . . . I . . ."

She withered, as if his touch had wounded her. He let go at once. "Franco? Something else happened didn't it? Something you haven't told anyone."

Cara crumbled into the chair, feeling as though her body were falling, picking up momentum, tumbling her head over heels down a jagged mountain. She pressed her hands firmly against the arms of the chair. "I don't know how to tell you. Sit down, Todd, I . . . something has changed our relationship."

His hands trembled as he unbuttoned his overcoat and threw it on the couch. Slowly, he sat down, his face filled with such concern that she lowered her eyes. Something in her manner told him to change his approach. She seemed to be on the verge of collapse. He had to handle her correctly or she might break in two. He did not move, although every muscle in his body ached to hold her in his arms.

"What has changed our relationship?" he asked softly.

She stared at him, her eyes suddenly cold and expressionless, as if she were beyond his reach. "Harrington, I'm pregnant."

'Pregnant!' he thought wildly. Obviously it wasn't his child. Cara hadn't seen him in months. Seeing the effect his reaction had on her, he quashed his feelings instantly. He was torn apart, yet he could not press too hard. He had to be gentle to find out what had happened. He sat on the couch quietly.

"Are you going to tell me about it?" he asked.

"Did you hear me?" she demanded.

Harrington nodded, unwilling to trust his voice.

"Don't look at me like that. What's wrong with you? I can't make the situation any clearer." Her emotions soared to such a pitch that she screamed. "Get out! I don't care about you!" Angrily, she left her chair and snatched up his coat, flinging it at him with all her strength. "Didn't you hear me! I told you to leave!"

He put his coat back on the couch, his stomach twisting in knots.

She watched him, wild-eyed. "I'm pregnant. It's not your child!"

"I hear you, Cara. Please sit down."

"Sit down! I don't want to sit down! I want you to leave at once! I don't love you! I don't care about you! Now go!"

"You say you don't love me . . . and I believe you," he lied, "but you still consider me a good friend, don't you?" She refused to answer, and he forged ahead. "Good friends can talk to one another. At least tell me what happened."

He saw her struggle. He summoned all his strength to remain seated instead of taking her in his arms.

"It's O.K., Cara," he urged gently. "You can tell me."

"Then you'll leave?" she asked so quietly that he barely heard her.

He nodded.

It was happening. She felt the wall around her heart slowly crumble, unlocking her heart and soul, leaving her defenseless against the horror. She was terrified.

"I . . ." Tears appeared in her eyes. The first tears since the incident. Quickly she wiped them away and gulped in air as if she were suffocating. He waited patiently. She swallowed hard, then tried to relate the facts as if she weren't a part of them. "He . . . was in the restaurant . . . he told me he loved me. When I . . . tried to get away, he attacked me . . ."

Harrington saw her starting to break. It was as he suspected. Ever so gently he said, "And then he raped you . . .?"

"Yes!" she cried out. "Yes! Yes! He ripped at my clothes. He ripped out my heart! He stomped on me until I wished I were dead. Now I'm just a living corpse, a body without a soul!" When she felt his hand on her shoulder, all the days of torment, all the anger and all the rage burst forth. "I can't bear it anymore. Please, help me. I want to die!"

She cried hysterically against his shoulder. Nothing, not even anger at the man who had violated Cara, could keep Harrington from remaining calm. He knew without question he would destroy Cara forever if he didn't remain calm.

He kissed her cheek. Then very softly, he touched her lips, and by instinct her arms went around his neck.

"Oh, Harrington! Why did he do it? Why did Vincent hurt me?"

His insides shook. He clenched his teeth so tightly that he thought they would crush. His arm muscles twitched. 'That goddamn bastard!'

"I'm sorry he hurt you, Cara, I'm so sorry . . ." He stroked her hair as she clung to him, weeping her heart out.

He thought of her, and he knew the violation of her body had truly damaged her soul. She who had been strong was made to feel weak and vulnerable. She who had been spirited found that spirit easily violated. The most precious gift that she had to give had been taken away from her, and she felt powerless.

He listened to her sob about Fred and Marcus and Vincent. "Don't worry anymore, my darling, I'll take care of you. No one will ever hurt you again." He swept her into his arms, took her to the bedroom, and cradled her in his arms like a child. "Oh Cara, why didn't you tell me? I should have been here with you."

"There was nothing you could do . . . I'm no good to you anymore . . . you promised me you'd go . . ."

She sobbed and sobbed until he felt as if he would burst from grief. He could no longer control his own feelings. Gently, he left her on the bed and stormed out of the room. Down the hall he staggered, pain exploding through his limbs. He doubled up his fist and smashed it through the closet door, then fell to his knees, dropped his head, and wept.

Minutes passed before he realized that Cara was behind him. He wiped his eyes and stood with his back to her.

"I'm outraged. I'm hurt and disillusioned by the injustice of it all!" He finally faced her. "I would give anything if it hadn't happened to you!"

With a trembling hand, she reached up and touched his cheek. "Harrington, I thought I could handle him and your father. It's my fault. Don't love someone who will bring you unhappiness. I will bring you only unhappiness. Can't you see that?"

His rage shimmered beneath the surface as he helped her back to the bedroom. He wanted to leave and find Vincent, but the tragic face of the woman he loved forced a higher priority upon him. Cara had a need, a hunger to hear words which he felt and had to speak.

Once Cara was on the bed, he held her hand and stared into her eyes as if to breathe back the life into her. "Our love has never been conditional, Cara. We're one in spirit. I love you. In my eyes you haven't changed, although I know you have in your own. Somewhere in your heart is the woman you were proud of. You loved that woman. I know she's a stranger to you now, and I know you don't know how to find her. You probably think you'll never find her. But she's there. I see her. Oh, God, how I see her. And I'm going to help you to see her again, too."

From his suit pocket, he took a tiny velvet box. With trembling fingers, Cara opened it up. Diana's diamond and emerald ring was inside. He lifted it out and placed it on Cara's finger.

When he held her in his arms, his hatred for Vincent resurfaced. He felt almost calmed by the vision of disfiguring the bastard. Still, Cara was first. If he wasn't careful, she might think he didn't love her, and he might lose her forever. He pushed his violent urges away again.

"One day when we're old, we'll rock together in one of those old wicker chairs and we'll look back on these days, and we'll say we triumphed. And then we'll laugh. Yes, we'll laugh. Because nothing, nothing in this world is more important than you and me." He pushed her gently from him and looked deep into her eyes with a strength that warmed her body. "Come to me, Franco. Let me make love to you and wipe away the memory of what was, so we can look ahead to our future."

Cara searched his face, seeing nothing but love.

"How can . . ."

"Because I love you, Franco," he said as she came into his arms. "Because I love you."

Two weeks later, on December 6, 1941, Harrington and Cara were married in a private ceremony at Newport, Rhode Island, by the justice of the peace. Diana, John Stevens, and Marcus Mancini stood up for them. Afterwards, Harrington and Cara were left alone in the old mansion where Diana was raised. They were unaware that Laster French and two guards specially picked by Marcus patrolled the grounds.

Diana reflected on her son's new life on the trip back to New York with John and Marcus. Harrington had told her about the rape. She had promised never to tell even John. But she asked the questions she knew any mother would. How would Cara feel about the baby? How would Harrington cope?

Dr. Smith had brought Winston Jason and Harrington into the world. He reported that Cara was in good health. That was something. 'But what about the baby?' Diana wondered again.

Wanting their problems behind them, Harrington and Cara had decided to begin their new lives in California after the baby was born. They questioned whether they would raise the child or put it up for adoption. The decision was theirs.

They had asked Diana to suggest a plausible excuse for their delayed return to California. Diana suggested a partial truth was in order: Cara wasn't ready for such a change so quickly after Fred's death. Conrad, Thomas, even John seemed to understand. So Diana carried their burden with them into their new lives. 'Their new lives,' Diana emphasized to herself as John and Marcus accompanied her into her Waldorf suite.

"Marcus," she said, her will suddenly reinvigorated. "Did Vincent Morello have an accomplice?"

Marcus closed the door. "I only heard a car. There had to be two men. Vincent couldn't drive and shoot a machine gun."

"I'm not surprised, are you, Diana?" John said, lighting a cigarette.

"No, no I'm not."

Diana was forty-four years old and still looked like a girl. After all she'd been through, she still had creamy white skin, unblemished and unlined. Her mouth opened slightly as if she were going to cry, but her determination triumphed, and John saw the fighting spirit he loved so much prevail.

"Gentleman," she said quietly, "I've made mistakes. I hope you're learning from them." She glanced at Marcus. "We'll need Laster's help and more men on staff."

"I've already handled that."

Diana nodded her approval. "Winston fired Vincent, but obviously hired him back for a one-night stand. Winston's directly responsible for all of this. I'm sure he's going to capitalize on this tragedy. I want proof when he does. From your investigation with Laster, we know for sure that Winston has personal files at the Todd Center. I'll want you to get them soon. Then we'll be able to implicate Winston."

On their wedding night Cara confided in Harrington. "I can't love this child. I don't want it."

"If you still feel that way after the child is born, we'll place it up for adoption. Who knows, it might even be a little girl," Harrington said, trying to be cheerful.

"Don't you understand, Todd. I don't want it even if it is a little girl. I wish I had the nerve to have an abortion."

"Come on, Franco."

"I'm sorry."

"No, no, I'm sorry."

He had cared only about her peace of mind, but Cara's thoughts of Winston kept her in turmoil. Winston thought she was carrying Harrington's child and Winston wanted an heir. With Diana's ill health, Winston only needed to bide his time for Diana to die, Cara reasoned brutally. Then, if he eliminated Harrington, Winston would feel he could take her child without a problem.

She lay awake hours after Harrington went to sleep, wondering about this on her wedding night. Was she going mad? She thought not. Soon she would have to discuss this with Diana.

The following afternoon, she and Harrington were sitting out on the patio overlooking the Atlantic. The cool breeze was biting. They were bundled up in overcoats, mufflers, and gloves. Harrington had his arm around Cara. They were shivering.

"What're we doing sitting out here, Franco?"

"Pitting ourselves against nature," Cara said, trying hard to regain her spirit. "If I almost freeze to death, maybe I'll care more about living."

"Jesus, Franco, nothing's that bad! Snap out of it," he said, a bit frightened by her words.

"You're right, Todd. I'm sorry."

"You're doing so well, really you are. I admire you, Franco. And if you need to talk about any of it, we'll talk and get you through it."

Tears welled in her eyes. "I can get through it, Todd, if Vincent pays for what he did to my papa."

He held her close. "Marcus and Laster are looking for him, Franco. Don't worry. I promise you, Cara. I will make him pay for *everything* he did."

They were startled by a scream, or so it seemed against the Atlantic wind. They jumped to their feet. A figure was running toward them across the lawn below.

"It's Laster French, Cara."

"The Japanese have bombed Pearl Harbor!" Laster yelled. "Pack your bags. I'm driving you back to New York!"

By dinntertime, everyone was huddled around the radio in Diana's suite. The WMCA announcer repeated the news of the bombing and urged listeners to stay tuned for further details.

The United States declared war on Japan. In New York, Japanese Nationals were rounded up by FBI agents. Many were sent to Ellis Island. The Japanese Consul General and staff were escorted from their Todd Center offices to their homes and placed under police surveillance.

John cancelled *My Sister, Kierston* because of its anti-war theme and immediately placed his new play, *The Glory*, into production. "There's a part for you, Harrington. You'll be rehearsing every day. Cara can stay with Diana and work in the suite. Of course, you'll want her nearby."

Harrington wanted to say, "And you would like Mother nearby, right?" But he refrained, remembering his grandfather's cautioning words about inhibiting them.

From Mitchell Field, American aircraft took off around the clock to patrol the Atlantic. Air raid wardens set up stations. School children, housewives, and businessmen were instructed on air raid procedures. Bridges, railroads, tunnels, and all public transportation routes were checked. A blackout was immediately placed into effect. The Empire State Building stood dark. The New York skyline looked like a strangely shaped geometrical range of mountains, barely discernable against the darkness.

On the ninth of December, Germany and Italy declared war on the United States. Flags were flown from private dwellings. Workmen installed air-raid sirens all over the city, and during those days, alarms rang out frequently, reminding New Yorkers of the battle cries across the Atlantic. Diana and Cara found the shelter nearest to the Waldorf and read the directions in the newspapers, which they were to follow in case of an attack.

Fifth Avenue was lined with flags. Society matrons took heed of Secretary of Agriculture, Claude R. Wickard's words: "Farmers are busy feeding the Army. Americans should start their own victory gardens." Many penthouse occupants spent the early mornings cultivating those gardens.

Diana and Cara planted vegetables in window boxes, and Diana was pleased that Cara tended them so diligently. Watching things grow was good for the mind, especially now that Cara had begun to show.

War bonds came in from Thomas and Conrad for Cara and Harrington's child. John toasted to Diana's future grandchild and happily confided to Harrington that Diana needed a child around, just as her father had, to revitalize her spirit. Only Marcus, with his cool penetrating instinct, sensed something was amiss.

By May, the Japanese took control of Southeast Asia. The headlines reported Allied ships being sunk almost daily in the North Atlantic and the Caribbean. The Battle of the Coral Sea saved Australia from a probable Japanese invasion.

Ships and tankers crowded the New York harbor. Sailors and soldiers on leave filled the streets. Harrington established

an impressive following as theatergoers attended *The Glory*.
Cara finally turned in her second draft of *My Immigrant
Father* and had the time for that long overdue conversation
with Diana.

It was the last week of May and they were having tea at
the Waldorf while Harrington and John were at the theater.

"I was thinking, Diana . . ."

"Yes, darling?"

"If Winston wants this child, let's give it to him."

"So, you've been thinking as I have that Winston wants
an heir. Marcus is aware of it, too." Diana poured tea from a
silver service and offered Cara a cup. "I'm happy you're
finally up to talking about this, Cara. It's been months."

Cara bowed her head. "I know."

Harrington had made love to her often. With tenderness, he helped her forget that rough cruel hands had ever
touched her body. When she held back, she knew Harrington
cursed Vincent. When she cried, she knew Harrington
wanted to kill Vincent. When she started to return his love,
she knew Harrington tried to forget about Vincent.

Cara unashamedly told Diana about this, then said,
"I've had these horrible nightmares, too. I usually wake up
screaming. Harrington's always there. It must be so difficult
for him."

Diana reached out and pressed her hand. "You're very
brave, Cara. I don't know how I would have coped."

"I do," Cara said softly. "Just as you always have. With
dignity."

Diana embraced Cara and then, still holding her very
tight, she said, "You aren't to blame, Cara. You never
encouraged Vincent. Vincent believed Joe's lies. You did
nothing to cause this tragedy."

"I've been asking myself about that. How did you
know?"

"Because I had a similar experience. When I realized
that Winston Jason was gone forever, I asked those questions
of myself, too," she said, stroking Cara's hair. "As I did, you
naturally assumed you were to blame." Diana held her at
arm's length. "You were raped, Cara. How often does that
lead to a pregnancy? Haven't you been asking yourself, why
you? Why on top of the atrocity do you have to live with a
constant reminder? Why did God or Fate or whatever you

believe in allow this to happen to you! Isn't that how you've been thinking?"

"Yes!" Cara cried. "What is the answer? Please, Diana, help me."

"I wish I knew."

"You don't know?"

Diana shook her head. "No, I don't."

"Then how did you accept Winston Jason's death?"

"I've always believed that things happen for a reason. I might not always know what it is, but I've always known I should make the best of a situation. Sometimes it can be a very humbling experience. But better that than quit. I've learned a great deal with that attitude. I hope I never stop."

"You're talking about logic—you've always made the best decisions you can from the information you've had."

"Precisely."

Cara stared at her thoughtfully. "Maybe I should make a logical rather than an emotional decision about the child's future."

"Yes, Cara, I know that's wise."

Cara felt at peace for some undefinable reason. "Thank you, Diana."

"Thank *you*, Cara. I've always wanted a daughter. You were heaven-sent, not only to my son, but to me. I love you. You have grown up to be an extraordinary woman. I am proud that you are a part of our family."

CHAPTER XVI

"Windsor Royal's a big place, Diana, but it does have that wall," Marcus said.

Diana had considered the numerous messages from Winston paired with her conversation with Cara and decided everyone would be safer staying at Windsor Royal.

"If my memory serves me right, my father told me Winston made it security proof," Marcus continued. "With the blackout, we'll have to get blackout curtains and post guards. Thank God, I've already served my active duty and Laster's with the FBI. He's going to have to moonlight on a regular basis. Hopefully, he can get some other agents to do the same. Now what about transporting Harrington to and from the theater? With the gas rationing in effect, we might get caught without fuel at Windsor Royal."

"Once I've stocked up the pantry, we won't be traveling much. And Windsor Royal has its own pumps, which I haven't used for the last few years."

"They're full?"

Diana nodded.

"Then it's settled. I'll drive Harrington to and from the

theater and he will be out of Vincent and Winston's reach."

Cara was delighted to be tucked securely away in Harrington's old bedroom at Windsor Royal. Their fond memories from childhood swept over her. The color returned to her cheeks. Her eyes glowed and her spirits were high.

Harrington was grateful to his mother. Cara's conversation with Diana had clicked. The nightmares still occurred. Cara still mourned for Fred. But her attitude towards confronting her pain was different. She allowed her grief to sweep over her, confronted it, and accepted it unashamedly. This process would continue for some time, but Cara was confident she could be healed and healthy.

In mid-June, Dr. Leonard Smith was summoned out to Windsor Royal. Cara's hands and feet had begun to swell, and she was spot-bleeding.

After examining Cara, the distinguished white-haired doctor smiled affectionately at Harrington. "I brought you into the world. What a delight it will be to deliver your child. Don't worry about Cara. I've given her a mild medication to ease her discomfort. She'll be fine. Your baby is healthy."

Harrington shook the doctor's hand, filled with relief. "I'm happy we have you, Dr. Smith. I was worried."

Diana took the doctor's arm. "Let's have tea, Leonard."

John stayed at Windsor Royal, and in the last week of June, he drove to Manhattan only to return with Thomas Garvin and his new wife, Katharine.

"Congratulations, Thomas!" Diana said, joyfully hugging him. "I'm so happy for you." She turned to Katharine and warmly took hold of her hands. "You are lovely, Katharine. Welcome."

When Katharine Garvin smiled, her face was extraordinarily beautiful. Her blue eyes shone with sincerity and depth, and her oval face became radiant. Slender in form, tall and delicate, she had an aura about her that denoted inner grace. Diana immediately felt a kindred spirit in the lovely young woman with the flowing raven hair.

Thomas had been drafted. The U.S. victory in the Battle of Midway showed the United States to have ingenuity and courage against the superior Japanese fleet. It looked as though the future held an Allied offensive in the Pacific theater. In one month, Thomas would be leaving for active duty on the U.S.S. *Washington*. Katharine understood his need to be among his friends. They would stay at Windsor Royal one month, in the suite where Sterling and Diana had resided on Diana's first visit to Windsor Royal back in 1914.

Harrington and Cara were quite taken with Katharine. For some indefinable reason, she reminded Marcus of Diana. John thought her enormously talented and urged Diana to have Katharine paint her portrait. Diana sat for the sessions dressed in a Mainbocher gown of emerald green adorned with the Darnley jewels.

Thomas often joined Katharine and Diana in the Renaissance Room for the sessions. He saw subtle changes in Diana and wondered why no one else mentioned it. She still had the lovely complexion, but around her eyes he saw faint lines of pain materialize in moments when she thought no one was watching.

Besides Dr. Smith's visits, Thomas noticed Dr. Frazier coming and going weekly. Seeing John's reaction every time the doctor walked through the door, Thomas dreaded to think about Diana's prognosis. John seemed worried enough for them all, so Thomas dared not ask.

Katharine, with her artist's eye, confirmed that Diana showed signs of stress. She and Thomas were both terribly concerned about her and about Cara, who had been confined to her bed during the last month of her pregnancy.

Diana sensed the Garvins' concern and tried to dispel their fears. She organized the days with activities and geared everyone, including Cara whom she worried about more than herself, to be as productive as possible.

In the mornings, while Katharine painted Diana's portrait, Cara worked on *Your Year With Mine*. By mid-afternoon, everyone met in Harrington's old room. Katharine brought the portrait to Cara's bed to show Cara her progress, and Harrington, Thomas, John, and Marcus joined them. Cara, secretive as ever, refused to show Harrington or any of them her script until its completion, but she seemed enormously happy with her progress.

Diana served tea and afterwards an early supper before Harrington went off to the theater with Marcus. Diana orchestrated the afternoon under the guise of making Katharine a part of their family. Stories were told, from Cara first finding Thomas on the street to Harrington's opening night performance. Diana, Harrington, and Marcus monitored the conversation to make sure Vincent Morello's name was never mentioned. They had many laughs and good times. It was a potent tonic for Cara and for Diana as well.

In mid-July, the Garvins' visit came to an end. Their parting was an emotional one.

"Promise me you'll stick around until I get back, Diana," Thomas said. "You're one of the people I'll be fighting for." He took her into his arms. "Take care, dear lady."

"I will be here, Thomas," Diana assured him, gently holding his hand and reaching for Katharine's. "I'll look forward to seeing the finished portrait, Katharine. And if you wish to visit any time while Thomas is away, Windsor Royal is at your disposal."

Katharine kissed her cheek. "Maybe after I've put the final touches to your portrait and Cara's baby comes I'll visit for a while and help."

"That's only a few weeks away! How lovely," Diana said, feeling revitalized by the thought. "Please do, Katharine. I know Cara will be as pleased as I."

On the baby's due date, Cara finally set aside her pen and paper. After an emergency delivery elsewhere, Dr. Smith was scheduled to come out to Windsor Royal. Cara would enter the hospital the following morning.

Cara lay in bed, her head propped up with fluffy pillows covered in satin. The curtains were drawn open to the late morning. One light, next to the bed, was on. It picked up the sheen of her golden hair. She turned her head with some effort as Harrington entered their room. "Hi."

She looked so pale and weak, and appeared in pain. Her condition startled Harrington. His pulse quickened.

"You don't look so good, Todd," she said, trying to joke.

There was something wrong. What had happened since last night when her cheeks were rosy and her eyes were alive?

"Come closer," she said suddenly.

He felt her tears against his cheek as she whispered in his ear. "Have I told you lately that I love you?" He didn't trust his voice. Instead of speaking, he kissed her. "Promise me something . . ."

"Anything," he said.

"Don't ever be afraid, Todd. And never let your father get to you."

He pulled back momentarily, a wave of raw emotion sweeping over him. He felt as though Cara was somehow slipping away.

"Promise me," she said firmly.

"I promise, Franco, but . . ." He heard voices. Then Dr. Smith entered with Diana and John. He kissed Cara. "We'll pick this up later, Franco."

Diana stayed with Cara while Dr. Smith examined her. Harrington and John walked just outside in the lane. The day was humid with a touch of a hot breeze. John wiped his brow.

"Have you told me everything, son?" he asked. "Somehow, I feel as though you haven't been totally honest."

Harrington was tempted to tell John about the baby, but he had promised Cara. Times like this, Harrington missed Sterling Darnley the most. "When the child is born, we'll all talk. Right now, I just want to know you're here for us."

John puffed on the last of his cigarette, took it from his mouth, and stomped it out. "I'm going to be by your side through this whole thing."

Harrington clasped John's shoulder. "You've always been here for me, John. Thank you. You're . . ."

John's eyes watered. "I love you, Harrington. Now tell me what's wrong."

"I'm worried about Cara. She acted so strangely before Dr. Smith walked in."

John had noticed her pallor. He too was worried. "Come on, son. Let's get back inside and see how she's doing. That'll make you feel better, just being close."

In the Grand Reception Room, they heard her scream. They ran up the stairs and down the hall into the bedroom.

Harrington cradled Cara in his arms, trying to comfort her. Dr. Smith was on the phone.

"Yes, I believe it's toxemia. Have the operating room ready! The ambulance should be here any moment!"

The ambulance screeched around the corner and skidded into the entrance of Philips Memorial Hospital in North Tarrytown. Attendants rushed out of the hospital. Cara's stretcher was lowered swiftly but gently.

"Get her into the operating room at once!" Dr. Smith

commanded.

Harrington ran alongside the gurney. Cara was white, her face distorted in pain. Harrington kept telling her everything would be all right, but she never heard his words. They raced down the long white corridor. As they approached the operating room, Harrington was crowded out of the doorway.

He stood, staring at the operating room door when a hand touched his shoulder. He turned around and faced Diana. Beneath her calm expression, she was so upset about Dr. Smith that she barely could contain herself. How dare the doctor overlook a toxemic pregnancy! She'd have a few things to say to Dr. Smith after the baby was born.

"Cara's in the best of care, Harrington. You've done everything you can."

"But I haven't."

John and Diana helped him into the maternity ward waiting room. Once seated, Harrington looked towards the door only to see Winston walk in. Something inside Harrington snapped. He felt it first in his stomach, then the cataclysm spread through his entire body. He jumped to his feet. "How the hell did you know we were here? Get out!"

Before Winston had a chance to answer, Dr. Smith, looking exceptionally nervous, entered the waiting room.

Harrington pushed by Winston and confronted the doctor. "Is Cara all right? May I see her?"

"I'm sorry, Harrington, you can't. Not yet."

"And the baby?" Winston asked.

Harrington grabbed Winston's lapels and shook him. "Don't mention the baby. Cara's the important one!"

John and Dr. Smith pulled Harrington away. "Get ahold of yourself, man," Dr. Smith ordered.

Diana was furious at Winston, but she controlled herself. "Harrington."

Slowly Harrington diverted his eyes from Winston to Diana. "What? What is it?"

"Cara is in critical condition. Please listen to Dr. Smith."

"All right, Mother," he said with effort and turned to Dr. Smith, who stood by impatiently.

"There's great danger for both the child and the mother. We're going to have to perform a Caesarean section."

"Do it, then!" Harrington said.

Dr. Smith hastily left, and Harrington turned to Winston.

"I know you're after the baby, but do you have to be so obvious?"

"You're not on the stage now, Harrington. Try behaving like a man or at least 'acting' like one if you prefer. Stop talking like a fool."

John turned bright red. "He's more a man than you'll ever be, Winston!"

"That temper of yours is going to get you into trouble one day, John. Everyone's hysterical. I suggest we all sit down and relax." Without waiting for a reply, Winston walked over to a chair.

Harrington started to follow him. John was there first and spun Winston around. "You've deserved this for years!"

He jabbed Winston in the stomach and clobbered him with a right. Winston stumbled backwards. John advanced and Diana signaled to Marcus.

"Get Winston out of here!"

Harrington held on to his godfather as Marcus pushed Winston up against a wall. "Let's go, Mr. Todd. It's over."

Winston straightened his suit. "I don't need an escort."

"But I think you do," Marcus said, taking Winston's arm.

When Winston was out of the room, they heard him call out, "We'll finish this up later, John."

Harrington seethed inwardly as he stared at the doorway. Then he returned his attention to John, inspecting his godfather from head to toe. Harrington was not himself at all. He started laughing. "You shouldn't have done that, John, but I'm glad you did!"

John hugged Harrington hard, looking over his godson's shoulder at Diana. His eyes watered with love and concern. Harrington was unaware of the severity of Cara's condition. "Forget him, Harrington. Think about Cara. As you said, she's the important one. She needs your thoughts. She's in danger."

As the minutes passed, Harrington became oblivious to everything around him. He concentrated on Cara and her indefinable presence. It was almost as if he could feel her pain and by sheer will was attempting to transfer more and more of it from her body to his own. 'Let me help you, Franco.

Take my strength. Come on, Franco. We've done it before.
Take it. Fight back, Franco. Fight!'

"Harrington?"

His expression was almost serene as he turned around to
face Dr. Smith. The grave faces before him held little
significance.

"We lost her, Harrington. I'm very sorry."

Harrington ignored the news about the child. "Please,
let me see Cara."

"We lost Cara," Dr. Smith said.

As he said the words, he noticed that Harrington was
unreceptive. He looked from the young man to Diana and
John. He grabbed Harrington, shaking him slightly. "Cara is
dead, Harrington."

Harrington looked down at the doctor as if he were out
of his mind. "I want to see Cara!"

John had never felt so old as in that moment when his
godson appeared so young. He threw a burly arm around
Harrington's shoulders. "Did you hear the doctor, son?
Please, Harrington . . ."

"He's mistaken. I know he is. Let me see her!"
Harrington tried to push away from John. "Let me go! I
want to see Cara!" He shrugged off John's arm and started
for the operating room, but Diana stood before him.

"God forgive me," she said. She slapped Harrington's
face, then drew him to her as her son started to focus on
reality. "Cara is dead, Harrington," she said softly.

"Dead?" Harrington said, still disbelieving. It couldn't
be. They were wrong. They were all wrong. He would never
accept Cara's death. Never!

Diana, white with anger, gestured for John and Marcus
to take Harrington out of the waiting room. Once she was
alone with Dr. Smith, she spoke in a low, soft tone of rage.

"He bought you off or blackmailed you, Leonard."

The usually distinguished doctor looked like he had
barely survived a severe beating. "Diana, I . . ."

"Don't, don't say a word. You can talk to the district
attorney."

She left the doctor swiftly and joined the men in the hall.
There was no time to grieve; she had to act. John took care of
Harrington while she spoke quickly to Marcus.

"I don't care how you get Cara's files. Break into Dr.

Smith's office if you have to, and get copies of the hospital records, too."

Marcus barreled down the hall.

When the news leaked from the hospital about Cara's death, reporters hounded Harrington. He faced them without comment. His spirit was locked to the vision of Cara lying lifeless in the hospital morgue. It was all a bad dream. He fought the idea that Cara was gone. Any moment now she would surprise him. He had no intention of answering questions based on a lie.

He stood between Laster and John in front of the hospital in the noon sun, his eyes clear but vacant, while Diana explained the situation to the press. Afterwards, they proceeded to the Church of the Good Shepherd to make arrangements for Cara's funeral.

Harrington refused to enter the church. While Diana and John went inside, Laster remained with Harrington outside. An hour later, Diana and John found him looking down the road, as if he were waiting for someone.

A special memorial service was held at our Lady of Pompeii Church in Little Italy. Family friends, acquaintances, neighbors all jammed into the church to pay their respects to Cara Franco Todd.

At the private funeral held at Meadow Hill Cemetery, reporters sneaked past the guards. They climbed all over the hilltop cemetery. They stomped over the fresh grass, marred headstones with their camera equipment, and took pictures of Harrington, Diana, John, and Marcus standing at the grave.

Harrington did not respond to the reporters' inquiries about Winston's absence. Nor would Diana. John and Marcus stood by them as Harrington looked to the valley and the Hudson River.

Harrington never did look down at Cara's grave. At last, when they were in the limousine, John tried to reason with him.

"Harrington, we really should stop by the hospital to see your son."

Harrington stared at him blankly. "I want to go home, home to Washington Mews."

Harrington turned to the window. John looked beseechingly at Diana. She cautioned John to leave Harrington alone.

Within hours of Cara's death, Marcus had broken into Dr. Smith's office. The filing cabinets were empty. Marcus had hurried over to Dr. Smith's Park Avenue apartment. Smith's wife had just been informed that her husband had died in a car accident on his way home from the hospital. Marcus had the hospital records, which stated clearly what they already knew. Cara had died in childbirth, the result of a toxemic pregnancy.

Diana struggled through the month of August, first trying to cope with Harrington's depression and then worrying about Thomas. Since June, there had been virtually no war news from the Pacific. Suddenly Buna-Gona and Guadalcanal filled the headlines. Thomas was aboard the U.S.S. *Washington*, which had become part of the South Pacific Force. Diana called Katharine. The women were grateful for each other's moral support and agreed that Katharine should travel east after the new year when Harrington was more himself.

At Washington Mews, Harrington seldom left the bedroom. No matter where he looked, he was reminded of Cara. He had been unable to remove her clothing from the closets. Diana had taken care of it. When he opened the doors, he was astonished to find the clothes missing.

When he shaved in the morning, he thought he saw Cara's reflection in the mirror, only to turn around to an empty bedroom. When he sat at the window, he often thought he saw her approaching the apartment. He'd rush out to the cobblestone road, only to find it vacant. At night, he either awakened at odd hours, thinking that he heard the clacking of the typewriter, or dozed, reaching out to feel Cara's warm body only to be startled awake when he found she wasn't there. With each disappointment he became more despondent.

Diana stayed with him for a few weeks. Finally, she asked if Harrington would return to Windsor Royal with her. When she received no response, Diana explained that she must take care of the baby. Marcus and John would stay with Harrington.

Harrington had barely heard her, so she kissed him and

held him without further elaboration. 'My son, my son,' she thought painfully. 'Please, God, help him. Oh, Father,' she thought, talking to Sterling, 'what am I going to do?'

Diana made three calls daily to Harrington from Windsor Royal. Harrington only listened. Still she phoned him, and she prayed while making her daily trips to the hospital.

One month after Cara's death, Winston appeared at the nursery and peered through the window. He smiled in delight as the nurse lifted up Cara's son.

"So that is my grandson. Spunky boy, isn't he? I think I'll name him . . ."

"His name is Jason Sterling Todd," Diana said. "And he will be placed in my custody until Harrington can take care of him. Laster . . ." Diana never traveled anywhere without Laster now. Walter Kent had helped get Laster leave from the FBI. "Would you please escort Mr. Todd out of this hospital. Harrington does not wish for him to visit or see his son. Would you please inform the hospital authorities of Harrington's wishes."

Diana heard from Katharine after the great Battle of Guadalcanal in November. The U.S.S. *Washington*, on which Thomas served under Rear Admiral Willis A. Lee, had triumphed in a second night battle with enemy ships. Diana and John were greatly relieved to hear that Thomas was well.

Further news in February 1943 that Guadalcanal was secured by United States forces reminded Diana, just as Sterling Darnley had by example, that one must never give up. Thomas was fighting for them all, and she had to coerce her son into doing the same. Harrington had to snap out of his depression.

Five and a half months after Cara's death, Diana summoned Marcus out to Windsor Royal.

"Harrington will never get over this unless we find Vincent. Have you considered my plans?" she asked.

Marcus nodded. "I'm ready; John is ready. Now all we have to do is wait. Can you wait?" Marcus asked bluntly.

Diana liked Marcus for this. "You are the only person I can talk to about my death."

"You'll never die, Diana. Too much of you is in each of

us. I suppose that's why it's O.K. with me that we talk."

Diana touched his hand, and then she kissed his cheek. "You're a dear man, Marcus Mancini."

"I'll always protect Harrington."

Tears filled Diana's eyes.

"Don't reproach yourself for not seeing him. You're doing the right thing. At this moment, he doesn't know what he's thinking, Diana. It's all right. He'll be a better man in the end if you follow your plans."

The nanny brought in Jason Sterling, then left. This was Marcus's first look at him. Diana cuddled the baby lovingly and then she allowed Marcus to hold him.

"He's going to look like Cara," Marcus said. "No one will ever know Vincent Morello was his father." He heard Diana gasp, and only then did he look at her. "I knew because Cara acted so strangely in that period between Fred's being beaten up and his being murdered. Also, she wasn't happy about the baby, nor was Harrington. No one else knows," Marcus said, looking down at Jason Sterling. The little guy was laughing joyfully and kicking his feet. "Hell, I thought I'd scare him. He's going to be a fighter, just like his mama."

"But if Harrington can't raise him, I will let Winston raise him."

Marcus studied her thoughtfully.

"First I want to see what information you get," Diana said, standing. "When are you planning the break-in?"

"On Sunday. The fewest guards are posted," Marcus said. "I've warned John and Laster to stay away. If I'm caught, you'll need them. Back me up."

"I'll talk to them," Diana said.

Marcus returned to Washington Mews only to find Harrington and John in an argument. 'At least Harrington's talking,' he thought and knew John felt the same.

"Don't talk to me about ideals!" Harrington was shouting. "Don't talk to me about hope and the future. Do you think he has ideals! He has no ideals, yet he wins!"

"So, you want to be just like him, is that it?"

"Why not?"

"And what about Jason Sterling?"

"I wish that child had never been born. Cara would still

be alive! I don't give a damn if I ever see him. He and Father deserve each other! Mother should let Father have him!"

Marcus wanted to warn John to keep his temper. But unsuspecting of Jason's true identity, John thought Harrington had stepped over the boundary of reason by rejecting his son. "My godson would never blame an innocent child for this tragedy. When you come to your senses, I'll be delighted to talk to you."

"To hell with all this crap. I'm going to California."

"You haven't been listening to me all these months, Harrington. Conrad is making recruiting films for the Armed Services and Thomas is on active duty in the Pacific."

"Then I suppose I'll have to work on Broadway until they return."

"There are other producers in California. I'm sure you could find work."

Harrington stared at his godfather with pain-ridden blue eyes. "I'll wait for Conrad."

As John left, he threw a script on the living room table. "Let me know if you like this."

Harrington glared at John and kicked a chair. "That's just fine. Everyone's leaving me now." He snatched up the script and headed for the bedroom.

As John left, he winked at Marcus. "He's going to be angry for a few days, but I think we're going to get our boy back. Look after him."

On Sunday afternoon, security guards stood at the main door beneath the Todd Center Crest. Marcus walked around the buildings. Using Laster's passkey, gotten from a friend at the FBI, Marcus entered through the basement. At the first flight of stairs, he fixed the wires to deactivate the alarm system. Then he walked the forty flights of stairs to Winston's private elevator and used a second passkey to trigger it to take him to the penthouse offices.

He picked the lock to Winston's office, entered, and quickly found the safe. Using the information Laster French had provided him, he managed to open it. Personal family files were inside. Marcus took them out. Personal business files were stacked behind them with the employee files.

"Get Cara's and Harrington's files first," Diana had told him. "Then the business files and the employee files. If you have time, get mine, but the business files first!"

Marcus quickly and carefully photographed all the pages of Cara's and Harrington's files. Then he proceeded on to the others, the business files of everyone from Walter Kent to Howard Dareel. An hour passed. He photographed the employee files. He stacked those up and started on Diana's file.

He was thinking how easy it had been when an alarm rang out, jarring him. What had caused it to go off? Hastily he placed the files in the order he found them and closed the safe, unable to complete his task.

He ran to the penthouse elevator and pushed the button. It was the only way out. His hand was on his gun. He rode the elevator down one floor.

"Hey! I heard the elevator bell. This way!"

Footsteps raced towards him as he sprinted to the stairs just in time to duck out of sight of two security guards. He was breathing heavily, but stood perfectly still.

"See anything?" the guard called out.

"Not a thing. I'm calling downstairs to check on this elevator. I'd swear you need a passkey to get into the damn thing."

Marcus heard more footsteps. Then he made a dash down the stairs. He was winded when he reached the bottom. He froze. Winston's guards were just outside the door. How in the hell was he going to exit the building?

Distant gunfire caught his attention. He heard a rush of footsteps. As the brigade of Todd Security stampeded for the front entrance, he charged towards the side door that opened onto Fifth Avenue. It was locked. He looked behind him, afraid a guard would turn the corner while he fumbled for the right passkey. Just as he managed to open the door, another alarm sounded. Marcus ran across the sidewalk almost getting sideswiped by a car crashing halfway onto the curb. He looked in disbelief at Laster French.

"Get in!" Laster yelled as he pushed open the car door.

Marcus jumped in. Laster gunned the car. Todd Industries guards rushed around the corner in time to see them leave.

"I'm glad you heard my cue," Laster said to him calmly. "It was John Stevens's idea."

"You fired those shots?"

"Easy does it, Marcus. You look worn out."

Laster's attention was fixed on the traffic. He handed Marcus a handkerchief to wipe the sweat from his brow.

"That's quite an alarm system Winston has," Marcus said looking over his shoulder. "We aren't being followed, are we?"

"Nope."

Laster dropped Marcus off several blocks from the Waldorf. Marcus was surprised to see John Stevens was waiting for him.

"Good work, Laster," John called out.

"Why don't you come up to Diana's suite," Marcus suggested. "She came into town especially for the occasion."

"I borrowed this car from a used car lot. I have to get it back. Marcus, take care of that film. Put it in a safe place."

As Laster drove away, Marcus noticed that the car had no license plates. He pointed it out to John.

CHAPTER XVII

S even months after the break-in, in September of 1943, Harrington opened in John's new play, *The Hero*. The critics, who once had hinted that Harrington's first Broadway performance in *Remember When* was a fluke, now hailed him as one of the finest actors on Broadway.

The Hero captured the essence of how war changed men. Harrington understood that transformation, having been through a war of his own. He realized that war was neither noble nor honorable, although it could make men noble and honorable. He struggled to recapture the honorable part of himself that had disappeared with Cara's death, but as the weeks passed, he came up empty-handed, and Marcus was beginning to irritate him. Everywhere he went, Marcus followed.

Harrington had rejected his former routine, and he now spent his evenings after the theater at the Stage Door Canteen next door to Sardi's. Located in the basement of the 44th Street Theater, the Stage Door Canteen had been donated by the Shuberts, and had been a speakeasy and nightclub during the twenties. On his day off, Harrington worked a three to four hour shift with other volunteers, waiting on tables and washing dishes. Anything to keep from thinking, even though Marcus hovered nearby.

Harrington liked rubbing elbows with the soldiers. Up to his old tricks, he often hopped up onto the stage to give an impersonation of one or another of the soldiers. His favorite was Burt Small, a Hollywood screenwriter who had worked for Coleman Productions, Conrad's company, and had been drafted the year before.

Burt asked him so many questions about Thomas that Harrington finally called Diana, embarrassed that he knew so few answers. Besides, he wanted to ask his mother why Marcus was following him.

Diana was greatly relieved to hear from him. They talked for over an hour, with Harrington catching up on all the news. Conrad had enlisted the aid of some high military brass to get Katharine on a plane to Hawaii to meet Thomas there on leave. Yes, Thomas and Conrad were well. Diana refrained from mentioning Jason, although she held the sleeping baby in her arms while she and Harrington talked.

"How are you, darling?" Diana asked. "I hear *The Hero* is sold out."

"I'm fine, only, Mother, Marcus has been like my shadow lately. What's his problem?"

"He broke into your father's office over seven months ago. He's just being cautious. Vincent Morello still hasn't been found. You need protection."

"Why didn't anyone tell me about the break-in? Wasn't that dangerous?"

"John told you, Harrington, and so did Marcus. You weren't listening."

"I'm sorry, Mother. I haven't been myself."

"We all know that, darling."

"What did Marcus take?"

"I think you should ask him."

That evening after the performance, Harrington had every intention of doing so when Marcus delivered the fan mail.

Harrington was dashing, rich, and a widower at twenty-three with an infant son. Rather than causing resentment among his fans, his rejection from the armed services seemed to gain him sympathy. Some female fans offered him written proposals of marriage while male fans asked him for money and advice about girls. Other than Frank Sinatra, he caused more of a frenzy with the bobbysoxers than any other musical or theatrical artist in Manhattan.

He usually waited until an hour after a performance to walk over to the Stage Door Canteen. Tonight, John dropped by just as Harrington was ready to seek out Marcus.

"Why not think about taking *The Hero* overseas in association with the American Theater Wing?" John suggested. "Maurice Evans was in the Pacific with *Hamlet* and Katharine Cornell has been overseas with *The Barretts of Wimpole Street*. Why not Harrington Todd in *The Hero*?"

Harrington wondered why John wanted him out of town. Did it have to do with what Marcus had found? His curiosity was peaked. He promised John that he would think about it and then started to dress for the Canteen.

"I'll see you tomorrow," John said at the door. "I'm happy you're in better spirits."

Harrington gave him a high sign and smiled as if he were in the best of moods. John left with a smile on his face. Then Harrington hastily finished dressing.

"Marcus!"

Marcus stood right outside his door with a bag of fan mail. "What's the trouble?"

"Come in and sit down."

Marcus complied and dumped the bag in the corner. When he sat down his eyes were on Harrington, but he seemed to be listening for something.

"I don't understand you, Marcus. For weeks you've kept the back stage door unlocked after everyone else has gone. Why?"

Marcus remained silent.

"All right, Marcus, I've had it."

"So have I, my friend. I will tell you nothing, because you'll just get in my way!"

"What's that supposed to mean?"

Marcus stood abruptly. "Leave it alone, Harrington. I'm in no mood for questions. I'll get you some coffee. You still have to go to the Canteen, and you look tired."

"Wait a minute! I want to know what you got out of the Todd Center."

"Not now, Harrington!" Marcus ordered and stormed

out of the room.

Harrington cursed under his breath and picked up his book, *For Whom the Bell Tolls*. What in the hell had gotten into Marcus, and what had he planned? He threw the book aside and picked up a script. *Your Year With Mine*. Damn John, this had better not be a love story. He had told John specifically that he wanted nothing to do with women. He flipped to the title page, then on to the first page, and then, slowly, turned back to the title page. *Your Year With Mine*, by Cara Franco Todd.

"My God," he cried out.

Was there really pain like this? It crashed around him, suffocating him in Cara's memory. He caressed the script, clasping it to his chest, and the void opened. Missing her wasn't enough. This image of her came to his mind's eye and he cried out "Cara! . . . Oh Cara!"

He was unable to shake her face from his vision; her delicate features, her loving eyes; her olive skin smooth as silk; her radiant smile; her voice saying over and over: "You can, Todd, you will!" She was gone from him. For the first time since her death, he cried like a wounded animal. Why did she have to die?

He heard the door open and didn't try to control himself. He turned to the dressing table. "Get out!" he ordered without looking up.

"You killed my Cara!"

Harrington spun around. Vincent Morello stood inside the room. Reason disappeared. All that mattered was that Vincent was there. Harrington rose to his feet, his adrenaline flowing.

"You killed my Cara!" Vincent repeated, reaching for a chair.

Harrington ducked as the chair flew past him and shattered the dressing table mirror. "Your Cara! You son of a bitch!" Harrington yelled.

He landed a crashing blow to Vincent's jaw. Flesh met flesh as bone crunched against his knuckles. The pain and the blood barely penetrated his consciousness. He yanked at Vincent by the shirt and threw him against the wall.

Vincent grabbed his right arm. As Harrington tried to push him off, he lost his balance and landed on the floor. Vincent tried to kick him in the head, but Harrington rolled away, jumped to his feet, and slammed a right hook into Vincent's jaw.

Vincent crashed into the wall, ducked Harrington's next blow, and came up with a knife in his hand. He swung the blade. Harrington jumped out of the way, but tripped over a chair.

Marcus, watching from the doorway, had wanted to give Harrington a chance to vent his anger before he took over. At the sight of the knife, he barged into the room.

Vincent looked astonished as Marcus drove into him. They fell to the floor. Before Harrington could move out of the way, Vincent landed on top of him and drove the knife deeply into Harrington's right leg.

Harrington yelled out. Marcus pulled Vincent off of Harrington and pinned him to the ground. He smashed Vincent's hand on the floor and the knife flew across the room. It landed beside Harrington.

"Pass it to me!" Marcus commanded.

Harrington slid the knife across the floor. Holding Vincent down, Marcus reached for the knife, grabbed it, and suddenly plunged it directly into Vincent's chest. Vincent screamed violently. Marcus stabbed him again and again. Then there was silence.

Harrington looked from the knife to the blood and then to Marcus. Marcus caught his breath and stood up.

"I'll call an ambulance, and your mother and your father."

"My father?" Harrington gasped, holding his bloody thigh.

"Yes, your father. Don't you think it's time we used him? After all, he sent Vincent here to kill you. You know he will not rest until you are dead."

*   *   *

Winston clad in an overcoat and still holding his winter gloves stood at the foot of Harrington's hospital bed, looking from Harrington to Diana to John.

Diana purposely had asked Marcus to include Winston in on this meeting. Although John was tense and ready to strike with the least provocation, Diana had been adamant.

"What happened?" Winston asked, pointing to Harrington's bandaged thigh.

Marcus finally had told Harrington everything: For

months, Marcus had waited, hoping to find the right moment, the moment he could trap Vincent and Joe without endangering either Harrington or himself. He kept Harrington on a schedule that Joe could easily trace. Winston and Joe Field had fallen for the setup, but had sent only Vincent. The plan had proved a bit more dangerous than Marcus had anticipated, and he had not trapped Joe Field and therefore Winston, as he had hoped.

"You know what happened better than I, Winston," Harrington said, vowing never to say "Father" again.

Winston shifted his eyes to Marcus. "Is that your opinion, Mr. Mancini?"

Marcus stood beside the bed at Harrington's side. He refused to acknowledge Winston.

"You look like a powerful man," Winston persisted. "Couldn't you have overpowered Vincent without killing him?"

"Yes," Marcus said simply.

"You do realize that if you gave that answer to the police you could be in serious trouble."

"Don't try that on me! If you don't take care of this, I'll bring you up on charges of conspiracy to commit murder, or better yet, I'll create a scandal that you'll never be able to live down. And you know I can do it."

Winston turned his attention to Diana, ignoring John completely. "Please tell Mr. Mancini that I'm as surprised as anyone about this, would you, my dear?"

With Dr. Smith dead, there was no way to pin Cara's murder on Winston, frustrating as that was.

Diana wanted Winston here to insure that his opinion of Vincent's murder was placed on the record. Everyone knew it was self-defense, but knowing Winston, he might one day wish to twist the facts and accuse Marcus or Harrington of murder. His statement to the police captain would keep Winston from ever using this incident, which he had instigated, against Harrington.

"I can't do that, Winston," Diana answered. "Marcus isn't bluffing. He's acting on my orders. I'm the one who will really create a scandal. I can raise enough questions to compel you to respond."

"To say nothing of what I can do," John added.

Winston viewed them with amusement. They had no

proof of his involvement in Cara's death or in Vincent's assault. Good. He turned to Marcus. "You're wasting your talents with Diana and Harrington, Mr. Mancini. Why don't you come to work for me?"

"Diana is a great lady. Harrington is a great man," Marcus said simply. "And you're scum."

"You're making a grave error," Winston said.

"You'd be making a mistake to hire me. You've been involved in the murders of my father, and Cara and Fred Franco. I wanted you, Joe Field, and Vincent. But it will do for *now* that Vincent is gone and Harrington's alive and recovering."

"Very well," Winston said to Diana. "You have your wish. I'll take care of this. The police were wondering about the multiple wounds. I will state that Vincent was an unstable employee who was trying to get to me through Harrington. Will that suit you?"

"I'll want to be with you when you tell them," Diana said picking up her coat. "Shall we go?"

Winston opened the door for her. They saw Joe Field out in the hall.

"Tell your guard to leave," Diana said with quiet vengeance.

"But Joe is just here to protect me," Winston said, smiling.

Marcus moved up behind Winston before John could and pushed his .45 into Winston's back. "Do as Diana says."

"You're forgetting yourself, Mr. Mancini."

"If I do forget myself, you won't be here to remember. Now do it!" Marcus whispered, for policemen stood in the hall and were now curious.

"I'll be out momentarily, Joe. Go ahead."

Joe Field bowed slightly, mocking Marcus, and then headed down the hall. When he was out of sight, Diana called out to the police captain. Marcus shielded his weapon. Winston and Diana walked beyond the threshold and the door swung shut behind them.

Marcus turned around and faced John. "I know it's hard for you to watch Diana in this position. But I couldn't let you take the risk. You might have pulled that trigger. Now put it away."

John was holding a gun. His face was beet red. Slowly he

placed the weapon back in his shoulder holster.

Harrington had watched John pull out the gun. What had happened to them all?

"Don't let him get to you. Promise me," Cara had told him. "It's over," Harrington said suddenly, surprising John and Marcus.

Harrington looked up at Marcus. Just as Vincent's death had jarred Marcus, Winston and Joe's presence and John's reaction reminded Harrington that he never again wanted to see that dark side of himself. Harrington remembered the words Marcus had spoken to him when he was being bandaged up and wheeled into this room just hours ago.

"Your mother used to tell us that there is no such thing as total control of one's life. Circumstances arise, some without warning, and those circumstances are fate. How one reacts to those events will determine whether one is master of oneself."

"How do you apply that to yourself, Marcus?" Harrington had asked.

"It was fate that my father died and that I became your protector. Killing Vincent made me master of myself once again. Your father and Joe Field murdered my father. I will get them one day, Harrington, but it will be on my terms, not theirs. Now, how are *you* going to live? Are you the master of yourself, too?"

John bent over his godson and gently stroked his hair. "Are you at peace with the demons at last?"

"Yes, John," Harrington said emotionally.

Marcus reached out and grabbed Harrington's hand. "Welcome back, Harrington. Welcome back."

CHAPTER XVIII

G ermany's unconditional surrender in May 1945 touched off pandemonium in Times Square, but tears of joy intermingled with those of sorrow, because President Roosevelt had died just a few short weeks before the victory.

"Everything's taken care of," Marcus told Diana in late July. "I've even finalized Fred Franco's last wishes. He should be resting happily now with his wife."

Diana was lying in her bedroom at Newport. John sat at her side. "I want to see the ocean," she said.

John helped her out of bed. She sat in the windowseat, a favorite place of hers as a little girl. Staring past the sweeping green lawn to the Atlantic Ocean, she said, "Almost everything, Marcus. I need to spend some time with my son." She glanced up at John lovingly, "And with you, darling."

Diana arranged to be alone with Harrington and John for a few weeks. Katharine Garvin agreed to take care of Jason Sterling at Windsor Royal. Hopefully, an Allied victory was imminent soon in the Pacific and Thomas would come home and join Katharine there.

Harrington still had not seen Jason Sterling. Once and

for all, Diana had to settle the child's fate. She had grown to love the little boy. He was extraordinarily bright for three and a half years old. What would Harrington wish to do with Cara's son and his own future? Diana could not rest until she was assured Harrington's course was set.

"Hello, Mother!" Harrington said.

'Harrington looks so handsome,' she thought proudly. Carrying himself with a sense of confidence, he crossed the bedroom with a slight limp. He shook hands with Marcus and then John. Afterwards he bent over and gave her a kiss on the cheek.

In the light, his blond hair shone with dark gold and his startling blue eyes reminded her of the ocean she had been watching. Muscular and trim, Harrington was dressed in gray slacks and a sportscoat with open shirt.

Harrington heard the door discreetly close as he sat in the chair beside his mother. They were alone.

"Mother," he said gently, "I'm fine now. I just want to make sure you are."

Diana smiled slightly and turned back to the ocean, almost at peace. "I've already told you about my will, darling. Have you thought any more about Jason Sterling."

Harrington had thought of nothing else. "If I don't take charge of him, Winston will."

"How would you feel about that?"

"Not good."

"But, he's Vincent Morello's child," Diana said bluntly.

"That shouldn't matter. He's Cara's son too."

"But it does?"

"Yes."

Harrington got up from the chair and looked out at the ocean, trying to picture what his life would be like with Jason Sterling as a reminder of all that had happened to him in the last few years.

"What will I think about when I look at him, Mother? Of Cara's rape and death? Of my being involved in his father's violent death?"

"Is that why you don't want to see him?"

Harrington sighed and sat down again. Leaning forward in his chair, he took her hand in his. His pain was so deep, so apparent, that Diana would have done anything to wipe it away.

"I think that's part of the reason."

"Harrington, I want to tell you something." She sat up straighter with effort and looked directly at him. "You have a destiny to fulfill. If Jason Sterling will keep you from achieving your goals—one's you've had since you were a child —then you won't be any good to him. If emotionally you aren't ready to be his father, then you should choose not to have him with you. Cara would have accepted any decision you made. The day before she died, we spoke. She had posed several questions. What if her child came between you? The child wasn't created out of love. Although it wasn't the child's fault, what was she to do? Protect the innocent, meaning Jason Sterling, and destroy the innocent, meaning the two of you? Although beginning to formulate her thoughts, Cara never was able to complete them. I just thought you should know that Cara was thinking along the same lines as you are before her death. The child was hers, Harrington. He's not yours."

"Do you love him, Mother?"

"Yes. That should have no bearing on your decision, Harrington. Besides, Winston can't keep Jason if you wish in the end to have custody. Thomas can take care of that. Why don't you think about it."

Diana watched her son struggle with his decision. She agreed with him that it was better he not see Jason Sterling until he made up his mind. In this instance, he had to think of his own mental well-being first. She knew her son. Once he saw Jason Sterling, he would remember his brother, Winston Jason. He might wish to take the boy for emotional reasons only and end up hurting himself forever. Harrington still had to overcome his own emotional problems. He needed time away from New York and away from Winston, time on his own, time for his career and his destiny . . . and possibly, time to find another woman whom he could cherish like he had Cara. Maybe he felt he could have all those things with Jason Sterling beside him. The decision was Harrington's.

In August, the first atomic bomb was dropped on Japan. News hit the States on Sunday, September 2, that Japan had surrendered to the Allies. Within the week, Thomas Garvin returned from Pacific duty while MacArthur was defending his policies as Supreme Commander for the Allied powers.

For everyone at Newport, the war was over. They were thrilled to have Thomas home. He spent a few days with Katharine at Windsor Royal. Then he made the trip to visit Diana while Katharine stayed with Jason Sterling.

Thomas appeared the same, maybe a little leaner and wiser. Harrington wondered what he had expected. He saw no visible scars, no limp.

Thomas held Harrington a moment longer than usual and spoke only for his ears. "We look the same, just a few years more experienced. We have a lot to talk about."

Thomas was not privy to Jason's true identity. When he heard that Harrington was struggling to decide whether to take custody of Jason Sterling or whether to leave him with Winston, he took a good hard look at Harrington.

'Why would Harrington wish to leave his own son with Winston,' he wondered? But as the days passed, he started to believe that Harrington should not take custody of Jason. He was not emotionally up to handling the responsibilities.

"I can draw up a custody petition that gives Winston temporary custody of Jason. Harrington will have the right at any time without notice to take over his son's care," he told Diana and Harrington. "And Harrington will have the right to visit Jason at any time, to talk to Jason at any time. I'll make sure the document is drawn up in such a way that Winston will not be able to contest it. I will have Winston sign it."

"I'll get someone on the Supreme Court to witness it, Thomas, in addition to you and Walter Kent," Diana added. "You are all well-known. If something were to happen to any of you, questions would be raised."

"Mother? How will Jason Sterling feel about living with Winston?"

She reached for Harrington. He sat beside her in the chair by the window seat. "I never told you, but I thought you might wish to make the decision Thomas has presented to you so I introduced Jason to Winston. I could not have supported this decision without having seen for myself how Jason Sterling and Winston got along."

Harrington was surprised and so was Thomas. Winston had instigated Cara's death and Diana let him see Jason before Harrington had made his decision?

Diana smiled slightly. "I know what both of you are thinking. But I've already told Jason Sterling about Harrington. Then of course, Jim Johnson is still at the stables and will be a very good influence on Jason just as he was on you, Harrington. Yes, Jason will be all right until you decide what you want. And never forget, Harrington," Diana said, thinking of what she had found in Winston's files. "Cara's mother died in childbirth. Winston probably prevented Cara from receiving the proper care. Quite obviously, however, Cara would have had complications anyway. I have the records from Florence. Her mother had a toxemic pregnancy, too."

Diana's condition worsened the following week, and John was at her side. She drifted in and out of consciousness. As minutes slipped into hours, she was only vaguely aware of the drone of voices and the scurry of activity around her. She felt neither pain nor discomfort, merely a glorious floating sensation as if she were suspended in a place all her own. She wanted to give in to it totally, to rest, to be free at last, but the thought of Harrington restrained her. She had to fight and hold on.

"Mother?"

Harrington's voice broke into her world. The touch of his hand slowly pulled her back into reality. Her eyes fluttered open and she took in his hazy features.

His eyes once again reflected an inner strength and wisdom beyond his twenty-five years. At the moment, they were full of concern. She wanted to touch his cheek and soothe his fear, but she couldn't move.

He stroked her hair as he spoke, trying to soothe her. "Everything's going to be fine, Mother."

"Harrington, we must talk about your father."

'Her voice sounds so weak,' Harrington realized, tightening his hand around hers.

Diana's mind drifted, and suddenly she heard Winston's words of long ago. 'I suppose you've drawn up your will?' A sense of urgency overcame her. Had she signed the new will? She tried to remember. Yes, and Thomas promised to protect Harrington's interests.

Harrington, her dear Harrington. She remembered

Harrington's first steps. How hard it had been to let him fall. Yet, she had kept her distance, and he had struggled before finding his own way into her adoring arms. As she had his entire life, she tried to curb her strong maternal instinct to protect, allowing him the freedom to fail. She had asked only that he do his best, and he had grown strong and independent, excelling on his own.

"Harrington," she said so softly that he had to lean forward to hear. "You're so gifted and you have wonderful friends . . . this is so important, Harrington. Come closer," she whispered urgently.

He moved onto the edge of the bed and stared at John momentarily. Their eyes locked. John tried to smile but had to turn his head. His eyes were full of tears.

Harrington tilted his head close to Diana's lips, overcome with grief.

". . . promise me that you'll never ignore the differences in men . . ."

He heard the pain in her voice and grimaced.

". . . consider those different from you as neither friend nor foe, but men whom you must deal with and can learn from . . . even your father . . . Promise me, Harrington . . ."

Her hand clung to his shoulder, and he took her into his arms. How fragile and thin she was. "I promise, Mother."

"I'm unafraid of where I'm going. Are you afraid of where you're going?" she whispered.

"I'm unafraid, Mother," he said, tears falling down his face.

"I'll love you eternally . . . you and John . . . and Winston Jason . . ."

She reached out a hand for John, and Harrington watched his godfather take her into his arms. Her eyes closed and Harrington knew she was gone. He got up from the bed and respectfully left John with Diana. Out in the hallway, he told Thomas that Diana Darnley Todd had passed away. It was a month before her forty-ninth birthday.

St. Patrick's Cathedral was filled to capacity for Diana's memorial service. Some of the mourners spilled out onto the steps and the Fifth Avenue sidewalk. A private family ceremony would take place the following morning at the Church of the Good Shepherd.

Huge bouquets of flowers and wreaths filled the sanctuary. Representatives of government, society, and the arts paid their respects to Diana. Walter Kent wept openly. The Dareels, the Christians, and the Shores sat in the same pew, wiping their eyes. Congressman Bates and Senator Johnson, Chief Justice Hall and Justice Burns sat behind Harrington, John, Conrad, Thomas, Katharine, and Jim Johnson. Winston sat in the front pew across from theirs with Raymond Baren.

After the memorial service, Winston played the dutiful husband, shaking hands and accepting condolences from those at the gathering unaware of his estrangement from Diana.

Those on the inside, like the Walter Kents, Chief Justice Hall, the Dareels, and the Shores, spoke only to Harrington's contingent.

With so many people present, Harrington's camp became indistinguishable from Winston's. Only the frustrated press, who somehow couldn't get Harrington and Winston into the same picture, questioned the coolness between the two men.

Two days later, Harrington drove out to Meadow Hill Cemetery with John, Thomas, Katharine, Conrad, Marcus, and Jim Johnson. Laster French positioned men outside the gates and surrounding the area. Harrington and his extended family deserved a private farewell with Diana.

Not a speck of sun slipped through the haze hovering overhead like a miasmic blanket. Rain was in the air.

Winston had refused to attend the service at the Church of the Good Shepherd. He had immediately taken up residence at Windsor Royal where Jason Sterling was living. Harrington tried to remind himself that he had made his decision and would abide by it no matter what Winston did. Still, he was filled with hatred and a tremendous grief.

They left the car and filed up the hillside through the open gate. Weaving their way among the headstones that bore the chiseled names of ten generations of the Todd family, they looked over the valley to the Church of the Good Shepherd and beyond to the curve of the Hudson River. It began to rain, and the wind whipped around them when they came to stand at the gravesite.

Although Harrington had held his mother in his arms and had felt the life leaving her, he still couldn't believe she was gone. He read the inscription on her tombstone:

DIANA DARNLEY TODD

November 7, 1897–September 27, 1945

It was simply stated, just as she had wanted. But how could a mere name and dates capture a life?

In his mind, Harrington saw Katharine's portrait of Diana; Diana's blonde hair, the lovely face, the clearness of eyes so like his own. He thought of all the times she had seemed happy, when her eyes had danced and she had been so vitally alive; and he tried to remember if she were ever sad, truly sad. He couldn't, yet he knew the pain and sadness she had shielded him from. She had taught him never to live for another, yet she had made the choice to live for him, to give him the opportunity to utilize his own talents so he would never have to experience her agony. But he, her son, felt unworthy of her sacrifice.

"The day before she died," Harrington said to them all, "Mother repeated to me something she had said before. That the scales of justice don't hang in balance by themselves. Whether fighting for an inner peace or fighting for an external balance with an adversary, one must fight for that balance—that is freedom." He stared out over the valley. "The night she died I promised her that I would recognize the differences in men and learn to deal with them. I'm going to keep that promise . . ." His body trembled. He felt as though his world was coming to an end. "He killed her, you know, but he's not going to win . . ."

Harrington felt a hand on his shoulder. Slowly he turned around. The stalwart, modestly dressed Jim Johnson gently looked into his eyes.

There they stood. The tall, elegantly dressed Harrington and the former stable boy, Jim, who had long been Harrington's close friend.

Without a word, Jim gave Harrington his response. Unashamedly he started to cry.

Harrington patted his shoulder. "It's O.K., Jim. Let it out."

Harrington felt a wave of emotion wash over him, and tears appeared in his own eyes. Jim hugged him, and Harrington finally cried too . . . for Diana, his mother, the woman who had given him his freedom.

Two days later, everyone joined Winston at Todd Industries' headquarters for the reading of the will.

"Sit down, please," Winston said, gesturing to the chairs and couches in his suite.

Thomas crossed the room and took the chair that faced the group. Harrington and John guided Katharine to a couch. Marcus and Jim Johnson sat beside her. Conrad took a chair between Harrington and John before Winston's desk.

"Would you like copies of the will to read along?" Thomas asked.

Winston looked at the summary of the will in the open briefcase. "That won't be necessary, Thomas. Leave me a copy after this is all finished."

"Harrington?" Thomas asked.

"I'll just listen, too, Thomas."

"Let's get on with it!" Winston snapped.

Thomas sat back in his chair and opened up the folder. "Walter Kent will arrive late. He's asked that I proceed." Clearing his throat, Thomas began the summary, commencing with the special bequests and eliminating the alternate beneficiaries:

> To John Stevens, I leave my half interest in the Randolph Lauren Theater, my half interest in the Stevens Summer Theater, half of my interest in the play, *My Sister, Kierston,* my First Folio of Shakespeare, and my estate in Newport, Rhode Island.
> To Katharine Garvin, I leave my Renoir paintings and my fourteen carat diamond bracelet.
> To Marcus Mancini, I leave my antique sword and shield, my first edition books on Napoleon, and the sum of one million dollars ($1,000,000.00).
> To Conrad Coleman, I leave my film library, half of my interest in the play, *My Sister, Kierston,* and the sum of one million dollars

($1,000,000.00).

To Thomas Garvin, I leave all of my shares of Garvin Enterprises stock including but not limited to all my shares of World Studios.

To Jason Sterling Todd, I leave all my property in Los Angeles, California, and a five million dollar ($5,000,000.00) Trust Fund to be administrated by his father, Harrington Todd, until Jason Sterling Todd's twenty-first birthday.

To Walter Kent, I leave one-fourth (1/4) of my Darnley Enterprises stock on the express condition and limitation that he may sell the Darnley Enterprises shares and other accumulated interests accruing therefrom to my son, Harrington Sterling Todd or to Jason Sterling Todd.

To Jim Johnson, I leave my thoroughbred horses at the Darnley Ranch in Kentucky and one million dollars ($1,000,000.00).

To Harrington Todd, my son, I leave three/fourths (3/4) of my stock in Darnley Enterprises, my suite at the Waldorf Towers, my china, my silver, the remainder of my art collection, my personal artifacts, the remainder of my jewels, the remainder of my books, and other tangible articles of a personal nature not otherwise specifically disposed of by this Will.

Thomas looked up to see Winston shaking his head and smirking. He seemed to be amused at Diana's bequests. Conrad sat between John and Harrington. He held their arms firmly, restraining them from doing Winston bodily harm. Katharine and Jim sat together quietly.

"There's one more specific bequest, but before we discuss that I want to review the disposition of the residue of the estate. Harrington, you are to receive two-thirds of the residue of the estate."

Thomas paused. He had objected to the next clause, urging Diana to bequeath Winston only that property they owned jointly. But she was adamant. If Winston wasn't left his share, she argued, he'd do everything possible to contest the will and tie it up in court for years.

If she left him a substantial share of money, the

newspapers would have a field day when he tried to contest:
"Billionaire Todd Sues for Paltry Millions." The papers
would accuse him of greed and smear his name across the
front page. Only in secret battles was Winston in his element.
He could face innuendo, but not facts. Maybe Diana had
been right in her decision.

"Winston, you are bequested one-third of the residue of
the estate, including the Darnley Ranch in Kentucky. For
your information, gentlemen, the estimated value of Mrs.
Todd's assets exceeds seventy-five million dollars."

Winston wasn't overly surprised at the turn of events so
far. He was waiting for the Cultural Center, and he also
wondered what Harrington proposed to do about Jason.

"As I indicated to you there's a last specific bequest,
which I'd like to discuss. The Todd Cultural Center in
Manhattan . . ." Thomas began.

Winston leaned forward in his seat and placed his elbows
on the desk.

"The Todd Cultural Center in Manhattan will remain in
trust until whichever of Harrington Todd's heirs that he so
chooses, either male or female, reaches his or her twenty-first
birthday, at which time it will be distributed to that heir.
Harrington and I are named trustees of that trust."

Thomas continued. "However, Winston, there is a
provision. Should you contest any part of this will, Diana
ordered that the Todd Crest now on the Center be replaced by
the Darnley Crest, and that the buildings be immediately
renamed the Darnley Cultural Center. Should you accept the
will without contest, the Todd Crest and name will remain on
the building, at least until Harrington's heir designate reaches
legal age. Also, should it happen that either Harrington or his
heirs die prior to the full distribution of this property, the
Cultural Center automatically will be renamed the Darnley
Cultural Center and will be placed in a foundation for the arts
with a designated board of trustees consisting of Thomas
Garvin, John Stevens, and Conrad Coleman.

"I have been appointed executor and trustee of the
estate, as you know, and I will receive five percent of earnings
from any trusts that I administer. The will is duly signed,
dated, and witnessed, as you gentleman may see for
yourselves."

Winston sat perfectly still, but Thomas could see the

color in his cheeks and the tension in his muscular arms. He was enraged, but didn't dare show it.

"Do you have any questions, Winston?"

"What about Jason?"

Thomas was ready for this. "Ring your secretary. I think you'll find the other witnesses are waiting."

"Witnesses?" Winston quickly picked up the phone.

Within the half hour, the temporary custody issue was settled. All the witnesses had received copies of their individual files, which Marcus had copied in Winston's office. Secretly, they were making their own plans to counteract Winston's invasion of their privacy. This was the first step.

Justices Hall and Burns, and Walter Kent, witnessed the custody document, as did Thomas. Thomas knew Winston was pleased and also unhappy. The signed document was iron-clad . . . almost. Winston could have the witnesses murdered, then buy off officials to have it revoked. But then, Thomas and these men were well aware of what Winston could do. They had taken the necessary precautions.

Conrad was awaiting Harrington in California, but before leaving, Harrington still had personal matters to settle.

"Marcus, you've been through so much," he said, ashamed he had thought only of himself. He walked over to his desk at Washington Mews and took out the deed to Franco's. "Would you mind accepting this with one condition?"

"I can't take that."

"Please. But rename it Mia Cara."

Marcus flushed, something he hadn't done in years. He grabbed his handkerchief and wiped the tears from his eyes. "My dear one," he murmured.

"For Cara, for Fred, and for your father," Harrington said emotionally, shoving the deed into his hands. "Excuse me now. I have something else I have to take care of."

That evening Harrington entered John Stevens's Park Avenue apartment carrying a gift under his arm.

"What's this?" John asked, peeling away the paper.

Maybe as a romantic, Harrington had come to believe John's heart had only belonged to one woman—his mother.

Watching her cope with life married to a man unworthy of her affections would have driven the man who truly loved her to desperate acts. John had shown remarkable restraint. And on top of it all, John Stevens was much more his father than Winston would ever be.

John gasped at Katharine's painting, caught himself, and slowly raised his eyes. "I thought you might have known about us."

John deliberately set the portrait against a chair and embraced Harrington. "God, I miss her, Harrington!"

Harrington wept openly. "I wish I could do something for you, John. Anything. You're my father!"

John hugged him, his eyes red with tears, his voice gruff. "You've brought me more joy in my life than anyone except your mother. Do more of the same and I'll always be a happy man."

Cara's movie, *My Immigrant Father,* came out at Christmastime to critical acclaim. Overcome with emotion, Harrington decided to see Jason before heading west in the spring of 1947.

"Jim keeps an eye on him," Marcus informed Harrington. That was the first time Harrington had heard mention of Marcus's contact with Jim Johnson at Windsor Royal Stables. Marcus thought of everything.

"Jim could leave Windsor Royal forever with Mother's inheritance."

"The money isn't important. His word to your mother is. He loves Jason. Jim's going to stay as long as Jason stays."

Katharine Garvin insisted on traveling east to accompany Harrington to Windsor Royal with a surprise all of her own. She was expecting a child. Thomas hoped for a girl whom they would name Kierston Cara Garvin.

Marcus drove Harrington and Katharine out to the country on a chilly March morning in 1947. Cold weather bothered Harrington's leg, although it had healed. On this day, as the sun passed behind the clouds, Harrington once again felt that dull ache gripping his thigh. For the first time in months, however, he felt a calm against the memories it stirred.

He peered out the front windshield as Marcus drove down Mayfair Road. At the gate, two security guards had taken up residence in the old gatekeeper's house.

Marcus pulled up, and one of the guards approached the car. "Your name?"

Harrington opened the back window. "Harrington Todd."

The guard peered into the car at Marcus, then at Katharine and Harrington. He nodded stiffly, as if Harrington's name meant nothing to him, and walked back to the guardhouse. They waited while he called the mansion.

The O.K. was sent down, the gates opened, and they proceeded down the two-mile drive.

Ahead, Harrington caught a glimpse of children playing in the forest. Winston's personal staff and security now resided at Windsor Royal. The families lived in the cottages across the creek on the eastern grounds. Their offspring attended school in the little schoolhouse a quarter of a mile from those cottages.

"They're the way we were as children," Harrington told Marcus and Katharine ruefully. "Eerie, isn't it?"

Harris Johnson had the privilege of greeting Harrington and his guests. "Is it possible?" he asked, taken aback by Harrington's appearance. Harrington was a man; he radiated a confidence that commanded respect without asking for it.

"Hello, Harris. I believe you know Mrs. Garvin."

"Why, yes, well congratulations! I see you're soon to be a mother!"

"And you know Marcus," Harrington continued.

Harris reluctantly tore his eyes from Harrington and Katharine and nodded his hello.

"Mr. Todd," Harris said to Harrington a trifle nervously as they entered the Grand Reception Room, "your father requests that you wait in the drawing room. He's in a meeting at the moment. If you . . . if you don't mind, he would prefer being present when you meet Jason."

They entered the drawing room. Harrington stopped short, startled to see an earlier portrait of Diana hanging over the marble fireplace. He was standing before it breathlessly, Katharine at his side, when he heard someone at the door.

"Hello, sir."

There in the threshold was the boy, Jason. He was Cara's image, but with black hair. Again, Harrington was overwhelmed with emotion. The little boy, almost five, dressed in a tailored suit, ran to him. He reached down and lifted Jason into his arms.

"Hi, there."

"Hello, Father," Jason said distinctly. They were just inches apart. Harrington noticed the color of Jason's eyes: blue with a dark rim around the iris. Jason took in all of Harrington's face as if he were comparing it to the version in his memory. In a clear voice, he said, "I'm happy you came. I didn't know what you looked like."

"Haven't you seen my picture?" Harrington asked.

"Pictures are different."

Harrington laughed, setting Jason down. He took his hand and led him to the couch next to the marble fireplace. Marcus and Katharine joined them.

"Yes, pictures are different," Harrington said, staring at Diana's portrait and thinking of Cara's photographs.

Jason threw his arms around Harrington, who bent down so Jason could kiss his cheek. Abruptly Jason's hands were gone, and his attention switched to Marcus.

"Are you Mr. Mancini?" Jason asked.

"Yes, Jason," Marcus answered.

"I thought so. Grandma told me you held me when I was little and that you saved my father's life."

Marcus winked at Harrington, totally taken by this bright little fellow. "I did, yes, and call me Marcus," he said, extending his hand to shake.

Jason looked with utmost interest at Marcus's huge hand surrounding his own. "You are very big."

Marcus cracked a smile in spite of himself. Jason touched his hand and examined it from every angle. "How long did it take you to grow this big?"

"I'm thirty-seven, but I was this big at sixteen."

Jason looked at him very seriously. "That's a long time." He sat back on the couch and studied them both, then his eyes drifted to Katharine and he edged forward.

"Hello, Mrs. Garvin. There haven't been a lot of girls here since you left and Grandma . . ." Jason stopped.

"Do you miss your grandmother, Jason?"

Jason nodded seriously, his eyes soft and sensitive. "Grandma and I had a talk, though. I understand about death. Grandma told me. She said she'd be looking over me." He stared at his hands a minute, then lifted his eyes and cocked his head, warming to Katharine's soft expression. "Do you play football?"

"I'm amazed that you should ask that question, Jason," Katharine answered. "Your father and mother told me they used to play football on the lawn in back. I used to play football, too, but with my friends back in California."

"Really?"

"Yes, really!"

Jason seemed very pleased by this news. He placed a hand on Harrington's leg and stared up at his father with that curious look again. "Jim says I take after you. So did Grandma."

Harrington's heart almost broke in two. "You're a very smart little boy, Jason."

Jason smiled. "Not yet, but some day."

They all laughed, and Jason with them.

When Winston's voice boomed in the Grand Reception Hall, Jason scrambled down from the couch and ran to the drawing room door. "Here I am!"

Winston appeared and lifted Jason into his arms.

"I was bad, Grandfather."

"Yes, you were. I told you to wait."

"I heard their auto," Jason chirped, "and I came down."

Winston's hair was no longer merely sprinkled with white strands. Still, he looked younger, much younger than the day the will had been read. He was trim and fit, more animated than Harrington had ever seen him.

Winston disliked the warm feminine quality that Jason found so appealing in Katharine Garvin. He nodded his head in Katharine's direction as his only acknowledgement of her presence.

"We certainly do appreciate your letting us come to visit, Winston," Katharine said softly, with a trace of reproachfulness. "We have all been having such a good time."

"We sure have!" Jason added brightly.

"Then you must have made quite an impression," Winston said to Jason with a wink. "What do you think of my grandson, gentlemen? Not only does he speak well, but he already can read and write. He plays all the sports you can think of and he keeps me young and active. I would say he's accomplished quite a lot in a short time."

"He's a charming little fellow," Harrington said. "Come here, Jason, let me look at you again."

Jason freed himself from Winston's grip and ran over to Harrington. "Are you going to California?"

"Yes, I am."

"Father?" he asked, reaching for his hand, "can I go with you?"

Winston raised an eyebrow, noticing that Harrington and Jason had established an immediate rapport. "Jason," he said sternly, "you can't be roaming around the country. You have your studies. Remember what I told you?"

Jason looked very disappointed.

Harrington bent down, even though it hurt his leg. "What did your grandfather tell you?"

"I've got to study hard, 'cause I'm going to Harvard."

"I see," Harrington said, smiling at him. "And are you having fun here?"

"Oh, yes, with the horses and my friends and Grandfather, but I'd like you to stay."

Winston again noted their exchange. Fortunately Joe Field had anticipated Harrington and Jason's affinity for one another. For over a year, Joe had searched through Italy trying to find a girl like Cara. Winston had never seen Marisa Benito in person, but her pictures showed an eerie similarity to Cara. Her history paralleled Cara's perfectly. Her credibility as an actress was being established. By the time Harrington met her, Marisa Benito would be a rising star. Hopefully, she would occupy Harrington's time and keep him away from Jason.

"Go play with your friends, Jason," he commanded suddenly.

"Will you come and meet them?" Jason asked Harrington.

"I'll be out in a minute. Have fun."

Jason raced across the room, then skidded to a halt. "Mrs. Garvin! Would you like to come with me?"

Winston watched as Katharine and Jason left hand in hand, then he turned to Harrington, a charming smile on his face. "I don't think it's wise for you to influence the boy. Here, he has a steady home life. You can't give him that. Don't put any ideas into his head about becoming an actor."

Marcus stood by silently, having to admit that once

again, Winston, with all his charm, would have fooled most people.

"I know you'd stoop to anything to keep Jason. You may raise him for the time being, but you can't prevent me from seeing my own son. I'm not going to dignify your comments further. We both know about the temporary custody order. By the way, what's Mother's portrait doing in here?"

"I thought it graced this room," he said, then changed the subject. "You're an actor, Harrington. It's no secret that they're notoriously unstable. I don't mean to be unkind, but does that sound like a healthy influence on a young boy?"

"I'm not interested in debating the merits of the acting profession with you today."

"You're missing the point, Harrington. I'm no longer angry at you. Jason is all that's important to me now. You can do as you wish. But I'll raise Jason and do with him as I choose, and there is nothing you or anyone else can do about it. If you try, you'll be tied up in legal battles so long that you'll have white hair and a cane before we get out of court. Now if you'll excuse me, I'll ask you to say good-bye to Jason. I'm sure it will be quite some time before you see him again." Winston walked to the door and turned. "Give it up, Harrington. Your mother failed and so will you. I'll destroy you if you get in my way. I mean to have what I want. You take heed of my words." He continued down the Reception Hall. "Harris! Have Jason meet me on the front steps. Harrington is leaving."

Harrington felt another surge of anger. He wanted to take the portrait of Diana. He knew it was ridiculous, but somehow he felt her spirit had become a captive audience.

"Not now," Marcus warned. "To fight him now would be to destroy what you're becoming. I'm sure Cara would not want that, even on her son's behalf." Harrington was staring at Diana's portrait. "He's goading you, Harrington. Don't you understand? By being charming, he's trying to undermine your confidence. Your move to California is just like opening night of *Remember When*. He wants you to doubt yourself, to fail. He's using your mother's memory and Cara's son against you, to play with your emotions. You've got to continue on with your life. We'll work it out. Why would you put yourself through that again?"

In response, Harrington could only shake his head that he couldn't. They walked through the Reception Hall to the arched front door. Jason ran up as they approached.

"You're leaving already? My friends . . ."

"Who said I was leaving," Harrington declared, taking Jason's hand. "I was coming out to see you, as I promised."

They headed for the great lawn where all of Jason's friends gathered around.

"This is my father, Harrington Todd. Michael, he's really here!" Jason said proudly.

"Boy, oh boy," Michael said, staring up at Harrington. "He's grand!"

Harrington looked at the children, and at Michael **Christian** in particular, who appeared to be Jason's closest friend. Harrington picked up the round, chubby-faced boy with the intelligent blue eyes.

"How are you, Michael?" he said man-to-man. Michael was all smiles, but unable to speak, so overpowered was he by Harrington's presence. Harrington set him down and shook his hand. "I'm glad to meet a friend of my son."

Jason stood by, so excited and bursting with pride that he looked like every single button on his suit would pop.

"Hi!"

Harrington noticed a little redheaded girl. "Hi," he said.

"That's Nicole Baren," Jason said distinctly. "She and her mother live here on the estate. Her father is away a lot on business. Oh, and Father, this is Bobby."

Harrington could hardly believe that this beautiful little redhead was Raymond Baren's daughter. He turned back to Bobby **Christian** now, another of Jason's buddies. "You look like a pretty healthy young fellow."

"Yeah," Bobby said, shy and awkward but obviously pleased.

For an hour, Harrington played with the children on the great lawn while Marcus and Katharine sat on the veranda watching and Jim observed from the stables.

Harrington placed his arm around Jason's shoulder and the boy clung to him happily. When he sat down on the lawn, Jason positioned himself close to Harrington and placed a tiny hand on Harrington's arm. Harrington laughed, and Jason squealed with joy, and they laughed a lot. The scene stabbed at Marcus's heart.

"It's a beautiful scene, isn't it," Katharine said.

"Remarkable," Marcus said emotionally.

"Do you think he'll take custody?" she asked quietly.

Marcus viewed Harrington and Jason again. "It's a possibility. Katharine, I respect your opinion. Tell me why Winston has Diana's portrait hanging in the drawing room."

Katharine considered her next words carefully. "Jason obviously adored Diana. I saw it whenever they were together. She taught him well and told him to trust Jim. Winston is unaware of Jim's influence, but he was well aware of Diana's. That portrait is there for Jason, to bind him to Winston. To Jason, Winston is Diana's husband. This was Diana's home. This is where his security is."

Marcus listened and knew she was right.

"Harrington! It's time for Jason's studies," Winston called out from the veranda.

Harrington shook hands with each of the children. Then he and Jason made their way back through the rose garden to the mansion. Jason chirped about flying to California one day as he and Harrington walked directly in front of Winston and through the library. Marcus and Katharine followed.

"Nicole said you are going to have a baby," Jason said to Katharine out in front of Windsor Royal.

"Yes, I am."

Jason stared at her stomach curiously. Then he rushed to the car and, with a struggle, opened the door for her.

"Thank you, Jason," Katharine said, getting inside.

Jason cocked his head and said very seriously, "Does having a baby mean you can't play football anymore?"

Katharine reached out and touched Jason's cheek. "No, dear child. I'll play again. Maybe with you one day soon."

Jason brightened.

Harrington crouched down and spoke to Jason. "Just remember, I'm very proud of you, as your grandmother was and your mother would have been. Can you remember that?"

Jason answered seriously. "Yes, sir."

"Don't call me sir. Never call me sir. I'm your father."

Jason threw his arms around Harrington's neck. "Yes, Father! Are you going to be away a long time? Grandmother said you might be. I'm supposed to be brave. That's what Grandmother said."

Harrington looked him in the eyes. "I don't know how long, but I'll be back. You just remember, I'll be thinking of you every day. And I'll call you every week." Harrington couldn't speak for a moment. He had never imagined that he would feel this way about Jason. But Jason was so much like Cara that he didn't want to leave him. His emotions choked his throat, but finally he found his voice. Then he said the words that he'd longed for Winston to say to him as a boy. "I love you, Jason."

Jason watched him curiously, as he had when they first met. "I love you too, Father," he said.

Before Harrington could answer, Jason scampered around the car and tugged at Marcus's pants.

"Take care of my father, please, Marcus."

Marcus patted Jason on the head.

"Good-bye, Mrs. Garvin!" Jason waved.

Katharine waved back from the window.

"Be safe," Marcus whispered.

Then they were gone.

CHAPTER XIX

On the evening of April 23, 1947, Harrington and Marcus slipped into a World Studios limousine.

Street lamps, set at regular intervals, looked like torch barriers along Rexford Drive. Their light shadowed the palm trees and graceful homes lining the street. Crossing over Lexington in Beverly Hills, the driver turned the limousine into line with other cars at the entrance to Conrad's home.

The moon was full against the galaxy of twinkling stars that appeared to cascade down into daylight. Up ahead, Conrad's two-story white French provincial mansion entry was lit up with kleig lights that gave the illusion of morning sunshine. The press corps was out in full force.

"So you think this party Conrad's giving tonight is a good idea?" Harrington asked.

"It's your formal introduction to the hierarchy in this town," Marcus said. "Conrad calls it image versus essence. Take it for what it's worth, no more."

Harrington stepped from the car, Conrad was there to greet him. Looking down at the little man with the powerful brown eyes, Harrington felt a sense of coming home.

Conrad enthusiastically shook Harrington's hand and winked at Marcus. "Why don't you let me introduce you to the crowd?" As an aside to his abruptness, he placed a hand on Harrington's arm. "We'll catch up later, Harrington, in a more private setting." Harrington agreed. Conrad turned to the crowd of reporters. "Ladies and gentleman of the press, our guest of honor has arrived. May I present, Harrington Todd."

Cameras clicked. The film began to roll. This film clipping was to be used on newsreels in the theaters.

"Harrington is starring in my film, *The Hero,* adapted from John Stevens's play. Principal photography starts this summer. We're planning on a 1948 Christmas release."

"How do you like Hollywood?" Jay Gansberg from the Los Angeles *Times* called out to Harrington.

"Judging by your welcome, I'm going to like it just fine."

Harrington had not been in Conrad's home since 1941. The memory of those frantic days when he sought a home for Cara escaped him momentarily. He tilted his head to scan the Rembrandts, Renoirs, and Monets displayed in the foyer with an impressive collection of Rodin sculpture and was reminded of Conrad's words: "My art collection allows me the opportunity to boast without bragging." That was the only egotistical statement Harrington had ever heard Conrad utter. Otherwise Conrad, like Diana, talked only of doing the best job possible.

The living room, formal and stately, with colorful English tapestries and mahogany antiques was softened with white and royal blue stuffed chairs and couches positioned in intimate sitting areas. From the sound of merriment filtering into the foyer, the guests found it as comfortable as Harrington always had.

"There you are!" John Stevens declared happily, bouncing up the stairs. "Hello, Marcus! Come on, Harrington, you really aren't surprised I'm here. You didn't think I'd miss your 'coming out party,' did you?"

Harrington embraced his godfather. "Knowing your feelings about Hollywood, John, I'm honored you made the trip. I thought you were off on a hunting expedition."

"What better place to begin than here," John said dryly. Those years with Diana in New York and Newport were the happiest of John's life. But now he was eager to get out into the wild, to smell some fresh air and possibly to feel closer to Diana in nature's arms. "Next week I'll be off to the Rockies."

The ring of laughter caught their attention. Katharine Garvin, surrounded by male admirers, was radiant even though well into her pregnancy. She had cut her auburn hair above her shoulders and it framed her ovalface. Her only jewelry was a diamond wedding ring and the diamond bracelet that Diana had bequeathed her. Thomas was talking to a group of studio executives. The Garvins saw Harrington and joined him in the foyer.

"We're all together at last," Harrington said happily, embracing them. Then seeing Conrad's serious expression, added, "I know. I know. This is business. Let's go to work."

John and Conrad escorted Harrington into the living room. He was introduced to major studio heads, executives, and Hollywood stars.

Thomas took the opportunity to talk to Marcus privately. They stood in an alcove near the steps where the crowd in the living room was visible to them.

"I've been using 'Diana's File,' " Thomas said, referring to the intelligence Winston had collected and which Marcus had photographed in Winston's office.

"Trouble?" Marcus asked, immediately on the alert.

"Nothing so dramatic. I took your advice. All new employees are checked against 'Diana's File.' "

"Good. Now what's this I hear about your hiring William Randolph Investment Brokers?" Marcus asked, referring to Winston's investment banking company.

Recently Thomas had asked his Vice President, Dave Britt, to inform Marcus of all Garvin-Todd business transactions. Marcus explained that Dave had told him about WRIB.

"I plan on using WRIB to make investments for our retirement fund. They're highly qualified, as you know," Thomas said, smiling as Marcus narrowed his eyes. "Winston called me personally to congratulate me on picking the best investment bankers."

"Stop talking around the issue. You want the enemy close," Marcus said bluntly.

Thomas remembered his Naval duty in the Pacific. The

enemy had been close and unpredictable. Danger. He seemed to thrive on it, just as he had as a boy. He snapped out of his reverie, feeling Marcus viewing him knowingly. Both their instincts were sharp. Neither of them would stop until they got Winston and Joe.

"I think you should save Harrington," Marcus said with a rare smile. "Arlene Habor has him cornered."

Thomas laughed. "My pleasure."

"Harrington, darling," Arlene Habor was. saying, "didn't I tell you back in New York that you should change your first name? Don't be offended. Of course 'Todd' should stay. But what do you think of . . ."

"I've grown rather fond of my name, Arlene. I think I'll keep it."

She flushed under his steady blue eyes, infuriated that he made her as uncomfortable as had the main line folks in her native Philadelphia. He's a newcomer to my town, she reminded herself. *My town,* that was the point. She had worked hard to gain prestige and power. A Todd or not, this young upstart would learn to show her respect.

"All right, dear, if that's the way you want it. Don't take my advice. You'll see how far you get without it."

"Hello, Arlene."

"Oh, hello, Thomas! A lovely party. I was just telling Harrington . . ."

"I heard." Thomas subtly gestured to Harrington to move on, noticing his impatient expression.

Katharine stood with John to the side of the crowd. "Harrington doesn't look very happy, does he?"

John watched Harrington move purposefully towards the bar. John was struck by Harrington's stature, so different from most of the other men here. He carried a sense of mystery with him and was unconscious of his charisma.

"He'll be fine—oh look, Katharine!" John said, greatly humored. "Roy Sharp is on Harrington's tail!"

"Knowing you, John, you'll probably let Harrington handle Roy on his own."

"That's right!" John beamed. "What better introduction to Hollywood!"

Harrington was at the bar when he felt a tap on his shoulder. "Broadway actor tries his hand in Hollywood, is that it?"

Harrington turned around with a drink in his hand. A gangling, unkempt man with darting eyes, stood before him. "Yes, Mr. . . ."

"Sharp, Roy Sharp, *Confidential Magazine.*"

Harrington stoically viewed the reporter from the notorious tabloid. Mr. Sharp had somehow crashed the party. Conrad had already warned Harrington about talking to reporters working for magazines such as *Confidential*.

"You've obviously figured out that film acting is a different game. It's who you know that counts. Being Conrad Coleman's 'new sensation' is pretty hot stuff. Conrad's track record kinda speaks for you both. Get my drift?"

"I'm sure Conrad is delighted that you're such a fan."

"Yeah, probably, but I also gave you a compliment."

"Save it until you've seen my work."

Roy shrugged indifferently. "Maybe you're right. But I wouldn't go around making an issue of it if I were you. Say, I heard you have a son. Is he with you?"

Harrington turned fully around and smiled guardedly at Mr. Sharp. "How long have you been a reporter, Roy? I find journalists absolutely fascinating."

Roy was so flattered, he ordered a drink and began rattling on about his supposed schooling at Columbia University. "Believe it or not, I started off interviewing for *Time* magazine. They had trouble a few years ago. I was laid off. Circulation was down. Going to be going back soon, though."

"Very impressive," Harrington said, not believing a word Sharp had said.

"Hey, now what's this about your kid, Harrington? Your wife died in childbirth, didn't she?"

Harrington had lost his patience. "Kids have a hard enough time growing up without reading about their lives in the newspapers."

"May I have a word with you, Mr. Sharp," Conrad said, startling them both.

"Mr. Coleman! Sure. My pleasure. See you later, Harrington."

Harrington watched Conrad politely escort Mr. Sharp right into Marcus's capable hands.

"Don't let him bother you," a gentle voice with an Italian accent spoke from behind Harrington.

She took Harrington's breath away. Graceful was not the word that best suited her. An Italian beauty? Still not enough. She was draped in a beautiful Dior gown of pale green. Harrington stared into green almond-shaped eyes and Cara immediately came to mind. Although brunette, taller and more shapely, it was her face that reminded him of Cara. His heart pounded heavily as he said the first thing that occurred to him.

"A friend of yours?"

"No, no, not a friend. When I first came to America, Mr. Sharp gave me a similar welcome."

Harrington watched her take a long thin cigar from her purse. He reached for her lighter. What started as a moment of politeness turned into an intimate gesture. Her delicate fingers guided his hand to light her cigar.

"Thank you," she said, staring deep into his eyes.

"So you've met," Conrad said, joining them.

"Actually, no," Harrington smiled, returning the lighter.

"This is Marisa Benito, Harrington. She is starring in her first film for MGM starting next week. Marisa, Harrington Todd."

"And I already know all about Mr. Todd," Marisa said in a husky soft Italian accent. "I saw him in *The Hero* on Broadway before coming here. You're a brilliant actor. The town's been buzzing about your arrival."

Harrington wanted to be alone with this exquisite creature, but cautioned himself. He had never been taken with just a woman's appearance. Was he attracted to Marisa because of her striking similarity to Cara? As his mind raced, Burt Small, the sailor from the Stage Door Canteen, grabbed him from behind.

"Hey, sport!" Burt said, shaking Harrington's hand. "I'm back from the stormy Pacific without a scratch!"

"Burt, good to see you!"

"Did Conrad tell you I'm adapting *The Hero* to a screenplay?"

"He did, and I'm delighted. Burt, have you met . . ."

Marisa had vanished.

"Business, Harrington," Conrad reminded him, seeing that his actor was bowled over by the youthful and beautiful Italian film actress. "Business."

The fanfare surrounding Harrington's arrival in Hollywood died down after Conrad's party. Wishing to start anew, Harrington placed the Roxbury home he and Cara would have shared on the market. He rented a small modest house on Almayo near World Studios and Rancho Park. True to his own taste and comfort, he left his Eastern attire in the closet and donned cowboy boots and a leather jacket. He spent all his waking hours at Coleman Productions.

Conrad had established many traditions in Hollywood including a strict dress code of suit and tie for himself and his staff. The first day Harrington walked into his office looking the part of the rebel, Conrad started to reprimand him, then stopped himself and looked at Burt Small.

"Times are changing, and I want to change right along with them. My gut tells me to follow Harrington's lead. He's natural, different, and I know he's got the talent. Revise the script to fit Harrington's rebel image. He's wearing his everyday clothes in the movie."

During the shooting of *The Hero,* Harrington could not get Marisa Benito out of his mind. When he lay alone in his bed at night, dreams of Marisa mixed with haunting memories of Cara and Jason. Then he would fall asleep only to be jarred awake by the nightmares about Vincent Morello. 'Is this what my life's going to be like?' he asked himself in utter frustration.

The Garvins called the first week in July. Kierston Cara Garvin was born twenty-two inches long, weighing seven pounds two ounces. Harrington watched Thomas and Katharine fondle their black-haired, blue-eyed baby girl, and his heart stirred. Thoughts of Cara and he living together, raising their children, filled him. He realized he would never forget Cara.

On December 11, 1948, a cool, clear evening in Los Angeles, the Garvins and Marcus drove in the limousine with Harrington and Conrad to Grauman's Chinese Theater. Their destination, *The Hero* premiere.

For months, Harrington had been working night and day. Here and there he had heard comments about the House un-American Activities Committee, but he hadn't paid much attention.

Thomas told them that the "Red Scare" had all the

major studio heads and presidents of major independent
motion picture companies grouping together in New York.
Wall Street had demanded that either Hollywood clean up its
motion picture industry of subversives or Wall Street would
pull the plug on funds.

"I used to think some of my cohorts were pretty damn
tough, but I was wrong," Thomas said. "Although I and a
few others opposed the idea of governmental investigations
into the film industry, we were outvoted."

"What is this Waldorf Pact that was signed?" Harrington asked.

"It's a document which literally throws open the doors
of Hollywood to HUAC to seek out and expose Communists." Thomas glanced mischievously at Harrington. "I
thought you might have asked Marisa to join us."

"I hope you're going to tell him to mind his own
business," Katharine said, nudging Thomas.

"It won't do any good, Katharine. You know that,"
Harrington said smiling. "You changed the subject, Thomas.
Are you worried about this 'Waldorf Pact'?"

"Worried no, cautious yes. We'll see. Look at the
crowd!"

Conrad had planned a huge media event, studding the
premiere with World Studios's star roster. Fans, crowded on
both sides of the street, crushed together behind barricades,
and filled the bleachers. Stobe lights lit up the sky. Camera
crews filmed the event.

Unlike his frenzied Broadway fans, the Hollywood
crowd greeted Harrington with silent curiosity. He looked
incongruous wearing his boots and leather jacket in contrast
to the tuxedoes worn by other male stars. Not until Conrad
stood beside him, did the fans realize they were looking at the
star of *The Hero*.

"Ladies and gentleman! Conrad Coleman has just
arrived," Arlene Habor called out to the crowd and her radio
listeners from a microphone at the podium. "And there's
Thomas Garvin, owner of World Studios. Mr. Coleman!"

Although almost a foot shorter than Harrington,
Conrad held Harrington's arm and escorted him to the
podium. "Miss Habor," Conrad said cordially, "you've met
Harrington Todd."

"Of course, Mr. Coleman, I hear your film . . ."

"I think your radio listeners would like to know about Harrington Todd, don't you?" Conrad interrupted. "After all, he is the star of my new movie, *The Hero*." Conrad stepped down from the podium.

Reluctantly, Arlene obliged Conrad. "Well, of course." She turned her full attention to Harrington.

"Harrington, that's a rather long name, now isn't it? Well, anyway, tell me how it feels to work with a great director like Conrad Coleman."

Harrington looked around the bleachers at the hundreds of people, waiting for his answer. "I . . ."

"Ladies and gentlemen, Spense Shore has just arrived!" Arlene interrupted.

Instead of being offended, Harrington stepped off the podium grinning in amusement. His smiled turned to curious wonder as he caught a quick glimpse of a voluptuous body draped in a soft blue gown of crepe de chine with sequins. He knew it was Marisa before she turned around and waved. He couldn't understand or resist her effect on him.

"I wanted to congratulate you," she said in her gentle, husky Italian accent, "After everyone sees the movie you will be showered with accolades. I saw *The Hero* at a screening last week. It's wonderful."

"Are you doing something afterward?"

Marisa pressed his hand. "Maybe some other time?"

"Next Friday."

"I'm at the Beverly Wilshire Hotel."

The Hero was a tremendous success, appealing to audiences of all ages, especially teenagers. Conrad was extremely pleased. He made preparations for Harrington to star in his second film, *The Restless*.

Harrington was oblivious to his budding popularity. Conrad had given him an opportunity to write. While preproduction on *The Restless* was in progress, he worked around the clock on a screen adaptation of Cara's play, *My Sister, Kierston*.

Marisa apologetically broke their date. Her first movie, having made a profit, secured her precious MGM contract for another two years. She was assigned to her second movie and was going on location for three months.

Harrington never mentioned Marisa, but he asked

Conrad if he could screen her first film. Conrad made the Coleman Productions's screening room available. Months later, when Harrington asked to screen her new release, Conrad confidentially told the Garvins he was worried about Harrington.

Conrad thought Harrington might be taking his rigid work routine too much to heart. He asked the Garvins why Harrington watched Marisa's movies. Wasn't it more appropriate to see her in person? Was Harrington afraid of human contact? He appeared to relate only to little Kierston Garvin whom he saw at least three times a week.

During Easter week, 1949, Marcus barreled into Harrington's office at Coleman Productions. Harrington stared at him in annoyance, his concentration having been interrupted.

"What the hell are you doing?"

"Listen," Marcus said.

"Hello, again," the radio squeaked, "this is Arlene Habor from Hollywood. An exciting newcomer to our film capital is breaking box-office records. Let me tell you something about him. He's a young Broadway star. He's worked his way up through the ranks, and at Christmastime his first motion picture for Conrad Coleman was released. America's teenagers are tired of war and tired of restriction, and it appears that they have found a new hero. His name is Harrington Todd."

Harrington stared at the radio dumbfounded as Arlene continued. "My sources tell me that clothing stores report a tremendous increase in sales in the new 'Harrington Todd' look. Don't be surprised, parents, if your teenage sons ask for leather jackets and cowboy boots for their birthdays or next Christmas."

All smiles, Marcus switched off the radio. "The old battle-ax obviously has had a change of heart about you. Get back to work. Shooting for *The Restless* starts next week."

"Wait a minute," Harrington said, turning from the typewriter. "What's this all about?"

"You haven't been paying attention to your fan mail, have you? There're thousands of letters in the mail room. I found a special one. Here," Marcus said, extending the envelope.

Harrington talked weekly to Jason on the telephone

despite Winston's disapproval. After each call, he was tempted to see Jason, but inevitably he found excuses to stay away.

Seeing Cara's son, loving him, looking out for him . . . he wondered if that relationship would help him to live in the present. Maybe that's why he was so intrigued with Marisa Benito. She was the future. The thought startled him. He mulled this over as he read Jason's note.

> Dear Father,
> I saw your picture in the newspaper! I think it is great! Jim says so too.
> > Love Jason

Harrington looked up. "I've been thinking a lot about Jason." Harrington noted Marcus's delight. "Can you believe he's almost seven years old!" He looked at the letter, shaking his head. "Cara's been gone almost seven years."

"Don't, Harrington."

"Do you ever think about Vincent Morello, Marcus? Do you have dreams about what we did?"

Marcus's rugged face softened. He placed a burly arm around Harrington's shoulder. "No, but I'm concerned that you do. Listen to me, my friend, don't rush into any decisions about Jason. Seven years or not, you might need more time. And a young boy is a mighty big handful. We've got Jim looking after him. You look out for yourself. You'll know when it's time to see him."

CHAPTER XX

O ne month before his eighth birthday, Jason was
cantering on his new thoroughbred. In the distance, he
heard the clanging of the stable bell, Jim's signal that it was
time to return. Jason pulled up Sable Lady at the creek. She
flared her nostrils and dropped her head to the cool spring
water while Jason looked at his wristwatch. Winston had set
his days to a severe schedule, and he had less than ten minutes
before he had to be seated for breakfast in the Garden Room.

He lifted his reins and turned Sable Lady around. To the
east, the soaring, jagged outline of Windsor Royal touched
the blue sky. The rose garden displayed a bountiful assort-
ment of color at its feet. To the north, the great lawn
shimmered with dewy green blades.

Jason laughed in childish delight and bent over to chirp
in Sable Lady's ear. "Come on, girl," he coaxed, "get me to
the mansion on time and I'll give you a carrot and a cube of
sugar for lunch."

Sable Lady danced at the news, already in tune with her
new master. Jason laughed. "Let's go!"

The swishing tailed, spirited thoroughbred, and her

equally spirited young master raced over the great lawn toward the stables.

Inside Windsor Royal, Winston strode down the wide spiral staircase. His feet brushed the brown oriental runner that lay snug against the white marble steps. Servants dusting the banister avoided his eyes and hastened out of his way. He passed them without a glance as Harris Johnson stepped to his side.

Since reestablishing himself at Windsor Royal, Winston slept only for a few hours a night. At first he worried that, like Winston Jason, young Jason might be abducted. Guards openly patrolled the grounds. Guardposts were manned around the inner wall. Windsor Royal's staff was on alert at all times to Jason's whereabouts. Everyone was held accountable.

Over the months, as he became more comfortable with his security arrangements, Winston still sat alone for hours in the drawing room. Jason had crept down the stairs on occasion and had seen him sitting before Diana's portrait. Winston wanted his grandson to think Diana looked after both of them. Besides, his memories of Diana were mostly fond ones.

Winston entered the Garden Room. Just as Diana and Jason had done, he and Jason shared an intimate hour together at breakfast each morning. Winston sat at the table in the alcove surrounded by huge white columns. He pushed back his starched French cuff with the diamond cuff link initialed WJT to look at his watch.

"Jim will see to it that Jason's on time," Harris said, reading his master's thoughts.

No sooner had he said the words than Jason wheeled into the room at breakneck speed and skidded into his chair. "I did it, Grandfather. I rode Sable Lady to the creek. I told you I would. Oh, hello, Harris!"

"I didn't tell you to be late," Winston said, as Harris smiled in greeting and poured Winston's coffee.

Jason's blue eyes shone merrily. "I'm not late, sir. It's 8:10 exactly."

"Stand up," Winston ordered. "Let me look at you."

Jason did as he was told, thrusting his shoulders back like a West Point cadet. His beige jodhpurs, black shirt, and black boots were ordered from Abercrombie and Fitch. They were a perfect fit. To Winston's delight, Jason resembled Cara rather than Harrington. He even looked a bit like Winston Jason. Black hair, olive skin, and blue eyes, he was a striking young boy, as bright and quick as most men Winston knew.

Once Winston nodded his approval, the maid set Jason's breakfast before him.

"Why did you decide to name your new horse Sable Lady?" Winston asked.

Jason finished chewing before speaking as Diana had taught him. "Jim says her coat looks like a sable, and she is a girl."

"And what is sable?"

Jason's brow furrowed in thought. "It's an animal that looks like a weasel. Jim says it has beautiful fur."

"That's true. But men use sable for a special purpose. What is it?"

"I don't know."

"Its fur is made into coats."

"Really! Do you have a sable coat, Grandfather?"

"Of course not!" Winston said irritably. "Sable coats are for women. Men don't wear furs. Never forget that!"

"I'll remember, but I'd like to see a sable coat. Then I'd really know if Sable Lady looks like sable."

Winston smiled broadly. Jason knew he had said something that pleased his grandfather.

"This is where every conversation should lead, Jason. We talked about your horse. You named her Sable Lady. From that we talked about sable, and now you want to see a sable coat. It just so happens that, at one time, our family owned stock in the Hudson Bay Company."

Winston explained that the first aristocratic Todds brought a special written privilege from William III to the new world. If the Todd ancestors had used that privilege correctly, the Todd Empire would have begun over two centuries ago. But they had lacked the vision to capitalize on the lucrative fur trade and many other export items.

"You don't like to lose money, do you, Grandfather?"

"Anyone can lose, Jason. Only a few can win. I am a winner. I accept life as it is and take advantage of every opportunity. If *I* don't, another man will."

"You're really important, aren't you?" Jason said with

enormous admiration.

"I am indeed. Did you know that without men like myself the entire world would collapse?"

"Do you mean that the ground would fall in and we'd all float away to outer space?"

Winston stared at his grandson in amusement. The little fellow wasn't joking. His habit of relating everything to outer space had begun when he first wondered how pictures materialized on the television screen. Fascinated by the air waves, the boy talked continually about one day earning enough money to own a television station.

"It's not quite that drastic," Winston said at last. "But enough for now. We'll continue this conversation over lunch. I have an urgent appointment, and you have your lessons."

After the mysterious break-in at Todd Headquarters, Winston had banished Raymond Baren to Washington D.C. Raymond ran a public relations firm to front for a lobbying organization for Todd Industries. Today, at Winston's insistence, Raymond had returned to Windsor Royal.

'My life could have been different, so different,' Raymond thought, 'if only I'd had money.' Then Winston couldn't have bought him. Then he wouldn't have helped Winston with his law school papers in exchange for tasting the rich life and all its luxury. 'My life is full of "if onlys,' " Raymond thought bitterly.

Everything depressed him: the Cold War, the Russians detonating the atom bomb. Apprehension rolled on the wave of fear, and he felt at the top of the wave, ready to crash at any moment. He hated his job. He hated Washington. And today, he wanted to tell Winston to go to hell, but he didn't have the nerve.

"How is Thomas Garvin doing?" Winston asked, closing the library door.

Raymond dropped into the chair before the desk. Winston took his seat behind it.

"Why are you so interested in helping Thomas Garvin? In the last year you let him buy an import/export business that's in direct competition with our subsidiary. I also understand that he bought an electronics company that underbid WJ Electronics for that Defense Department contract to manufacture surveillance equipment. What are you up to?"

"You've been away too long, Raymond. I ask the questions around here. Now answer me!"

Raymond sighed inwardly. "Garvin Enterprises is approaching number one in net revenues in California. And I have the information on Joe Field right here." Raymond took a sheet of paper from his pocket.

Winston had requested he uncover any incriminating evidence on Joe, who had once worked at the FBI. Joe was obviously in Winston's bad graces. Raymond didn't dare ask why. "I have names, dates, and times. Joe blackmailed many businessmen. They had gone under and were more than willing to talk." He placed the papers on the desk. "I'm staying on at the estate with Sue Ann and Nicole for a few days. If you need me, I'll be at the cottage."

Winston guarded his thoughts. Sue Ann would not be sharing his bed this evening. All those years while Diana was alive, Sue Ann had been growing up on the neighboring ranch to the Darnley's Kentucky Estate. After Diana's death, Raymond had been in charge of liquidating Winston's share of Diana's holdings. The Darnley ranch was sold to Sue Ann's father, and Raymond married Sue Ann as part of the deal. To Winston's mind, the twenty-eight year old Southern belle was as much his asset as Raymond's. Winston just preferred to be a silent partner.

"Have a good time," Winston said amiably. "Now, if you'll excuse me, I have some paper work to do before my next meeting."

Harrington was still on a promotional tour for *The Restless* in August 1950.

"I had no idea so many people would relate to this film," he said in amazement.

The Restless had been inspired by some interesting perceptions expressed by Thomas, who talked regularly with those of his army buddies having difficulty adjusting to society. Conrad had decided to have a script written. Using an ex-soldier as the lead character, Burt Small created *The Restless*, about a soldier's misfortunes of coming home, being misunderstood by his family, and being carted off by unfeeling, embarrassed parents to a sanatorium.

Marcus had to agree about the enthusiasm for the film.

People stopped Harrington on the streets. Ex-soldiers cheered him outside theaters. Teenagers followed him everywhere.

"You represent something they like," Marcus told him.

"I'm just playing a part."

"But it's the way you do it that appeals to them."

Harrington looked out their Kansas City hotel window. "I wish all this were enough, Marcus. But I feel empty."

Marcus reflected as Harrington returned to his packing. They were heading for New York tomorrow. Harrington had called Windsor Royal alerting Winston to his possible visit with Jason. Harris Johnson had said Winston and Jason were out of town. Although Harrington sensed Harris was lying, he had not pressed the point. As he told Marcus, "I could call Jim. I could call Thomas. I could get in if I really wanted to. But maybe I should wait a while even to visit. I'm not sure what Jason's expecting from me, and first I'd better decide what I expect from myself."

All during his early life, Harrington had known exactly what he wanted. Since Cara's death, he'd been in a turmoil. Everyone—the Garvins, Conrad, and now Marcus felt Harrington had to get over Cara. Only then could he make a rational decision about Jason. Marcus suggested to Conrad that they nudge Harrington along.

When he and Harrington returned to Los Angeles in September, Conrad held the answer in his hand. "First you're starring in *My Sister, Kierston* this fall. Then you're set to do *The Lonely Cowboy*."

"*The Lonely Cowboy*?" Harrington asked.

"Here's the script," Conrad said, shoving it into Harrington's hand. "I'm loaning you out to MGM. They've set Marisa Benito to co-star. You'll have a couple of months in between films. Principal photography doesn't begin on *The Lonely Cowboy* until the spring of '51."

When Harrington walked off with the script, Marcus told Conrad, "I didn't think you could work that fast. It's just what he needs."

Conrad shook his head. "I didn't have anything to do with it. Miss Benito refused to do the project unless she could co-star with Harrington Todd."

Every day for as long as Jason could remember he met

Jim at the stables. Late in September, while Harrington was on location with *My Sister, Kierston*, Jason was eating lunch with Jim.

"Do you have something for me?"

Jim reached into his shirt pocket and unfolded a newspaper clipping about Harrington, one of many such clippings he had given Jason in the past years. "Here's the latest."

Jason finished off his sandwich and wiped his hands. "Oh boy, this is great!" Jason said, looking at the article.

Newspapers from all over the country were delivered daily to Windsor Royal. Winston read them by noon, then the staff filed them in a huge research room in the basement. Often, during his free hour before dinner, Jason combed those papers. He pasted every article he could find on Harrington into a scrapbook, a surprise for his father, for the next time he saw Harrington.

He took the magazine article and read it. "Father's making two more movies. I wish I could see them!" He stared at the article about the movies, *My Sister, Kierston* and *The Lonely Cowboy*, then folded the paper and put it into his back pocket.

"Jim?"

"Uuumhm?"

"Have you heard anything lately about the world falling apart?"

Jim eyed Jason curiously. "Last time I looked it was still around."

Jason laughed, and he turned serious. "Jim? Did you and Father ever play football or go horseback riding or any of those sorta things?"

"Yeah, but not until he was ten. He was sickly as a child."

Jason sat down on the grass, crossed his legs in front of him and leaned forward. "You mean like in *The Restless*?"

Jim laughed. "Naw, that was just a movie. Sometimes people get actors and characters mixed up, but that's okay. It's part of the fun."

"Well," Jason said intently, "did he have a cold?"

"Sometimes. Once he caught pneumonia. It's a disease in the lungs."

"Boy," Jason said, wide-eyed. "Was he in bed a lot?"

"He had a pretty rough time of it, but he was a smart child just like you. He read a lot and was always friendly."

Jason thought silently for a moment, then wrinkled his nose. "I don't think I'd like to be sick."

Jim ruffled his hair. "You don't have anything to worry about. You're a tough guy."

"Do you think so, Jim?"

"Sure. Now enough for today. I think I hear Bobby and Michael on the lawn."

Jason jumped to his feet. "See you later." A lot of things Jim said made sense. His grandmother had told him they would. He was going to have to ask his grandfather about the world though. If Jim hadn't heard about it falling apart, then maybe he'd gotten it all wrong.

"You took me literally, Jason. I was actually referring to our society," Winston told him that evening at dinner. "Men need me. They have to be governed and ruled, otherwise the world will fall apart."

"But it's a free country, isn't it, Grandfather?"

"This isn't a free country. Granted, there is more freedom in the United States than elsewhere, but this freedom doesn't mean every man is created equal. That's a myth."

"I don't understand," Jason said, cocking his head.

"One man is equal to another only if he is equal monetarily. If he uses that money correctly, he will gain power —power to rule. The masses don't accept this. That's why they remain ignorant peasants."

"Peasants? What do you mean, Grandfather?"

"It's really very simple, Jason. Let me illustrate. I can send out an order right now to have a building constructed. Thousands of men will earn wages working on that building. After they've poured all their sweat into it, after they've carefully put every ounce of their knowledge into its construction, whose building will it be? Mine," Winston said triumphantly. "People don't say John Doe's Center in New York; they call it the Todd Center, and the peasants don't give a hoot about the architect."

"But you need builders, don't you?"

"Of course, but there's a price for every man. I can pay it. The workers, the technicians, the architects, they all work for your grandfather. They're followers—mere peasants.

Without me, they wouldn't have a job. Their very lives depend on me. Why? Because I have the money."

"Don't you work for anybody, Grandfather?"

"No one," Winston declared.

Jason thought about this. "Mr. Simmons says people all over the world are starving. Since you're the ruler, maybe you should help them. They need food."

The lines in Winston's face deepened into angry grooves. "You listen to me. I just told you men get what they deserve. People who don't earn a living starve. That's their problem. No one deserves a handout."

"But Mr. Simmons says they can't help themselves."

"The world is better off without them. Unfortunately, they seem to come from healthy peasant stock. They're the most stubborn, pugnacious group I've ever seen. If their will to help themselves were as strong as their will to demand help from others, then maybe the world would be better off. But that isn't the case, nor will it ever be. There are peasants and there will always be peasants.

"As long as someone else helps them to pay their mortgage, to own a car, to sit by the radio or that new infernal contraption, television, and allows them to save a few pennies a year, they'll be content. That's why they will remain peasants. We'll let them defend the country. We industrialists will run it!"

Jason cocked his head and opened his eyes wide in disbelief. "I like television. It isn't infernal. It's the future. I've been telling you about it for a long time. I thought we agreed."

"There is a vast difference between escaping into fantasy and looking at the business that produces fantasy," Winston said severely. "You're going to view television as a business. The peasants never will. But we'll discuss this later." Winston stood up. "I have to speak to Mr. Simmons."

Jason watched his grandfather march out of the dining room. What was all the fuss about? He supposed his grandfather didn't like to hear about starving people. He told himself never to mention hungry people again. He also reminded himself that he should watch out for those peasants. They must be a horrible group to make his grandfather so angry.

After dinner that evening, Winston entered the Windsor Royal library, locked the door, and opened a secret panel in the wall. He walked in, closed the door behind him, and descended the secret staircase to the "Operations Room."

After the break-in at the Todd Center, he had this secret room constructed. A large oval table occupied the center of the main room. A switchboard of ten phone lines hooked into a panel at Winston's chair. Rows of files extended down the northern wall. A bathroom, kitchen, and bedroom lay beyond the closed door next to a television set built into its own console.

Here, Winston communicated with his contacts from all over the world. Private investigators' reports, photos, and various types of incriminating evidence were gathered and filed to use against anyone who got in Winston's way.

Joe Field, using the alias "Bill Reed," as he normally did when in the field, had gone to work for Garvin Enterprises in their maintenance department four months ago. Winston sat down to wait for his usual Sunday evening call.

"Harrington's agreed to star in *The Lonely Cowboy*," Joe confirmed an hour later from Los Angeles. "The setup is perfect. Harrington's screened every one of Marisa's movies and Marisa's been infatuated with Harrington ever since seeing *The Hero* on Broadway. Both think the other wants to co-star in *The Lonely Cowboy*."

"It's taken you long enough to get your plan into the works," Winston said irritably. "This girl had better come through. We've spent years cultivating her."

"Don't worry, Mr. Todd," Joe said confidently. "Marisa is young. I can control her. Besides, she needs the money. About Garvin. He has a huge land deal going down in Orange County within the month."

"Send me all the pertinent information. I'll let you know what to do. And what about John Stevens and Conrad Coleman?"

"Everything's in motion."

The following morning, Jason stomped into the Garden Room for breakfast, flushed and upset. "Mr. Simmons said you fired him. Why?"

Winston's face turned to the cool stillness of the bronze statues in the Renaissance Room.

"I don't care if you are angry. Mr. Simmons has given me lessons all my life. Since I was two years old! I like him and so did Grandmother!"

Winston raised a brow. Diana, of course. Sorry, my dear, he thought. "Sit down, Jason." Although Jason was furious, he did as he was told. Only then did Winston continue. "Sometimes you might enjoy a person's company, but that person isn't good for you. I know your grandmother would agree. Mr. Simmons has outlived his usefulness."

"I don't understand."

"He's not of our station. He has no earthly idea what to teach the heir to the Todd Empire. Take my word for it, Jason. Now shall we forget about Mr. Simmons?"

Winston watched the little boy muster up his courage to accept that Mr. Simmons was gone. Winston was amazed at his affection for the bright little fellow. He got caught up in the excitement of sharing with his little ally.

"Let me tell you about some disturbing news I heard this morning," Winston said. "Did you know Hollywood is full of communists?"

"Oh!" Jason said at once. "Are they going to hurt Father?"

"Don't you worry, Jason, I won't let them. I'm afraid your father has difficulty taking care of himself, but you and I will see that he's protected."

Jason looked at Winston in adulation. "Grandfather, you're the greatest man in the world."

"Well, my boy, since Harrington is our flesh and blood, you and I will make one exception and protect a peasant . . ."

"Father isn't a peasant," Jason said, alarmed.

"I'm afraid he is, Jason. He needs us to look after him."

Jason sighed heavily, gazing off into space. "Father is a peasant." He returned his eyes to Winston. "I think you'd better wait and tell me about the peasants when I grow up, Grandfather. I just don't understand."

Winston chuckled. "Don't you worry, Jason. I'll teach you."

After lunch Jason ran through the rose gardens along the path to the stables. Running down the long wide aisle in between the stalls of thoroughbreds, Jason spotted Jim in the grooming stall, brushing Distant Darkness, the stud who had fathered Sable Lady. He climbed up on the wooden railing to watch.

Jim was stalwart. The muscles in his back rippled beneath his shirt as he worked. He heard Jason rattle the boards, kicking his feet impatiently on the planks. When he called out his greeting, Jason didn't answer.

He turned around, his gentle eyes taking in Jason's angry expression, and knew Jason was in need of a man-to-man talk. Jim immediately threw the dandy brush into his grooming kit and gathered up the box.

"Come on, kid."

Jason jumped off the plank. They walked down the stable aisle, filled with the familiar smell of hay and horses.

Jim entered the tack room, left his box, and gave Jason a boost up the ladder to the hayloft. He climbed up behind him, tugging at Jason's pants, but Jason was in no mood to play. Since the stable hands were eating lunch in the dining hall, they would have at least fifteen minutes alone.

They nestled down in the hay. It was cool in the loft, almost damp. Jason lay on his stomach. Jim lay on his side about four feet away, his head propped up by his big right hand.

"Well . . .?" Jim questioned him.

"Mr. Simmons is gone."

"Gone? Why?"

"Grandfather said he wasn't good for me."

Although Jason told him everything, Jim never commented on Winston's actions. He didnt' think it would be fair to Jason.

"Mr. Simmons was my friend."

"Look at it this way. You'll make many friends when you go to school this fall."

Jason sensed Jim didn't like the idea that Mr. Simmons was gone either.

"Jim?"

"Ummmmm?"

"What do you think of the peasants?" he asked suddenly.

"Peasants?"

"You know, the majority of people in the United States who can't take care of themselves?"

Jim turned his head and stared at Jason. The little guy was so intense. 'What the hell was Winston doing to him?'

"Well, what do you want to know?"

"What kind of people are they?" Jason asked very matter-of-factly.

"Some aren't so bad."

"Is Father a peasant?"

'So that's what Winston's up to,' Jim thought heatedly, falling back against the hay. "Why would you think your father is a peasant?"

"Because Grandfather said so. He said Father can't take care of himself and that's why he's a peasant."

"Well, Jason, I guess you have to make up your own mind about that. From what I heard, your father's doing a pretty good job in his work."

"Pretty good!" Jason said indignantly. "He's the best actor in the whole world."

Jim tilted his head and looked at Jason humorously. "I guess you answered your own question then, didn't you?"

The tension left Jason's face. He began to laugh. "Oh boy, Jim, I'm sure glad you're around."

They laughed together and then grew silent.

"I sure would like to see Father," Jason said.

"It won't be long now. You'll see him soon."

Jason accepted Jim's word.

The filming of *My Sister, Kierston* ended in late November and Harrington spent the following months into 1951 revising *Your Year With Mine*. In early May, he flew up to Middlefork to work on *The Lonely Cowboy*. In his thoughts, he wondered just how he and Marisa would get along.

Middlefork was located along the outskirts of Boise, Idaho. Beyond the miles of undeveloped land and past Bear Valley, where a goldmining process had stripped the land's natural resources, Middlefork stood out as an oasis in the mountain valley, with its hot springs, lodges, cabins, and stables.

At dusk, after the first week's shooting, Harrington hopped into a jeep. He followed a curving dirt road to the airstrip between the mountains. Stopping at the edge of the field, he waited.

Something magical had happened to him here away from the city. Being in the country triggered recollections of

Windsor Royal. For the first time in years, the memories were happy. Why? Thinking back to when he was eight years old, struggling with rheumatic fever, he vividly remembered reading *Tom Sawyer* aloud to his friend, Jim. They had laughed a lot that summer of 1928. Now Jim was there again for another little boy of eight, the boy Harrington called "son."

'Jason,' he thought, 'Jason, Jason, have I hurt you by staying away? Your letters don't accuse me of abandoning you. Has Jim been such a friend that you don't begrudge me my freedom? If so, what a special little boy you are.'

His heart was full, his thoughts jumbled as he heard the distant sounds of the plane bringing Marcus and four-year-old Kierston Garvin for a visit.

He shaded his eyes, watching the plane circle the area and slowly descend. He started up the jeep and drove towards the plane as it landed. The plane door opened almost immediately.

"Har-ring-ton!" Kierston screamed.

Harrington waved. "Hello, Kierston!"

Over the last four years, he and Kierston had become fast friends. Dining with the Garvins every Sunday, when home and not working, was one of the joys of Harrington's life.

He watched Kierston adoringly as she ran to him, black hair flying behind her. She was as energetic and precocious as she was sensitive.

She crawled right up inside his jeep. As Harrington lifted her into his arms, he looked into blue-violet eyes, then at the smug expression on Kierston's beautiful little face. "You little devil."

She hugged him tightly, giggling in delight. "It took a long time to get here. Marcus got sick all over everything!"

"You promised not to tell!"

Harrington tried to keep a straight face. Marcus was white as a sheet. "What's the matter, Marcus? An old Army veteran like you lets a little girl get the better of you in a single-engine plane?"

Marcus grunted. "Might as well have taken my chances flapping my arms."

They drove back to the lodge and settled in, after being introduced to the cast and crew. Then they all gathered in the dining room for dinner. Kierston took an immediate liking to Marisa.

Every time he was in her presence, Harrington thought of Cara. During these first two weeks of shooting, Harrington and Marisa's relationship had been strictly business. Yet, speculation among the other members of the cast and crew was that Harrington and Marisa were on the verge of a romance.

Marisa took out a long thin cigar after dinner and announced to the room, "Gentlemen, the poker game is about to begin."

Poker chips and two decks of cards materialized. Marisa was joined by six players and a few friends who wanted to watch.

Marisa smiled gently at Kierston and winked. "I want you to stay right here beside me. You're going to be my good luck charm."

"If you have any more luck," one of the crew members called out, "I won't have a nickle to show for this job."

Marisa shuffled the cards. "Aren't you going to play, Mr. Todd? Mr. Mancini?"

Harrington held up his hands as if he were being robbed. "I've been rescued by my friend here," he said, nodding to Marcus. "Maybe tomorrow night."

Marcus had spent time with Marisa before going to get Kierston. He liked the young woman greatly. "Tomorrow night for me, too," he said, "and we can talk about our homeland."

Harrington walked over to Kierston and lifted her up. "And it's your bedtime, squirt."

"But, Harrington! I'm Marisa's luck!"

Marisa watched Harrington talk quietly to Kierston, explaining about her bedtime and the fun things they'd do tomorrow, and she thought of her Uncle Julio's words. "To know a man, a woman need only look at the way he handles women. If he's good to his daughters, he'll appreciate the child in you. If he's close to his sisters, he'll be a good friend. If he's respectful, but is independent of his mama, he'll respect your strength. If he's dominated by any one of the women in his life, run!" Her Uncle Julio laughed uproariously about this last rule. Marisa adored her uncle. She smiled to herself now, thinking thus far her uncle would approve of Harrington.

"Now off to bed." Harrington kissed Kierston on the cheek and handed her over to her nanny's arms. "We'll look in on you later." As he and Marcus left the room, he called out over his shoulder, "Good luck, gentlemen!"

Harrington and Marcus walked back to Harrington's cabin and sat on the porch overlooking the rugged Middle-fork River.

"What's the trouble?" Harrington asked.

Marcus stared out into the darkness, feeling the gentle cool breeze, and Thomas's words came to his mind. "Harrington looks like he might have another chance at happiness. Don't worry him before we have all the facts."

Six months ago, Garvin Enterprises' land deals started falling through, a shipping line was bought out from under Thomas, and Thomas lost an import contract with a European shipper to a competitor with a lower bid.

Garvin Enterprises had an excellent security team. Although industrialists, like Winston, had tried to spy on Thomas's company, the agents had been discovered and prosecuted. For three months, his security had been under scrutiny. All of Thomas's employees were found to be loyal. A mole was invisibly buried within Garvin Enterprises. Thomas thought it was Joe Field, and with good reason.

Marcus had found out that Todd Industries obtained the import/export contract Thomas had sought; a Chicago developer with a P.O. Box had bought the highly prized Orange County property and a new Houston land deal; and Raymond Baren had been lobbying for Garvin Enterprises to obtain defense contracts without Thomas's permission.

Todd Industries would do well with a California defense plant. Winston wanted Thomas to set up that framework. Then behind the scenes he'd maneuver Thomas's other divisions to fail. If Thomas lost enough money, his loans would be called in and he'd be cash poor and jeopardize the company's growth. Eventually Winston was banking on Thomas being forced to sell out completely.

When the trouble began, Thomas set up a special telephone line outside of Garvin Enterprises to "Anaid," a new subsidiary of Garvin Enterprises, unknown to anyone except Marcus, Katharine, and David Britt. Marcus had conducted his search for Joe Field from Anaid's West

Hollywood offices. Thus far, he had found that Thomas's phone had been tapped with his own Garvin Enterprises surveillance equipment.

Marcus had checked all employee clearance files and attached photographs. If Joe was involved, he had obviously destroyed his own file. Thomas insisted that the tap be left on his phone. For the moment, they wished the saboteur to feel safe, as they had arranged for a Chicago land deal to be their bait.

"As I told you on the phone," Marcus finally said, his thoughts heavy. "I heard something about Conrad. A rumor is starting . . ." Marcus glanced at Harrington. "One of his staff told a friend of a friend . . . who told Burt Small . . . you know how rumors are started. Anyway, it's going around that Conrad is a communist. Roy Sharp is somehow involved."

Had Marcus been less serious, Harrington would have been sure he was joking. "You don't think that anyone will believe that, do you? Who would take Sharp seriously?"

"I'm not sure. Do you mind if I think out loud for a minute?"

"I wish you would."

"Remember the newsletter I told you about?"

"*Counterattack*?"

"That's the one. Well, another newsletter has recently been published. It's called *Red Channels: The Report of Communist Influence in Radio and Television*. . . . No, Conrad's name isn't in either of those, but John Stevens's is."

"John's!"

Marcus nodded solemnly. "Laster French, I told you he returned to his job at the FBI . . ."

"Yes . . ."

"He says some former FBI agents are behind *Red Channels*. They call themselves American Business Consultants. Their offices are right on Madison Avenue. They're no better than Roy Sharp. They gather information from back issues of the *Daily Worker*, the Communist paper . . . get names, information on groups. Then they accuse anyone in the magazine, even anyone who reads it of being a Communist. People are given citations. Then they're forced to prove their innocence."

"How'd John's name get in there, for Christ's sake?"

"That's what he wants to know. He's on his way to Washington right now. Lord help the members of the House un-American Activities Committee. He just got back from a hunting trip and he has a beard. He'll probably scare the hell out of 'em."

"He went alone?"

"Thomas sent one of the lawyers from his New York law firm along. I alerted Laster French. We thought it best not to have a fight on the steps of the Capitol. You know how John can get. Anyway, I'm flying on to Washington. Something's amiss, and I want to find out what it is. When I get back, I'm going to pay Roy Sharp a visit."

Before daybreak the following morning, Marisa sat out on her balcony overlooking the Salmon River. Unable to sleep, she decided to try and sort out her thoughts.

Over the last five years, Bill Reed had orchestrated her life and her career. Between Bill and her Uncle Julio, she had finally gained a sense of self-confidence. She had scars which kept her from love. She appeared to be a sophisticated lady, but the child in her heart was predominate.

Before she met Harrington, she wondered if she would ever love anyone. Now that something special was happening between them, she was afraid she couldn't handle it.

"You can't sleep either?" Harrington called out.

She was startled out of her reverie and glanced over to the neighboring balcony where Harrington stood. Her heart beat heavily. What was he doing up? Her dishabille made her blush. She wanted to rush inside her room, but he had disappeared into his own and reappeared with two glasses and a bottle of champagne before she could move. Swinging over the railing, Harrington landed right on her balcony.

Marisa smiled up at him, masking her inner feelings. "You do that very well."

Harrington laughed at himself. "I've never done it before in my life." He placed the glasses and champagne on the table and dropped into a chair beside her. "I don't have any sense of protocol in these sort of things. Champagne at daybreak just seemed like a romantic idea."

Another blush was coming. She felt it and averted her eyes. He would think she was inexperienced. She wanted to seem grown-up. The first time they met, at Conrad's, she had seen his discomfort with the revolting Roy Sharp and boldly walked up to him. But she couldn't hold the posture. The moment she found an out, she had disappeared.

Harrington was so attracted to her, he was momentarily lost in her beauty. Yet something made him hold back. Now that they were alone for the first time, he studied her carefully. In her movies she looked so womanly. Her figure was most provocative, her face filled with a foreign worldliness, strong and determined, sexy, yet, yet, what? She seemed so vulnerable now, youthful, innocent, and shy. 'That's it,' he thought in wonder. Although she looked like a woman in face and body and gesture, played poker and smoked a cigar, beneath the facade she was just a girl!

"I think you're lovely," Harrington said gently. "From our first meeting I thought you were older, now I see that you must be . . ."

"Twenty-one," Marisa said, flushing.

She got up, unaware of the striking picture she presented. The whisper of a gentle breeze fluttered her aqua peignoir into caressing folds around her body. Wisps of brown hair danced against her cheeks. Her almond green eyes were ablaze as she told herself she was acting like an utter fool.

She reached for a box of the slender cigars. "Maybe I'll have some champagne," she said, once again feigning confidence. Trying to act mature and graceful, she started to light her cigar.

Harrington noticed her hands trembling. Very carefully, he got up and took away the cigar and tossed it into the river below. "I'm just as nervous as you are. You don't have to pretend with me."

"I . . ."

He tilted up her chin and gently kissed her. He wanted to know everything about this girl who had stirred emotions in him he thought were dead.

How they made it into her bed, he never knew. 'Why did she seem so different now that he held her naked in his arms? What was she doing?' Marisa was crying. He gathered a sense of reality around him and stopped before they began. Softly, he whispered, trying to understand, "Marisa, haven't you ever made love?"

"No," she answered. "Please . . ."

'My God,' he thought. He closed his eyes, trying not to think about the magnificent, curving, soft body beneath him. 'What has happened to her,' he wondered. 'Why does she cry? Embarrassment?' He thought not.

"We'll take it slow," he said, feeling a sudden protective-ness intermingled with desire. He dried her tears. "It's O.K., Marisa. I don't have it figured out either."

"I want it to be you."

"I do, too," he said honestly. He lifted her chin and looked deep into her tearful eyes. "We can help each other, green eyes. Maybe we can mend one another's wounds. When you feel like it, I want to know what happened to you."

Marisa buried her head in his shoulder, unable to speak. Somehow her reaction reminded him of Cara and the rape, and he found tears appearing in his own eyes and was unable to control them.

On Sunday evening, Winston walked swiftly into the "Operations Room" full of determination and purpose. The lights were on. The large oval table was covered with papers.

"Welcome back, Joe," Winston said, shutting and locking the door behind him.

Joe Field sat in the chair beside Winston's. His stern face, the brown cold eyes, the bald head all blended together to give Joe the look of a mercenary.

"I talked to Marisa this morning. She's in love with Harrington," Joe reported as Winston sat down.

"Has she paid for herself yet?"

"I'm negotiating two more movies with Conrad. Once the contracts are signed, we'll be in the black. Too bad we have to cut her loose. She could be a goldmine."

"It's all relative," Winston said, thinking Joe's idea of a goldmine and his were vastly different. "Now what about Thomas Garvin?"

"He's flying up to Middlefork early. I thought Marcus might catch on. According to Marisa, all the top executives are clearing out of Garvin Enterprises. That Chicago land deal I told you about last week might be Marcus's. They won't find anything though." Joe looked at Winston proudly. "I did a good job, didn't I?"

Joe was getting too cocky, knew too much, and secretly loved Marisa Benito. It was time Raymond planted that evidence on Joe with the FBI. Implicated in his own crimes, Joe would become a fugitive from justice and would have no choice but to remain loyal to Winston.

"Your return to Windsor Royal was well-timed," Winston said, ignoring Joe's thank-you request. "You lay low for a while. Communicate from here with Marisa. They won't be able to trace the calls. Have you set up Marisa yet?"

"By the time Marcus figures out what happened, Harrington's going to think Marisa betrayed him and his friends. There's also her history in Sicily, which we'll be able to use in the press."

"Grandfather, do you ever have any fun?" Jason asked Winston curiously that evening at dinner.

Considering the question, Winston thought about Sue Ann Baren. Desiree Richards had been the ultimate consort until he bedded Sue Ann. The girl had a lustful appetite and the most provocative lips he'd ever seen. He reproached himself. He must be getting bored to dote on Sue Ann. Besides she was forever suggesting she should provide him with a proper heir. He'd have to be careful of her.

"Of course. Why do you ask?" he said at last.

"You always wear a suit and you never play."

"There are many different ways to enjoy oneself, Jason. When you're older you'll have fun wearing a suit, too."

"Is that when I'll work for you?"

"That's correct."

"But, Grandfather, it takes a long time to get old, and I want you to play with me now."

"It won't be as long as you think," Winston chuckled.

"Grandfather," Jason said seriously, "I've been thinking about what you've told me. Don't you ever help anyone? Wouldn't you help me?"

"You, of course, and only a handful of others. Otherwise, no. Not unless I get something in return. If you do a favor, you will one day be able to ask a favor. But it is to your advantage never to ask someone first. It is also to your advantage never to ask that a favor be returned unless it's absolutely necessary."

"Why?"

"It's called leverage."

"Leverage?"

"Let's say you ask a friend a favor. I don't know . . . maybe you want to ride his bicycle. He consents. Now, if he ever asks a favor of you, you will have to grant it, won't you?"

"I never thought of that, Grandfather."

"You should have. So what do you think happens when your friend asks to ride Sable Lady? Let's say he has only an hour to ride and it's just when you're ready to ride her."

"Oh!" Jason said wide-eyed.

"What would you do?" Winston demanded.

"Couldn't he ride her after I do?"

"I'm afraid not. He has only an hour. It's the same hour as yours."

Jason felt the burden of someone else riding his beautiful new horse. With a long face he answered, "I guess I'd have to let him ride. But I wouldn't like it."

Winston looked satisfied. "What if you said no to your friend?"

Jason thought. "He might get angry?"

"That's right. Now there are times when you can say no to someone, but you must be prepared for the consequences. Your friend would never do you another favor after that. But it's to your advantage when someone asks a favor of you. Let's say he wishes to ride Sable Lady and you let him. Then you don't ask to ride his bike. That is when someone becomes indebted to you. Then you can ask him a big favor one day. And he'll do it, because he wants to ride your horse again. Do you understand?"

Jason sat up very straight, his head cocked. "I'm not going to ask anyone any favors, that's for sure."

"Winston?"

"I thought you were back in Washington," Winston said, surprised to see Raymond in the doorway.

"May I speak to you just a moment in private?"

Reluctantly Winston got up and joined Raymond.

"I wanted to relay this message personally. I've just heard that Marcus Mancini's in Washington asking questions about you and that Madison Avenue group that publishes *Red Channels*."

Although he appeared outwardly calm, Winston's mind raced. Did Marcus know he was behind the group? No, Joe Field had protected his anonymity just as he had with Marisa.

"Will Marcus never leave me alone?" Winston shook his head sadly. "Raymond, I have many worries these days, yes, many worries. As you know, Joe Field has been heavy on my mind. I think that information you have on him should be put into the right hands . . . anonymously, of course, but just the same, into the right hands."

Winston was stringing him along, but Raymond was too pleased about being back in Winston's confidence to protest. "Is Joe connected with that Madison Avenue group?"

"I have my suspicions," Winston answered. "Just do as I ask, Raymond."

"What about Marcus?"

"He can't do any harm." Winston patted Raymond on the shoulder. "Thanks for dropping by. It means a lot to have you so concerned."

"One other thing," Raymond called out as Winston again sat down in his chair. "Thank you for the land, Winston. Sue Ann told me we could finally build a home here on the estate."

Raymond's gratitude was transparent. To live on Windsor Royal in a home of his own was the strongest endorsement ever given by Winston to any employee.

Winston almost laughed out loud. Raymond had no idea that the land was for Sue Ann.

"I'm happy you're pleased, Raymond. Don't forget about Washington. Our contract with the Army will double our profits this year at Todd Aeronautics. You keep those boys on the hill and at the Defense Department happy . . ."

"You can count on it. Bye, Jason."

When Raymond left, Jason looked puzzled.

Winston understood. "The gift of land was a favor I bestowed on Raymond."

Jason shook his head. He didn't understand Winston's intentions and was unhappy that he had to see Nicole Baren all the time—maybe for the rest of his life! "Boy, Grandfather, I wonder if I'll ever figure you out."

Winston threw back his head and laughed. "One day you'll understand, Jason. One day."

CHAPTER XXI

On the first Saturday in June, after a month of filming *The Lonely Cowboy* in Idaho, Harrington sat before the typewriter working on his second draft of an adaption of Cara's play, *Your Year With Mine*. Marisa was in the bedroom reading the pages he had completed. Harrington wanted Marisa to co-star with him in the movie.

"Oh, Harrington!" Marisa declared, running out into the living room. He turned around in his chair, and she settled excitedly at his feet. "Your script is so wonderful! Did you and Cara really feel that way about one another?"

He looked into her eyes and was lost in them. "Yes. Why does that please you?"

"Because, my love, it makes you different. You're so talented, Harrington. I love that about you. You can express something special to make others feel good."

"Thank you," he said genuinely.

She smiled brightly. "You're welcome." Her phone rang out on her balcony. "That must be Bill. I'll fix lunch for us after the call. I'll only be a minute."

Harrington shook his head in amusement. Her conver-

sations with her agent were never just a minute. He turned
around to the typewriter and went back to work.

"Hello, Bill," Marisa answered cheerfully. She heard
Harrington's typewriter clacking and the river sweeping by
below.

"You haven't called," said Joe Field, known to Marisa
as Bill Reed.

"Yes, I have. The Beverly Hills Hotel said you checked
out."

Bill laughed. "I was just testing you, honey. Wanted to
make sure you hadn't forgotten about me."

Marisa smiled. "How could I forget about my benefactor? Did you send my check to Florence?"

"Yes, honey, and your mama is fine. She spoke about
your father last week. It's her first time. An encouraging
sign."

A chill went through Marisa. "What did she say?"

"I don't know any more than that. Maybe you should
call her doctor."

Marisa sat down. "I will. And thank you, Bill."

"Since when have you had to thank me, honey? You
know how I feel about you."

As Bill continued to talk, Marisa heard the phone ring in
Harrington's cabin. She hoped it was Jim calling with Jason
on the line.

"Marisa? Are you listening to me, honey?" Joe asked on
the other end of the line.

"I'm sorry, Bill, what did you say?"

"I'm going to be in and out of hotels for awhile so let's
get down to business, then I want to hear all about
Harrington."

Marisa brightened. "Harrington is very special . . ."

"Business first, Marisa. O.K.?" Joe said, warming up.
"Number one, MGM has agreed to loan you out. Coleman
wants you to co-star with Harrington in two more movies."

"Harrington told me about *Your Year With Mine*, but I
didn't know . . ."

"Conrad wanted it to be a surprise. Let Harrington tell
you."

"It's wonderful news!"

"I thought you'd like it," Joe said, trying to match her
mood. "By the way, Arlene Habor's gotten a tip about you

and Harrington. She wants to do a phone interview with you."

"I never discuss personal things," Marisa said, frowning.

"Why don't you talk it over with Harrington? I don't want to offend Arlene. She's a powerful force in Hollywood. Besides, if you don't talk to her, she'll make something up."

An hour later, Marisa entered Harrington's cabin and kissed him. "Come," she said in her gentle Italian accent. Then she tugged on his arm.

He followed her outside to the balcony where lunch was set for two. The river crashed against the rocks below them. The sun warmed their faces. He smelled her scent blown his way by a gentle breeze. They ate hamburgers, a favorite of Marisa's since coming to America.

"Bill says that Arlene Habor wants . . ."

"Don't tell me. A phone interview."

"How did you know?"

"She called while you were talking to Bill. I told her our relationship was private—actually none of her business."

Marisa laughed joyfully. "I do enjoy you so, Harrington Todd! You are loyal. Are you sure you are not Italian?"

Harrington smiled. "You don't have the market on honor you know."

"I know that," she said reflectively. Her eyes gazed out at the river beyond while she listened to the rapids cascade past the support poles of their cabins. "Sicilians are even loyal for the wrong reasons sometimes."

"Sicilians?" Harrington asked.

Marisa realized her divulgence and bowed her head. "I am from Florence. But I was born in Sicily."

Although the mention of Sicily reminded him of Vincent Morello and gave Harrington the chills, he tilted her head up with his fingers. "Why does that bother you so?"

His touch brought a strong desire to her body. She tried to focus in on his words, to tell him why the island of her father was a source of sorrow to her. But when he kissed her, she couldn't resist him. He had been patient and caring. Now it was her turn.

She had never known such pleasure existed as when they made love that afternoon. His touch was extraordinarily gentle as if she were a budding flower plucked and made to blossom. She felt safe with him, one with him, and yet she knew there was more she had to learn. She flowed with her feelings, forgetting everything except the exquisite pleasure he brought to her. In return, she learned from him of his needs and saw the passion in his eyes. Smiling at her with joy, Harrington forced her out of herself to act with him in a union that brought them both enormous pleasure.

Later that evening, she snuggled up to him, her head on his shoulder. "I love you, Harrington. I have a lot to learn. But I am strong. I will overcome and I will share myself with you as long as you wish."

Harrington had propped up his head with pillows, and he held her in his arms. "Marisa?"

She placed her hands on his chest and looked up. "Yes, my love?"

"Tell me something about yourself."

"All right, my love. It is time."

Marisa Benito had been born in Palermo, Sicily, in 1930. Her mama, Carmen, took Marisa to Florence where they stayed with Carmen's brother, Julio, and his American wife, Mary.

In her teens, Marisa learned some English from Mary. Then the Nazis came to Florence. Mary was arrested in 1943 and executed as an enemy of Italy's Fascist Party. This was a severe blow to Marisa who valued her aunt's friendship and guidance.

Where should she turn? Her mother was ill. Mary was dead. Marisa had no friends. There were many reasons for her shy and suspicious nature. Seeing her problem, Uncle Julio became her protector.

Although the retreating Germans had destroyed Florence's historic quarters on either side of the Ponte Vecchio in 1944, Julio's cafe had miraculously been spared. Marisa worked in her Uncle Julio's establishment as his hostess. The Germans had fled, and De Gasperi, with the support of the Allies, had finally gained control of Italy.

Soon the people of Florence saw Americans dining in their restaurants. Hotels were full, the streets crowded. Bill Reed was one such American, a businessman from New York who entered Julio's one evening and was greeted by Marisa Benito.

For two weeks, Bill Reed dined at the front table, near to Marisa's station. While Marisa greeted Julio's customers and practiced English with the American soldiers, Bill Reed befriended Julio. When Julio told her Bill Reed wished to make her a proposition, she sat with both men to hear it. Bill wanted her to sign an exclusive contract. Bill would receive fifty percent of all her future earnings. In return, he would make her a movie star.

"I am not an actress," she said in a gentle, thick Italian accent.

"But you are exquisite, Marisa," Bill assured her. "And you have star quality."

She was only fifteen, but she had seen the worst of life, and she was cautious. People always commented on her beauty, but she did not feel beautiful. "I don't know about acting."

"Don't worry," Bill said, "I'll take care of everything."

Marisa glanced at her uncle. Since Mary's death, he had taken ill and was unable to work full time. Although Marisa tried to keep the employees honest, they stole from her uncle when her back was turned. Instead of going to school, Marisa was working full time. Her uncle needed help; her mama needed care. The weight of her family was on her shoulders, and they meant everything to her. She wondered if Bill Reed might be a way out of this situation for all of them.

"Don't do it for me," Julio said. "We can manage."

"I will do it," Marisa said, ignoring Julio, "if my uncle can be with me, and my mama taken care of."

In April of 1946, Bill Reed snuck Marisa and Julio onto an American Air Force plane, which landed at Mitchell's Field. They settled into a beach-front home in Boston and Marisa's whirlwind education began.

She was taught English, diction, etiquette, and acting while she was tutored in American history, math, and science to earn her American high school diploma. For one year, Bill traveled between Boston and New York to oversee her progress. During that year, she attended the New York theater only once to see Harrington Todd in *The Hero*. The audience's reception to Harrington instilled a will to succeed in Marisa.

"Do you think I could get people to love me like they love him?" she asked Bill.

"There's no doubt about it. One day, I promise, you will work with Harrington Todd. He's a class act, and he's going to Hollywood where you'll be."

Bill endeared himself to Marisa by keeping his word. Her family was provided for; her mother was even moved to a fine sanatorium outside of Florence, and her uncle's health improved. When her year-long education ended and Bill told her she was ready for Hollywood, she and Julio had a tearful parting.

Julio returned to Florence and Marisa arrived in Hollywood in March of 1947, one month before Conrad's party. Bill was beside her, guiding her career for three more years. He stayed at the Beverly Wilshire Hotel and seldom left his room, while she worked at MGM in Culver City, attended parties, and finally met Harrington.

After starring in her first movie, Marisa was sought out by powerful men—politicians, American and foreign financiers, and businessmen. A few of her dates knew of Bill and appeared skeptical of his credentials. She never saw them again. Marisa was blinded with loyalty and became protective of Bill. No one had ever been so good to her. She was totally devoted to him.

After Bill told her about Harrington's request that she co-star in *The Lonely Cowboy*, Bill returned to the East Coast. He still handled all her business, but he explained that his paternal devotion to her had been transformed into that of a friend and mentor. She was free to live her life. It was 1950, and and she was twenty years old.

Marisa curled up beside Harrington when she finished her story and promptly fell asleep, leaving Harrington to stay awake with many nagging questions.

'What had happened to Carmen Benito?' he wondered. Marisa never explained why her mama was in a sanatorium. What about her father? And who was Bill Reed? Bill had accompanied her to *The Hero*. Many other fine productions were having long runs in 1944. Why just his play? And what was this about him wishing her to co-star in *The Lonely Cowboy*? Didn't Marisa understand that he was under contract to Conrad? Conrad had loaned him out to MGM. He didn't have any say about a co-star. It was his understanding that Marisa wished him to co-star in the movie.

The following morning, he placed a call to Garvinhouse, Thomas's Beverly Hills home.

Every summer, Thomas flew his Garvin Enterprises executive staff up to Idaho to stay at his Middlefork Ranch for a two week "think-tank session." Thomas owned all of Middlefork. He had built the executive house expressly for business. Ten bedrooms, a huge conference room, and a household staff served his executives' needs. The home was located a mile away from *The Lonely Cowboy* location. Thomas was arriving in Middlefork within the week, but Harrington wanted to talk to him and Marcus now.

"Not only was I loaned out to MGM, but you're making a profit on their location. Pretty smart," Harrington told Thomas.

"You sound happy, Harrington. I'm looking forward to meeting Marisa. So is Katharine. How's my daughter?"

"Mischievous as ever. She and Marisa are off on a hike."

"I wonder who's in the lead," Thomas said, amused. "I suppose you really called to talk to Marcus though. He's been inaccessible lately. I'll put him on."

"Thomas . . . I want to talk about Marisa and . . ."

Thomas had already passed the receiver to Marcus.

"Hello, Harrington. Sorry I haven't called. I know you're upset about John. I'm still digging."

Marcus had returned from New York without a clue as to how John's name had been placed in *Red Channels*. Although John had forced HUAC to retract his name from the pamphlets and had given the press the story, the newspapers didn't make a splash about it. Neither the public, nor politicians, nor the press seemed to want to offend HUAC with the country in its present mood.

Roy Sharp had not granted Marcus a meeting at his office, so Marcus waited for Roy to return home to his Sunset Boulevard apartment. Marcus had no qualms about strong-arming Roy. He finally got a confession. Roy had started Conrad's rumor based on an anonymous phone caller's tip.

"Laster French called *Confidential*," Marcus said, filling Harrington in. "Roy's been fired. There's also been publicity about his dismissal. Possibly that will discredit him with whomever he told about Conrad. I'm also having him followed. I'm not sure he was telling the truth."

With Marisa on his mind and Conrad's problems troubling him, Harrington still had a moment to pause and listen carefully to Marcus's voice. His old friend was disturbed by much more than Conrad's rumor. He was spending hours at Garvinhouse. 'What was up,' Harrington wondered.

"Is Thomas all right, Marcus?" Harrington asked, taking a shot in the dark.

"I'll fill you in later. By the way, Conrad's already found you another love story. You've got part of the summer off. Then he's made a deal with MGM. He gets Marisa for *Your Year With Mine* and *Tomorrow My Love*."

"Conrad should have a pair of wings and a bow and arrow," Harrington said drolly. "Leave it to him to think of business during a crisis. . . . Marcus, don't keep me in the dark. I want all the details about Thomas. I have something important to talk to you about as well. Call me after your meeting."

But it wasn't until the following morning that Harrington received Marcus's call.

Marcus filled him in on everything from Anaid to Raymond Baren's unsolicited lobbying for Garvin Enterprises to Garvin Enterprises' phones being tapped. Thus, the late call. Marcus was at Garvinhouse, where the lines were clean.

"It's not as bad as it sounds, Harrington. David Britt tripled the company's South American sterling investment through Anaid. Thomas is losing money, but Anaid, Garvin Enterprises' defense contracts, and World Studios are turning a profit. If the banks call in any loans, they'll be covered."

Thomas had also reconsidered WRIB's advice to invest in China. With Chiang Kai-shek driven to the island of Formosa, the Korean War underway, Truman and MacArthur not seeing eye-to-eye, and China a potential threat to the United States in Korea, he didn't think that was sound advice. At the end of the month he was going to Europe anyway to meet with the Chinese representatives, but only for future contacts and good will, not for current investment.

One day the situation in the Far East would settle down, and he'd have the contacts established. But he didn't intend to inform WRIB.

"I know Joe's behind this, Harrington, but I can't find him anywhere. There are the initials BR printed beside Joe's name in 'Diana's File.' Possibly those initials stand for an alias. The hell if I can find him though. I've looked through every photograph under J,F,B,R. Nothing.

"This afternoon, a police artist is coming over. At least I'll have a picture to circulate. Maybe someone will recognize him. I have to be careful, though. He still might be working for Garvin Enterprises, or somewhere nearby. I'd like to nail him. Other than that, I'm just going through film footage of everyone who had access to Thomas's security safe files. I've been at it a month. That's why I haven't seen you, my friend. We didn't tell you because we didn't want you to worry. Now what's important from your side?"

Harrington had listened to Marcus for half an hour. It was Marcus's turn. Harrington filled him in on Marisa's history and his questions about what she had not told him.

"I don't doubt Marisa. I think something horrible happened to her in her early life. She might even be manipulated by her supposed mentor, Bill Reed. His initials are right. Possibly, it's nothing, Marcus, but I think you should check him out."

Through the week, Marcus had daily conversation with Harrington. Even though Roy Sharp was out of work and could do no more damage, the rumor about Conrad's communist leanings had spread through the Hollywood community like the flames that scorched the Los Angeles mountainsides during the desiccated summer months.

By the end of the week, another of Thomas's profitable divisions was under fire as he boarded Garvin Enterprises' private jet with his executives for Middlefork.

IATSE, the theatrical labor union, threatened to call a union strike unless Conrad was banished from his offices on the World Studios lot. Further pressure was brought to bear to deny Conrad's movies distribution through World Studios. Thomas had received desperate phone calls from World's corporate executives worried about the company's survival. He had made up his mind to ignore the hysteria. He would maintain the status quo until Marcus found Joe Field.

Harrington at once started organizing his friends to gather in Middlefork. John was flying in from the East.

Conrad agreed to a week away from Coleman Productions.
The two men would stay with Katharine and Thomas in the
executive house. Harrington filled them all in on Marisa's
story and his doubts. Although he wanted to make sure about
Marisa, he asked everyone to treat her with understanding,
for he loved her and believed she was innocent of any
wrongdoings.

The artist's sketch and the lead on Joe's possible alias
being Bill Reed both produced positive results. Confirmation
of Joe's identity came through Garvin Enterprises' maintenance department. Fortunately, neither Winston nor Joe
knew anything about 'Diana's File,' nor did Marisa. Therefore, their finding that Joe was really Bill Reed was a valuable
secret for them, and it created questions in their minds about
Marisa.

Katharine was still an artist, but in recent years, she had
become involved in Thomas's business. Katharine's strongest
asset was her ability to assess people.

Tonight, as everyone gathered around the dining table,
Harrington took in her delicate features. Missing from her
expression was that radiant charm he had always found so
pleasing about her. She was obviously worried.

Since her arrival, Katharine had spent time with Marisa.
Until a month ago, Marisa had never ridden a horse. With
gruelling determination, Marisa had mastered the sport and,
like Harrington, opted to do her own stunts. Katharine liked
her courage and her softness. Marisa was exquisite and sexy,
with a magnificent figure, but she had a kindness, a
vulnerability, and she obviously adored Harrington as he did
her. Katharine thought Marisa was innocent and was being
manipulated. It worried her that Thomas did not.

Conrad and John were old pros at this sort of thing and
kept Marisa entertained while everyone waited for dinner.
Thomas showed more reserve than usual. His manner
reminded Harrington of their younger days when Thomas
was ready to fight.

At dinner, Harrington focused on the sunset. The
evening's retreating sun glared in the June sky like a fiery orb
of erupting lava. 'Beautiful,' he thought. 'Everything else is
just a bad dream.' Their salads were served, and he returned
his attention to the table, playing out a game he hoped would

have a happy ending.

"I hear Roy Sharp is still giving you a hard time," he said to Conrad, "even though he's lost his job and has Laster French breathing down his neck."

"Please don't worry, Harrington," Conrad said, winking at Marisa. "I'm afraid Harrington's dislike for Roy Sharp might be equal to yours."

Marisa laughed. "My accent. He always criticizes my accent and calls me an Italian bombshell. I thought it had something to do with the war when I first read the word."

They had all agreed not to mention any of Thomas's business, so Conrad chuckled, although furious that Thomas was in potential financial danger. "Roy Sharp can't ruin my name. We mustn't take this seriously."

"Many good people have been blacklisted," John said firmly. "I do take it to heart. Rumors started just like yours. No solid evidence ever comes up and then . . ."

Conrad sobered. He knew some of John's New York friends were in trouble. "I apologize, John. You're right."

John looked sentimentally at Conrad. "I just worry about you, old friend."

"And I you."

Marisa watched the two men's exchange, and she squeezed Harrington's hand. "It's rare to see such good friends. You all are. I like you for that."

Conrad smiled at Marisa. How could one help but like the girl. "You and Harrington certainly have become popular," he said, livening up the mood. "Arlene Habor is touting you as the romantic couple of the fifties. Where'd she get all that background material and those photographs?"

Marcus was puzzled by Arlene's build-up and had told Harrington, "I don't like it. I feel you're being set up for a fall."

Right now Marcus was on a plane to Florence to see Marisa's Uncle Julio and her mama, Carmen Benito. Hopefully what he found could be used to protect Marisa, as well as the rest of them.

"I have no idea where the photos came from," Harrington said finally. "Arlene disliked me for the longest time and then became my most ardent supporter. What about you, Marisa?"

Marisa paused for a moment while the salad plates were

taken and the main course of Beef Wellington was put before them.

"I thought Arlene was a very strange lady, but Bill introduced us and said it would be good to be nice." Marisa laughed. "I didn't follow his advice, although I'm sure Bill's heart was in the right place."

'Dear old Joe doesn't have a heart,' Thomas thought, thinking Marisa either naive or the best actress he'd ever seen. He changed the subject then, and shared his thoughts of the times.

With MacArthur's return to the United States, Senator Joe McCarthy of Wisconsin accused the administration of "Twenty Years of Treason": Roosevelt had caved in to Stalin at Yalta, and Truman had solidified Communist control of the Chinese mainland when he recalled MacArthur. Although Thomas disliked McCarthy, there seemed to be some truth in his words, however crudely they were spoken.

"We could handle McCarthy if he didn't have such a profound affect on our people," Thomas said, disturbed. Thomas had government contracts, and both he and his employees were required to swear their loyalty to the United States. As Chairman of the Board of World Studios, Thomas knew that blacklisting was rampant in Hollywood.

"Doesn't American law say that you're innocent until proven guilty?" Marisa asked, remembering her American schooling in Boston.

"Yes, but blacklisting encourages the very opposite," Harrington answered.

"McCarthy's making such a stink," Thomas explained, "that attitudes towards freedom of expression, which is the very basis of the entertainment business, and attitudes towards the 'freedom' to steal government documents, somehow have become confused."

"When I first came to Hollywood," Conrad said, "no respectable citizen would talk to me. I tried to find a place to live and came across sign after sign that read: 'No dogs or actors allowed.' Although I was a director of sorts, movie people were typecast as bums. For decades, moviemakers have had their share of problems, some minor, others more serious like the blacklisting. But we're here to create, to express, not to dote on man's banal prejudice—unless it has something to do with a film, which I might make on this very subject one day."

"Nevertheless," Thomas said, "when he returns from Europe, Marcus will have a full report for us."

"I suppose you talk to Bill often, Marisa?" Katharine asked, trying to have her reveal more to them.

"I do nothing but talk to Bill Reed," Marisa joked before Harrington could tease her about the lengthy conversations. "I'm very happy to be working with Harrington and with you, Mr. Coleman. Bill told me we begin in August. I've been trying to get Harrington to go see Jason beforehand. Can I get anyone to help me?"

Harrington watched Thomas and Katharine exchange a quick glance. At once, they joined in with Conrad and John voicing their hearty endorsement of Marisa's proposal.

"Marisa hasn't had a proper introduction into our circle. Therefore, she doesn't know about my family. Don't you think she deserves to hear about Winston?"

"I have wondered," Marisa said, referring to the conversation she had just heard. "I don't really understand why Harrington's father would wish to harm all of you."

Thomas liked the idea that Harrington was being so open. Again, they'd have an opportunity to study Marisa's reaction. The dishes were cleared and coffee and liquor were served.

Harrington started the story, painting a picture of his life with Diana and his estrangement from Winston. Lastly, he spoke of Cara and Jason.

"I don't know quite how to explain it," Harrington told her. "Winston wanted an heir. We knew somehow he was involved in Cara's death. I wasn't myself after she died. I agreed to let Winston have temporary custody of Jason. That doesn't sound very noble, but those are the facts. I was out of my mind. I think I blamed Jason for her death."

Everyone at the table nodded, then John elaborated on Harrington's story, telling Marisa about Dr. Smith's diagnosis of Cara and about Smith's death and the disappearance of Smith's files. They each skirted the issue of Vincent Morello, guarding Harrington's heart—for Marcus had let them in on Harrington's feelings about taking Vincent's life. If Harrington wanted to talk about Cara, Vincent, and Fred Franco, he'd do it in his own way. John did end his story with details of Fred Franco's death and their suspicions, but lack of proof, about Joe Field's part in it by Winston's orders.

Everyone noticed that Marisa didn't flinch at Joe's name. Obviously, she knew him only as Bill Reed.

Over dessert of chocolate mousse, Thomas told Marisa about his first meeting with Harrington at Franco's. Conrad described his and John's one venture with Winston in *The Rich in Spirit*. Katharine told Marisa about Diana and her struggles.

After three hours of conversation, Marisa turned to Harrington, disbelief, wonder, sorrow, and tears intermingled in her expression.

"My love," she said genuinely. "I now understand you better." She looked around the table. "Thank you so much for sharing your stories. I've known such men as Winston, but I didn't know these things happened in America. I . . . He would have done well in Sicily. Remember the Kefauver hearings?"

Everyone remembered them well. They were the first Congressional hearings seen on television—the subject was the investigation of organized crime.

"My Uncle Julio said the Mafia in Sicily came from Sicilian criminals. He might have been right. Not even historians can agree. Winston is a criminal, too, don't you think?"

"That's putting it mildly," John said, emotional at having relived Diana's story. To get his mind off of his beloved, he focused his curiosity on Marisa. "I remember Cara's father telling me that the Mafia developed from the Compani d'armi, hired guards who protected the feudal landowners' families and land."

"Oh yes," Marisa said reflectively, knowing a great deal on this subject from her uncle. "Others say the Mafia began some time during the Inquisition. What do you call it? A state of mind—a protection of one's self respect . . . to guard themselves mentally against the wrath of foreign invaders. And yes, still others say it originated in 1282 when the peasants rebelled against the French."

"The Sicilian Vespers?" Katharine asked.

Marisa nodded.

"There was a source of power in silence, wasn't there?" Katharine added, remembering what Cara had told her.

"The *omerta,* the silence, was a shield. Sicilians barred

displays of weakness from their enemies with their silence," Marisa said.

Harrington was surprised that Marisa knew so much about the Mafia. After all, she had said she left Sicily right after she was born.

"My point," Marisa was saying, "is that Winston seems like some men I have known. He exploits the weaknesses in others for his own benefit."

"Precisely," John said firmly. "Couldn't have said it better myself. The man's an exploiter who I'd like to see hang from the nearest tree!"

Harrington noticed Thomas was even more skeptical of Marisa by the evening's end. He had thought Marisa was possibly naive, but the last part of this conversation showed she was quite aware. Katharine had her doubts, too. John and Conrad didn't look happy. Harrington sighed. Even if he was a fool, he didn't believe Marisa was guilty.

When Harrington and Marisa bid farewell at the door, Thomas reminded Harrington, "I have the Artisanmanor file with me. You can sign the papers tomorrow."

"Artisanmanor?" Marisa asked.

Harrington had set up a foundation in Diana's name, the money from which was going to buy land from Thomas where the first Artisanmanor—a school for the promotion of the arts—would be built. Conrad, Thomas, and John Stevens were board members. Publicity on the school was due out in another week.

"What a lovely idea," Marisa said.

"I can't believe you've never been to Florence," Marisa exclaimed in wonder. "London, then? Paris? Madrid? Rome? The Riveria?"

Harrington shook his head. "I've never had the time."

They had shot the rapids that morning in the Salmon River. This evening they were having a candlelight picnic out in the forest. The campfire crackled beside their blanket. Marisa curled up her long legs and sipped the Cabernet Savvingnon Harrington had just poured for her. It was their last week on location.

"For such a worldly man, you certainly haven't seen much of it. What do you do all day when you're not making films?"

"I always had work to do."

"On what?"

"For the last few years, I've been writing when I'm not acting, and learning from Conrad about producing, editing, scoring music, dubbing, and . . ."

Marisa narrowed her eyes and interrupted. "Oh, Harrington, you really must get out more often. How can you write without experience? How can you live in such a confined world!"

"Somehow I've survived."

Marisa shook her finger at him, then leaned over and kissed him fully on the lips. "Yes, you survive, but are you living?"

"That's not the way I look at it, although I would like to see some of the world. What about you? This country must be very different to you."

"You are different. Most of the world's people are the same."

Harrington found this curious. "Then why do you want to travel if everyone's the same?"

Marisa came into his arms. "Because if I traveled with you, at least the world would look different."

Harrington, lost in his own thoughts, gazed into the darkness. Marcus had been in Florence only a few days, and they hadn't heard from him yet. Harrington was impatient.

Sicily seemed to be the key to Marisa's life and maybe to his own. Vincent was from Sicily. Why did the past always crop up in his life? Was it a sign? Was he supposed to forget about Jason? The thought disturbed him somehow. Recently, on the phone, Jason had asked when he would see him. He didn't want to hurt the little boy. What was the answer?

Marisa had waited patiently for him to break out of his own reverie. She was lying down with her head in his lap, staring at the fire. How lovely she was. The creamy olive skin. The piercing almond green eyes. 'But who is she really?' Harrington asked himself for the hundredth time.

"Why don't we go to your homeland?" he suggested.

She looked from the fire up into his eyes. "Sicily?"

"Why not? We can fly to London, spend a week, then on to Sicily and afterwards Florence. I'd like to meet your Uncle Julio. Why didn't he ever come back to America?" he asked, staring down at her. "I barely know anything about you,

Marisa."

"You won't learn in Sicily," she said, leaving his lap. "I haven't been there in years. Florence is my home."

There was an edge to her voice. He didn't understand. "Listen, Marisa, give me a chance to understand. Don't you see? I know you have this agent, Bill Reed. I know you have a mother, but I don't know why she's in a sanatorium. You never talk about your father, your friends, your early schooling, or anything."

"Isn't it enough to know me as I am?" she asked quietly, denying the promise she had made to herself to tell Harrington everything.

Harrington wondered why she was holding back. "You're right. None of the past matters. Hell, you're just getting to know me, too."

"But I would like to know you better," she said. Then realizing what she had said, she started to laugh. "You're right, I admit it. Let's start all over again. I'll take you to Europe and maybe to Sicily if you take me to see Jason."

"You name the date. I'm getting everything I want."

She got caught up in his excitement. "July!"

"July? That's in a couple of weeks!"

"We leave in two weeks."

CHAPTER XXII

Jason had one week of summer left at Windsor Royal before leaving for Europe. Winston was taking him for his ninth birthday. Jason intended to make the most of this week. This morning, he hastened to the stables after breakfast, but stopped dead in his tracks at the stable door.

He had seen Mrs. Baren often at Windsor Royal. She was pretty enough, with her copper colored hair. But she didn't have the same quality Jason had instinctively seen in Katharine Garvin long ago and in his grandmother. Nope, Mrs. Baren was O.K. and that was about it.

She bent down and kissed his cheek. "How're you, honey? Isn't this nice? Nicole is riding this morning, too. You'll be able to ride together!"

Jason looked past Mrs. Baren to Nicole. Her flaming red hair was tied in a ponytail with a yellow bow. She wore a white blouse and beige jodhpurs. Brown boots covered her delicate little feet. His first thought was that this week's vacation was not going to be as much fun as he thought if Mrs. Baren insisted that he ride with her daughter every day.

Mrs. Baren seemed all atwitter, fussing over him as he

waited for Jim to bring out Sable Lady. A stable hand was helping Nicole mount her horse, Silver.

"Is your grandfather at the house, honey?"

Jason nodded, thinking it was a stupid question. Winston was always at the house. He watched Mrs. Baren's fluttering hand wave at Nicole. She kissed him again and flew out of the stable towards the mansion. Nicole turned in her saddle and stared expressionlessly after her mother.

Although he could ride circles around Nicole, she really had improved since the last time they rode. He was surprised. Sable Lady was a faster horse, after all, and Nicole wasn't as aggressive as he, of course, but he had fun riding with her just the same, even if he wouldn't admit it to anyone.

"Why don't you wait up for Nicole?" Jim scolded.

"She's just a girl; I can't slow down for her!"

Nicole tossed her hair in open defiance, her little body heaving in frustration and her hands clenched. "Some day I'll win. You just wait and see!"

Jim looked after them curiously. Jason was a terrible tease. He'd hold back the reins on Sable Lady until Nicole thought she had a substantial lead, then loosen the reins and breeze past her, waving to rub it in. Jim shrugged and walked back into the stables laughing. He had known Nicole almost as long as he had Jason, and she wasn't one to give up easily. It would be a very interesting week.

On Wednesday afternoon, late, as a cool breeze softened the humid summer day, Nicole led the way past the creek, through the forest, up an old trail to a hilltop that overlooked Windsor Royal.

"How did you find this place?" Jason asked.

"I don't spend all my time with you," Nicole said, tossing her hair and looking down to the valley.

"This is a perfect spot," Jason said, turning Sable Lady. "Wait here. I'm riding back to the house to get my camera."

"I'll go with you."

"No," Jason yelled. "You'll only slow me down. You're just a girl, remember?"

During the following three days, Jason brought his camera to the hill and insisted Nicole pose for him, much to her discomfort.

"The pictures yesterday were very good," Jason said. "But you didn't hold your head right. Get over there on that rock. Lift your chin. No, not that way, Nicole. To your right and up. Steady now. Good. Freeze. Nicole you moved!"

"Stop ordering me around," she said, infuriated.

Jason put down the camera. "I'm only telling you what to do because you don't know."

Nicole tossed her hair and stomped her little foot. She turned from him and marched to her horse.

"Hey! I'm not finished yet!"

Nicole guided Silver to a boulder, stepped onto the rock and mounted. "I don't care!"

When Jason galloped up to the stables, he saw Jim eating his lunch out back. Jason took a few pictures of Jim sitting under the old sycamore tree before jumping off Sable Lady and leading her over to the bench.

Without looking up, Jim handed him another article on Harrington. Everyone else was at lunch, so they were alone. Jason sat down next to Jim in the shade, still holding Sable Lady's reins, and looked at the article.

"Who's this lady with Father?"

"His co-star, Marisa Benito," Jim said, batting a fly away. "They're doing another film together in a few months called *Your Year With Mine*. Your mother wrote the script. She was a very talented woman, Jason."

"Was she, Jim?"

"Sure was. You don't think your father would make her screenplay into a movie if it weren't good, do you?"

"Of course not!"

"Well, then, you have your answer."

"Did my father like my mother?" Jason asked.

"He loved her, Jason. She was grand. Truly grand."

Jim finished his sandwich, folded up his napkin, and put it in a paper sack.

"Grandfather says women have their place. They can never equal men. Men rule the world."

Jim looked at Jason knowingly. "Having trouble with Nicole?"

Jason scratched his head and grinned. "I sure don't understand her. Grandfather says there's nothing to understand. Just love them and leave them. Don't let a beautiful woman tie you down."

Jim laughed. "That's tough to do."

"Why?"

"Women have a spirit all their own. A good woman should be prized just like a good man. Each is an individual. You can't put labels on people. Look at your grandmother, now she was the finest lady I ever met," Jim said with affection. "I learned a lot about life from her."

"But Grandfather said if he were smarter, he would have kept her in her place. He told me to learn from his mistakes. I'm not supposed to ever let a woman get the better of me."

Jim brushed off his work clothes and picked up the sack. "Come on," he said, refraining from commenting on Winston's advice. "Help me unsaddle Sable Lady."

Jason walked Sable Lady into the stable with Jim and they unsaddled her and put her into her stall. Jim went to the tack room, returned with his grooming kit, and began to wipe her off with a rag.

Sitting on the planks, Jason watched intently. "What I don't understand is what Grandfather means by 'place.' Should a woman be locked up?"

Jim looked amused. "I don't think that he meant it like that."

"What did he mean, then?"

Jim sighed. "I thought you and I made a pact that I wouldn't comment on your grandfather's advice."

"Okay," Jason said, unruffled. "Tell me your opinion."

When Jim completed wiping Sable Lady, he picked up the dandy brush. He nudged Sable Lady and her head turned towards Jason.

"Do you enjoy riding your horse?"

Sable Lady nuzzled Jason. "She's a great horse."

"And she is female, right?"

"Yes."

"She's faster than Nicole's stud, isn't she? And you think she's smarter, too, don't you?"

"Yes, but she's my horse."

"You mean you take credit for it all?"

Sable Lady pushed Jason, and he almost fell off the plank. "Hey," he said laughing. "Stop that."

"That's what will happen when you don't respect your woman," Jim said simply.

The phone rang and Jim hastened to answer it. When he returned, he told Jason, "Your grandfather wants to see you at the house. Important business, he says."

Winston was in the Operations Room. Joe had spoken to Marisa, who had glowing news. She and Harrington were visiting Jason this afternoon then heading on to Europe. She had told Joe confidentially that Harrington wished to see her homeland. Knowing her history, Joe had played it just right.

"Of course," Joe had told her, "you have ghosts from the past. Maybe it's time to be brave and confront them. Since you love Harrington and he loves you, possibly you can face your past together. What better way to heal wounds than with the person you love?"

Winston chuckled to himself. Listening to Joe explain his role as the doting confidant really was a hoot. Possibly, just possibly, Joe's plan might work after all and once more turn Harrington into an emotional cripple. Right now, Joe was sneaking into London to plant documents in Marisa's room, and Roy Sharp was on his way to Rome. He'd have plenty of photographs for the papers before Harrington and Marisa returned from their trip.

In the meantime, he and Jason had to get going before Harrington arrived. Within the hour, Winston and Jason were on their way to the airport. Harris Johnson, Jim's father, and still head of the household staff, watched them leave. He wondered why Winston wished that he keep their destination a secret. But Harris never questioned Winston's orders.

In the early afternoon, Harrington and Marisa drove up Mayfair Road to the guardhouse.

"This is where you lived? Where's the house?"

"A couple of miles up beyond the gates."

Harrington was driving a Mercedes 280SL convertible. The same guard, the one who had greeted Harrington uncivilly in 1947, stepped out of the guardhouse and came over to the car. Rough and pugnacious, he viewed first Harrington then Marisa as if they were not only unwelcome, but trespassing.

"Would you tell Mr. Todd, Harrington Todd is here," Harrington called out.

"He's not here."

"Then let Harris know I'm here to see Jason."

"Mr. Todd's grandson is not here either."

Harrington's hands tightened on the wheel. "Open the gates."

"Suit yourself."

Marisa had looked forward to seeing Harrington with his son. Harrington was as disappointed as she.

Out at the stables, Harrington spoke to Jim and found out they'd just missed Jason. He and Winston were on their way to Europe. Jim watched Marisa reaching out to touch one of the fillies.

"Did anyone know we were coming?" she asked.

"No," Harrington said.

"Winston knew, Harrington. Jason was just riding a few hours ago. I didn't think they were leaving until day after tomorrow and then, poof, they were gone to London."

"That's where we're going," Harrington told Marisa. "We'll catch up with Jason there."

Marisa had liked Jim at once. "Harrington has told me how you look out for his son. He is lucky to have someone like you."

Jim saw something in Marisa's eyes. She wasn't just beautiful. She had compassion and a deep sorrow. He smiled at her. She was different from Cara, not quite as spirited, but she had a heart.

The stable phone rang as Jim accompanied them out of the stable, and they heard footsteps behind them and Harrington's name being called.

"Mr. Mancini is on the phone," the stable boy informed Harrington. "He says it's urgent!"

Winston and Jason were staying at Claridges in London in the Mayfair District. Winston had scheduled meetings all week, and the morning following their arrival, Jason went out with one of the security guards to tour London. When he met Winston later at Les Ambassadeurs, a man was sitting with Winston at the table.

Les Ambassadeurs was a quiet, dignified club. Dignitaries from all over the world gathered there. It was filled with history. Peace treaties had been discussed and pacts signed here. The large room in which they sat had oak-paneled walls with a handsome carved wooden mantle; chairs and tables were arranged throughout the room.

"Jason, I'd like you to meet Thomas Garvin. Thomas,

my grandson."

At the sight of Jason, Thomas thought his heart would break. Jason was the spitting image of Cara, all except the black hair that recalled Winston and Fred Franco.

"How do you do, Jason?" Thomas said, extending his hand. "We haven't seen each other for many years, not since your grandmother was alive."

Jason looked up at a man of medium height. He was athletically built, with broad shoulders, a slender waist, and a healthy head of wavy brown hair.

"Very well, sir," he answered. "Father told me about you when we talked on the telephone."

Thomas smiled and asked Jason what had most impressed him about London.

"Big Ben," Jason answered.

"Big Ben?" Winston queried.

Thomas held Jason's eyes and smiled, ignoring Winston. "So," he said, "time is important to you."

Jason liked Thomas for understanding. "I never knew how important until I saw Big Ben."

"That's very wise of you, Jason."

"He's my grandson, isn't he?" Winston said proudly.

Jason continued to stare at Thomas with a trace of admiration and curiosity. "Why are you in London?"

"I'm here on business, to talk to some men about possible trade with China. Your grandfather's firm, William Randolph Investment Bankers, WRIB, set up the meetings."

"China?" Jason said wide-eyed. "It sounds like a very big place."

Thomas laughed. "It most certainly is."

"Well, Thomas, the world is getting smaller. Who would have thought we would bump into one another in London?" Winston smiled affably. "I must congratulate you. I've been hearing your name lately in the most impressive company . . ."

Although a cool expression fell over Thomas's face, he still smiled. "That's interesting. I've had a little trouble lately."

"Really? Anything I can do?" Winston asked, feigning concern.

"No, no," Thomas laughed. "Don't misunderstand me," Thomas said, sensing Winston was immediately on the alert. He purposely was doing this with calm in front of Jason so Winston could do nothing but listen—yet by doing this, he could watch Winston's reaction. As long as he was careful, Jason would never know he and Winston were mortal enemies. "Anaid is doing quite nicely. It's salvaged whatever losses I had with Garvin Enterprises over the last year."

"Anaid?" Winston asked in spite of himself.

"Oh, I forgot to mention it to WRIB. It's a little subsidiary of Garvin Enterprises. It's guarded my parent company very well, and it should, considering . . ." Thomas took a pen from his suit coat and wrote down, "A-n-a-i-d" on a slip of paper. "Jason, why don't you spell it backwards?"

Jason was ready for the task. "D-I-A-N-A." Jason looked up joyfully. "Diana! That was my grandmother's name!"

"Yes," Thomas said happily. "I named the company after her. It's in California," Thomas said, feeling Winston's hot stare.

Jason's face brightened at the mention of California. "Tell my father I said hello, will you, Mr. Garvin?"

Feeling compassion for the little boy and further anger towards Winston, Thomas defended Harrington. "I surely will, but I wish you could have told him yourself. Your father stopped off at Windsor Royal to see you," Thomas said, ignoring Winston's displeasure. "Unfortunately, he missed you by only an hour."

Jason cocked his head, staring deep into Thomas's eyes. "Grandfather decided we should leave early." Jason brightened. "So he was coming to see me!"

"He sure was."

Jason was so delighted that he beamed. "I knew he hadn't forgotten me. I just knew it."

"He'll never forget you, Jason. Isn't that right, Winston?" Thomas said, hiding his outrage.

"Of course," Winston said magnanimously. "I'm sure Harrington will find the time to see Jason some time soon. Jason, Mr. Garvin is interested in television."

"I already knew that, Grandfather. Father told me," Jason said, liking Thomas Garvin very much. "Are you going to get into TV, Mr. Garvin? Father told me you were."

Thomas laughed. He had heard that this little boy was bright. "Yes, I am."

"I think that's smart," Jason said thoughtfully.

"You do?" Thomas said, humoring him.

"Yes."

"Well, Jason," Thomas said kindly, "I think you're pretty smart, so let me tell you a story, O.K.?"

Jason sat forward eagerly. Winston was ignored.

"Radio began during the first World War," Thomas said. "Later on, they decided to sell the surplus of radios. It was lucky, too, because during the Depression a lot of people listened to President Roosevelt's fireside chats. He made them feel good because they were hungry and they needed someone to tell them everything would be all right. Television is a combination of radio and movies being brought into the home."

Jason was delighted with the story and squirmed in his chair to get comfortable before making a very important comment. His feet just brushed the floor. His young face was very serious.

"Being here has made me think alot. It's too bad we didn't have TV during the last war. If everyone saw all the big mess from the bombs, maybe the war would've been over sooner. Don't you think?"

Thomas looked at the serious, sad expression on the boy's face. Jason seemed too mature for his years, as if Winston's age had rubbed off on the child. Thomas hoped that was all that had rubbed off. But Jason was something special, that was clear. "That's a very good possibility," Thomas said.

"I don't know for sure," Jason continued, "but I don't think people will want to see another war on TV."

"I don't think they will either," Thomas said.

"Bright boy, isn't he?" Winston said, waving to the waiter. "Would you like something, Jason, Thomas?"

Both declined.

Winston started to get up, concealing his anger behind a mask of compassion for Jason. Thomas seemed not to notice as he continued to talk to Jason.

"You and your grandfather should come and visit us in California one of these days."

"Jason has his studies, Thomas," Winston said with an edge to his voice. "Having a child of your own, I'm sure you know that one can't be too careful about the raising of a child. Unfortunately, Jason, it is time to go."

As they stood outside Les Ambassadeurs saying good-bye, Jason spoke to Thomas.

"I'd like to see your studio some day, and don't forget to say hello to my father and Mrs. Garvin. Did she have her baby?"

"Yes," Thomas said. "Our daughter's name is Kierston."

"My mother wrote a play about a 'Kierston.'"

"That's who our daughter is named after. We knew your mother well."

"Really, Mr. Garvin? You liked all the girls in our family, didn't you?"

"I surely did."

Winston interrupted Thomas as he started to talk about Cara. "As you can see, my grandson has many interests." Jason started to interject his questions about his mother, and Winston placed a possessive hand on Jason's shoulder, cautioning him. "Curious minds are invaluable when directed on the proper course. Good-bye, Thomas."

Thomas watched them get into the limousine. Jason waved and smiled as the car pulled away. Thomas waved back, thinking that Jason would one day be his own man. Then his thoughts turned to Marcus. He turned on his heel and hurried to the telephone. He had to call Sicily before catching his plane at Heathrow.

Marcus had told Harrington to forget about London and instead to meet him in Palermo, Sicily. Harrington was dreading the visit to the island where Fred Franco and Vincent Morello had been born. But Marcus had insisted.

"You'll both find your answers here," Marcus had said firmly. "I've already rearranged your reservations. Just get to the airport within the hour."

Now they were flying across the Strait of Messina, and Harrington saw Sicily as the plane made its descent.

"There's the island!" Harrington exclaimed.

Marisa followed his gaze to the window and the sun's rays, which shimmered across the sea, crystalizing the rippling water. The sunlight danced on the soaring mountains that erupted from the island's edge, leaving crevices darkened and peaks illuminated. The plane actually looked as though it were heading straight for the mountains, which soared above their vision. Huge hunks of rock and earth were seen at eye level and higher still, and then, at the last minute, the plane changed course, flying parallel along the coastline before settling down at the Palermo Airport.

"You told me the island was mountainous, but I didn't think it would look like that!" Harrington said in astonishment.

Marisa laughed at his wonder. "This island, like its people, is very rugged."

"Rugged? I don't think of you as rugged," Harrington said, kissing her. "I think you're wonderful."

They drove to the Villa Igiea Grand, which was just off the Piazza Belmonte and faced the Tyrrhenian Sea. The hotel was a rambling two-story villa. The tourist season had begun and sunbathers lounged on the terrace overlooking the swimming pool and the Tyrrhenian Sea.

The day was hot and bright, and it took Harrington a moment to focus when entering their bedroom suite. Marcus was sitting in the parlor. From his expression, Harrington knew Marisa was innocent. Harrington looked more closely at Marcus and saw something so tragic in his eyes that Harrington walked over to give him some assistance. Then he saw a man beyond Marcus, in the bedroom. Julio Benito entered the parlor.

Marisa opened her eyes in total surprise and excitement. "Uncle," she said, throwing her arms around his neck.

Harrington scrutinized Julio Benito, from his European suit to the head of wavy black hair. He was taken with Julio's face. There was a sadness in the features. Actually the man looked as though he was crying through a brilliant smile. He greeted his niece with tender affection.

With an arm around his niece, he looked directly into Harrington's eyes. "Marcus says you love Marisa."

Harrington nodded.

Marisa cocked her head to the side, staring up at her uncle. She was unaccustomed to the tone in his voice. "What is the matter?" she asked.

"And you love him. You've told me so."

"Yes, yes!" Marisa said joyfully. "What is this all about? Why are you acting so strangely?"

"Come here, Marisa. Sit with us, Harrington. Please."

Harrington glanced at Marcus who was joined by Julio in the sitting area. What the hell is going on? When they were all settled in, Harrington beside Marisa on the couch, Julio opposite them in a chair and Marcus now standing by the fireplace, Julio smiled kindly at Marisa.

Julio had insisted that he break this news to Marisa. His niece had been through much in her life. How to begin?

"Marisa, something has happened that you and I are in the middle of. You did not know some things, nor did I. You were young. I should have known better, but I was sick and upset about Mary . . . but that's for later. Marisa, you and I, we did not know people would get hurt. You must not blame yourself."

Marisa looked from her uncle to Harrington. "Do you know anything about this?"

"Not everything," Harrington said.

"I want to know what you know first," Marisa said.

"I'm the one who should explain," Marcus said. "I don't think it's fair that Harrington should. It might appear . . ."

"You're wrong," Harrington interrupted. "She deserves to know from me. No matter how it makes me or any of us look."

Marcus flushed. Julio liked Harrington for being honest.

"You told me a wonderful story about your benefactor, Bill Reed . . ." Harrington began.

"Is that what this is about?" Marisa demanded, suddenly angry. "You don't even know him! Why doesn't anyone like Bill? He's been good to me, to my family. Uncle, tell them."

Before Julio could say anything, Harrington did. "But I do know Bill Reed."

Marisa faced him squarely. "I never introduced you."

"No, you never did. I met him long ago, although his name wasn't Bill Reed. His name still isn't Bill Reed. Bill Reed is Joe Field. You've heard us all talk about Joe Field?"

Marisa stood up. "I don't believe you."

Marcus came forward and took a series of photographs from his pocket along with proof of Joe's involvement in many crimes and a copy of the warrant for his arrest. He handed Marisa the information.

She grabbed the photos and started looking through them. "This isn't Bill. He isn't bald. He's . . ." She stopped

short. She stared incredulously at the photo in her hand.
Then she rushed through the remaining photos and documents, lastly looking at the documented history of his crimes,
ranging from extortion to murder, and then at the warrant.
When she lifted her eyes, she was horrified. "You don't think
. . ." Tears came to her eyes. Bill had helped her. He'd
cultivated her. "He . . . Bill is my agent. How could he work
for Winston? Why would they go to such trouble? You can't
be serious!" But they were serious. She could see it.
"Harrington," she said, turning to him, "what must Thomas
think?"

"He was the most skeptical of you."

"He was hurt by me?"

"No, no, Marisa," Harrington said, flushing brightly.
"Really, you mustn't think that. Joe . . . I mean Bill—well it's
Joe Field—used his alias to not only fool you but to fool
Thomas. He worked at Garvin Enterprises. Thomas lost
money, but it wasn't because of you. Everything's fine now."

Marisa was dumbfounded. "And you, Marcus? What
did Bill-Joe do to you?"

"Long ago he murdered my father."

Marisa gasped. "Murdered? If I had known," Marisa
said helplessly, "then I could have helped you, isn't that
right?"

Marcus shook his head firmly. "But there was no way
for you to know. Don't blame yourself."

"And Conrad?" she said to everyone in the room. Then
her eyes fixed on Harrington's. "And you, my beloved? And
Jason?"

Harrington got up, and Marisa broke down. He reached
her just in time. She cried hysterically in his arms. "I've
betrayed you, Harrington. I'm so sorry." Harrington left the
men where they stood and took Marisa into the bedroom and
closed the door.

Julio shook his head. "Harrington's father, this Winston
Todd, is a man of cruelty. If you had not found me . . ." he
shook his head. "My heart weeps to think of how horrible
Marisa and Harrington's nightmare would have been."

"It's unwise to tell them," Marcus said. "They both need
to discover the rest themselves. In essence, Winston might be
saving them both."

Julio smiled, bittersweet. "Only because Harrington has

a wise and talented friend like you, Marcus. Otherwise Winston might have destroyed their love."

"We aren't through yet. Are you sure you don't want to wait a few days?" Harrington asked Marisa over breakfast the following morning.

She shook her head adamantly. "If you are with me, I'll be fine."

Julio was still unsure. "Maybe tomorrow."

"Today," Marisa said. "You made a special trip down here to show me something, Uncle. I don't like to keep people waiting."

They piled into the rented sedan.

"Tell me everyting you can remember," Harrington said, sitting in the backseat with Marisa while Julio drove, heading towards the heart of Palermo.

Marisa thought back, "I don't remember much about Sicily. I was too young," she said, looking out the window. "I was born here, but my mama took me to Florence within a year of my birth. My papa brought me back here when I was so young, and only for a few months."

Julio glanced at Marcus sitting beside him in the front seat. His eyes mirrored the tragedy of Marisa's life, and Marcus sighed inwardly.

They passed a church decorated with rows of flowers in colorful assortments. In front of it, a crowd of people clad in black were dabbing their eyes with handkerchieves as pallbearers solemnly carried a casket from the church. As Harrington watched the pedestrians stroll by without a glance at the mourning crowd, he knew that he and Marisa could not look away. They had to confront their problems. He glanced at her and noticed she was shivering. He reached out and took her hand.

"Five years before Marisa's birth," Julio told them, "Benito Mussolini came to power in Italy. Four years later, he sent Perfect Mori, a retired policeman, to Sicily to wipe out the Mafia. Although Perfect Mori didn't succeed, he did make it very difficult for the Mafiosi. Mussolini did not understand or wish to acknowledge that the Mafia was so strong a belief in the minds of the Sicilians. But then, like all invaders of the island, mainland Italians did not understand the Sicilians' ways. You understand the Sicilian history and you will know why Marisa's papa was betrayed and became a tyrant."

Sicily had been damaged extensively during the war. Harrington saw a few new buildings among the rows of vacant lots loaded with heaps of brick, stone, and scraps of wood piled higher than a man could reach. Old homes, converted to apartments, stood stained and worn against the foggy day.

"For centuries, foreign powers ruled and enslaved the Sicilians," Julio continued, his voice taking on that expert tone again. "They raped their women, tortured those who opposed them, and left little hope in the lives of the Sicilians. The mountainous regions divided cities. Communication was difficult. Sicily never was a united country, just many different towns, villages, and cities with individual forms of local government, and varying standards and beliefs."

He pointed out numerous examples of Arab and Norman influence from the San Giovanni degli Ermiti designed by the Arabs to the La Martorana, which was a Norman Church.

They parked the car and entered the La Martorana.

"Phoenicians, Greeks, Romans, Byzantines, Normans, French, Spanish, and the Bourbons rolled into Sicily in successive invasion waves over the centuries," Julio told them as they walked through the church.

Suddenly Marisa stopped.

"I remember some other things now. Uncle, didn't you tell me about a man my father knew who was a member of 'The Honor Society.' Didn't he betray papa?"

"Yes on both counts. Remember when I explained about the Mafia to you? To belong to an organization whose power came from silence and secrecy was very intense. Your papa was manipulated. You see, with some men, manipulation is an art. Our people are extremely intelligent, don't ever think otherwise. They have made a study of men. They know their weaknesses and their strengths, and they knew how to capitalize on both."

"Your father is such a man," Marisa said to Harrington.

"Yes, my love, he is."

"Doesn't it hurt you?"

Harrington glanced at Marcus then smiled down at her.

"It used to. I never even admitted it to myself for the longest time. Winston is my father, Marisa. My blood. But I had to learn to accept him for who he was. Then it gave me the strength to be who I am."

Outside of La Martorana, they were surprised to find movie fans gathered around their car. Children handed Marisa flowers. Women and men shook Harrington's hand. Marisa held his glance and laughed. "Remember? I told you, you were loved all over the world. You didn't believe me."

Harrington took her in his arms, right in front of everyone. "I only need you love, dearest."

He kissed her then and the crowd smiled, whispered, pointed, whistled, and giggled. Many people approached as Marcus snapped them out of their trance.

"We'd better move on or we'll never get through the crowd."

Harrington patted the child closest to him on the head, then edged open the car's passenger door for Marisa. She got inside and he slipped in after her. As Julio slowly moved the car from the curb, people waved, shouted out their names, and threw flowers on the car. None of them saw Roy Sharp behind them, photographing their departure.

Julio drove them through the center of Palermo, past the Palazzo dei Re' Normanni, which was built by the Normans and was now the center for the Sicilian Parliament. Harrington was too busy listening to Marisa to notice that Roy Sharp was following them in his car.

"My papa was . . . what do you call it . . . framed, isn't that right, Uncle?"

"Yes, my beauty. Perfect Mori thought your father was a Mafioso, and he was imprisoned and tortured. What could he do? He told the truth and they did not believe. By the time of his release in 1928, your mama was in Florence. She rushed back to Sicily."

They drove through the back roads of the Via Papa Sergio, a road which ran along the sea up into the mountains about eighty miles from Palermo. Marisa saw the rocky hillside and somehow it seemed familiar.

"Where are we, Uncle?" she called out, a strident tone in her voice.

It was Marcus who turned around as the car lumbered along the dirt road into the village and stopped among peasants clad in dark muted clothing. "We're in Milocca."

The village meant something to both Harrington and Marisa. Each saw it in the other. Silently, they left the car, unable to speak.

Harrington looked down the rutted road lined with disheveled houses made of mud, straw, and rock, Below, orange groves filled the small valley where children were working right alongside their fathers. Mothers peered curiously from curtained windows as Harrington inspected the scenery.

Beside him, Marisa said softly, "This is where my papa was born. He brought me here to the village of Milocca."

"What is this," Harrington demanded of Marcus. "Some kind of sick joke? Vincent Morello was from Milocca."

Marisa's reaction to Vincent's name went unnoticed by Harrington as Marcus forcibly led him down the road.

"He knows Vincent Morello!" Marisa said, throwing off Julio's hand from her arm. "How does he know him?"

"That's what you are going to find out. Now come along. Someone is waiting to meet you."

The man inside the house lay in a bed at the window. He was blind and obviously enjoyed the warmth of the sun on his face. He must have been sixty. His face was like that of a saint. Harrington looked at Marcus.

"He's a priest."

Marisa and Harrington were mystified, but drawn to the two chairs beside the bed. Marcus and Julio waited outside.

"Marisa? Harrington?"

"Yes?"

The man smiled, showing beautiful teeth, a rarity among the peasants. "I'm so happy you came to see me at last."

The man was dying. He spoke in a soft, thickly accented English and took deep breaths in between his sentences. Still, he appeared serene, as though welcoming the rest he was about to take.

Finally, with effort, he talked again. "I am a man like you who has been wronged by Vincent Morello. Harrington," he said in this thick Italian accent, "Marcus told me that Vincent attacked you and that he killed Vincent in self-defense. Marisa, we have much to thank Harrington for. Vincent killed Cara's father. He also hurt you, Marisa, indirectly."

"He raped my mother," Marisa said softly. "My papa thought I was Vincent Morello's child, and my papa hated me because of it."

Harrington looked at Marisa anew. Was he reliving the past?

"Did your father ever tell you that?" the old man asked gently.

Marisa's lips trembled. "I don't remember."

"Was it your mother who told you?"

Marisa tried to recall. "She was out of her mind so much of the time. Maybe she did mention it."

"You see, Vincent left Sicily before you were conceived, but your mother never forgot the rape and got confused.

"Vincent Morello put his identification on your papa, and your papa was arrested and imprisoned and tortured. Vincent forced himself on your mama. He raped her, violated her. When the authorities arrested him, they found out Vincent was a Mafioso, and your papa was released.

"Your mama came back to Palermo to be with your father, in 1927. Vincent Morello had escaped from prison in 1929 and sailed directly to America. You were born in 1930. Then your papa found out your mama had been raped. That's when all the confusion began. Your mother had harbored the secret and it drove her insane. You, the innocent child, were caught in your mother's confusion and influenced to think you might have caused your mother's illness. You didn't."

He had said the words so gently, Marisa felt no pain, just an enormous relief. That's exactly what she'd thought all these years.

"Are you sure about this?" Marisa said, trying to put the new facts in their places. "Why did my papa bring me here then? Why am I afraid of this place?"

"That is easily explained. Your papa was dying. He wanted you beside him. With your mother's interpretation of the facts, you were mixed up, too. You were just a child. It was I who took you back to your mama in Florence."

"You! I remember you now!"

The old man's smile was radiant. "You were beautiful then when I could see." He reached out with trembling fingers and touched her face. Marisa leaned forward. "And I see you still are. Now you must let me talk to Harrington alone. Then you and I will have a private conversation. I'm sorry to be so abrupt, but you are late and I have just a little time."

Marisa kissed his forehead then joined the men outside while Harrington spoke to the old man.

"Marcus told me of your situation. He did not betray your confidence. It is safe with me. First, you have your father to thank for our meeting. Joe Field visited me in Palermo a few years ago and then again recently. Your father wanted you to relive your experience with Cara through Marisa. I am glad Marisa is adjusting to the truth. Joe wanted me to lie. He think's all priests are corruptible especially Sicilians." The old man laughed, "And I was for a very long time."

He choked, and Harrington handed him a glass of water. He drank gratefully.

"You must get over your guilt about Vincent," the priest told Harrington quietly. "Your son—Vincent Morello's son, Cara's son, should not be with your father."

Harrington heard the urgency in his voice.

Harrington felt comfortable enough with the old man to say, "Why should I take your word?"

The old man smiled so serenely, Harrington wondered if he had heard him.

"I am a priest," the man said gently. "I am also Vincent Morello's brother. I've come home to die in our parents' home."

CHAPTER XXIII

J oe Field was waiting for Winston in the Windsor Royal
library. Once the door was locked and Winston was seated
behind his desk, Joe thrust a series of magazines in front of
him.

Winston took the April 1952 issue of *Confidential
Magazine* with Harrington's photograph gracing its cover
and opened to the place marked. He glanced at the article and
saw his grandson's picture and name in print along with little
Kierston Garvin's. The story was written by Roy Sharp.

"What's this?" Winston demanded.

"Kierston's picture was obviously taken with Harrington
in Idaho. I know you didn't want Jason's photo in there, but
it sure does make Harrington look like a terrible father. Look
at Kierston's face! She's horrified. Jason doesn't look much
better."

Confidential Magazine under the byline of Roy Sharp
had printed a series of articles with photographs of Marisa
and Harrington's visit to Sicily. The rest of the country picked
up Roy's story.

Facts, dates, and quotations were made up. All the old

clippings of Vincent Morello were in the tabloid. Marisa was
raped instead of her mother. Harrington and Marcus
murdered Vincent Morello who had murdered Cara's father
and abused Cara. Harrington's life was colored as troubled,
filled with bad luck. Winston had given strict orders to
Arlene Habor. No mention of him or Jason. For months
now, Harrington's story had been bantered about and hashed
and rehashed in every tabloid throughout the nation. The
press refused to leave Harrington and Marisa alone, although
neither he nor she had talked to a one of them.

World Studios Stage 3 was surrounded with security
when shooting ended on *Your Year With Mine* in November
of 1951 and filming began on *Tomorrow My Love* in March
of 1952. Harrington knew all of the crew were loyal to him
and to Conrad, and therefore to Marisa. It was a closed set.
Although the press stood vigil outside the World Studios lot
on Pico Boulevard, no one was admitted without Thomas
Garvin's consent.

"Was this your idea, Joe?" Winston demanded.

"Well, sir, I saw that Custody Order that Garvin sent
you. Harrington wants Jason back. I thought it would help—
that you would be pleased."

Winston frowned. Thomas Garvin had fired WRIB and
hired its toughest competitor. Back on his feet because of
Anaid, Thomas was confident about using World Studios as
a blanket of security for Harrington and Conrad, although
Conrad's rumors still lingered. Everything was too quiet.
Almost as if carefully planned.

"Don't ever do anything without my permission,"
Winston said irritably, although he was secretly pleased. "By
the way, Joe, your little plan didn't work quite the way you
thought, did it. Marisa and Harrington seem to be coping
despite all the revelations you put them through."

Joe had been trying to figure out how Marcus had found
him out, but he wasn't about to tell Winston that.

"You thought it was a good idea at the time. I don't
know what went wrong. Obviously we underestimated their
love for each other."

Winston came forward in his chair and pounded on the
table. "Don't make me laugh! You were supposed to plant
those reports in Marisa's hotel room in London. You never
did. They would have made her look like a traitor."

"You know Harrington and Marisa never made it to London. They headed straight on to Sicily."

"But you left London before you knew they had rearranged their flight to Sicily. As soon as Thomas Garvin arrived in London, you fled back here to New York. My point is that you didn't follow orders. Now we're in a bind. Marisa's out of reach. We don't know what actually happened in Sicily except from Roy Sharp's photographs, which were all full of love and nothing I can use.

"We need information, Joe. Arlene and Roy are totally ineffectual without it. World is locked up tight and Harrington's new home in Malibu is impregnable. Marisa's the key. Are you sure they don't know about you?"

"That's why I returned from London!" Joe said, trying to clear himself. "I didn't want them to detect me."

Winston leaned back in his chair, his elegant hands laced in front of him. "Precisely."

Joe stared at Winston nervously. "Well, they don't know about me. There's no way."

Joe had missed something. Marcus had been in Europe, too. Covering his tracks carefully, Marcus had evaded Winston's bodyguards. No one knew where he had gone or who he saw. But Marcus must have discovered something, which had helped Marisa and Harrington through their crisis. Why else would they have left for Sicily so abruptly? After the trick Joe had pulled on Harrington and Marisa, Winston was actually surprised that Marcus hadn't retaliated. Maybe the custody issue was the beginning of it.

"Call Arlene," Winston said suddenly. "Let her know I'd better read an article tomorrow about Conrad in the Los Angeles *Times* or she'll not only lose her job but her national reputation!"

"Why? She's been loyal."

"I don't tolerate mistakes!" Winston said, pointing to *Confidential Magazine*. "She'd better get control of that Roy Sharp byline! And tell Mr. Sharp to keep his nose clean!" Winston rose. "Now, let's get downstairs. I have to call my attorney."

An hour later, ten-year-old Jason ran down the hall carrying a newspaper under his arm and skidded to a halt at the library door. He knocked impatiently. When his grandfather didn't answer, he tried the doorknob. To his dismay, the door was locked.

As Michael Christian said, Jason's grandfather sure didn't need this huge old house. He spent most of his time in the library. Often Michael and Bobby had to wait to play with Jason who had to wait to ask his grandfather's permission before they went on one sort of expedition or another.

Today was no exception, except that Jason didn't have Michael and Bobby to keep him company the entire morning. Winston had shut down his Windsor Royal business operations. All Todd Industries employees were relocating to Manhattan.

'Well, I'm not waiting any longer,' Jason told himself. He had read a lot about Conrad Coleman in the newspapers. Conrad Coleman was his father's friend. His grandfather had to help Conrad Coleman. He was in trouble!

Jason ran back down the hall and entered the Renaissance Room, crossed to the French doors, which opened onto the veranda, and raced outside over the marble floor on the veranda to the French doors of the library. He peeked in, but the curtains blocked his view. Brusquely, he rapped on the beveled glass.

When his grandfather didn't answer, he twisted the doorknob. Much to his delight, the door opened. He pushed aside the curtain and entered.

"Where are you, Grandfather?" he asked puzzled, looking around the empty library.

He walked over to Winston's desk and started to sit down when he saw the copy of *Confidential Magazine*. His eyes opened in excitement upon seeing Harrington's cover photo. But when he looked inside and saw the picture of Harrington, himself, and Kierston with the headline, he let out a screech.

Before he knew what he was doing, he was running out of the library with the magazine. He ran and ran, fighting back the huge wave of emotion thundering in his chest.

"Jim! Jim!" he yelled, flying into the stable corridor. "Where are you, Jim!"

It was 5:00 P.M. The stable hands were gone. Jason was beside himself with frustration. He felt his hands tremble as he looked again at the magazine.

"What's all the hollering about?" Jim said, coming into the stable.

"Just look at this!" Jason declared, running up to him.

Jim took the magazine. "Who gave you this?" he demanded.

"Is it true? Did Father abandon me? Doesn't he care about me at all?"

"It isn't true," Jim answered vehemently.

"Then why did they print it?"

"You answer my question first. Where did you get this?"

Jason had never heard Jim raise his voice. Neither had the horses who were peeking out curiously from their stalls.

"It was on Grandfather's desk," he answered at last.

Jim led Jason to his office where he pulled out a stool to let Jason sit down. When an animal was hurt, you got close and soothed them. People were no different. Jim opened up the magazine and got close to Jason to show him he cared.

"Now, you've never seen me give you any pictures like this have you, or any articles? And you haven't seen any articles from your grandfather out of this magazine before, have you?"

Jason's mind immediately went to work. "No," he said, staring at his own picture with Harrington.

"Now, look at your part of the picture, your face," Jim said. "You haven't seen your father since you were nearly five years old. You didn't look this way when you were four, now did you?"

Jason peered down at the magazine. "I sure didn't."

"I'll say you didn't. This picture's been taken in the last year. See how tall you are? And look at your face. Why, you're ten years old, a young man now, not a kid."

Jason smirked and shook his head. "Don't get carried away, Jim. I'm still a kid and you know it." He reached for the magazine to inspect it more closely. "Boy, am I dumb. I should have seen that before you did. Why that's the picture of me that Grandfather had taken out on the great lawn— and the picture of father—that's from his first movie. I have that picture in my scrapbook!" His fingers touched the page as if trying to figure something out. "How did they put those pictures together and make them into one?"

"I don't know," Jim said. "You're the photographer."

"Yeah," Jason said, so relieved he was now intrigued.

"If a paper would do something like that, do you think they'd print the truth?"

"No," Jason said emphatically. Still staring at the magazine he asked, "Is this really Mr. Garvin's daughter?"

Jim nodded. "That's what your father said. Beautiful little thing, isn't she?"

Suddenly, Jason closed the magazine and looked at Jim long and hard. "So you do talk to Father. You said he told you about Kierston."

Jim nodded. "Oh boy, I let that slip."

Jason looked at Jim's startled expression and wondered why he felt so funny. All of a sudden, he wasn't so confident about things. Although his grandfather had said he was supposed to be a man, he caved in to a new sensation and, to his bewilderment, started to cry. "I miss my dad, Jim," he sobbed. "I want to see him!"

The poor little guy, Jim thought, hugging Jason. Always so reasonable. Jason probably should have let out these emotions long ago. Damn Winston! Jason cried and cried into Jim's shoulder and Jim wondered what to say.

Sniffling a bit himself, Jim tried to think of something to say. He knew Jason would be embarrassed for crying once he recovered. "When something builds up in ya, well, if you don't let it out, then you end up kicking in the stable door like Old Silver," he rambled. "I'm glad you're crying. I'm sorta teary myself. Don't fret, boy. Your father loves you. He's even tried to see you, Jason, but somehow your grandfather always finds out when he's coming and takes you away."

Jason looked up startled, tears rolling down his face. "He's tried to see me, Jim? When?"

Jim told Jason about all the times since the call he made to Harris when on tour with *The Restless* in 1950.

Jason's brow furrowed. "Why would Grandfather do that, Jim? Why didn't Father tell me he'd tried to see me?"

Jim sighed, knowing he had overstepped his bounds.

"Your father didn't want you to worry, so he never said anything. . . . Your grandfather? . . . Well . . ." Jim groped for words. "That's hard to say . . . uh . . ."

"Grandfather doesn't like Father?"

Jim pondered on how to answer. He was in over his head. "They're different. You know, like Old Silver and Sable Lady here at the stables. Old Silver's very aggressive like your grandfather. Know what I mean?"

"I think so," Jason said as he wiped his eyes with his

sleeve. "Yeah, I do. Grandfather needs attention."

"Yes, and your father doesn't want you hurt. He would die if he knew you'd been hurt," Jim said. "Just like I would."

Jason threw his arms around Jim's neck. "I love you, Jim. Why, if you weren't here I think I'd be in a lot of trouble. I'll never forget you. Never. And I'm happy you talk to Father. I'm happy he tried to see me. It . . . it hurts not to see him, Jim, but I think I understand. Can you give him a message, though? Just tell him I love him, will you, Jim?"

Tears again appeared in Jim's eyes. "I'll tell him, but I think he already knows."

Jason jumped off the stool and picked up the magazine. "I'm going to put this back."

Jim blew his nose and smiled sheepishly. "Good idea."

"Bye, Jim," Jason said cheerfully, ". . . and thanks."

Jim watched Jason go, thinking he was probably the most resilient person he knew.

On Friday morning Arlene Habor's column read:

"Conrad Coleman is a disgrace to the fine upstanding patriots who are a part of the motion picture industry. Although his motion pictures were at one time hailed as classics, after careful review of each film, it is undeniable that they have slipped their messages throughout America, corrupting the moral fiber of this country, feeding on America's people, infiltrating our free society with Communist propaganda.

He is now being harbored on a World Studios' lot, by none other than the Chairman of the Board, Thomas Garvin. It is time for loyal Americans everywhere to stand up and be heard. A dangerous man, like Conrad Coleman, should be banished from World Studios' lots—and the free world!"

"It worked," Marcus said. "The custody issue set him off. We can proceed. Are you two up to it?"

Harrington and Marisa faced him, sitting on the patio of

their Malibu home behind guarded gates. They had both been relaxing, sunning, when Marcus came to visit. They had isolated themselves. For the first time in their lives they truly were having a vacation. Both golden tan, clad in white bathing suits, they looked healthier and happier than Marcus had seen them in months.

As drastically as Vincent Morello had changed their lives, Carlos Morello had pieced them back together. They were changed people. Ironically, Carlos had died a few hours after their return to Palermo. It was as though their past had died with him.

"I hate having Jason in the middle of it," Harrington said.

Marisa touched his arm. "He should be with you, my love. You're his father."

Harrington had not been able to disclose Vincent Morello's violation of Cara. Jason had to be protected for now and always. He and Marcus were suspicious after the series of articles in the papers. What did Winston know? The stories about Marisa were eerily similar to Cara's history.

"Jason should be with me. You heard what Jim said. Jason was devastated when he read that *Confidential* article." Harrington squeezed her hand, then got up and restlessly walked over to get a drink. "Anyone else?"

"Wine," Marisa called out, glancing at Marcus and signaling he should continue.

"Give me a Coke," Marcus said. "I know this might sound strange, but I'm worried." When Harrington returned, he completed his thought. "If Winston uses Arlene as a scapegoat, she could be in real danger. She knows too much. She could expose him and Joe and Winston's whole operation. We could use Arlene as our star witness. Same for Marisa, at least where Joe's concerned."

"My heart's breaking for Arlene," Harrington said, narrowing his eyes. "How is Roy Sharp doing?"

"Singing, thanks to Marisa."

"Does Winston have any idea?"

"Absolutely not. We have Roy talking to Arlene every day just like he's supposed to."

Harrington kissed Marisa full on the mouth. "You've saved us all, kid. All right. Let's call Laster."

One month later, Thomas and Katharine threw open the doors of Garvinhouse to the press, members of the motion picture industry, and politicians. The invitations read that Thomas and Katharine were having a special screening at Garvinhouse's two-hundred-seat theater. The title of the movie was not disclosed.

Harrington was on edge tonight. The FBI had questioned Winston about Joe. Winston flatly denied he had anything to do with Field. He opened up Windsor Royal to a search. The agents came up with nothing. J. Edgar Hoover told Laster French that if he ever bothered his good friend Winston Todd again, his career was over. Harrington was apprehensive about Joe's anonymity and, therefore, Marisa's safety.

Thomas had also done his part trying to ascertain what evidence the House un-American Activities Committee had against Conrad and trying to garner support for him. When Congressman Bates told him to be "careful of the company he kept," Thomas told him he might take his own advice. Then he told Bates what was in "Diana's File" regarding his life. Bates did a fast turnaround.

"So here we are, my love," Marisa said, reading Harrington's thoughts. "We don't have Joe, but we have Bates."

"You're getting pretty sophisticated with the score card."

"Tonight," she said, kissing him, "we'll hit a home run as you Americans say."

Harrington laughed as they crossed the hall to the Garvinhouse library. Thomas and Conrad were in there alone. They crept past, giving their friends some privacy.

"This should be an interesting evening," Thomas was saying.

"I know you never allow the press or the general populace into Garvinhouse," Conrad said quietly. "I know you've been pressured by unions, lost employees, and have felt the repercussions from Wall Street for letting me use your facilities. You've even lost clients. Saying thank you isn't enough."

Thomas joined him at the study window, which overlooked Beverly Hills and downtown Los Angeles. The stars twinkled over the city lights like flickering candles. They stood there quietly for a moment and then Thomas said:

"Did it ever occur to you in 1928 that you were taking a huge risk, helping a ghetto boy? Especially one who had a chip on his shoulder and a juvenile record a mile long."

Conrad chuckled, straightening up his five-foot-six-inch frame, which was clad in an impeccable brown gabardine. "No, it never did."

They looked out the window once more. Thomas placed a hand on Conrad's shoulder. Conrad had embraced him in the same way on their first meeting. It was a singular moment for them both, one that stirred memories. At last they heard the approaching voices and proceeded down the hall.

"Do you think Marcus will make it?" Conrad asked.

"I'm sure of it. The plane's already landed."

A steady flow of VIPs filtered through the doors of Garvinhouse. They were led through the entry, past the old oak living room to a large open foyer. There, doors had been thrown open leading to the two-hundred-seat screening room, which had an enormous library adjacent to it. Typical of Thomas's no-nonsense approach, the library was purposely placed in view of the screening room where guests, who watched movies for entertainment, were reminded that the motion-picture industry was a combined art form and business.

Marisa and Harrington joined the crowd.

"This is my last night as a secret agent," she whispered joyfully.

Harrington laughed. "I'm going to enjoy this."

"Me too."

Arlene Habor came into the library, flanked on both sides by photographers.

"Harrington, darling," she said, coming up to him and Marisa. "Why it's been ages since we talked. And you, Marisa, how stunning you look! I've heard that *Your Year With Mine* and *Tomorrow My Love* are going to be huge successes. I'm delighted for you."

Harrington and Marisa had been listening to the slim, balding senator from California, who continued talking in spite of Arlene's intrusion.

"You Todds are quite a family," he said genuinely. "I heard your little son is a very bright fellow. What are his aspirations?"

"Excuse me, Senator, would you please?" Arlene said

rudely, gesturing for him to step back so that her photographer could take pictures of Marisa and Harrington.

Harrington guided Marisa around Arlene and resumed talking to the senator. "He says he's going to work at Todd Industries. And I tend to believe him."

The senator chortled in amusement. "I have a child about . . ."

"Harrington, dear, if you must talk to the senator, please look towards the camera."

As Harrington turned around, the camera started clicking. Pressure was building, and Marisa's heart was too full. She opened her purse and took out a long slender cigar and lit it. She winked at Harrington, hoping to lighten his mood. "Do you like it?"

"Very becoming," he said. "Senator, what do you think?"

Arlene had instructed the photographer to stop. "Marisa, dear, please get rid of that horrid cigar."

Harrington laughed, turned to the senator, and totally ignored Arlene.

"Everyone in this town is afraid they aren't interesting enough, Senator. Marisa was spoofing and out of character, but many actors think they have to maintain their image at all costs. That's what sells tickets. That's what keeps the public intrigued. Unfortunately, artists are afraid the myth will crumble. It's such a fragile line. And people like Arlene Habor know it, isn't that right, Arlene?"

"Why, what are you talking about?" Arlene asked, bewildered.

"You dangle that thread over people's heads reminding them that with one flick of your pen you can tell the world they're frauds. But as for me, I'm not about to let some frustrated actress from yesterday's yearbook dictate my life. So if you don't mind, I'd like to talk to the senator without your interference."

"Why are you saying this? I'm your biggest fan!" Arlene said in total confusion.

But Harrington didn't hear her. Kierston had wandered downstairs and stood in the library doorway in her nightgown. "Will you excuse us a minute?" he said to the senator.

He and Marisa walked through the gathering. Harrington swept Kierston up in his arms. She rubbed her eyes.

"I thought you were asleep," he said, walking her down to the foyer.

"Yes," Marisa said. "We would have come upstairs and said good-night."

Kierston placed a loving hand on Harrington's shoulder and smiled sleepily at Marisa. "There was too much noise for me to sleep." Kierston opened her eyes wide. "You didn't want to stay in there, did you?"

It was intriguing and touching that Kierston was more perceptive than most of the adults they met—and all the more amazing because the little darling had been having troubles at school. Her classmates had bedeviled her about Conrad being a Communist. Kierston was having nightmares.

Harrington and Marisa were upset that even Kierston was involved.

"No, we didn't," Harrington said. "We'd much prefer to be with you."

In the hall, Harrington sat down in a large leather chair with Kierston in his lap. Marisa sat beside him. Kierston was wide awake now and said, "Will you and Marisa take me to the drive-in theater?"

"Sure, what would you like to see?"

"*Your Year With Mine* and *Tomorrow My Love*."

"Your wish is our command," Harrington said, holding her close.

Over the noise, Marisa heard Katharine calling out Kierston's name. "I'll go tell her where Kierston is." She kissed Kierston then Harrington and left for the staircase.

Kierston was playing with her hair, looking thoughtful. "Everyone's been sad lately."

"Don't fret, Kierston," he said, trying to comfort her, for he would have preferred facing a firing squad rather than hurting her. "See how much fun it is to grow up?" he asked, his eyes dancing with affection.

Kierston giggled, then grew somber. "Daddy says older people sometimes carry heavy loads." She shook her little head in bewilderment. Then she stooped over, her back hunched. "But I don't see people walking around like this."

Harrington threw back his head and laughed, much to Kierston's delight and surprise.

Katharine suppressed a smile, and glanced at Marisa. They were coming down the stairs and saw Harrington tickle

Kierston. "He loves her as if she were his own."

Marisa detected apprehension beneath Katharine's charming façade. She was terribly worried about Kierston.

"It will almost be over tonight, Katharine. Harrington's as worried about Jason as you are about Kierston."

Katharine squeezed her hand at the bottom of the stairs. "I know everything's going to be fine." She laughed suddenly. "If only I could get my daughter to stay in bed."

After Kierston and Katharine disappeared up the stairs, Harrington and Marisa greeted the New York *Times* columnist and old friend of Diana's Sol Chandelier and Harrington's reporter friend Jay Gransberg of the Los Angeles *Times*.

Thomas saw the reporters from the library and came out into the hall. "Thank you for coming, gentlemen. Now that you have arrived, I think we can begin . . ." David Britt nodded from the doorway. "Yes, we can begin," Thomas said, sounding mysterious.

David Britt asked for everyone's attention in the library: "As you all know, for the last several months a rumor has been circulating through Hollywood that Conrad Coleman is a Communist. Thomas Garvin would like to say a few words on this subject."

There was a crescendo of whispers and then silence as Thomas stepped forward. Harrington and Marisa stood in the doorway. Katharine weaved through the crowd to Thomas's side.

"During the last several months, a cloud of suspicion has surrounded my friend Conrad Coleman." He watched as reporters began to take notes. "Congressman Bates from California, who is a member of HUAC, told me that his committee had no evidence to support this rumor. He suggested I make inquiries at the American Legion and IATSE to find out if they had any evidence to support the suspicions. Those two organizations denied emphatically having any knowledge or information concerning Conrad's ties to the Communist movement. The rumor has remained despite the absence of one single shred of evidence.

"Conrad Coleman has a distinguished military record, having fought for America in World War I and served his country in World War II. He's been decorated with the highest military honors. He supports this capitalist society and all his films deal with freedom of choice and how success comes to those who work. To my mind accusing Conrad Coleman of anything un-American is a mockery of our system."

All eyes turned to Conrad as he addressed the press and members of the industry:

"Normally, I would never defend myself against such accusations," he said, "but I have many friends who have supported me and are now feeling the pressures and repercussions of that support. I will leave my views on this to be interpreted through my work. I, along with all my friends, are very happy you could come here tonight to finally hear for the first time, as I will hear for the first time, what evidence there is to link me with the Communist Party. Arlene Habor has consented to tell us her findings."

"Me?" Arlene said, in sudden embarrassment.

A murmur went through the crowd as all eyes turned to her.

"Well, now, Miss Habor," the California senator said, "if this is true, the United States Senate would very much like to hear what you have to say. Possibly we should call you before the Senate Committee."

The press scribbled down the senator's words.

Arlene composed herself, straightening her hat and smoothing her dress. Attempting an appearance of sincerity she began. "I have nothing to say."

"That's something new," someone in the crowd called out, causing the tension to momentarily fill with laughter.

"I don't know if this will help or not," Marisa said innocently. "But I heard that you had some information about *The Rich in Spirit*."

Her words had the proper effect on Arlene. "Well, I, well, I do have information. But I didn't think this was the place or time to talk about it." She pulled herself together and said condescendingly, "According to my sources, when Conrad Coleman was filming *The Rich in Spirit*, he associated with Communists. In addition, John Stevens wrote the film, and he is a friend to the Hollywood Ten!"

"And here I thought you liked me, Arlene."

The crowd shifted their attention to the doorway where John Stevens and Marcus stood beside Harrington. Dressed in a three-piece black suit with his wild white hair combed,

John held himself with the dignified carriage of an elderly statesman. He was, and looked, above reproach.

He shook hands as he came forward, making his way to Conrad's side. "We certainly do meet on the strangest of occasions, Conrad."

Then John surveyed the room, commanding a sober mood. "I am much more of a quote-un-quote liberal than my friend here," he said, glancing at Conrad. "I'm also proud to say so. Ah Thomas, I can see you aren't exactly happy with the way I'm proceeding. Well, I've never been one to apologize for my political affiliations." He noted that Arlene Habor suddenly looked quite smug. "Arlene, is that all the information you have? That I'm friendly with some writers?"

"Isn't that enough?" Arlene said indignantly.

"You're smarter than that, Arlene. What else is on your mind?" Arlene refused to speak. "One day, madame, I can assure you, you'll be most embarrassed by your accusations . . ." He turned again to the others. "Earlier I said I've never apologized for my political affiliations. The reason is, I don't have any. I've never backed a party. I back the man. Now as far as Conrad and our film *The Rich in Spirit* . . ."

"That is suspect, too!" Arlene declared.

"You, my dear woman, as of a year ago, were one of Conrad's most ardent supporters. Look through your archives and you'll find copious words of praise over a period of years about his films. And you will also find, if my memory serves me, an equal amount of praise of me! Of course, I never read the stuff myself: Conrad told me about it."

In spite of the serious moment, John received a laugh.

"Nevertheless," he continued, "Thomas has graciously lent out his screening room to you, his guests, so that you may view *The Rich in Spirit*. For those of you who have seen it, indulge us and view it again." He glanced at Conrad. "Old friend, do you have anything to add?"

Conrad looked at the reporters. "Concerning the evidence now laid before me, I demand a hearing by the House un-American Activities Committee to refute these accusations. I will also be calling witnesses to testify on my behalf." He almost added, "In particular, Winston Todd, since he financed *The Rich in Spirit*," but he refrained. They had other plans for Winston.

Arlene felt the crowd turn against her. She was desperate to get away and yet had to stay to try and salvage her reputation. She knew she had no choice but to continue on the same course. "I will not be a party to watching a Communist film!" she said, heading for the door, hoping some would follow.

No one did, but Harrington stopped her midway across the room.

"There are a couple of other things that have come to our attention, Arlene. You have been known in this city for many years to be a reputable journalist." Harrington took a file from David Britt. "I have here the most astonishing news . . ."

"What's that?" Arlene demanded. "What are you talking about?"

The crowd started to move towards Harrington when Marisa joined him.

"Let's see," Harrington paused. "Where would you like me to begin? With your alias perhaps? All this time I thought you worked for the Los Angeles *Times*. They were surprised to learn you also worked for *Confidential Magazine* with Roy Sharp. As a matter of fact, Roy Sharp never wrote an article. He was your front man, wasn't he? Roy Sharp is actually your alias."

"I don't know what you're talking about!" Arlene said, trying to push through.

"But Mr. Sharp does. Here's his sworn affidavit," Harrington said, showing a copy to Arlene. "I also have copies of checks payable to Roy Sharp—and he was even kind enough to supply us with a copy of your contract with *Confidential*. You see, the contract reads Roy Sharp, but the social security number is yours. Therefore, you get the checks. We can always confirm this with your bank . . . I think your credibility as a journalist is over."

Thomas came forward and handed Arlene a subpoena. "You have been properly served. Harrington and Marisa are suing you and *Confidential* for slander. Many other actresses and actors are following their lead. You'll be hearing from me in regards to their cases as well . . . possibly a class-action suit."

A buzz went through the crowd. Arlene was white.

Harrington stepped aside to allow her to pass alone. Marcus stood firm. She had to squeeze through the doorway.

She turned back to Harrington. "Do you know what you've just been a party to?"

"It's called justice, Arlene."

"Fans can be fickle, and I do write a column, which your fans read."

"After tonight you won't," Jay Gansberg said. "You're going to make the headlines tomorrow, Arlene, and it won't be in your column, but on the first page of the *Times*."

"That goes for the New York *Times* as well," Sol Chandelier added.

Marcus and Harrington followed after Arlene, down the hall out. Harrington caught her by the arm.

"Marcus insists that I do this. Why, I don't know. Especially after what you've done. But he wants you to have security. Your life is in danger!"

Arlene glanced at Harrington in bitter contempt. "Dare say who is going to threaten me?"

"Winston Todd," Harrington said simply.

Arlene broke into laughter. "You're the one who should fear him, not I. He will take care of everything. Before it's over you two-bit nickle-and-dime Adonis-façade of a no-good actor, you will be walking the streets begging to talk to me."

She turned on her heel and walked out the front door of Garvinhouse as Harrington looked after her incredulously. Then he laughed.

"Marcus! I didn't think she had it in her! Maybe for the first time in her life, Arlene actually was telling the truth."

Marcus grinned in amusement. "Who's pulling whose leg?"

Winston was furious. He had to reschedule his plans to Europe when he received word the following morning of what had taken place at Garvinhouse. Now he was stuck in the library. Again. And with Joe. Again.

The phone buzzed and Winston picked up the receiver. "Yes, Harris. No, you needn't pack the trunk. This will be a short trip. Yes, the Middle-East . . ." he said, drawing out the conversation to make Joe more fidgety. Although he wasn't going anywhere, he wanted Joe to think he was. "Saudi

Arabian oil. Do you have Jason's things packed for Groton? Yes, he's going to summer school. Good. Oh, and Harris, did you place the Conrad Coleman article at Jason's breakfast plate this morning? Good." He hung up and returned his attention to Joe. "Now what about Arlene?"

"Uh, well," Joe said nervously, "she's lost her job."

Joe showed Winston that day's New York *Times* and Los Angeles *Times* about Arlene.

"She defied me!" Winston stormed, throwing the paper in the trash. "I don't tolerate mistakes. That rumor about Conrad would have lingered on for months if she had done as she was told. She was never supposed to use that information on John Stevens!"

"I think Arlene was O.K. Marisa Benito was the one."

"And who's to blame for Marisa? You told her Arlene worked under an alias, didn't you?"

Joe flinched, but avoided the question. "At least Arlene never divulged her source. I think . . ."

"I pay you to carry out my orders, not to think! Get rid of Arlene. And take care of Marisa!"

"Yes sir," Joe answered with startled attentiveness.

Winston paused, sitting motionless in his chair, waiting for his words to sink in, then very deliberately came forward in his chair, calmer now, with the air of a respectable gentleman who really detested having to dirty his hands by being so explicit with someone who should have known how to do his job. He pushed back his chair and contemplated the situation.

His contacts at HUAC had started pressing for information about Conrad's Communist ties. He had told Joe to forget it. But he was furious. Because of Joe's stupidity he was going to lose some valuable contacts. Bates, especially, was acting strangely.

"Once this is cleared up, I think you should leave the estate for awhile."

"I'd like some time off, but not now. Thomas Garvin told the FBI I was in the East. With you questioned, and the house searched, you can kinda see my predicament, and yours if I was picked up."

Winston smiled expansively. "They won't be looking for you at my London home."

"London!"

"Of course," Winston said, guiding him to the door. "You're heading back to London. This time you have to promise to stay there."

They opened the secret paneled door. Winston fastened it shut behind them.

"Is everything up to date in here?" Winston asked, opening the solid wood door to the Operations Room.

"Sure, let me show you."

Much to Joe's surprise, Raymond Baren was already inside.

Winston closed the door.

"How do you think Marcus got your alias, Bill Reed, Joe?"

Again Joe was surprised. How had Winston known they had found him out. He nervously flexed his right hand, although he tried to appear outwardly calm.

"I have a hunch he must have photographed those special employee files in your private safe at headquarters, otherwise how would he have known?"

Winston nodded at Raymond. "That's the same information Raymond had. You've exonerated yourself, Raymond. Welcome back to the fold."

"Grandfather, can't you help Father's friend, Conrad Coleman?" Jason asked Winston that evening at dinner. "The newspaper says he's in trouble!"

"How do you know who Conrad Coleman is?" he demanded.

Jason didn't flinch. "I read the newspapers. Like the article in the morning's paper."

"What have you read about him?"

Jason sat up very straight. "That he makes Father's movies. That he is known all over the world. His films are supposed to be classics," Jason said with distinct expertise.

"I see," Winston said. He wiped his mouth and leaned back casually in his chair. "So you think he's an important man. If he's so important, why can't he help himself?"

Jason thought about this long and hard. "I don't know."

"You don't know, because Conrad Coleman is not an important man. The news media writes about him and you believe what you read. Let me show you an example of what I

mean." Winston picked up the *Confidential Magazine* Jason
had placed back in Winston's library. "This magazine prints
lies. It's not worthy of any discussion except to make this one
point. As you can see, your father's picture is on the cover.
Now before I show you what's inside I want to emphasize that
it prints untruths." Winston opened the magazine.

Jason stared at the headline. He wanted to tell Winston
he had seen it, but that would have given Jim away. With
restraint, he listened to Winston's explanation of the facts.
They were just as he and Jim had concluded.

"Is Conrad Coleman an important man or not? He gets
himself into a bind that he can't get out of. I've shown you
that newspapers and magazines can print lies to make people
look good or," he said, pointing to the magazine, "bad.
Everything in Hollywood is created, a fantasy. You can't
believe anything you read about the city or its people.
Therefore, I think it's a total waste of time to be filling up
scrapbooks with clippings that aren't true."

Jason was surprised that his grandfather knew about his
secret treasures. His grandfather seemed to know everything.

"It's beneath you to think of Hollywood," Winston
continued. "You and I have more important things to do."

Jason's brow furrowed. "But your pictures have been in
the papers, and I've read all sorts of articles about you. Are
they lies, too?"

Winston regarded Jason with cunning, thinking that the
little fellow was developing quicker than he had expected.
"There are three ways to print a story. For you—against you
—or just the plain truth. My stories are the truth. Your
father's stories and Conrad's have been printed in their favor,
but they haven't been the truth. Now those lies are catching
up with Conrad. As you mentioned earlier, he's been
portrayed as an extremely influential man. But," Winston
said, flipping his hand, "when he's put to the test—when he
has to defend himself against accusations that aren't true, he
can't. He's not that powerful or important. Whereas, I am."

Jason's eyes lit up. "Then you can help Mr. Coleman?"

"Not so fast, my boy," Winston cautioned. "There is a
lesson for you to learn. I have told you that men get what they
deserve. I'll help Coleman because you asked. But I'm doing
it for you, not for him. I'm doing you a big favor, and you're
indebted to me. Someday you'll have to return that favor.

Even if it means letting me ride Sable Lady!"

Jason looked upset. He hadn't quite realized what he had done. "Yes, Grandfather."

"Now what about those scrapbooks. Do you still think it's important to waste time working on them?"

"I suppose not," Jason said sadly.

"And are Conrad and your father important or not?"

"Not as important as you, Grandfather."

"Then it's settled," Winston said firmly. "Because you asked, I will give the peasants a helping hand, but just this once. If they get themselves into trouble again, I won't lift a finger. I have a business to run."

"Father's not a peasant," Jason said, defending Harrington.

Winston sighed. "I'm afraid it's true. Regrettable as it may seem, your father decided to be one of them, and now of course the press prints lies about him, too. I don't understand why he joined them, but that's the case."

Jason's face dropped as Winston continued to talk through dinner. He didn't even pick up his fork. He would have said a lot more to his grandfather. It was a big mistake not letting him see his father. But he didn't say anything because he might hurt his grandfather.

For many years, he had snuck downstairs at night. Winston was usually sitting sad and alone in front of his grandmother's portrait in the drawing room. Jason didn't know quite what to make of it, just that it made him feel sorry for his grandfather. Somehow, he sensed that he was his grandfather's only real friend.

At 8:00 P.M. Eastern time on Friday, May 15, 1952, Todd Industries' Public Relations department called the major newspapers and television and radio stations in New York. Winston Todd was holding a major press conference at Todd Industries Headquarters the following morning at 9:00 A.M.

At 7:00 P.M. Pacific time on Friday, Sol Chandelier contacted Harrington at Garvinhouse with the news. Winston would comment on the accusations against Conrad.

At 9:00 P.M. Pacific time, Conrad and John joined Harrington, Marisa, and the Garvins at Garvinhouse.

John was irate. "I'd like to blast the bastard right out of the water!"

"Calm down," Thomas cautioned. "We have a lot of work ahead, John. Marcus, what's the status on Arlene Habor and Joe?"

"No news. You know how that makes Laster and me feel. We want Joe bad," he said darkly. "And Arlene spotted Sy outside her apartment this morning. She called the police. He's been warned to stay away or he'll land in jail. He's surveying the area, but he can't stay close enough to help her if she's in trouble. I talked to Laster. His hands are tied. As you can imagine, his association with us hasn't done much for his popularity at the agency. I think he might quit before they fire him. Right now he's on vacation leave . . ."

"We'll always help Laster. Assure him he needn't worry about a job. As for Arlene, well, Arlene's her own worst enemy," Thomas said irritably. "Now, I've already spoken to Walter Kent and Congressman Bates to garner support. Bates has already started the word circulating in D.C. that Winston had purposely set up Conrad, smeared John's name, sabotaged Garvin Enterprises, and even tried to damage his own son's career."

Walter Kent suggested that Winston would support Conrad to protect himself. Walter had his own personal loyalties for Diana's family. He was intent on discrediting Winston at any cost. In "Diana's File," Winston had notes indicating he was trying to set up Walter in a stock scandal. Fortunately Walter got the information in time or his name would have been ruined. Walter had been delighted to hear that Thomas was going to broaden Garvin Enterprises' power base and move Katharine and Kierston to New York, as much for business as for Kierston's well-being.

On Saturday morning at 9:00 A.M. Eastern time, Winston's news conference began.

> "When I read Arlene Habor's column last week, I was shocked and dismayed to hear about Conrad Coleman's predicament. I am setting the record straight. I financed *The Rich in Spirit*, and I can assure you that I hold Conrad Coleman in the highest regard. Through his art, Conrad has represented our country admirably, here and abroad. Whoever has accused him of being a Communist is sorely misinformed."

The chairman of HUAC followed Winston to the podium and read a terse statement condemning Arlene Habor's attack.

At 7:00 A.M. Saturday, Pacific time, Arlene Habor's telephone rang, jarring her out of a deep sleep. A reporter from the New York *Times* asked for a statement. "About what?" she demanded, rubbing her eyes. When she was informed about Winston's press conference, she abruptly hung up the phone. 'That bastard!' she thought, heading for her desk. While the phone rang and rang, she hunted for incriminating letters addressed to her from Joe Field. They were gone. Shakily, she rushed to the bathroom and took three tranquilizers. Then she sat down at the typewriter and forced her memory to recapture the essence of Joe's letters. Into the afternoon, she worked on preparing a statement. At 3:00 P.M. Pacific time, her phone was still ringing. She picked up the receiver, pushed down the button to hang up on the caller and clear the line, and called her city desk. In a very self-assured and authoritative voice, she began to read off her statement.

"Hold it Arlene . . . I said hold it. Goddamnit! You don't work here any more."

Arlene panicked. "At least hear my story! I have substantial proof. There were letters written from Winston Todd's agent. He was the source of my evidence against Conrad and now the bastard is using me as a scapegoat."

"You're a desperate woman, Arlene. I know Winston Todd has a controversial reputation, but he would never make a public stand if you had information like that. He isn't stupid. You've already embarrassed me once. How could you have worked for *Confidential*? To say nothing of defaming Conrad Coleman! I'm writing a letter of apology to our readers for your Friday article. Don't humiliate yourself by making me say no to your rebuttal. There isn't a respectable newspaper in this nation that will print a word you write. Now, if you'll excuse me, I have a letter to write."

Arlene hung up in despair. If her editor was against her, everyone in town would be. She took the phone off the hook. Tomorrow she would take her information down to the newspaper. Now, she just wanted to rest. Back in the medicine chest, she found a bottle of sleeping pills. "Curious," she said to herself, "I thought I'd run out."

"Miss Habor!!"

The knock on the door startled her. "Who is it?" she asked suspiciously, coming out into the living room.

"Sy Gottleib. Thomas Garvin sent me."

"Go away!" she cried. "Leave me alone!"

"I'm staying right here. You need protection, Miss Habor!"

She turned on her television full blast to the evening news, drowning out Sy's pleas for entry. Portions of Winston's and the HUAC chairman's statements of that morning were being reported to the television viewers.

Arlene crumpled onto the couch, crying hysterically. How had this happened to an outstanding American like her?

When Arlene's phone continued to be busy, Harrington got worried. He wanted Winston backed so far into a corner he could never get out. "The woman's a fool. You were right, Marcus. She needs protection. First, I'm calling police headquarters, then I'm going over there to see her myself!"

"Mr. Todd, well, this is a pleasure," the police lieutenant said. "I'm sorry about all this, but Miss Habor . . ."

"I know what she said," Harrington answered, "but Marcus Mancini and I are leaving for her apartment. If you're not at her apartment by the time I get there, I'm going to tell the press you're working for Winston Todd!"

"That's your father!"

But Harrington had already hung up.

When Arlene didn't answer her Fountain Avenue apartment door, Harrington looked at Marcus. "Let's break it down."

With Sy's help, the door almost fell off its hinges.

Harrington did not believe his eyes. Arlene was lying unconscious in her apartment, a bottle of sleeping pills in her hand.

"Jesus, Marcus, we've got to get her up!"

Harrington was trying to lift her when the police arrived.

"Don't touch her, Mr. Todd," the police sergeant said.

Ambulance attendants entered as Harrington backed away.

Harrington flew into a rage when the police held Sy

Gottleib for questioning and sped Arlene away by ambulance without police protection. Marcus had to hold him off.

"Harrington," he said severely, outside on Fountain Avenue, "pull yourself together. We'll go to the hospital. I'll call Thomas from there. He'll get Sy out."

Within the half hour, they were in the halls of USC Medical Center. Arlene was dead. When he phoned Thomas about Sy, Thomas reported that Laster had called from New York. Joe Field's corpse had been found on the New York City docks.

On Monday morning, the autopsy reports showed that Arlene had taken the equivalent of an entire bottle of sleeping pills. The authorities officially declared her death a suicide. In New York, Joe Field's body had been cremated by "mistake" before it could be examined.

Two days later, Harrington heard from Walter Kent. Winston had booked a solid week of social functions with Desiree Richards.

"She's beautiful and charming," Walter told them, "and still Winston's most valued mistress. She's Washington D.C.'s most gracious hostess. Popular, respected, and highly regarded by the New York elite—a perfect choice to help him diffuse the new rumors flying around the Capitol and New York City about his tampering with the results of Joe Field's and Arlene Habor's autopsies. She's been telling everyone that Winston turned his back on Hollywood long ago and barely knew Arlene Habor. And once Winston knew of Joe's misdeeds, he turned Joe in to the FBI. It's on record."

Thomas had all of Marcus's proof of Joe's infiltration of Garvin Enterprises. They had Roy Sharp's testimony. Roy was heavily guarded, ironically, at Conrad's home. Roy had met Joe, alias, Bill Reed. He had spoken to Arlene on countless occasions about their benefactor, Winston Todd. In addition, Laster might press for an investigation of the L.A.P.D. regarding its handling of Arlene's death. Hospital officials would be questioned. The hospital records would be found missing. Many questions could still be asked. Joe's sudden cremation could create similar questions. With all of that, it was still a long shot that they could get at Winston.

"Joe's gone," Marcus said. "Laster and I are frustrated that he didn't get life sentence in prison, but maybe he will elsewhere. And everyone else is safe. We almost got him,

Harrington. He'll think very carefully before he does anything again."

"Is that enough?" Harrington asked.

Marisa shook her head. "It is not, but it's all you're going to get, as you Americans say."

"Except," Thomas volunteered, "for the custody issue."

CHAPTER XXIV

Jason stood in the open front door of Windsor Royal a week later, peering down the hill to the forest. Suddenly, a Mercedes limousine appeared at the clearing and began its ascent up the road.

"They're coming, Grandfather! he yelled.

Jason was already out in the graveled circular drive when Winston's voice boomed out.

"Jason! Come back here immediately!"

Jason looked at the car approaching and back at his grandfather. Dressed in his new blue slacks and white shirt, he reluctantly ran back across the drive, his black shoes clickety-clacking on the marble stairs as he raced to his grandfather.

The hum of the motor grew louder. They watched the car cross over the bridge and circle to a stop in front of them. Harrington alighted from the limousine.

Jason could barely contain his excitement. He looked in awe at his father's startling appearance. There he was, the tall, handsome man he had studied so very often in the newspapers and magazines, but had not seen for five and a half years.

In utter happiness, Jason gazed curiously at the black leather coat and cowboy boots, the white shirt and the blue slacks and the easy manly way his father walked towards him. Jason thought he remembered Harrington's hair being lighter, but he had never forgotten Harrington's eyes. They were the same intense blue and they were staring at him now, almost laughing.

As Harrington mounted the steps, Jason smiled happily and his heart danced. When he started to move to greet Harrington, Winston contained his enthusiasm with a firm grip on his shoulder. Harrington was not to be denied. He scooped Jason out from under Winston's grasp and threw the four-foot-six-inch boy into the air, landing him on his feet. He crouched down to Jason's eye level.

"You look great," Harrington said in a man-to-man tone, his voice filled with affection.

Jason threw his arms around Harrington's neck. "I've missed you, Father. I'm so glad you came!"

Harrington guided Jason down the steps with a hand on his shoulder.

"Where are you going?" Winston demanded. "Dinner is being served early today."

Harrington turned around, an affectionate hand still on Jason's shoulder. "I hope you don't mind," Harrington finally said evenly, "but I've invited Thomas and Katharine to bring Kierston out here to meet Jason later today. Dinner will have to wait until they arrive. Oh, and by the way, I'm spending a few days with Jason. I've asked the Garvins to join me."

Throughout the afternoon, Jason felt he was in heaven. Harrington and Marcus accompanied him to the stables.

"Jim! Jim!" Jason shouted, running ahead of Harrington and Marcus down the stable corridor. "Look who's here!"

Jim walked out of the stable office grinning happily. "Harrington!" Jim called out.

"Jim, I don't know how to thank you for all you've done."

"I told him that, too," Jason said.

Harrington laughed. "I'll bet you did."

"Jim's almost as big a fan of yours as I am," Jason said

proudly.

Jim watched approvingly as Harrington pulled Jason into his arms and looked deep into Jason's eyes. He spoke warmly, but firmly. "I'm just a man, Jason. As an actor, I'm just an image on the screen. Right now . . . right here, I'm real. I'm your father, and I think you're very special. If anyone should be a fan, it's me. I'm a big fan of yours."

Jason's eyes glistened. Suddenly shy, he said, "That makes me feel good."

Harrington hugged him. Jim and Marcus stood by, proud of both their charges.

Harrington talked to Jim alone briefly and vowed one day to repay Jim for all his positive influence on Jason.

"No need," Jim told him. "He's brought me joy, Harrington, more than I can tell you. Besides, you and Mrs. Todd did the same for me. I've just passed it on. Now, spend some time with your son. Seeing the two of you together makes me happier than talking to you myself."

Jason showed off Sable Lady. They played football on the great lawn. Marcus watched them throughout the afternoon, and tears came to his eyes. He blew his nose more than once. When Harrington settled down with Jason under a tree near the stables, Marcus waited in front for the Garvins.

"Father," Jason said, looking up at him in earnest. "Have you ever had bad dreams?"

'Vincent Morello,' Harrington thought. How horrible those dreams had been. Harrington held Jason close. "I have had nightmares, Jason. Are you?"

"Sometimes," Jason said.

'He sounds so vulnerable,' Harrington thought, feeling Jason's heavy sigh. He kissed Jason's forehead, held him protectively, and gently stroked his hair. "We all need help, Jason. Kierston's had nightmares, too. She's seen her godfather, Conrad, her parents, and even me attacked by irresponsible people in the last few years. She doesn't understand either."

"Well, I can help her," Jason said. "Sometimes it's good to talk about things. Father? I know you don't want to tell me now, but one day will you explain about Conrad and all of you?"

"Of course I will, " Harrington said.

"Harrington!"

Kierston scooted excitedly across the great lawn with Marcus and the Garvins following her. Harrington scooped her into his arms, laughing.

"Kierston, I'd like you to meet Jason."

Kierston's head swung around, her hair flying to the side. She was so excited to see Jason that she tried to wiggle out of Harrington's arms. When he set her down, she froze momentarily in awe. Harrington held his breath as she finally stepped forward.

Jason smiled slightly. Eyes, the color of forget-me-nots, drew him in. "I'm sorry about your dreams. . . ."

A momentary sadness crossed Kierston's face, then she shrugged, too fascinated by this older boy to dote on her problems. "Daddy says they'll go away. I believe him."

"They certainly will," Thomas said, finally catching up to his daughter.

Katharine reached out and gently stroked Jason's cheek. "It's so good to see you, Jason," she said softly. Then, overcome with emotion, she drew him into her arms.

Jason had not felt a woman's warmth in many years, and he was a bit startled by Mrs. Garvin's reaction, yet, somehow, he liked it. He looked up at her, trying to appear grown up. "You've gotten thinner, Mrs. Garvin," he said.

Thomas smiled in amusement. "How are you, Jason?"

Jason told Thomas he was fine and thought how much he really liked the Garvins. Boy, did he, and he wanted to let them know it.

"I can help Kierston," he told them boldly. Then he patted Kierston on the head as if to let her know she'd be all right. "I've had bad dreams, too. We'll talk about yours and mine, and then we won't have the dreams anymore. They'll just be stories. Come on. Oh, and I can show you the horses, too. And you'll meet Jim!"

Kierston flushed shyly, happy she wasn't alone with her nightmares. If Jason had dreams and he was all right, then she would be all right, too. Willingly, she let him lead her towards the stables.

Everyone was quite relieved when Winston excused himself from dinner that evening. An unexpected business meeting in Manhattan called him to the city for two days.

Having time alone with Jason meant more to Harrington than he had thought. Windsor Royal held mixed memories for him. With Jason, he recaptured the best of them.

"This is exactly where we used to have the picnics," Harrington called out the following afternoon. He set down a huge basket filled with sandwiches and cakes and waved to Thomas.

"Nope," Thomas said, placing an enormous cooler beside the creek further south along the edge of the great lawn. "It was over here, Harrington."

Katharine carried the second picnic basket; Kierston some linens; and Jason a football, a camera, and a third basket with the tablecloth.

Katharine laughed. "Until you two decide where we're going to setup, I'm putting everything between you."

The Garvins marveled at Jason's effect on five-year-old Kierston. Usually rambunctious and independent, Kierston listened attentively to Jason and trailed after him like a shadow.

This afternoon, Jason was eager to take pictures of everyone. While the adults setup the picnic, he took a couple rolls of film, then he found a perfect spot for his photo session with Kierston. He started shouting out his orders to Kierston just like he had with Nicole.

"Hey, that's not bad, Kierston. I like the football. Yeah, but get over there next to the tree. No, Kierston, don't sit on the ball! Hold it."

Harrington happened to be watching when Kierston moved from the grass to sit down near a tree. He smiled to himself. Kierston was on the verge of losing her temper. Harrington nudged Thomas and Katharine. Silently, Kierston took her time in following Jason's commands. Pursing her lips, she stared at Jason in open defiance. Jason was oblivious to her mood. He was too wrapped up in his work, looking at the scene and Kierston's position, and focusing his lense.

"That's perfect, Kierston!" he called out. "Perfect . . . now smile! One . . . two . . . smile, Kierston! . . ." Kierston smiled as he ordered, but when he yelled "three!" she stuck out her tongue and Jason took the picture. "Kierston!"

Kierston laughed gleefully. Jason fumed. He put down his camera and started towards her. Her eyes opened wide and then narrowed in rebellion. She awkwardly hurled the football. Jason caught it. His anger vanished. He looked at the football in surprise.

"Hey! That was a good throw!"

Suddenly Kierston angrily ran right at him. Jason laughed, dropped the football, and readied himself for her tackle. She plowed right into his stomach head first, and he playfully tumbled to the ground, pretending she had knocked him over all by herself.

"Hey, why'd you do that?" he asked her from his reclining position.

She sat on top of him and declared, "Because you aren't very nice!"

"Don't give in, Kierston," Marisa exclaimed in her gentle Italian accent, surprising everyone with her arrival.

Harrington, delighted to see she had arrived early, walked over and greeted her with a kiss. Jason and Kierston watched curiously. Thomas and Katharine waved. It was Marisa's time to be introduced to Jason. She had purposely waited a day so Harrington could have some private time with Jason. Marcus had brought her in from Manhattan this afternoon for the picnic.

"Jason," Harrington said, "I'd like you to meet Marisa. Marisa, this is my son, Jason."

Kierston held Marisa's hand, smiling up at her adoringly. "Marisa is my friend."

Jason liked her at once. She was just like his grandmother and Mrs. Garvin. And a real knockout. "Do you play football?" he asked.

"I have never had that pleasure," Marisa said. "Would you like to teach me?"

"Well, I . . ." Jason flushed a little.

For the first time, Harrington saw Jason for what he was: a ten-year-old who didn't quite know how to react to such a beautiful lady.

"I taught her how to ride a horse, Jason. You teach her football. If you can't, I'm sure Kierston can."

"No, no," Jason said, acting very grown-up again. "I'll take care of it, Father. Don't worry."

"Or I will!" Kierston chirped, following after Marisa and Jason.

That evening at an intimate candlelight dinner in the

Garden Room, Jason was full of questions for Harrington.
Where did Harrington live? What did he do every day? How
did he like California? Harrington smiled and interrupted
him.

"Hold on, one question at a time. First of all, I don't
own a home in California. I own a duplex in New York,
though."

"Why don't you live in a big house, Father?" Jason
asked curiously. "You could buy one just like Grandfather's if
you wanted to."

"I don't need it, Jason. If you and I and your mother
had lived together all these years, I might have felt differently.
Our home would have existed for our needs. If we had felt
good in a big house, we would have had one. But it would
have been what we wanted, not what someone else thought
we should have."

Jason glanced at Marisa. "Where do you live?"

"Sometimes with your father," she said honestly, "and
sometimes in a hotel."

Jason thought about this. He wanted to know if they
were going to get married, but it wasn't right to ask. Marisa
read his thoughts anyway.

"We haven't thought about marriage," she said, startling him.

Jason blushed, then he smiled. "I guess it's none of my
business anyway. I wasn't very polite."

Marisa thought he was a charming little boy. "Never feel
that way. You ask anything you want. If I don't understand,
I'll ask your father. He's a good teacher of English and many
other things."

"I'm sure glad everyone's here," Jason said suddenly.
"It's like I was having my birthday or something."

That's all Kierston needed to hear. "Did you get our
presents?" she demanded to know.

"Presents?" Jason asked perplexed.

Harrington explained that Kierston had helped him pick
out Jason's gifts for various holidays and whenever Harrington saw something special he thought Jason might enjoy.

"I've never received any presents," Jason said, visibly
upset.

Harrington gave a quick look to Thomas and Katharine.
Then he shrugged it off. "It's not important, Jason. Just

know I was thinking about you and so was Kierston."

"But what happened to them?" Kierston asked, bewildered, then suddenly very upset.

Harrington watched Jason cover up his own hurt for Kierston. His eyes began to dance just like Harrington's as he told Kierston, "My grandfather loves presents. He probably just thought Father and you sent them to him."

Kierston looked horrified, then puzzled. "I bet the clothes don't fit."

Marisa left that evening with Marcus, having created a favorable impression on Jason. The following morning, Jason led Harrington and Marcus through the east wing of the mansion to his workroom, where he proudly displayed his photographs and wanted to demonstrate just how *Confidential Magazine* had placed two separate pictures together into one.

He explained that he had taken one of his favorite photos of Harrington, from *The Hero* premiere, and carefully cut away the background of the photo, leaving him with just Harrington's face and torso. Using the same process, he had cut out a picture of himself. Then he pasted both his and Harrington's pictures on a black sheet of paper and carefully brushed black paint around their images to blend the scissor-marked photos into the black background paper. Afterwards, he took snapshots of the board.

The result of this repeated process was a series of photographs, which he had pinned on the wall around the room. In one picture he stood with Harrington in a *Your Year With Mine* promotional photo. In another, he and Harrington were outside Grauman's Chinese Theater at the premiere of *Tomorrow My Love*. He had worked all weekend on the process and had developed the pictures in his darkroom. Harrington was deeply touched. While Jason showed him every picture, Harrington sat with his arm around Jason's shoulder.

"You did a beautiful job, Jason."

"I wish I had a picture of Mother," Jason said. "I'd like to make us both a picture of the three of us. Marisa, too!" Jason added.

"It's O.K., Jason," Harrington said gently. "Marisa would understand. I don't need to send you a photo; I have one right here." He pulled out his wallet and took out his favorite picture of Cara. She was standing at the Todd Center, where Harrington intended to take Jason very soon.

Kierston came in with Thomas and Katharine and admired Jason's work. Jason was only too happy to explain the process all over again to her and the Garvins. When Kierston declared his pictures were better than *Confidential Magazine*'s, Jason thought she was pretty darn smart.

Little did either of them know that Harrington and Marisa's lawsuit was about to make *Confidential* defunct.

Jason was sorry to see the Garvins go.

"This isn't farewell, Jason," Katharine Garvin told him. "We'll see a lot of you. We're living in New York now."

Jason grinned. "That's great!" He shook hands with Thomas and then he turned to Kierston and patted her on the head.

Kierston smiled, very pleased, then she got into the car. As they drove down the drive, Kierston looked out the back window, waving good-bye to her new friend.

Winston returned for dinner that evening. He noticed that Jason was a bundle of energy, so happy to be with his father that he could not wipe the smile from his face. He felt a twinge of jealousy. If Jason so desired, he could leave with Harrington this evening. Winston had Harrington's permanent custody order in his drawer. There was nothing he could do. Winston wondered if he would lose his heir after all.

They sat around the forty-foot rectangular dining table. Over head a chandelier glowed. A silver vase in the middle of the table was surrounded by crystal, silverware initialed WJT, and hand-painted China place settings. The room was accoustically perfect. Everyone could hear each other, but Winston had used the largest table in the mansion and assigned seats so that Jason and Harrington could barely see each other.

The head butler poured the wine while his first assistant followed behind setting an individual plate of caviar in front of each person.

"I was sorry about your trouble in Hollywood, but then trouble seems to follow you everywhere, doesn't it, Harrington?" Winston said. He was sitting at the head of the table with Harrington opposite him in the distance. "I'm glad I could be of some help."

"You were only too kind to deny your own rumor," Harrington said, placing his hands flat on the table and staring down at his father with a touch of anger and pity. Winston had no conscience. He didn't care if he brought this up in front of Jason.

Jason sensed his grandfather and father were angry at each other. His heart pounded heavily. Desperately, he tried to think of something to distract them.

He cocked his head and smirked at his grandfather. "What's a kid got to do around here to get some attention, anyway? I know you're the greatest businessman in the world, but do we have to talk about business now? We're having a party."

"You're absolutely right, Jason," Harrington said from down the table.

Winston flipped a hand casually in the air and his diamond cufflink sparkled against the glow of the chandelier.

"Jason," Winston said suddenly, "this is probably as appropriate a time as any to answer that question that's been bothering you." Winston explained to Harrington and Marcus. "Jason has quite a curious mind, as you know. Recently, he asked me why people buy certain products and not others. I'm sure you gentlemen will find my dissertation most interesting."

Without waiting for a reply, Winston explained to Jason:

"Let's use your father as an example. A gifted public relations man can sensationalize an actor, get the fans' blood boiling, create excitement and an image for his client as we do with our products. An actor is a commodity to be sold, just like any other product: tobacco, oil, cotton, actor. There's really not much difference between them."

Harrington laughed. "Really, Father. An actor isn't an object. You can't buy and sell him like a pack of cigarettes."

"Why not?" Winston said, taking a healthy bite of his steak.

Harrington viewed Winston with amusement. "Because an actor has free will."

Winston raised a commanding brow. "Very good, Harrington."

"And," Harrington continued, "a passion for his work, very similar to an athlete."

"You mean like a baseball player?" Jason asked curiously.

"Sure. Like with a baseball pitcher, an actor has a team. There's an agent, manager, public relations man, lawyer—all of whom will try their damnedest to help him pitch a great game. Just like in baseball, success depends on timing, talent, the player's determination, and the determination of the professionals working with the player. Even when all the elements are right, success isn't guaranteed. An artist has to have a special appeal, something only the public can determine."

"The most indefinable element in the entire formula is charisma," Marcus added.

"It's no different with products," Winston said, wiping his mouth. "Many people are involved in the introduction of a product to the public. Sometimes it works and sometimes it doesn't. As you say, it's the public who decides. Granted, the actor might be more complex than a material product. I give credit where credit is due, but the fact remains that he is sold to the public as part of a media package. The actor's most unique quality is that he charges the public to love and adore him! That's true hype!"

"Gosh," Jason exclaimed. "That's a pretty good deal!"

Winston grinned. "It's a great deal, and it's also a pain in the neck for anyone associated with him. I prefer my products. As your father aptly pointed out, they talk back only in dollars and cents, not with irrational emotionalism."

"Let's not get carried away, Father," Harrington said easily. "It's quite obvious that the buy-and-sell process cuts across all industries and vocations. A man's main asset is himself, and if he's a successful man, he's selling himself every day of his life. Ideas, products, talent, and money change hands as a result of one person convincing another of his abilities."

"Gosh, Grandfather," Jason said, "isn't that the truth? That's what you do."

Winston smiled, all eyes on him. "Again your point is well taken, Harrington. But being an actor is nothing to brag about. A man who parades around in women's makeup, dressing in ridiculous costumes, and orating at the top of his lungs, isn't a man at all, and surely isn't worthy of much respect."

Harrington laughed out loud. "I hope I do more than that."

"You sure do," Jason interceded. "You make people feel good."

"Thank you, Jason," Harrington said, smiling.

Jason suddenly left his chair and walked down the room to Harrington's side. His young intense face turned upward so he could look Harrington in the eyes. "I have a present for you. May I get it?"

"Of course."

Jason signaled to a butler, who walked the length of the banquet room and set Jason's scrapbooks before Harrington. Marcus joined them.

"What are those, Jason?" Winston called out.

"The scrapbooks, Grandfather."

Harrington flipped a page of the first volume. The scrapbooks started with clippings from Harrington's first Broadway show, *Remember When*.

"Do you like them, Father?"

"Very much," Harrington said, choked with emotion. "They're just beautiful. Did you do this all by yourself?"

Jason nodded his head up and down, very pleased.

"It must have taken you a very long time," Harrington said, smiling at him.

"Half of my life."

"That is a long time," Harrington said gently, deeply moved.

Jason was extremely happy and edged forward to touch his arm against Harrington's. Harrington placed his arm around Jason's shoulder as he turned the pages. Suddenly his hand froze. Staring back at him was an article about Vincent Morello. He felt Jason's shoulder beneath his palm, and Vincent Morello came vividly to his memory. He turned to Jason, Cara and Vincent's son, his look so deep and searching that Jason was jarred a bit.

"That's when Marcus saved your life."

At that moment, it seemed as if he and Jason were alone in the room. He smiled at the boy as his mind and heart flooded with memories. He soaked in Jason's innocence, he basked in Jason's smile. He felt himself being drawn to the boy more than to any person in his life. He realized that he had been holding his feelings in check. He had been keeping in touch with Jason as a duty, as a responsibility, and his ego had been flattered by Jason's attention. But at this moment, with their eyes fastened to each other's, their smiles warm, and their faces happy, Harrington's heart opened up. Vincent Morello's memory faded into oblivion as he received Jason's love and gave back his own in return.

Still staring at Jason, he pushed back from the table, stood up, and took Jason's hand. "I think you and I should have a little talk while Marcus admires your work, don't you?"

"All right, Father," Jason said happily.

"Where are you going with him?" Winston demanded.

"We'll just be walking out front."

Jason and Harrington walked along the gravelled drive. "I'm not going to see you again for a long time, am I?" Jason said, matter of factly.

It was dark. The mansion was lit up and dim specks of reflected light danced on their path. The moon cast a warm light on the vast acres and the rolling lawns.

"I have a few choices, Jason. Your grandfather only has temporary custody of you. I can have you live with me, or I can let you live here. I wanted us to talk about it."

"Jim told me about how you'd come to see me. Why did Grandfather let you come now?"

"Because he had no choice. It had been long enough that we'd been apart, and so many things had happened. I think he knew he couldn't keep me away."

Jason thought about this. He wanted to say more about it to his father, but he didn't. He knew grandfather had been wrong in keeping him away from his father. But Jason didn't want to say anything that might hurt his grandfather. After all he felt he was his grandfather's only true friend. "I understand," he said looking up.

"I think you do," Harrington said, "but it amazes me."

"Because I'm just ten," Jason said, "doesn't mean I'm naive."

Harrington laughed. "Well it should. Most boys your age don't have your abilities." They walked on to the path beside the lake.

"I know, but I do understand. And I also know if I weren't here, you and Grandfather would get along better."

Harrington's heart sank. Why did Jason feel that way? "That's how it must seem to you, Jason, but it isn't true. Your grandfather and I never got along. We're different. We barely know one another. We'll probably never get along. Your grandfather's attitude towards me has absolutely nothing to do with you. You must remember that. And if he and I get angry at one another—it's not your fault. Do you understand?"

Jason nodded, but Harrington noticed he wasn't convinced. 'He's just a child, a boy of ten,' Harrington thought. Questions filled him. Could he watch Jason's happiness turn to sadness? Could he bear to watch him grow up to be cynical? The boy hadn't had a chance to be a boy!

They were at the path alongside the lake. Harrington sat on his haunches and took Jason into his arms. "I love you, Jason, I really do." He was surprised by the depth of his emotion. He no longer knew how to define it. It was not Jason's striking resemblance to Cara. It was not the love Jason bestowed on him. It was an exquisite feeling, which drew them together now. "I want to take you with me," he said, surprising himself, for he had vowed under no circumstance to pressure Jason. Why did it hurt so very much to think of leaving Jason?

"I love you, too, Father, and I'd like to go with you . . ." They sat down on a bench beside the lake and Jason continued.

"But you see, I figured something out. You saw Sable Lady . . ." Harrington nodded. "Well, I guess you could see that she's the best horse in the whole stable. And I guess you could also see that she knows it." Jason laughed.

He grew serious. "But Nicole has a horse named Silver. Remember we saw him out at the stables?" Harrington nodded again. "Oh, and I forgot, Silver and Sable Lady are going to have a colt while I'm at school."

"Is that so," Harrington said.

"It is. Anyway, Silver used to be the king of the stables. Jim says he used to like all the attention he got before he got older." Jason sighed. "Well, I thought about this for a very long time."

"I'm sure you did."

"Oh, I did," Jason said seriously. "Sable Lady gets all the attention now. She's so beautiful, and she's the best horse in the stable. I think she likes to be alone a lot because she gets tired of everyone being around her all the time. And then there's Silver. Well, he likes attention. And he misses not having it. He makes this big scene when no one pays attention. Everyone thinks he's very clever about getting attention, too."

"Why is that?"

"Because he's smart. He can do tricks and everything." Jason lifted his eyes to the stars. He was about to windup his reasons for staying with Winston. He wondered whether he should tell his father about Winston sitting before Diana's portrait all the time. No, he had to keep to himself why he knew for a positive fact that his grandfather needed him very much. He scratched his head and looked at Harrington. "So you see? You're like Sable Lady. And Grandfather is like Silver. I'd like to be with you, but old Silver would die if Jim and the stable hands weren't around."

Harrington felt a lump in his throat. This little boy was remarkable.

"I'll respect your wishes," Harrington said at last. Yet, he wondered whether he was doing the right thing. Jason was a brilliant little boy, but did he really understand what he was saying?

"Don't worry, Father. I know what I am doing." Jason took Harrington's hand. "Pretty soon I'll be grown up and I can come to California. But I promised Grandfather I'd take care of him. I have to keep my promise."

So that was it. Winston had played on Jason's loyalty. A promise was a promise. Harrington sighed. "Then make me a promise, too . . ."

"Oh, I'd like that."

"It's a big decision you're making tonight, Jason, and I won't try to change your mind. But if that choice of yours ever becomes too difficult for you to deal with, I want you to contact me. Promise me you will . . . and that you'll call if you need me."

Jason threw his arms around Harrington again. "I promise."

Winston was waiting for them at the top of the steps. Marcus was carrying the scrapbooks to the car. With a subtle gesture, Harrington indicated to Marcus to lead Jason away so that he could confront Winston alone.

"What you try to do to grown men is one thing," Harrington said, "but if you ever try to harm Jason, I'll come after you."

"So you couldn't convince him to leave," Winston said with satisfaction.

"I didn't press the issue. He wants to stay here. So therefore I'm staying in Manhattan," Harrington said, his words surprising even him.

Winston raised a brow. "Have you decided to retire, Harrington?"

"I'll be working with John, this time on Broadway in his play, *The Challenger*. I'm asking for a cease-fire, Father, for Jason's sake. I think you know everyone's paid dearly for our dispute. You and I are the only ones who can stop it. I want to see Jason and I want your guarantee that Marisa is safe, that all my friends are safe."

Winston looked at his son thoughtfully. This was just what he wanted. "I didn't know you exerted that much control over Thomas Garvin," he ventured.

"I can assure you, there'll be a truce. For how long, I can't say. You see, we have enough evidence to place you in a very difficult position. You know it. I know it."

"When would you like to see Jason again?"

"Next week."

"All right, Harrington. Jason will visit you next week. Give Conrad my regards, and of course, John Stevens. Marisa is safe."

Harrington walked away without looking back and joined Marcus and Jason by the car.

"Will you make a promise, too?" Jason asked as Harrington stood before him.

Harrington again sat on his haunches to look at Jason man-to-man. "Anything."

"Don't ever forget me, Father."

Harrington put a hand to his chest, feeling the pain of departing. He gently touched Jason's cheek and then let his hand fall to rest on Jason's shoulder. Looking him squarely in the eye, he said what he knew Jason needed to hear, for he couldn't have loved Jason more if he had been his own son. "You are my son, Jason. We are part of one another. If I forgot about you, part of me would die. And I want to live for a very long time. As long as I do, you will live within me.

We are one in spirit, Jason. I'll think of you every day, until we see one another next week."

Jason's eyes grew larger and larger. "Next week!"

Harrington drew him into his arms. 'I'll never desert you again, Jason,' he thought emotionally. "I'm staying in New York for awhile. We're going to see each other often."

CHAPTER XXV

T*he Invisible Power* premiere was set for Christmas 1957. Although Conrad kept the story a secret, speculation ran high that unlike Arthur Miller's *The Crucible*, a play symbolizing the McCarthy era through the Salem witch hunts, Burt Small had created a true-to-life script about the treachery of the McCarthy era toward the newly founded Coleman/Todd Productions.

On December 6, 1957, Harringtron and Marisa joined the invited guests and critics crowded into the Rivoli Theater on Seventh Avenue for the New York premiere.

A tremendous crowd waited outside the theater behind barricades as mounted police patrolled the area. Television lights doused the entrance to the theater. CBS and NBC networks covered the event live.

Harrigton and Marisa had been voted the biggest box office draw of the decade. Their pictures appeared on the covers of major national and international magazines. Newspapers, gossip columnists, comedians, and talkshow hosts described Harrington and Marisa as the most romantic acting duo of the fifties.

When Harrington and Marisa stepped out of their limousine, the crowd greeted them with an outpouring of adoration.

Happier than he had been in years, Harrington greeted the crowd with a stunning smile. Over the last five years, Jason had stayed with him often at Washington Mews. They had pored over Cara's photo albums, laughing and crying at stories Harrington so beautifully told about Cara. Many a Saturday night, they dined at Mia Cara, still a festive, elegant restaurant, thanks to Marcus. They visited the Todd Cultural Center, explored New York, and played football in Central Park. Jason became reaquainted with John.

Mysteriously, he remembered somewhere in his infant soul that John had been a part of his early life and special to his grandmother. Conrad came East whenever he could to stay with the Garvins. He was quite taken with Jason. As reminiscent of the days when John and Conrad influenced Harrington, Cara, and Thomas, John and Conrad now became strong influences in Jason and Kierston's lives and in those of their friends, Nicole, Michael, and Bobby.

It had been five years of peace, which probably would be over after tonight's premiere. Harrington and Marisa had insisted on starring in *The Invisible Power*. The movie, if Winston so desired, would be his motive for declaring another war.

Harrington smiled at Marisa as they walked into the theater. "It seems like we've been in this situation before."

Marisa's heart was his, and she laughed. "Don't we ever learn, my love?"

Winston daringly accepted the premiere invitation. He guided Jason into the theater late, making a grand entrance, much to the crowd's delight.

"I don't know why he never took me up on that job offer," John said, having to admire Winston's nerve. "He's a great actor. Why did you let him bring Jason?"

"Don't excite yourself," Harrington said in concern.

"Stop treating me like an invalid, Harrington, I'm as healthy as an ox."

But John was ill. The pallor of his skin was whitish yellow. His tall body was unusually thin. His greatest joy lately came from Kierston and Jason and their friends.

"Hello, Uncle John."

At eleven years old, Kierston had become quite the young lady, John thought, admiring her beauty. He smiled to himself thinking of Jason's expression every time Kierston was nearby. Five years Kierston's senior, Jason teased her unmercifully and often pretended indifference when John had no doubt he loved Kierston deeply.

Since that game of football with Kierston, which John had heard about from Thomas and Harrington, Jason had learned to talk to Kierston by gently prodding her rebellious spirit without ever showing disrespect. John thought that Jason's major design for his life included Kierston. They were mysteriously linked, just as Harrington and Cara had been and as Harrington and Marisa now were.

While Jason declared his future was with Todd Industries, Kierston, although an artist by Katharine's teaching, insisted her true vocation was as an actress and possibly one day a producer/director. She had attended the Stevens's Summer Theater. Soon she would be returning to Los Angeles and would enter Harrington's Artisanmanor. She read constantly and only had time for a few friends, all of whom were older than she. She had attended school with Nicloe Baren. They were best of friends. Otherwise she stuck close to Jason, Michael, and Bobby.

Kierston and the other teenagers had enjoyed the luxury of being kids as well as facing the inherent problems of growing up. Soon John planned to challenge them, especially Jason and Kierston. Unfortunately, they had a responsibility to which they had been born. This generation had to stop Winston.

Thomas and Katharine agreed with John. Harrington disagreed. Jason, he thought, should have a childhood unhindered by nagging doubts about choices he should make later in life.

John smiled to himself. Harrington was a wonderful, devoted father and, like most parents, blinded at times to his own child's thoughts. Jason had been soaking up information since he was a young boy just so he could make up his own mind about his future challenges. Winston had had the advantage of teaching Jason his way of thinking. Harrington, only by example, had shown his way. John didn't give a damn what anyone said. He knew Diana would approve.

In the following years, Jason would hear about his family history and so would Kierston. Actually, John knew that Harrington wanted a rest himself away from all the turmoil. Possibly that was another reason why he insisted on only being an example. Katharine and Thomas, however, were a bit rougher on Kierston. She was living in high style, without the benefit of street life to educate her.

Katharine had sadly had four miscarriages. The Garvins had decided Kierston would be their only child. Thomas treated Kierston with a hint of a son in his mind—she was to carry on his name. Katharine understood this and cultivated Kierston's feminine side. Staring at Kierston now, John saw all their efforts growing in this young girl, who had no idea of what the adults in her life were grooming her for—possibly, too, she had those inherent qualities already. After all she was Thomas's daughter.

"Where have you been, Kierston?" John demanded in his gruff tone. "Sit next to me."

She settled between Marisa and John, her full white skirt ruffling below her knees. "I just saw Jason. He's with his grandfather. Why didn't he come to the theater with you?" she asked Harrington, who sat on the other side of Marisa.

"It was my suggestion," Jason said, standing in the aisle. "Hello, Father!"

Jason, now fifteen, stood five foot ten. John noted that he radiated the intensity that a curious intelligent person possessed. A handsome kid. Tonight, he wore a navy blue blazer with gray slacks.

He greeted John and Conrad with a handshake, wishing Conrad luck. Then he crossed over them in the row and stopped in front of Kierston.

"You're going to give me an excuse to come to California now," he said, referring to the Garvins' return to Los Angeles at the end of the month. "How am I going to keep you out of trouble otherwise?"

"You haven't been around much anyway, has he, Harrington? I have things to do with my life besides waiting for him, don't you think?" Kierston said, smiling.

Jason had worked every summer since he was ten. From errand boy to dock worker, he was bent on learning everything about his grandfather's business. How else was he to know how to run Todd Industries one day? Winston was teaching him about the stock market. Under Winston's tutelage, Jason invested his earnings in Todd Industries stock in addition to the $100,000.00 Winston had given him as an advance against his inheritance.

"You don't have to wait, Kierston," Jason said. "You have to catch up."

She poked him in the ribs. "You'll be sorry you said that."

"Yeah, probably."

Nicole Baren, sitting behind them, huffed, fluffed her hair, and put a hand on Kierston's shoulder. "I know he's going to eat his words."

Harrington suppressed a smile when Michael Christian spoke to Nicole.

"Lay off, Nicole, Harrington said we all have to stick together. Right, John?"

John glanced behind him and looked over his glasses. "Right, Michael. Isn't that right, Conrad?"

Conrad eyed Nicole. "I'm happy at least Michael was listening."

Nicole bent over and kissed Conrad's cheek. "You don't scare me."

"I must be losing my touch," Conrad said, patting her hand affectionately.

Thomas and Katharine entered and sat in the row in front of them with Walter Kent, now Ambassador to the Court of St. James under Eisenhower. Mel Christian, Jr., Chief Executive Officer of Todd Industries took his seat between his sons, Michael and Bobby. The Barens sat on either side of Nicole.

Just as the lights dimmed, Winston entered through their row. As he crossed to sit beside Jason, he nodded charmingly at John and Conrad, winked at Kierston, shook hands with Harrington, and nodded in amusement at Marisa before he sat down.

When the curtain opened, Jason settled down in the seat between Winston and his father, unaware of the strange experience awaiting him. The film began with a quote silently rolling over the screen, and the crowd was still.

"This is no time for men who oppose Senator McCarthy's methods to keep silent, or for those

who approve. We can deny our heritage and our
history, but we cannot escape responsibility for
the result. As a nation we have come into our full
inheritance at a tender age. We proclaim ourselves, as indeed we are, the defenders of
freedom, what's left of it, but we cannot defend
freedom abroad by deserting it at home. The
actions of the junior senator from Wisconsin
have caused alarm and dismay amongst our allies
abroad and given considerable comfort to our
enemies, and whose fault is that? Not really his.
He didn't create this situation of fear; he merely
exploited it, and rather successfully. Cassius was
right: 'The fault, dear Brutus, is not in our stars
but in ourselves . . .' Good night, and good
luck."

> EDWARD R. MURROW
> March 1954

Jason knew something about Joe McCarthy now that he
was older. The senator had been discredited and had
ultimately died. What stayed in Jason's head as the music
soared from the speakers and the picture came on the screen
was the concept of "exploitation of fear." He shelved the
thought in his mind and returned to the movie, unaware that
he had edged a bit closer to Harrington in the process.

While watching the film, the old questions about
Harrington and his grandfather returned. Harrington had
spent hours in makeup each day while the make-up artists
crafted him into a sixty-five-year-old man. He captured
Winston to perfection, using Winston's mannerisms—
especially the rise of the brow and the flip of the hands. He
left no mistake about whom he portrayed.

The relationships between Harrington, Marisa, and
Winston, and between Winston and Conrad, were portrayed
in the film, although disguised, masterfully interweaving a
message into entertainment. The film's strongest statement
came from Conrad's character after he had been maligned by
Winston and his career almost destroyed. "We are both men
of accomplishment, but I want to capitalize on the greatness
of the human spirit while you want to bankrupt mankind.
Curious isn't it that men respond more readily to you than to

me?"

The thought took Jason's breath away. There he sat between his father and his grandfather. He could feel the tension. Suddenly their differences crystallized.

Winston worked in order to gain power and money without regard for people. Harrington thought of what he wanted, then he inspired others with the same spirit to work with him, and prosperity and acclaim following naturally. There was a big difference. Yet, each man succeeded in his own way. Jason wondered if one day he would be asked to choose between the two, and knew that day was coming.

As the film ended and the credits rolled, a dedication to Jason froze on the screen just before the World Studios insignia. "Why don't you let Jason know it's a present to him," Kierston had suggested to Harrington. "At least his grandfather can't take the film away." Jason stared at the dedication in surprise. So this was Harrington's explanation to him about Winston and Conrad and Winston and Marisa and the whole mess a few years ago. He knew now he would see this film many more times, alone, without anyone's knowledge. He felt Harrington's arm around his shoulders, and he looked up at his father with glowing pride.

"You were wonderful, Father," he said, "And thank you."

Harrington only nodded his understanding, for Winston was watching, and he didn't want Jason in the middle any more than he already was.

Thundering applause, cheers, and accolades filled the post-screening hour. The critics rushed off to meet newspaper deadlines. At last the audience left the theater.

Winston was polite and attentive throughout the film. He wanted Jason to remember him standing and applauding innocently. After all, wasn't a motion picture a fantasy?

"A most provocative subject matter, Conrad. My compliments," he said afterwards. "And congratulations to you, Harrington. A splendid performance. Yes, and even you, Miss Benito, were captivating. Ah, Thomas, I see you enjoyed it as well."

"I·thought it rang with realism, didn't you?" Thomas said.

Winston chuckled. "I'm going to miss you, Thomas. When are you returning to the West Coast?"

"In a few days. My work's down here for awhile. David Britt will be heading up our New York headquarters."

Thomas was being modest. Garvin Enterprises had quadrupled its profits in the last four and a half years; its reputation was impeccable. Winston knew this and smiled slightly as he watched Walter Kent leave the theater. He made a mental note to have Raymond talk to Walter. Undoubtedly, he'd stop being Thomas Garvin's champion unless he wanted his private life as a homosexual exposed. He found it humorous that all those years he had thought Walter was after Diana's affections.

"Have David call Raymond," Winston said at last. "We'd be delighted to help him in whatever way we can."

Mel Christian, Jr., was talking to John and Conrad. His father had come to the Todd Gala years ago when Diana was alive. Winston had bought out their clothing store and now Mel Christian, Jr., worked for Todd Industries. Fifty, Boston born, good family tree, a Harvard graduate, Mel Christian, Jr., was in John's estimation the most cultivated and respectable executive at Todd Industries.

"Sorry about all that mess in Hollywood, Conrad. I should have called. Honestly, I didn't know what to do. A coward's way out, I'm afraid, but just the same, I was thinking about you. And you obviously found your own way to fight the matter. The film was brilliant."

Conrad also respected Mel. They knew one another through various political organizations. He accepted Mel's comment as the truth. Winston didn't let his executives in on all his underhanded dealings. "Thank you, Mel. I appreciate that."

Jason, Kierston, Michael, Nicole, and Bobby stood apart from the adults. Bobby, the oldest among them, whispered to Jason only enough for their group to hear.

"I want to see that movie again."

Michael nodded in agreement. "Scarey stuff."

Nicole tossed her red hair. She thought of herself as Kierston's older sister. "I don't need to see it again. Jason's grandfather is mean. That's all I need to know."

Kierston looked over at her mother and father. Winston was talking to them. She had questioned her father about Winston. After all, she had the feeling that he had caused a lot of problems with her family and friends when she was younger.

"He doesn't think like we do," Thomas had told her. "In a few years, I'll tell you more about it."

"Come on, Kierston," Nicole said, taking her hand. "Jason doesn't agree with me."

Jason, Michael, and Bobby watched the two girls walk off. Michael adored Nicole. He idolized Jason. "I wish you would talk to Nicole."

"I can't do anything about it," Jason said, watching after the girls. "She doesn't like Grandfather, but I do."

"Try to explain," Bobby said, his square face set in a serious pose. "Remember? We're supposed to stick together."

"I'll try," Jason said, "but I don't think it'll do any good."

The Invisible Power swept the Academy Awards, giving Harrington his first Oscar as Best Actor, and Marisa her first nomination. Conrad won his sixth Best Director Award; Coleman Todd Productions its first Oscar for Best Picture.

With this type of success, Harrington was on the lookout for any sign of retaliation from Winston. Month after month, through 1958 and 1959, Marcus reported that Winston was pulling in the reins on Jason. When they visited Jason at Harvard in 1960, he never complained, although they noticed his bodyguards were doubled and his mail was handed to him opened.

Kierston's life was different. In 1959, at the tender age of twelve, Thomas and Katharine gave her independence. She flew alone to Florence where she spent the summer with Marisa and Julio. Kierston saw Sicily and the best and worst of Italy, Germany, France, and England. Nicole arrived for the last half of Kierston's European summer, and she and Kierston hiked through portions of the Italian Alps.

In 1960, Kierston spent half the summer in Los Angeles at the Artisanmanor and half the summer under John Stevens's tutelage. The same held true for the summers of 1961 to 1962, until Marcus finally put Kierston to work waitressing at Mia Cara.

Jason visited Kierston every chance he got. They rummaged around their fathers' old neighborhood with the added advantage of their fathers' experience to guide them.

Michael and Bobby tagged along. Nicole even joined in, although she usually stayed close to Kierston or Michael.

Bobby had enrolled at MIT; Michael had followed, enrolling at Harvard with Jason. Nicole attended Vassar. The young men accepted Jason's lead and even coordinated their majors toward Jason's goals. Michael went for an MBA. Jason was in a combined undergraduate/law-school program. To Harrington's mind, the trio would be an unbeatable combination. They met every chance they got to organize a prospectus for Jason's computer company. Whatever else they discussed, they kept to themselves.

Yet, with all their goals and mutual aims, their shared experiences had a different effect on each and ultimately caused Michael and Nicole to drift apart from Jason and Bobby. Harrington noticed that Jason used all his knowledge and experience for one aim—his future with Kierston and Todd Industries. Harrington had endorsed this behavior because he had been driven similarly with work and Cara. Bobby Christian was of the same mold, but his brother Michael, and Nicole Baren, drifted in a different direction. They became socially conscious and entered the youth movement with unusual zeal. Fighting for civil rights, equality, and justice, Michael and Nicole ultimately isolated themselves from what John Stevens called "their chosen destiny."

"It's a reality," John told Harrighton firmly. "They didn't ask to be born into this situation, but they have been. You're a good man, Harrington, and you wished to forget, because it's too painful to think that Jason, Kierston, and all their friends will have a life like yours. But they will, and you have to help them prepare for Winston."

At least two weeks of every summer, the five friends gathered together. Kierston was the magnet, bringing the singleminded Jason, and Bobby, and the socially conscious Michael and Nicole, together. Conrad and John usually participated in their visits. Harrington and Marcus always did. As Diana had with him, Harrington tried to instill in them the belief that they could do anything they wanted if they did their best.

In the summer of 1963, they were rendezvousing at Windsor Royal, and anticipating Jason's upcoming twenty-first birthday.

Marcus drove Harrington out to the country the third week in June. "You should see *Breeze*, Marcus. Kierston is wonderful!"

Kierston had just starred in her first feature film. Harrington had written the script, a tribute to Winston Jason, Jr., about his feelings towards the loss of his brother. He had used a female perspective, instead of a male one, so Kierston could play the role.

"Has Jason seen it?" Marcus asked.

"I promised to screen it for his birthday. I hope our new script will bring some peace between the warring factions."

Especially over the last year, Jason and Michael had become political adversaries. Recently, their conflict had taken on a new dimension. Now they argued about Winston. Like Nicole, Michael had a hell of time tolerating Jason's close relationship with his grandfather.

"It didn't help when Michael was arrested last year in Birmingham, Alabama. Jason's a tough taskmaster, but Michael made a promise he'd be responsible to their mutual goals. He's been absent a lot from those weekend meetings at Harvard."

Harrington glanced at Marcus curiously as they traveled through the Manhattan sidestreets towards the Bronx. "Have you been snooping around?" When Marcus didn't answer, Harrington laughed "So you're as curious as I am about Jason's whereabouts lately. What's he been doing?"

"Something in California. I don't know what. Couldn't keep up with him." Marcus smiled slightly. "He's pretty foxy about dodging detectives." Then Marcus sobered. "He's had to be. Winston's still got guards on his tail."

"But he told Winston to lay off a couple of years ago."

"That doesn't mean Winston will stop, or have you forgotten?"

"No, no," Harrington said, "I haven't forgotten."

"And never do," Marcus warned. "John was right. Jason's time is coming."

CHAPTER XXVI

A half hour after Harrington's departure from Manhattan, Jason pulled up to Windsor Royal and parked his Porsche. He looked up at the mansion and thought of his grandmother. He and John had often spoken about her since his sixteenth birthday. They'd talked about everyone. Jason knew everyone's background, including Harrington's.

Jason hopped out of the car and got his luggage. That initial discussion with John seemed like twenty years ago instead of five. He remembered thinking at that time, that he needed to be alone, to sort things out. Now everything was in order. With John's help, he had altered the course of his life. No one but John knew about it. He had chosen his destiny. This summer it would be Kierston's turn.

Just the thought of kissing Kierston's warm soft lips brought a smile to his face. He loved Kierston Garvin and wanted to spend his life with her.

He entered Windsor Royal with his luggage and dropped it in the Grand Reception Room. Raymond Baren was walking towards him, and he stuck out his hand.

Raymond shook it as he took in Jason's towering figure,

321

the thick black hair as dark as ebony, the blue eyes that were direct and filled with confidence. Just looking at Jason made Raymond want to hide.

Raymond seldom smiled anymore. His medium frame bulged out at the waist. His double chin was accentuated by the tightness of his collar. The clothes he once had taken care to press and clean were sloppy and wrinkled. He could see that Jason was shocked by his appearance.

"Jason, your grandfather wants to talk to you before we leave for Europe." Raymond said the words simply, without malice. He appeared to want to say more, but didn't. He just pointed to the library and left Windsor Royal.

Winston continued signing a stack of letters as Jason fell into a chair in front of his desk. "I'm happy to hear you didn't join Michael Christian's anti-segregation organization at school," Winston said.

For a large man, Winston was extremely graceful. Jason liked to watch the crisp sharp movements of his body, which so clearly showed the thoughts that Winston could not bring himself to express. Right now, for instance, he wanted Jason to stay put and criticize his own friend. Jason complied . . . halfway.

Winston glanced up. "You aren't thinking about joining him in the future are you?"

"No, but I do believe a man should be able to eat sitting down where he wants," Jason said. "And alone, if he so chooses. So why don't you grant me my civil rights and call off your bodyguards. I asked you two years ago, and I still see them around."

Winston dropped his pen and raised an eyebrow. "All right," he said, feigning a concession. A few years ago, he had decided that Jason could take care of himself, abductors or not. He had only meant the guards to be a warning. He was and always would be "boss." Beside, lately they hadn't been able to keep up with Jason. What was he doing out in California, anyway? Winston intended to find out. He had already hired new guards who were quicker on their feet. "But be careful, Jason." Winston smiled. "This is your first summer without working. Relax, enjoy yourself. I hear your father's visiting you with Marcus and all your friends will be here this summer."

Jason rose. "That's right. You have a good trip."

"Oh, and Jason, when I return I'll have a birthday present for you. After all, this is the big one—twenty-one."

"Thanks," Jason said. "Again, have a good trip." As Jason walked out of the library, he almost collided with a frantic Sue Ann Baren. "Excuse me," he said.

She merely nodded, tossing her red hair as Nicole did. Then with a flutter of hands and flying chiffon, she closed the library door after Jason.

"Winston! I have wonderful news!"

Winston flipped his hand at her in dismissal. "I'm leaving on a trip, Sue Ann," Winston said, ignoring her. "I don't have time."

"You have time for this," she said, proudly standing before his desk. "I'm going to have your heir!"

"It isn't mine," Winston said. "You'd better go talk to your husband."

"Winston! I'm telling you the truth!"

Winston stood. "I said it's not mine, Sue Ann." He rounded his desk and headed for the door. "I'll see you when I get back. Your husband's waiting for me out front. I suggest you go home and take care of your lovely daughter."

Upstairs, Jason had changed into his riding attire. He was walking down the hall when he heard Winston's car rolling out of the drive. He paused a moment, thinking he also heard something else.

Seldom did he visit Winston's personal quarters. A noise drew him to the wood-and-mirror paneled dressing area. Harris was bending over a suitcase atop a gilded daybed, trying with all his might to close it. Although a strong seventy, Harris Johnson was stooped over so far that, when he walked, he always looked as though he were about to fall over.

"Let me help you with that," Jason said.

"Oh, Jason, you needn't trouble yourself."

"No trouble." Jason pushed the suitcase top down over some sable coats and latched it shut. "What's grandfather doing with these fur coats? Did he leave them behind?"

Harris never knew why Winston did anything. How could he answer that question? It also seemed peculiar that Winston wanted this suitcase given to Sue Ann Baren on Jason's birthday. He shook his white head in wonder, grabbed the suitcase handle, and stuck the riding crop back in Jason's hand.

"I don't know, Jason. Come along, it looks like a fine day for riding."

Jason wondered what Winston had in mind with those fur coats, but forgot about it as he weaved his way past gardeners manicuring the roses. From behind him he heard footsteps and turned around.

"I'm still trying to catch up to you," Kierston said, smiling.

Every time he saw her, he was struck by her extraordinary beauty. High cheekbones, smooth olive skin, and exquisite piercing blue eyes with a violet rim around the irises. At sixteen, she had a strength of character clearly indicated by her straight posture, the way she held her head, the steadiness of her gaze. Yet there was a hint of vulnerability beneath the surface that made her all the more appealing.

"I was wondering where you were," he said, coming to her. He had kissed her many times, but today was special. Today, he was going to be kissing a woman.

Strong arms pressed her body. The thought of resisting him came only after he had dominated her body and lips, and once enclosed in his arms, Kierston knew she never could resist. She gave of herself unthinkingly and without inhibition. He sought out her lips, opening her mouth, and bent her over until her back arched under his weight, balanced against the strength of his arms.

He couldn't get enough of her. He wanted all of her. He was past reserve, past all sense of time or moment. He felt the softness of her body, the arms thin and strong, yet soft. Her breasts pressed against his chest and he held her closer so as to hear her heartbeat.

"That was a wonderful hello," Kiersten whispered breathlessly in his ear. "I wish we weren't in your grandfather's rose garden."

Jason laughed, coming back to reality. He didn't let her go, but he noticed the gardeners nearby smiling.

"I just wanted you to know I missed you."

"I wish I had thought of it first. Next time I will." Kiersten said, still holding him.

They heard the sound of hooves and watched Nicole race Silver towards the creek. Kierston was staying at the

Barens' home. Nicole had been upset all morning. Kierston explained this to Jason as they rushed for the stables.

"Remember what I told you last week about Sue Ann?" Kiersten asked him.

"I remember."

"That's what Nicole's upset about."

Kierston knew what was on Jason's mind. John was preparing them for the future. She had only heard Cara's story although she was sure Jason had learned much more. They had a lot on their minds—a future to decide upon. Yet, Kierston refused to give up a friendship because she was under a new type of pressure. Nicole needed their help.

At the stables, Kierston mounted first. "Let me ride ahead. O.K.?"

Jason nodded.

Jim studied Jason's handsome figure atop the thoroughbred. "I suppose I'm meddling, but what the heck. If you know what's good for you, don't push that flaming ball of fire too far. She's much more spirited than this horse you're riding. She's had a pretty tough time."

"We'll take care, Jim. Don't worry."

As Jason galloped over the great lawn, Harrington, Michael, and Bobby hurried through the rose garden, looking after him.

"Looks like Jason's heading right into an argument and doesn't even know it," Harrington told Michael.

"I'm sure glad you're here," Michael said. "Let's hurry. I don't want Nicole getting too wound up."

They rushed on to the stables.

Far in the distance Jason saw Kierston and Nicole cross the creek and disappear into the woods. He urged Sable Lady on. Across the back acres stood the old homestead area formerly used by the Todd staff. Paths threaded along in between trees leading to cottages. He walked Sable Lady III through one back yard after another. A half mile up the hill he saw Silver grazing. He trotted Sable Lady up the trail.

It was a warm day, not yet humid. The light shimmered through the trees. He reached the hill and dismounted, leaving Sable Lady III with Silver II and Distant Darkness IV.

He stood before a cottage somewhat larger than the others around it. He boldly walked up to the front door, and instead of knocking, tried the knob. It opened. Nicole was on the couch sobbing in Kierston's arms.

"Get out of here!" Nicole said, jumping to her feet.

He closed the door and walked towards them. He was about to speak when, overcome with tearful frustration, Nicole slapped him as hard as she could across the face. Jason didn't move, but his expression almost made her step back until her rage took over. The thought of her mother in Winston's arms rooted her to the ground.

"You're just like your grandfather. Now leave me alone!"

"I'm really not," Jason said evenly. "I didn't know about the affair until Kierston told me last week. I'm sorry about it, Nicole, but it's your mother's choice. I just wish you weren't unhappy. But it's her problem. If she's unhappy with your father, she should have left him rather than having an affair with Grandfather."

"That's downright heartless!" Nicole cried out.

Jason looked at Kierston and shrugged. Then he looked back at Nicole. "But truthful. I don't blame your father for your mother's actions."

Nicole turned a vivid red. "What about your grandfather! I suppose he had nothing to do with it, either!"

"Jason!"

They heard Harrington's cheerful voice. Nicole hurriedly dried her eyes and Kierston and Jason went to the door.

"We're in here, Father!" Jason called out.

Harrington opened the door. "Come here, Red." Nicole cried some more in his arms, and then he made everyone sit down. Michael and Kierston comforted Nicole, and Bobby entered and sat beside Jason as Harrington spoke to them. "All right, it's out in the open, right? Jason, you finally know about the affair?"

Jason was surprised. "You knew, Father?"

"Yes, for many years." Harrington looked at Nicole. "Jason didn't know, Nicole."

"Why didn't you tell me?" Jason asked.

"It wasn't your problem," Harrington said matter-of-factly, turning to Nicole. "Listen, Red, I'd do anything to take away your pain, truly I would, but I can't and neither can Jason. I hope you don't blame him for Winston's actions. If you want to be angry, you'll have to focus on Winston."

Nicole looked at Kierston. Kierston had told her the

same thing. "I guess you were right."

Kierston hugged her. "I just care about you, Nicole. It doesn't matter who's right." She glanced at Jason. "JT, you can be pretty blunt at times."

Jason's eyes danced just like Harrington's. "You can take it, Kierston."

"Oh, yes, you've seen to that. My parents have, Conrad and John have, but Nicole is a different story. It's lucky she's our friend, too. Otherwise, you and I might forget about our hearts."

Nicole hugged Jason. "I'm sorry, Jason."

Jason held her, looking over her shoulder at Kierston. "I'm sorry, too, Nicole. For once, Kierston is right."

Kierston threw a pillow at Jason and ended up hitting Nicole in the leg. Nicole danced out of the way.

"Hold it. Time out, everyone. Truce!"

Jason laughed and said, "At least now I know why everyone was acting so strange."

Bobby, the quiet young man, nudged Jason. When he spoke everyone tuned in. "You just have that effect on people."

Jason laughed the loudest of all. Kierston smiled. It had been good to let off a little steam. She was struggling to become an adult prematurely, and the teenager in her was rebelling.

Harrington was enormously relieved that everyone was joining in on the fun. "I'll talk to the owner of Mia Cara. I think he'll give Kierston the night off. Let's go have dinner, and I warn you, no politics tonight. Strictly friendly conversation."

Mia Cara had prospered through the years with Marcus at the helm. Whenever Harrington was in New York, Marcus spent his evenings at the restaurant. Otherwise, Marisa's Uncle Julio managed the establishment. When Carmen Benito had died, Julio returned to the States. He often tended the bar, too. A sense of poetic justice, Marcus felt, and Harrington and Marisa agreed.

Mia Cara still catered to an exclusive clientele, only the faces were younger, the dress more casual. Mia Cara had become a hangout for New York youth. Tonight, the topic of conversation centered around Medgar Evers being shot in the back in Mississippi.

Harrington, Marisa, and Marcus sat at a window table while the five friends had a chance to catch up on the year they'd spent apart. They sat in the corner booth with the map of Sicily above it, where Harrington and Cara had sat many years ago.

"What did you mean earlier, Kierston," Nicole was asking, "about John and Conrad and Jason making you tougher?"

Kierston tossed it off. "I was just trying to win a point. I'm so happy we're all together. I'm starving. If you like the food you serve, you know it's a good place to eat!"

They ordered, then Kierston directed their conversation to John Glenn and Scott Carpenter orbiting the earth.

"One day we'll explore all the planets." Jason sounded excited. "In the near future, communication satellites will be placed in stationary orbit. Men will be linked together by satellite communications, television, and radio, and we'll be able to see what's going on in every part of the world as it happens. Todd Industries has already bought a television station in New York, and WJT Aeronautics is in the process of manufacturing one of those satellites." He looked at Kierston and she smiled and understood.

Bobby did too and said, "When you think about such prospects, such horizons to conquer, the vastness of what man doesn't know and what he will discover—well then, at least to me, I have to concentrate on what happens only in my own life, otherwise I'll get bogged down in all of it and never attain my goals. Jason taught me that." He looked at Michael and ruffled his curly long hair. "We haven't been trying to leave you out, Michael. You're my brother. I love you. We've just got a lot to do."

"Yeah, you're right. I keep getting off track."

Nicole put her arm around him. "It's only because you have a heart. But I guess Jason's right . . ."

The table all chimed in with her. "Again!"

Everyone laughed.

August 15, 1963, Jason Sterling Todd turned twenty-one years old and Harrington and Kierston joined him for the celebration along with Marcus, John Stevens, Conrad, and Marisa. The Grand Banquet Hall was set for the occasion.

Twenty-one candles in sterling silver holders lined the long forty-foot table.

John and Conrad and the Garvins gave him one thousand shares of Garvin Enterprises stock.

Kierston, Nicole, Michael, and Bobby had bought him fifty shares of Todd Industries stock. Marcus, Marisa, and Julio pitched in and bought a round-trip ticket for two to Europe.

He looked at Kierston. Youthful and beautiful, Kierston was dressed in a pale yellow sundress, full in the skirt and tight at the waist with narrow straps holding up the bodice. Even in the shadowy glow of the candlelight her violet eyes stood out against her tan.

"I wonder who I'm supposed to take on this trip?" Jason said teasing her and taking her hand.

The feel of her skin was like an electrical shock. His expression was youthful and reckless. His heart pounded as he bent over and kissed her.

"If you're taking Kierston, you'll have to wait awhile for the trip," Harrington said. "She's starring in *The Accused* next month."

"Isn't that the surprise for Michael and Nicole?" Jason asked, as Harrington had suggested he should.

"What surprise?" Michael demanded to know.

Kierston smiled. "Harrington wrote the script for you. It's about a young couple who help a black man in the South."

"Really!" Nicole asked. "Are you dying your hair red, Kierston?"

"Give me a break, Nicole," Kierston laughed.

"I have a copy of the script in my room. After dinner, and the screening of *Breeze,* I'll get it for you two. Now . . ." Harrington was seated between Jason to his right, and Kierston to his left. Harrington smiled at her when he handed Jason a large manilla envelop. "I have something here, Jason, which is near and dear to my heart, as it was to your grandmother's. Happy birthday, son."

Jason opened it up and stopped short. He hoped his expression did not give him away. He glanced over at John, who tried to conceal a smile that spread over his lips anyway.

"Well," John demanded. "What do you think? Conrad wants a full report."

Jason had never been more excited. He couldn't believe that he thought along the same lines as his grandmother had and his father did.

Harrington tried to catch his eyes. "I guess your silence means you like it a lot, right?"

Jason laughed. "Father, I don't have the words. One day soon, I'll tell you just how much this means to me. Thank you!" He shook Harrington's hand across the table and a special look passed between them.

"There's one more piece of good news," Conrad said grandly. "Harrington, did you tell them about your phone call from the President yesterday? I didn't think so. Jason, your father has been asked to found the 'Presidential Award.' The House and the Senate unanimously agreed that Harrington was the only member of the Hollywood community to organize this National Award. It's to be given every five years to artists in every creative field."

"Similar to being knighted in Britain," John said, bowing slightly. Then he coughed and everyone was silent.

Kierston immediately produced a glass of water. John hated everyone fawning over him. Most of the time he seemed so healthy that they forgot he had cancer. Possibly because he kept smoking those cigarettes. When he had caught his breath, he looked at everyone present.

"This is a celebration. We have much to be grateful for. Let's get on with the festivities."

At once Jason switched the focus from John to Harrington, just as John wished. "Congratulations, Father, that's a real honor. When will the first awards be given?"

"1966."

Suddenly the lights went out at Windsor Royal. The twenty-one candles flickered brighter. Through the wide Banquet Room windows, they saw that the exterior lighting was gone, too. The hallway outside the Banquet Room was pitch black.

"What happened?" Kierston asked.

"It's probably Mr. Prescot fiddling around down in the basement," Jason said, standing. "I gave him some ideas for lighting the outside of the mansion, and he wanted to check our electrical system to see if it could take the extra wattage." He picked up a candle. "I'd better get downstairs. I want to make sure everything is all right."

Everyone joined him. The house flickered with the light of candles carried from the table as Jason lead the way down the hallway to the stairwell. "Watch your step. There's a landing and then four more steps," Jason warned.

Just as they made their way into a large corridor, the lights burst on. They could see old Mr. Prescot coming from far down the corridor.

"Everything's fine," he yelled. "Just a fuse."

"This is like a whole other house," Kierston said, looking around as she blew out her candle.

"I can't believe I've never been down here," Nicole exclaimed.

The ceilings were high. Wooden beams ran the length of the mansion. A series of rooms lined the hallway on either side, stretching all the way down to the room into which Mr. Prescott now disappeared.

"My grandfather has all sorts of papers stored here. Says he likes to study history. This is where I found those articles on you," he told Harrington.

Marcus and Harrington glanced at one another, thinking that Winston might have a secret room here. John didn't look at anyone as he walked ahead of them all.

"What's over there?" he asked, leading the way.

He entered a research room. Rows and rows of bookcases filled with newspapers from all over the world lined the walls.

Jason had stopped short.

"What's the matter?" Marcus asked him.

Jason pointed to the far wall. "I don't remember a door being over there." The door was unlocked. He felt for a light switch and couldn't find one. "Anyone have a light?"

The flickering candles lit their way once again as they entered one darkened room after another. Jason couldn't be sure where or how things had been changed in the basement, but he knew they had. He was walking along, deep in thought, and almost stumbled to the ground.

"Look out," Kierston said, "you'll step on another box."

Jason held the candle high. Packages in all shapes and sizes, stacked one on top of the other, covered the floor. Kierston picked up a gift with a baby boy on the wrapping. She found another with a football player. Then she looked up at Harrington, who was holding a candle above her.

At once, he knew what the packages were. "Well, I guess we've seen enough," Harrington said, trying to distract everyone. "Let's get back upstairs."

Jason paid no attention to him. He picked up one gift after another. "Is there a card with any of these?" he asked. "Here's one!" He opened it.

> MARCUS AND I WERE JUST THINKING OF YOU AND WANTED YOU TO HAVE SOMETHING TO REMEMBER US BY. KIERSTON HELPED US PICK THIS OUT.
> I LOVE YOU, FATHER

Jason ripped open the box. Inside, he found a blue cashmere sweater meant for a young boy. He stared from it to the hundreds of presents, and he wanted to open every one. Gifts represented the giver. What had his father bought for him? He thirsted to know even more about Harrington. A wave of indescribable pain crushed his chest. His father had taken time to buy him presents, and Winston had hidden them from him. He was so angry he had trouble talking.

Marcus cleared everyone out except Kierston and Harrington, who took Jason by the shoulders and made him stand up. They looked at each other in the eye.

"It doesn't matter," Harrington said firmly. "You and I have much more between us than things—gifts. Got it?"

Jason only nodded.

Harrington glanced at Kierston, who still held a candle. He nodded at her to talk to Jason and then he left, using the trailing candlelight of the others to find his way back to the lighted center hallway.

"Come on, Kierston," Jason said at last.

She heard his voice shake, but his hand firmly grasped hers. Kierston's eyes slowly adjusted to the light as they found their way back to the research room.

Once back in the light, Jason held up the sweater. "Grandfather's going to have to learn to keep his nose out of my personal affairs," was all he could say.

As they left the basement, Kierston placed a hand on his arm. Anger still permeated his features. "I told you the clothes wouldn't fit him."

The remark was so unexpected that Jason stopped short, then laughed in spite of himself. "You're wonderful, you know that?" He dropped the package and took her into his arms instead. He smelled the fragrance of her hair, the sweetness of her skin, and he kissed her soft mouth.

"Kierston," he whispered at last, breathing heavily, "you have to grow up quickly, okay? Do you understand?"

"I know," she said. "I love you, Jason."

He had tears in his eyes. "And I love you."

Upstairs, everyone had cleared out, much to Jason's relief. Hopefully his father wasn't too upset. He and Harrington would have a long talk tomorrow. Kierston was staying at Nicole's, so he walked her back through the estate to the Baren home.

"I'm building something for us," he said.

"What?"

Jason drew her close as they walked along. "You'll see soon. John wants to talk to us next week."

"You keep reminding me," Kierston said and shivered. "Jason, I have this funny feeling . . ." He held her closer. "Maybe it's just the argument the Barens had before Raymond left. He told Sue Ann that she'd be receiving a surprise from your grandfather today. A good-bye present, a suitcase with sable coats."

They heard a sound like a shot echo in the forest. They froze, straining to hear. An instant passed; then they knew it was a shot, and that it had come from Nicole's house. They ran frantically towards the Barens'.

"Someone help! Help me!!"

Nicole's screams reached them as they threw open the front door. They raced up the stairs. Nicole was on her knees, crying beside her mother. Mrs. Baren was lying lifeless on the bed, blood trickling from her temple and a gun dangling from her hand near the floor.

"Kierston, please," he pleaded, "get Nicole out of here!" He grabbed for the phone to call Harrington and the police, averting his eyes from the body before him.

Harrington chartered a plane, and they flew to Kentucky for Sue Ann Baren's funeral. Jason couldn't shake the sight of Sue Ann Baren from his mind. During the funeral, he held Kierston and Nicole's hands while Nicole sobbed against

Michael's chest.

Raymond Baren continually shifted his eyes from the gravesite to Nicole. He had told no one that Sue Ann was pregnant at her death. Something in his manner had changed. He was sober, yes, but his heart was in his eyes. He appeared to want to reach out to Nicole, but was lost as to how.

Winston had sent a wreath, which Nicole would not accept. Jason saw it conspicuously set outside their circle at the gravesite.

Curiously, Jason had only learned today that Mrs. Baren's ranch, where he stood, used to be his grandmother's.

"Your grandmother bequeathed it to Winston, who ordered Raymond to sell," Harrington had told him. "That's how Raymond and Sue Ann met. Nicole's grandfather bought the ranch."

'Why, Grandfather?' Jason thought. 'Why do you have this affect on people?'

Everyone flew back to New York. Kierston and Jason stayed with Harrington and insisted Nicole join them for a few days.

"You knew it was going to happen, Harrington," Marcus warned Harrington privately. "It's begun again. And it will get worse. Jason has to get used to it. Winston will never change."

Nicole grieved for her mother. She wanted to hate her father. Michael and Bobby showed up. Marisa tried to soothe her, but it was Kierston she sought out. They talked by themselves in Harrington's bedroom. Finally Nicole agreed to listen to Harrington.

"Try to talk to your father," Harrington beseeched her. "As much as I've been at odds with him, I know he's hurting. I think something magical might happen if you reach out. You're the only one who can."

Nicole bowed her head. She needed her father now more than ever. "All right. I'll try."

That evening, she and Raymond dined alone at the Baren home.

"What are you thinking about, dear?" Raymond said.

"I'll be perfectly honest, Daddy," she said, trying to hold back her tears. "I've wanted to hate you, but I can't. But I do hate Winston, and I know you and he are as thick as thieves. I also know you've done some shameful things."

Raymond viewed her with surprise, and she pressed on. "I love you in spite of it, but you should know it's particularly due to Kierston, Jason, and Harrington, and all of my friends."

When Nicole explained Jason's deductions about Sue Ann, Raymond gasped in shock. "You and Jason knew about your mother and Winston!"

"I knew and I told Kierston, Michael, Bobby, and Jason. And we were all aware of why she committed suicide."

Raymond had bowed his gray head, shaken that she had known about her mother, and utterly disgraced. Not only had he inadequately held his wife's affections, but he had stayed on at Todd Industries, working for the man who had bedded his wife. He was degraded and humiliated. At least Nicole didn't know her mother had been pregnant.

"You knew and you're still here?" He choked with emotion.

Nicole was thunderstruck. Had her father been more shattered by her mother's death than she realized? Very quietly she went round to his chair. "I miss her, Daddy!"

"After all I've done to you!" Raymond said, standing, gulping in air. His voice was filled with bewildered pain. His eyes looked like they saw something horrible.

"Don't torture yourself, Daddy," she said helplessly.

His thoughts ran wild as he took in her beautiful features. This young girl was his daughter. His daughter! A part of him! It was as though he were seeing her for the first time. She had been as unappreciated as any person could be. His heart sank. She had stayed with him in spite of his faults. He told her this, then said, "What had I ever done for you?"

"I don't know, Daddy," she said, helplessly, "but you're all I have." The thought startled her. Why had she never considered this before? "I'm so miserable! If I could only reach out to you; if you would only take me in your arms. Oh Daddy, we've never even hugged!" The words weren't enough. She needed desperately for him to know she understood him so he in turn could understand her. She fumbled for the words, her eyes evasive as she searched. "I'm really different from the people you've known. I don't really want anything from you, except . . ." Tears appeared in her eyes. "Except . . . well, I want you to love me. And I want you to be happy. I really do. Believe me, I understand, because I'm having problems, too."

Raymond felt the first surge of parental concern in his life. He gently held her hand. "We're both vulnerable . . ."

"I would never take advantage of you, Daddy."

"You don't understand, Nicole. I've done terrible things."

Nicole started to cry. When he pulled her close, she threw her arms around his neck. "If only you knew, Daddy!" she sobbed. "I've done terrible things, too! I've been a horrible friend to Jason—I'm having trouble coping! I hate Winston so much that I also disliked Jason!"

Raymond's eyes lifted to the ceiling, considering that which his daughter thought horrible. Compared to his actions, her confession was pale. He told her as much.

"I know all about you, and what I don't know, I can imagine," Nicole said tearfully. "But I still love you."

He guided her into the living room, still holding her close, and they sat down together. "Please don't cry, dear," Raymond pleaded. "Why, do you know, you're the first person I've ever opened up to? I've never had a confidant, a friend." 'This is a new experience, to say the least,' he thought, bewildered at his peace.

Nicole wiped her eyes. "I can believe it."

He smiled in response to her affectionate expression. "This might take some doing. I'm set in my ways. I don't know if I can break old habits, but I suppose it's time to try. I'm sixty-five years old, but I'll try."

She told him she wasn't expecting miracles, for he still had to deal with Winston, who should not see the new Raymond Baren emerge until Raymond was ready to leave Winston for good. Raymond choked back his emotions, suddenly realizing the only way he could make that break was to rely on Nicole's love.

"When one is addicted it has to be a clean break . . ." she responded. Then she cried again for her mother, and Raymond Baren did what any father would do. He hugged his daughter, giving her comfort, and in turn felt a deepening sense of comfort himself.

"I was going to call you," John said, looking at the young couple standing in the hallway outside his Park Avenue apartment. "Come in."

Jason sensed a longing in John's voice. It was after 9:00 P.M. on August 22. Kierston looked around the room and immediately spotted Diana's portrait over the mantel. Jason noticed it, too. They gravitated to the seats nearest it, somehow finding comfort there, as John always did.

"Happy Birthday again, Jason."

"Thank you, sir."

"Are you two all right? That was a pretty nasty thing that happened with Mrs. Baren . . . you being there and all. Want to talk about it?"

While Kiersten listened, Jason gave John a detailed description of the funeral, leaving out his observations about Mrs. Baren's body. He didn't want to upset John, as he had his father.

On the flight back from Kentucky, Jason had told Harrington how upset he was about Mrs. Baren. "I know Vincent Morello didn't commit suicide or anything, but you did see him mortally wounded, didn't you, Father? Did it bother you?" He and Kierston had noticed that Harrington and Marcus were visibly upset by the question.

"I've seen men die," John told them. "It's god-awful. I noticed you didn't bring up the body, so I'll just mention it right out. You'll think about it a long time. But you'll get over it. It's natural what you're going through."

"Thank you, sir," Jason said in relief.

"I appreciate it, too," Kierston added.

"Don't thank me too soon, you two. I'm about to add another burden to your shoulders. I want to talk to you about Diana and Harrington. Are you both up to it?"

For two hours, Jason and Kierston listened. During that conversation Kierston knew the course of her life was changing. When John had finished and waited for a reply, Jason looked at her, and she couldn't find words to express herself.

"I think I need to be alone for awhile," she said finally.

Jason understood. That's exactly how he had felt.

Kierston never questioned why they immediately got on a plane for California. She was lost in her thoughts, even as Jason drove them in a black Ferrari into the Bel Air Mountains. When he turned off of Bel Air Road to a private drive, she absently watched him punch the computer panel built into the Ferrari dashboard. The gates opened.

Only when they neared the hilltop did Kierston sit up in startled attentiveness. A magnificent home had come into view against the twinkling lights.

"Stop the car!" she commanded.

Kierston opened her door, stepped out, and stared up at the home. Lighted wood and glass swirled around against the full moon in twisting geometric designs. She had never imagined such designs and forms combining together, but there they were. A round roof swept into a high plateau in the center. From the plateau, the roof curved down in an arch and swooped up again into a rectangular form. Glass covered its exterior in solid bold columns. Trees surrounded the property. There were no other homes in sight.

"It's magnificent!" Kierston said excitedly as she slipped back inside the car.

Jason nodded. "I was hoping you'd say that."

Inside the home, Jason guided her into a foyer with a forty-foot ceiling that expanded with astounding grace into a living room overlooking the city. He showed her the screening room with its glass dome that opened to the stars and became an observatory. There was only one bedroom suite, and it was the only room furnished in the house. They walked out to a veranda, which overlooked a swimming pool and a tennis court. He led her to the end of the veranda to a small round table covered with white linen on top of which was a bottle of chilled champagne.

Jason held her chair, and she sat down, suddenly awakening to all her senses. The fragrance from a bouquet of roses in the center of the table tantalized her. The warm night breeze danced by her bare arms. Her own soft breathing filled her ears.

He reached out and took her hand. "You O.K.?"

She smiled at him. "Yes." She looked around her. "It's so beautiful here, Jason. It's perfect." She stared at him once again. "So this is what you've been doing. I can't sit still. It's just too lovely."

Jason watched her grasp the balustrade and arch her back. Her face basked in the glowing moonlight as her long black hair swung down to her hips. He loved the natural way she moved and acted, almost as if he weren't even there. It was too intimate a moment for him not to be near her.

He came up to her from behind. "I love you, Kierston."

She turned around without hesitating and whispered back. "I love you, too."

He kissed her then and with the touch of her body against him he lost control. He wanted to consume her body. His hands felt her breasts and thighs. He wanted to know everything about her. Everything that she had become.

Her head fell against his arm, her senses whirling, making her dizzy. He held her firmly and kissed her until he thought she might cry out. When he released her lips, he held her so close that his lips brushed hers as he spoke. Her eyes fluttered open in a daze, so totally was she disoriented that she could barely focus on the eyes blazing inches from her own. He tightened his arm around her waist and touched her hair with his left hand. His eyes drifted from her face down to her bosom rising and falling against her shirt. His lips curved up into the trace of a smile. Pain and joy seemed to radiate from his face.

'What's come over him?' Kierston thought wildly as he kissed her once again. She moaned, her arms around his neck, her lips on his, her body molded to his. Her hands felt the texture of the muscles of his shoulders, the smoothness of his neck and the roughness of his cheeks as she touched his face, feeling their lips together, their bodies together. She clung to him as she had never known she could cling to anyone. He had always been a part of her, ever since she had first heard his name.

He swept her into his arms and carried her inside and up the stairs to the bedroom.

"Put me down, Jason," Kierston said, her words almost a whisper.

He did as she asked, but it almost pained him as they stood apart.

Her hands slipped over his shoulders. Her fingers unbuttoned his shirt and slid it off. She felt the smooth skin of his chest while he stood quietly, his arms idle at his sides. It took all of his will power to restrain himself from tearing at her flimsy clothes.

Her lips touched his chest; her hair skimmed over his skin until he thought he would go mad. Her hands encircled his neck, and she kissed him, bending him towards her. His arms ached from restraint. He couldn't take it any longer.

Her pants fell to the floor, her shirt on the chair. He swung her into his arms and they tumbled onto the bed.

Her spirit was mounting in such force, that he had to dominate her for the moment to keep up with her insatiable urge. He crushed her into the bed. His lips and his hands explored her body until she cried out and reached for him, wanting him with all her passion. He made love to her gently, alleviating her pain as she opened to him. It was a warning and a strength, that love, that act of his piercing into her, challenging her and consummating life and love. She took him willingly, fiercely, experiencing the pain and moaning in pleasure that she should take this from him, bear this, and then find exquisite pleasure. To suddenly awaken from the pain and crave him all again aroused her feelings even more. She explored them, flowed with them, concentrating on nothing but the pleasure of his body against hers, and it drove her to climax with him at one and the same time. They lay still, but he did not leave her.

He held her body and rolled to his back, remaining inside her. Their lips inches apart, he studied her mouth, wet and still hungry; he smiled in tenderness and exaltation.

"You were magnificent . . ."

"So were you, Jason . . ."

As she lay her head on his chest, he stroked her hair. Then he felt her begin to move again, slowly. His hands slid down her back to her hips as she sat up, then she bent to kiss him as he began to grow inside her again.

The following morning, Kierston lay with Jason in bed, looking at the sunlight coming through the open skylight in the bedroom.

"Jason? When did John tell you about your grandmother and your father and all the other stories I heard yesterday?"

Jason looked down into her eyes. "What makes you think he did before yesterday?"

"You took it too calmly—and this home—you told me last night before you fell asleep that you want me to move in here. You were holding me so tightly. John told you a long time ago, didn't he?"

"Three years ago," Jason said, holding her. "And I meant every word I said last night."

CHAPTER XXVII

Jason and Kierston spent a few days in Los Angeles. Then she had to prepare for *The Accused* and he had to return East. Winston returned to Windsor Royal. Although Jason didn't speak to him personally, Winston left word with Harris that he wanted Jason to travel with him to Europe at the end of the month.

They took off for Europe, Jason well aware that Winston knew he was in receipt of his grandmother's inheritance. Winston never mentioned Sue Ann or the presents Jason had cleared out of the basement. He only said he was happy Jason was keeping him company for the next three weeks.

Jason waited for Winston to mention Diana's inheritance as they first traveled to France to witness the unveiling of the design for the new supersonic Concorde, and then flew on to the Sixth World Petroleum Congress in Frankfurt. But it wasn't until the flight home that Winston brought it up.

"I forgot to tell you, Jason," Winston said so casually he yawned. "Your grandmother left you the Todd Cultural Center."

341

"You told me you owned and built the entire Todd Center complex," Jason said, already knowing this wasn't true.

Winston chuckled. "I think I've done quite enough in my lifetime. The Cultural Center is of little significance to me, as I'm sure it is to you. Our future plans are a far cry from owning a few buildings."

Winston hid his delight, but to Jason it still glared visibly. Jason settled back and closed his eyes. 'Why did he love his grandfather?' he asked himself for the hundredth time. Every other word out of Winston's mouth had a double meaning. Yet, Jason would give anything to make Winston understand that he didn't have to be destructive to get his way. Jason knew he and his grandmother were the only people to whom Winston had ever showed any emotion. Ah, his grandmother. She must have been something. Too bad he couldn't talk to her. John Stevens would have to do.

And what of his father? Harrington had spoken to him the evening of his return from Los Angeles.

"Are you still planning to work for Todd Industries, son?"

"Yes, Father."

"If you work for your grandfather, you know he'll control you forever. John told me about your conversation after Sue Ann Baren's funeral. You know your grandfather hired Vincent Morello and Vincent Morello tried to kill me. You learned that your grandfather fought me and tried to discredit everyone associated with me. You know about your grandmother's history, your mother's, and mine—you have seen *The Invisible Power* and you still want to join him?"

"Yes, Father, I do."

Harrington reached for his son's arm. "You wouldn't work for him out of fear, would you?"

"No."

"Jason, Jason," Harrington had said, "I've seen men change, but only when their will has been so strong that they seek relief from what they are. In their lives it's an everyday struggle—but the key to these men is that they desperately want to change. Your grandfather will never change . . ."

Jason had wished he could put Harrington's mind at ease, but it was too soon. He hated to see Harrington worry, but it would only be for a little longer.

He opened his eyes. Winston was staring at him.

"You're looking rather serious, Jason. Is there something on your mind?"

Jason laughed, but told himself he'd have to be more careful around Winston. "Not everyone's as deep a thinker as you. There was nothing on my mind."

Although Jason was smiling, Winston raised an eyebrow. "You wouldn't be conning me now would you, Jason?"

"There you go again, Grandfather."

Winston laughed uproariously. "You are delightful, Jason. I'm happy you're coming aboard at Todd Industries. I'm looking forward to the New Year of 1964."

"San Jose? What's Jason doing here?" Harrington asked Thomas two months later in November of 1963 as Marcus drove them down a San Jose side street.

"An equally important question is, what are all of Thomas's security doing working for Jason?" Marcus said irritably.

Laster French, Jack Combs, Sy Gottleib, and Al Smith had all disappeared from Garvin Enterprises without as much as a good-bye. Marcus had finally caught up with them. It had taken him a month.

Thomas was still thinking about the morning headlines in the *Wall Street Journal*. Walter Kent, former Ambassador to the Court of St. James, had become a member of Todd Industries's Board of Directors. 'What did he have on you this time, old friend?' Thomas thought sadly, for he thought Walter a fine man. 'It must be something that horrifies you or you would never have betrayed Diana and her memory or violated the provision of her will.'

Legally, Harrington had the right to file a lawsuit against Walter Kent and Winston. Although Harrington still held the controlling interest in Darnley Enterprises, Winston had gobbled up a substantial portion of the company. Walter had handed over his share of Darnley Enterprises to Winston. For now, Harrington was weighing his options.

At the end of the road, he and Marcus saw the roof of a building peeking out above a twelve-foot-brick-and-plaster wall. Two guards stood at the entry behind a thick brass and wrought-iron gate.

"Thomas! Look! There's Laster French," Harrington exclaimed.

"Laster's here; they're all here," Marcus said. "I've already told you."

He stopped the Mercedes 280SE and honked the horn. Sy Gottleib and Al Smith peered out between the wrought-iron bars. Al was a former undercover CIA operative who was a master of disguise. After having worked for Harrington long ago, Sy Gottleib had rejoined the FBI.

"No need to worry, Mr. French, we're friendly," Thomas told him as they got out of the car.

Laster's deep blue-gray eyes were held in reserve. He motioned to Al Smith. "Sorry, Thomas, we can't let you in."

"Get Jason," Marcus said.

"Who says he's here?"

"Get him or I'll storm the gates."

"That won't be necessary," Jason called out.

Jason, Kierston, Bobby, and Michael walked through the inside parking area.

Thomas was shocked. Kierston was here? "I thought she was working with you," he said, turning to Harrington.

"We wrapped up two days ago."

"Then she should be at school," Thomas said, irritably.

"I suppose we should show them what a thriving business we have," Jason said to Kierston and Bobby.

Kierston nodded in agreement while Bobby narrowed his eyes in caution, and then, understanding, smiled. "Sure, why not."

"Open the gates," Jason ordered Laster. Once everyone was inside, Jason said, "I didn't think you'd find us so soon."

Kierston walked along with her father.

"I'll talk to you later," Thomas said in the most controlled voice Kierston had ever heard.

"Please don't be angry, Father."

"If I knew what you were doing, I wouldn't be upset at all," Thomas responded. "But since I don't, I'm angry as hell!"

Jason fell back into step with them, next to Kierston. "Don't get so heated up. Kierston's the mastermind behind all this. You should be proud of her."

"I am not," Kierston said.

"You gave me the idea."

"And I didn't even know it."

Inside the building, they walked through the expansive lobby past a receptionist and a secretary.

"What does Lascom stand for?" Thomas asked, viewing the insignia.

"Laser Computer Corporation," Jason responded.

"Computers? Is this a project for Todd Industries?" Harrington asked.

"I don't know," Jason said honestly.

They proceeded through a series of large research laboratories into the body of the plant. It was as silent as Cheops's Tomb.

"Are you opening for business or is this just a showcase?" Thomas asked.

"Opening for business, but . . ."

"President Kennedy's been shot," Michael cried out suddenly. "We just heard it on the radio!"

They ran back into the reception area where televisions were hooked up. Jason hastily flipped them all on. The news about the shooting filled the screens. Entranced, everybody's eyes were fixed to the televisions.

"The one great President we've had. Jesus!" Michael exclaimed wildly.

Harrington hugged Michael. Thomas held Kierston and Jason. Marcus stood with Bobby. Everyone grouped together in stunned silence. Just hours later, John F. Kennedy was officially declared dead. They were watching Vice President Johnson sworn in when John Stevens called Jason.

"Are you watching the news?"

"Yes, John."

"Horrible, isn't it. So disheartening. I hate to add to your burden, but . . . are your father and Kierston with you?"

"Yes."

"I need you all, Jason. My time is near."

Jason, Kierston, and Harrington flew together into New York and Marcus drove them to John's Park Avenue apartment. They found John propped up in bed. Although he was dying of lung cancer, he was smoking a cigarette. He greeted Harrington warmly, and then turned his attention to Jason.

"Well, Jason," he said gruffly, "we haven't seen each other for a few months. I hope you've been working hard." He looked over at Kierston standing in the doorway. His expression softened. "Has he been working hard?"

John was putting up a brave front to hide his failing health and energy. "Yes, he has," she said, coming in and kissing him. "You need to talk to Jason and Harrington so I'll be outside with Marcus."

Quietly she closed the door.

John was whiter than the sheets covering him. Although his body was thin and gaunt, his spirit had not left him. "Sit down," he commanded Harrington.

"Jason, we've never discussed this, but your grandmother left you the Cultural Center for a reason. What is it?"

Jason didn't miss a beat. "As it was her weapon, she wanted it to be mine."

"That's right, Jason! Harrington, you've done well by your son!" He laughed until he could hardly breathe.

Harrington helped John drink a glass of water. "Please, don't excite yourself, John."

John looked up lovingly at Harrington. Harrington sat down right beside him on the bed. The love between them was obvious.

"Don't you see, Harrington?" John said, trying, but failing, to be gruff. Harrington had to lean close to hear his words. "I have to be sure you're taken care of, that everyone's taken care of. This can't go on for another generation." John waved to Jason to approach. Jason pulled up a chair near the bed next to his father. "Do you remember everything I told you, Jason?"

"I remember every word."

John sighed as if relieved. But he had to be sure. "Remember, don't make any moves until you're prepared. I know you're going to be impatient, but weigh your options. And, Jason . . . when you need a breather—when you've been in the trenches too long—get the hell out for God's sake and visit with this man," John said, holding tightly to Harrington's arm. "He's the greatest human being I've ever met. You understand?"

"Yes, I understand."

"Now tell your father what you really think of your grandmother's inheritance," John said.

Jason smiled slightly. "It's quite a coincidence. I've already started building a Todd Center West, Father."

John saw Harrington's surprise. "He understands everything, Harrington. Diana would have been pleased. By God, he's almost a reincarnation of her! First the Center and then a satellite network. You know your grandmother was instrumental in the first broadcast on closed circuit television for the 1939 World's Fair, don't you, Jason?"

"A satellite network?" Harrington interrupted. "What's this all about?"

"He'll tell you later, Harrington," John said. "Just give me a minute alone with him . . . tell Kierston I want to see her, too . . . just a minute with Jason though . . ."

"Please, Father," Jason said. "I . . ."

"He has a lot to tell you, Harrington," said John. "Just let us talk first."

Although Harrington was apprehensive about Jason's future, he allowed John his request.

"Come closer," John urged the young man when the door closed. "Good. Now listen to me, Jason. To be a wise leader, you must surround yourself with men such as yourself who in turn will pick men like themselves to work under them. Tempt men with inspiration not with fear, and compensate men handsomely who are unafraid . . . and for God's sake don't forget about those secret files your grandfather has locked away! Now tell me again about Lascom, about what you have in mind," John said, closing his eyes.

"Lascom stands for Laser Computer Corporation. It will manufacture computers for business and ultimately for home use. A special division will manufacture computers for spacecraft."

As Jason continued, John heard the young man's voice lighten, just as he had wanted. Jason was talking about one of his passions.

Jason explained that advances in computer technology allowed for the utilization of lasers to condense the size of computer memories onto silicon chips, thereby drastically reducing the size of computers. Lascom intended to develop this new form of computer technology in the future, but for now, it would market larger computers within two years.

Bobby Christian, who had left Remington Rand to

become Lascom's president, would keep in close contact with the Stanford University research faculty. Jason's contacts had proved invaluable, and the scientists admired his innovative ideas.

"You already know I hired Laster French and Al Smith away from Thomas. He knows I've done it, but not why."

"You must tell them all now: your father, Thomas, Marcus, Michael . . . I know Kierston already knows. She's quite a young woman, Jason. Protect her . . . be sure to protect her!"

Jason nodded. "I will, John, don't worry."

"I know it's been rough on you, but it will get rougher. You must let everyone know. They'll be involved, whether you like it or not. If your grandfather doesn't already know, once he confirms in his own mind that you can't be controlled, everyone will have to be on guard. In the last few years, your behavior has bought you time. You know the reasons why that will soon be over. Now are you ready with Lascom?"

Jason sighed. "We're ready, John. Lascom will go into operation after the New Year, regardless of what happens."

John grabbed his hand. "You get that son-of-a-bitch, Jason, do you hear? Don't you dare let your feelings for him get in the way of your reason!"

Jason gripped John's hand tightly in return. Then he leaned over, and to John's surprise, he kissed his forehead. "Don't worry. I'll take care of everything."

John saw the cold eyes, but felt the soft gesture. Inside Jason's heart was a tremendous love for Harrington Todd and Kierston Garvin. Tears appeared in John's eyes, and he was unprepared for Jason's reaction. Jason took him into his arms and allowed John to cry against his chest.

"You can die in peace, John. I promise you. Neither Harrington Todd nor Kierston Garvin will meet the same fate as my grandmother and mother."

CHAPTER XXVIII

It was Christmas Eve, 1964. As Winston's chauffeur drove the limousine through the Windsor Royal gates, Jason studied the trees, all were bare except for the evergreens, whose graceful branches were mantled with snow. His thoughts were on John Stevens. He still missed him.

John had died three weeks after his visit. The New York *Times* heralded him as an American writer who had been a legend in his own time. That would not have impressed John. "My proudest moments were when guiding you and sharing my life with your father and your grandmother."

Harrington's loss was almost equal in pain and sorrow to the loss he had felt after Diana's and Cara's deaths. He had decided to create a one-man show entitled simply—*John Stevens,* which would take up where *Remember When* had left off. Harrington was starring in it. Conrad would direct. Jason insisted upon financing it. Harrington had also been asked by President Johnson to get the Presidential Award ready as planned by 1966. He intended to have John Stevens receive the honor posthumously.

At the clearing, Jason looked ahead to Windsor Royal and told himself that tonight would be as much for John as for his mother, father, and grandmother.

He glanced at the lawn, sweeping down from the mansion in a winterland of white. The sky looked as though an artist's brush had swept strokes of gray and white between the twinkling stars. The car was fast approaching Windsor Royal. Hurriedly, Jason reviewed all that had transpired since November.

His Todd Industries employment contract had been drafted and included a full disclosure of Lascom. Although everything was ready at Lascom, nothing had been implemented at the time he submitted his contract. He truthfully disclosed Lascom's minimal staff, and its meager assets, and had stipulated that Lascom was exclusively his company.

Winston and Mel Christian, Jr., a member of the Board of Directors and Chief Executive Officer of Todd Industries, had signed the contract and returned it to him without comment. The following day, he put money into the Lascom account and pre-typed orders were sent out for Lascom equipment.

It was now December. He carried the official title of Vice-President in charge of Special Projects for Todd Industries, and Lascom's production was in full swing. Within a year, Bobby would implement his detailed plan, which included a day-by-day management calendar, and Lascom would hopefully turn a profit.

Harrington, the Garvins, Marcus—everyone knew a portion of his plans, but Kierston alone knew what tonight meant. Thomas had, however, surprised him with an offer.

"Jason, if you have any trouble with your grandfather, you can count on me. I might even be interested in buying Lascom one day. I'd like you to have alternatives, for your spirit and your protection."

Jason had found his ironic. "And I was considering that one day I might make you an offer to buy Garvin Enterprises."

"Who knows," Thomas had said to Jason's surprise. "You might need her one day. After all, I'm complimented that you implemented my Anaid idea. I suppose there's no better catalyst than flattery to win my support."

The two stone fireplaces were ablaze in the medieval Banquet Room. The table was set with gold china and French crystal. As Jason took his chair, he noted that Winston looked especially pleased with himself tonight.

"I was at the Todd Center today," Winston informed him. "As you know, we hire our men on Christmas Eve."

Jason had heard this many times. Winston continually told him his tactics for weeding out the men from the boys.

"Were there many applicants?" Jason asked, picking up a wafer and spreading it with paté.

"There were, but few were hired," Winston said, joining him in an appetizer. "I was amused by the fresh-faced idealists. Our legal department was in need of two good men. We found only one. I'm afraid the young fellows these days have no understanding of Montaigne's words: 'There is as much freedom and latitude in the interpretation of the laws as in their creation.'

"Justice doesn't have anything to do with legal decisions. It's the person whose interpretation is approved who's victorious. I'm never for hiring a man with a liberal education. The liberal arts broaden the imagination but don't do a blasted thing for a businessman except confuse him. Not only do they take time away from work, but they fill a man's head with dreams instead of realities. Somehow, I always think of creative men as indecisive. I like dealing with men like you, who meet issues squarely and make decisions. Actually, that's why I bothered going to the interviews at all. I wanted to size up your competition. You have none."

Jason sat back as the butler cleared the plates and placed a salad before him. His grandfather wasn't very subtle. Jason had known for years that Winston pumped himself up with his pontifications, but twenty-two years of it was enough.

"There's very little room at the top," Winston was

saying, "but every man wants to get there. I've never met a man yet who wasn't eventually willing to destroy himself trying. Fear and money, that's what . . ."

"Who are you trying to convince, me or yourself?" Jason interrupted with a smile.

"What?"

"I've had time to observe," Jason said, changing course. "Corporate men fear failure every day. They're on the line to make money and decisions. They fear they'll not make enough money. They fear they'll make the wrong decisions. They fear men coming up the ladder. They fear those men will out-perform them and take away their jobs and their prestige. They're so afraid that they compromise their principles. They fear so much that they demand their wives and children succumb to the same pressures. They insist their family kiss the ass of every corporate official above them. They employ protégés who will cover their backs or who will bail them out of trouble if they make a wrong decision. They use others' ideas as their own. And being enmeshed in fear, they won't let anyone close to them.

"They are careful of what they say. They are careful of whom they offend. They are pleasant and dependable while beneath their pathetic, conniving natures they dislike most of the people around them and wish to God they could find a job they enjoyed.

"I think it's all a waste of time and energy. If they fear their work, that fear will permeate every other area of their lives. If that's the way they want to succeed, to be driven, let them. If they embrace that system, they'll eventually destroy themselves. I don't want to think about such men nor have them around me. They'll get in my way."

"Those are noble words," Winston said with guarded eyes. "I wish you luck."

In silence Jason finished his salad and sipped his glass of wine. The second butler returned and cleared their plates again, placing the roast turkey, dressing, cranberry sauce, garden potatoes, and green beans before them. Jason immediately started eating, keenly aware of the quiet interrupted only by the crackling of the fire.

Winston sat very still. In the shadows, deep lines creased his brow. Suddenly, he chuckled in amusement.

"You're still young, Jason, and delightfully naive. I'm going to have to keep my eye on you a little more carefully. You're off the track a bit. Fear is a tool used to coerce men to work. Of course, those who are unafraid are the only ones who can use it."

Jason sighed, suddenly bored again. He got up from the table. "I have something to show you." He left the room.

When he returned, the plates had been cleared. A silver service was placed to his left with coffee pot, creamer, and sugar. Cups were at their places.

Jason unloaded papers and rolled up charts before Winston.

"What is all this?" Winston demanded.

"Your Christmas present. A Todd Center West."

Winston looked up at Jason and down to the papers. He began to go through the files. Then he opened the architectural plans and studied them. He pored over the information in silence for twenty minutes and finally looked up.

"Why didn't you consult me? You aren't experienced enough to take on a project like this."

"I've already taken it on. I bought the land myself. The plans are drawn up; the city O.K.'d the permits and zoning. The land is leveled. Everything is ready for an April construction date."

"You're a bright boy, but there's no use pushing yourself."

Jason tapped the sheets. "The figures are here. Everything is ready."

"You'd better let me decide what's best for Todd Industries, or is it that you have decided that you should run things now that you're working for my company."

"This is what you hired me to do. You placed me in charge of special projects. This is the first. I have many others already in progress."

Winston frowned. "Are you suggesting that I don't have

ideas of my own?"

Very calmly Jason faced him, his eyes were direct, unwavering. "Don't, Grandfather, not with me."

"What do you mean?"

"The position you hired me for had no restrictions. And don't tell me I'm inexperienced. You hired me, and you have the experience to know what men are qualified to do. You've tried these tactics on everyone. Don't try them on me."

Winston stared at him, feigning bewilderment. "I don't know what you're talking about."

Jason sat back. "Yes, you do."

"I really don't," Winston said, looking at the plans. "Anyway, this isn't a new idea, Jason. I thought of it twenty years ago."

Jason refrained from mentioning that the original Todd Center was Diana's idea. Leaving him the Cultural Center in her will was ingenious. It was almost as if she had foreseen this day. "No, you didn't," he said finally. "Twenty years ago it wouldn't have been feasible. First, it was wartime and building materials were restricted. Second, Los Angeles wouldn't have supported a Center at that time."

"How dare you contradict me!" Winston stormed. "I raised you to be an 'employee' of Todd Industries. I didn't raise you to try and steal the company out from under my nose! You'll have to pay your dues just like I did! I'll not have you building anything in the name of Todd without my say so!"

"God only has one 'd' in His Name. Maybe you should eliminate one 'd' from yours!" Jason said, coming forward, his eyes dark.

Winston raised an eyebrow. "I didn't know you'd turned into a humorist."

Jason already knew the answer to his question, but asked it anyway. "Are you telling me you don't want me to build anything for Todd Industries, that my title is figurative?"

"Exactly."

"And that you don't want me to make a move without

your approval?"

"Precisely. What did you expect. I've given you every-thing. I've made you who you are. You're my grandson, isn't that enough? Your function is to one day oversee my empire, and I will choose that day."

"You made me who I am? I didn't have anything to do with it?" Jason asked quietly.

"Well, of course you're a bright boy. You're my grandson. But it was I who gave you every opportunity."

"You did present opportunities. But just because you raised me, that doesn't give you the right to take credit for my entire existence. It doesn't give you the right to meddle in my personal affairs. And it doesn't give you the right to paint whatever image you wish of me before the world. The purpose of my life is not to be a professional grandson. I do not choose to live my life through yours. I don't want a title at Todd Industries that binds me to a meaningless existence.

"If you don't want me involved with this Center and other projects like it, you should never have hired me as Vice-President in charge of Special Projects. If you don't believe in my abilities, then you most assuredly should not have hired me for that job. I should have been placed at the bottom of Todd Industries, starting out as a junior executive."

Winston's large frame was straight and rigid. His white head of hair was combed to perfection. His dark eyebrows loomed over his eyes. Jason knew exactly what he was thinking: Winston was putting him through the first test—the first of many—and he was weighing how far to push him. His next words would appear to be a concession, to make amends —but instead, they would deepen their conflict.

"I can't start you out as a junior executive," Winston said at last. "You're overqualified. You've been working your way up the ladder since you were a teenager." He frowned and came forward in his chair. "If this Center means so much to you, go ahead, Jason. It's yours. But remember, I've given you the opportunity to go ahead. It's really too small to quibble about. Call it the Jason Todd Center West if you wish. But after this, you are to consult me before you attempt to secure another project."

Jason deliberately reached for a manila envelope in his inside pocket. He took out two documents and signed them. Afterwards, he handed them to Winston.

"What are these?" Winston demanded.

"The deed to the land and my resignation."

Winston threw them onto the table. "I said you could have the Center."

"Don't insult me by taking my years of work and handing them back to me as your gift to me." Jason stood. "If I had wanted this Center for myself, I would never have felt any obligation to show it to you. Although it was with my own money, I bought the land for Todd Industries. I was working for Todd Industries. Now I am not. The Center remains where it was intended to remain. With you.

"You've lied to me. You've tried to control me. You've had me followed after I asked you to stop. You've restricted my phone calls, my mail; you've dictated whom I can see and whom I cannot. You've tried in every way imaginable to control me. But I cannot be controlled, because neither you nor Todd Industries has a hold on me to the point that I will lose myself for either of you. You are so deathly afraid that someone will betray you, that someone will get the upper hand, that you try to destroy those who wish only to build and never even dream of betraying you. I am such a man. Since you don't understand this, I no longer have any moral obligations to you."

"Sit down," Winston said sternly.

"I won't sit with a man who trusts me so little that he spies upon my every move. I won't sit with a man who has to exploit others to build. Do you want me to remind you of the circumstances that kept my grandmother under your roof? Possibly I should remind you of what you did to my mother and father. I'm sure you remember Vincent Morello. The list is very long: Raymond Baren, Joe Field, Arlene Habor, Sue Ann Baren, Marisa Benito, politicians, businessmen, former executives of Todd Industries, those who are working there now, world leaders, and religious prelates."

"How dare you accuse me!" Winston declared in stormy indignation. "You're lucky to be a part of my world at all!"

Jason stared down into the cruel gray eyes. "I'm no longer a part of your world. You're lucky I stayed here as long as I did."

Winston began to chuckle. "What have I wrought?" He shook his head. "Judas or Brutus, my boy, you are the spitting image of your father!"

"Thank you."

Winston glared at him. "That was not a compliment, Jason, believe me it was not. Now sit down and stop talking nonsense."

"You stand, Grandfather. I won't sit with you . . ."

"All right, Jason," Winston said, abruptly standing. "What will it take to keep you at Todd Industries?"

Jason had anticipated these words. His eyes fastened on Winston without a flicker of emotion. "You will remain what you have always been, Grandfather. You will never change. I accept that . . ."

"Yes, well, what do you want then?" Winston demanded.

"Anyone, living or dead, who has, is, or will be associated in any way with Harrington Todd or Kierston Garvin will be, from this day forward, free from any of your influences or exploitation whether it be a direct or indirect action—none will be manipulated—none will be plagued by the memory of the dead or plotted against by one who is living . . . I will be the one exception. You let me have free rein to work and build in the way I wish, and I personally will be your 'sport.' You raised me. Now I'm giving you the chance to convince me in whatever way you wish that I should be like you. Isn't that a much more enticing game? You can even keep your secret room downstairs. You can try to influence me in any way you wish, but only as it relates to business. My personal life is my own."

Winston's face had hardened into cruel lines. "What room are you referring to?"

"The room downstairs in the basement, I believe you

call it the 'Operations Room,' where you've hidden files on everyone from Presidents of the United States to captains of industry and union men, from heads of foreign governments to U.S. senators. From Harrington Todd to Thomas Garvin. The list goes on and on."

"How did you find out about that room?"

Jason had not known for sure until this moment, but he was not about to tell Winston that. Marcus had informed him about the secret files. So had John Stevens. When he had found Harrington's gifts in the basement, he had seen that there had been rooms constructed there that were not accessible from the basement. Marcus, Harrington, and John had noticed it, too. The entrance to the room was probably in the library where Winston spent so much time. He had not cared to search for it, although it would have been easy for him to gain entry.

"Forget about the room. It's yours to do with as you wish. I don't intend to infringe on your territory. Forget about everything except the offer I'm placing before you. I will stay, but the battle will be between you and me, exclusively."

"Since you're being so critical of my business ethics, how do you rate yourself, working for Todd Industries while on the side you've been building your own company, "Lascom? Maybe you're more like me than you think."

"Lascom was formed as an alternative for my life. I can build my own empire, Grandfather. I don't need you."

"So you were trying to show me, is that it?"

"To the contrary. I don't like to waste time. If you and I couldn't work things out, I had Lascom. I wasn't trying to show you anything."

"So you don't trust me."

"No."

"I don't trust anyone either. Doesn't that make us more alike than you think?"

Jason smiled. "I didn't say I distrusted everyone, Grandfather, only you."

"And if you could trust me?"

"If you agree to my terms, I'm willing to take the gamble that you will keep your word, and I in turn will think of Lascom as just another investment, not a company where I could focus my career."

Winston smiled. Jason was such an innocent, or was he? Lascom was already setting up for business, and at a hectic pace. Was Jason truthful to the end? Maybe Jason didn't realize how far he had already come over to Winston's ways. Well, he'd find out from Al Smith. Winston regarded his grandson with interest.

"I thought I told you never to let a woman turn your head."

Jason turned so cold that Winston had trouble looking him in the eye. "I won't discuss Kierston."

'He'll never win,' Winston thought with satisfaction. 'Yet he'll present a most unusual challenge. Unlike Diana and Harrington, Jason was willing to play the game, a high-stakes game with his own soul on the line—his soul versus my empire.'

"Sit down, Jason, please," Winston said, all at once amicable and charming.

Jason did sit down now. He watched Winston pour their coffee, artfully, like a gentleman of breeding. Jason knew he was biding his time. Winston would agree to his conditions only if he were granted something in return. He waited to hear what it was.

"So, Jason, you decided to come to your father's rescue and protect your ladylove," Winston said dryly.

"Yes."

Winston considered this, and then the thought came to him that he had waited for. He smiled broadly.

"What if I could prove to you that your father is not the man he seems? If I could prove to you that he has lived a lie— what would you say to that?"

"You're overstepping the boundaries, Grandfather. I told you—you may not in any way interfere in Father's life. I won't listen to anything you have to say about him."

"All right, Jason. It's you and I. You know very well that

you've laid a proposal before me, which, if I accept and then breach, will damage Todd Industries. If you leave, you will destroy my legacy. If I destroy you, I destroy my legacy. I commend you on your strategy. I'm in checkmate. We both know you're a man of honor, and you're forcing me to be one."

Winston sank back in his chair, chuckling. "I will agree to everything, but you must give me your word. I will not interfere with your father or Kierston or your personal life. But first, you are to continue listening to my advice. You don't have to take it, but you must listen. Secondly, if I wish to show you how I run things, you must take the time to understand fully how I operate. Thirdly, I will continue to work in whatever way I choose so long as my actions don't encroach on the boundaries you've laid out."

"Or any of my business associates. No games in my department at Todd Industries. I'm your only sport, remember that."

"Agreed, but no one is to know about our agreement. And most important, if you ever find out that your father is not the man you thought he was, then you are to do things my way. If you agree to this, we have a deal."

Without hesitation, Jason stuck out his hand. Winston shook it.

"Welcome to my world, Jason. I'm proud of you. I'll be seventy-six years old next month. I'll live another ten years at least. You will give me the most exciting years of my life. I raised a worthy opponent or partner, time will tell me which."

"I'm glad you see things my way," Jason said.

"Before I die, Jason, you will see things my way. I won't have to lift a finger."

"Just keep your hands where I can see them."

"I intend to, Jason. From now on you will see every move I make." Winston's eyes glistened. "I honestly think I love you, Jason."

"I know you do, Grandfather. That's why I'm here."

Winston was taken aback. "What do you mean?"

Jason's heart filled with sadness, for he had wished to

say he loved him, too. But he warned himself to be careful. "It isn't important, Grandfather." As Jason expected, Winston shrugged off the comment, which was a further verification to Jason of his position, yet it brought pain. Part of his grandfather had been dead for years, or possibly had never been cultivated. That alone was what made him so dangerous, and yet so frail.

CHAPTER XXIX

In June of 1965, Winston drove by Todd Industries's headquarters, having dropped Shaun Miller, his latest mistress, at the Plaza after dinner at "21." The chauffeur slowed per his instruction to allow him to peer up at the second story. Lights were on in Jason's suites. His grandson had been too busy to notice that his position, with all its privileges, was wreaking havoc with company morale. Winston ordered the chauffeur homeward and sank back against the seat to reflect.

Many of his executives were unhappy with Todd Industries's management and had thought that Jason might be just the man to help them with job transfers, raises, and more autonomy in their work. But Jason's special privileges had angered them. Unfortunately, Jason had performed better than Winston had anticipated. Jason had won back the respect of Todd Industries's executives through hard work, showing he wasn't being handed anything. He actually worked at his job, and harder than anyone else.

Through the spring, Jason and his staff worked around the clock double-checking labor details, costs, contracts, and prospective lessus before the Todd Center West ground breaking in April. By the end of April, forty percent of the space at the Los Angeles Center was leased, while at the newest Center, in Chicago, thirty-five percent of the space was reserved by June.

Winston chuckled to himself. He'd taught Jason well. Now Winston had to find another way to keep his executives at bay. It was imperative that Jason have as few allies as possible when he tried to take over Todd Industries.

When Winston entered his office the following morning at 8:00 A.M., he noted the curious glances of his three top executives. Across the oak paneled suite, they lingered near chairs positioned in a semi-circle in front of his massive writing desk. Never had he called them together this early in the morning.

Slowly, he walked around his desk where his secretary had left seven newspapers lined up in a row. When he sat down, they followed suit.

Raymond Baren placed his right leg over his left and an arm over the back of his chair. His shoes were polished, but the soles were worn, which was evident as his right foot nervously moved up and down. Mel Christian, Jr., dressed in navy blue, sat with his feet planted on the floor. He had picked up a paper to study. Kurt O'Daniel, prissy and meticulous, always looked uncomfortable. His left eye twitched behind thick black-rimmed glasses. The spectacles, made of clear glass, were used to disguise Kurt's nervous tick.

With a steady, deliberate hand, Winston displayed the front page of the *Wall Street Journal*. "Jason has become Todd Industries's goodwill ambassador in just six months. I'm proud of his progress and furious about his working quarters." Winston let this sink in. "I left it to you to decide where our new Vice-President in charge of Special Projects was to set up his offices. Where did you put him? On the second floor!"

"Do you want Jason to have new offices?" Raymond asked.

"Thank you for clarifying my position, Raymond," Winston said disparagingly. "Would anyone like to volunteer his space?"

No one spoke. Their offices were on the top floors. Having worked their way up the corporate ladder, they had no intention of slipping down a rung or two in appearances.

"I have another alternative," Winston said casually. "Possibly it wouldn't matter where Jason worked as long as he had everyone's full cooperation."

"But he does, Winston," Kurt declared defensively. "I hope Jason didn't insinuate that I . . ."

"Jason wouldn't bother," Mel Christian, Jr., said.

"That's where you're wrong, Mel. Jason told me he's been hearing complaints about the way Todd Industries is being run."

Raymond sighed inwardly. Jason had never said anything of the kind. Mel agreed with him, but Kurt was visibly upset. 'Nitwit,' Raymond thought.

It was obvious that Jason was too popular, which meant too powerful. Winston inevitably played his executives against one another so he stayed in command.

Winston wrapped up the meeting by "strongly" suggesting that everyone make daily visits to Jason on the second floor. He would expect a report from each of them at the end of each working day. What better way to keep an eye on Jason and again build up executive resentment towards his grandson?

"You stay, Raymond," Winston said as the others filed out. When the door closed and Raymond was back in his chair, Winston continued. "You appeared to be bored by the conversation, Raymond, or is it that you agree with Mel that Jason is a refreshing change?"

"I agree with Mel."

"Then maybe you'd like to oversee the Washington operation again, Raymond."

Raymond surprised himself by being delighted with the

same suggestion that had devastated him twenty years before. "All right, Winston."

'So, my old ally, you're shifting ground,' Winston thought. "I want you to speak to the appropriate people about getting new defense contracts and also about paving the way for Jason to get FCC approval for a television station. You'll oversee the operation from New York."

"You're pushing very hard for Jason."

"And I'll continue. Our boy doesn't understand the inner workings of the corporate world. He can learn the hard way, but I don't want us to lose money in the process. By the way, that award Harrington's organizing. The Presidential Award. I want you to promote Harrington around our nation's capital. By all rights, he should be receiving that award."

Raymond gasped. "I can't do that. How would it look for him to be the first recipient of an award he founded! Besides, I think it's going to John Stevens."

Winston overruled him. "Once you've promoted Harrington in Washington I want the word to reach Jason that I was behind this boost for his father. Do you understand, Raymond?"

"No, I don't."

"Well," Winston retorted dryly, "you understand enough."

The smoldering summer of 1965 erupted as blacks destroyed Watts in Southwest Los Angeles. Although out of the riot area, the Todd Center West, under construction, was near enough to be a concern to Jason, who had his staff monitor the riots on television.

Michael Christian was deeply affected by the riots; his heart was with the people. Michael still wore his natural curly hair long. His concession to the establishment was a tailored suit. His distinction was the loosened tie and white socks. Winston had a fit every time he bumped into Michael and mumbled about the rabblerousers who were tearing down the country. Jason had thrown dozens of memos regarding

Michael's attire into the trash.

In the midst of a staff meeting this summer morning, Jason's emergency line rang. Michael Christian stopped in mid-sentence, looking from the television to Jason. 'Not more bad news,' he thought, waiting.

"I told you never to associate with liberals!"

Jason sighed. "I'm in a meeting."

"Remember the pledge? You're supposed to listen. You have to keep your promise," Winston stormed. Jason gestured for Michael to clear out the staff as Winston continued. "These filthy peasants picketing our corporations, plundering our property, expounding on love and equality are downright un-American. They call themselves flower children of all things. By God, you'd think they want the entire corporate world to be plowed under and go into the floral business! Next they'll be asking us to turn the other cheek in international waters!"

"What's your point?" Jason said, losing his patience.

"You'd better warn Michael Christian about his friends. If those idiots don't stop picketing WJT Aeronautics, I'll have my men kick the shit out of them! You have your television on. Take a look! And tell Michael to cut his hair!" Winston hung up.

"Turn up the sound, Michael," Jason said, slamming the receiver down.

Released a week after New Year's, *The Accused*, unlike the rebels' raging denouncements on TV, treated the subjects of injustice and bigotry rationally. The film had been nominated for an Academy Award as Best Picture and Kierston had received a Best Actress nomination.

The thought of Kierston was like a warning to Jason. "If all goes as planned," he had told her, "there will be months in the future when I won't see you. You'll be guarded, but I also want you to learn to protect yourself."

She had reminded him of her upbringing and that she had learned how to shoot a gun during the filming of *The Accused*. She was an expert markswoman.

"You have to go to target practice every month," he told

her. "Soon, you'll have bodyguards at your side at all times. I don't know when Grandfather will strike, but it will happen. Maybe not this month, maybe not this year. I would have preferred you not get involved in this . . ."

"My decision is final," she had told him. "If you're a target, I will be one as well."

Marcus had become the general of Jason's security force with Laster French, Sy Gottleib, Jack Combs, and Al Smith his lieutenants. Whether Winston struck now or years from now, Marcus and his men were on the alert, undercover, positioned and ready on both coasts. For safety, only Marcus and he knew about all their security arrangements.

Jason had to admit he was more concerned for Kierston than for himself.

"Get the staff back, Michael. Kierston's coming in for *John Stevens* a few days early. I don't want her waiting for me until midnight."

Kierston skipped down the Waldorf hallway, throwing a football in the air. Harrington let Jason use Diana's former suite. The door was cracked open. She pushed it aside.

Jason stood in the middle of the dimly lit room, a bottle of Dom Perignon in his hand. A smile crossed his face as he took in her figure. Clad in jeans, a jean jacket, and wearing a baseball cap, Kierston looked like a youngster, better yet, a street kid.

"I'm flattered you dressed for the occasion," he said, amused. "At least you could have gotten it straight. Didn't anyone ever tell you they wear helmets for football?"

"They told me," she said, closing the door, "but I'm from the school of hard knocks."

Jason laughed out loud. She had this way of making him feel lighthearted, free. "Champagne?"

In a youthful boyish gait, she strutted across the room. "Sure, mister."

In exchange for the glass, she threw the football over his head. He caught it, at the expense of half a glass of Dom Perignon.

"You've lost your touch," she said.

"Have I really?" He whisked off her hat, and the black hair tumbled over her shoulders and down her back. He pulled her near, cupping her face with his hands. "Have I really?" he whispered, kissing her.

"Is this what they call a blitz?" she sighed.

He placed her glass on the table and drew her closer. "Exactly," he answered.

There were many things on his mind but he didn't remember a one. Smelling her fragrance, the sweetness of a spring bouquet, deadened his senses to the outside world. He took in her every feature, his fingers gently outlining her lips, then kissing them.

She could always make him forget. She had the power to consume him, to make the endless hours of preoccupation with Winston disappear. She could wipe away all the hours he spent carefully considering his plans. She could lessen his pain from all the sleepless nights, when his patience had just about left him, and he thought if he'd had a gun, he would have used it. But then everything would have been lost, and his work would have been for naught. His dreams would have vanished; his visions, his accomplishments, and his purpose, and he would not have her, his exquisite love in his arms with the moon shining in through the window onto their bed. He would not be discovering that a woman could help him to forget the pain he felt from living and working in a foreign way in order to guard his visions for another day . . . and in the end, for a far greater purpose.

"Kierston," he whispered.

She didn't let him speak. She wanted him to forget everything just for a moment, just as she had to forget. For she saw a man with a warm and true heart turning colder and more distant by the moment. Was this what it took to deal with Winston? If only she could take his place for a few seconds a day. But she knew his torment came from more than Winston. It came from his frustration that he was held back from accomplishing what he knew he could.

His hands traveled down her body, feeling her soft

breasts and her thin firm legs. Then he possessed her, and she thought to herself that if love were a weapon, she would be dead. She loved him so much it was almost too painful to consider.

Mia Cara was the only restaurant in town where Jason was assured of privacy. He and Kierston dined there the following evening with Michael and Nicole in their favorite corner booth. The Beatles were playing in the background. The ambience was as festive as ever.

"Thanks for the draft deferment," Michael said quietly. "Don't want to say it too loud around here. You'll have guys standing in line."

It was because of his work on projects of national security that Jason was exempted. Articles had appeared about his satellite designs, some of which had been bought by the government. Using Michael as his assistant, Jason had continued his satellite research for WJT. Ultimately, they hoped to use them for Todd Industries International Satellite Network.

"You're welcome," Jason said, smiling. "I wish I could give a deferment to every man of fighting age." He sighed. "Have you been watching the news lately? The media's almost being used as a weapon. It's dangerous."

"But it's also a powerful force," Michael said seriously.

"Communication is the most volatile, powerful weapon in the world today. If used incorrectly, we'll all be in a lot of trouble," Jason said with equal intensity. "The sixties will be remembered for protests, social unrest, assassination, space —but I wonder if people will consider that this was the time when television brought the world into everyone's living room and people were forced to become acquainted with one another.

"America sees the world on that little screen. It becomes a very personal matter when a man is accused of being a bigot right in his own living room." He shrugged, as if trying to unburden himself, yet his shoulders were still stiff with tension.

"Maybe so," Michael said, "but some people need to have their eyes opened. I like your compassion though."

"So do I," Kierston said spiritedly. "That's why I know he's going to love my good news."

Marcus came up to the table. "Only you, Harrington, and Conrad think it's good news . . ."

He caught Jason's eye. A signal went out. Jason turned to Kierston.

"I'm all ears."

"Next year your father is planning on taking time off from *John Stevens* to direct a movie. I'm starring in it with an actor named William Wall."

"Even though *John Stevens* hasn't opened yet, I'm glad Father's thinking ahead," Jason said, amused. He looked up at Marcus. "That doesn't sound so horrible."

Marcus grunted. "It's a remake of *Your Year With Mine*."

A chill ran down Jason's spine. His mother had been writing that play just before her death. He turned to Kierston, grabbing her arm. "Are you out of your mind?"

"I loved that movie," Nicole said, defending Kierston. "Your mother wrote it. What's wrong with you, Jason?"

"I can't believe it!" Jason said.

"You liked it, too, didn't you, Michael?" Kierston asked, paying no attention to Jason.

"Are you listening to me, Kierston?" Jason demanded. "I think . . ."

"Don't hassle me, Jason. I'm intent on doing the project and I'm not superstitious."

"It has nothing to do with superstition, Kierston. It has to do with Grandfather."

"What about Winston?" Michael asked.

"I don't want to talk about him tonight," Kierston said.

"She's determined," Marcus shrugged. "Your father is determined. Conrad is determined. You don't stand a chance."

Jason shook his head. "How did I ever fall in love with an actress?"

Kierston smiled. "I guess it was just good luck."

"I still don't like it."

"Let me do this, Jason. I'm not questioning what you're doing . . ."

"Yes, but . . ."

"It's my choice."

"You're a damn fool nuisance, you know that?"

"I could say the same of you."

"She's right about that," Michael piped in. "I've wanted to say it for years, too."

"Me, too," Nicole chimed in.

What could he say? He knew it was true.

To Harrington, the opening of *John Stevens* brought back memories of years past. Two years prior to the Cultural Center's completion in 1934, Diana and John had shown him the site. "Soon the Center will be standing here," his mother had told him. He was then twelve years old. "And one day I'll write a play and you'll perform in it at the Cultural Center Theater," John had added.

Harrington remembered their words and the special glance between them; he had felt then as though he were in on a glorious secret. He told Jason and Kierston about it in his dressing room after the performance. Marisa sat beside him.

"*Remember When* was to have been that play. But your grandmother decided at the last minute not to wave a red flag."

"I see," Jason said, narrowing his eyes. "So instead, you've decided to wave a red flag with *Your Year With Mine*."

Marisa lit a thin cigar. "He's right about that, my love."

"I know he's right."

Harrington kissed Marisa's hand. A look of adoration passed between them. Marisa smiled, then turned to Jason.

"It's for your mother."

How generous Harrington was to let Marisa say it, Kierston thought, loving Harrington all the more. Marisa understood that he had never gotten over Cara.

"And for you, Jason and Kierston," Harrington added.

"You see, I'm revising the script again. You and Kierston are the subjects of the remake. It represents who you are. It's my contribution to the choices you've made; Kierston's contribution to her beliefs; and something for you to watch whenever you need a lift. That's what art is all about."

Harrington's actions touched Jason's heart, eroding another layer of loyalty he felt for Winston who had tried to care but failed. Money could never buy the essence of a man.

"You have not changed, Father. Yours is a pure spirit."

"Why does that please you so, Jason?"

"Because, Father, I care about you above all men."

At that moment, they appeared more like brothers than father and son. Harrington spoke, gazing at Jason with the deepest affection and love. "Remember when you decided to remain at Windsor Royal? You were ten. I told you to contact me if your decision ever became unbearable? Do you remember?"

Jason smiled. "Yes, I remember."

"I'm not questioning you now," Harrington said. "I support any decision you make. Whatever you do, whatever you become, I know you have good reason. Just remember, I'll always be there for you."

'What an extraordinary man he is!' Jason thought, embracing Harrington.

"I'm so proud of you! Both of you!" he said, including Kierston in their embrace. "All of us," he added, taking Marisa into his arms.

Jason laughed in delight. "Father! Whose opening night is this anyway? We're proud of you! The play's going to be a huge success!"

Raymond, Nicole, and Michael were waiting for them outside. Harrington shook hands with Raymond and received congratulations from Michael and Nicole.

"Bobby sends his best," Michael told Harrington. "He'd have been here if he could."

"I have no doubt. From what I read about Lascom, he must never get any sleep."

The press pursued Harrington outside the stage door.

"Guess what, Harrington," a reporter called out. "Someone told me you wanted to be the first recipient of the Presidential Award."

Raymond cringed. It was only a second's reaction, but Jason caught it. Then he focused in on Harrington. He was relieved to see his father was so quick on his feet.

"I've heard it all now, boys. You're pulling my leg, right?" When other reporters said they had heard the same thing, Harrington laughed. "The joke's on you. If I'd wanted an award that badly, do you think I'd have been modest? I'd have taken top billing and called it the Harrington Todd Presidential Award."

The question and Raymond's reaction had placed Jason on the alert.

"Raymond," Jason said as they waited for their cars, "why don't you accompany me to the Chicago Center site tomorrow?" Meanwhile he thought, 'Let's see if Nicole is right about her father.'

The following day, Raymond walked with Jason among the Chicago construction crew. Jason appeared equally interested and equally firm with everyone as he questioned a laborer here, a contractor there.

"Why do you talk to the blue-collar workers?" Raymond asked as they flew back to New York.

"Men who've been working on assembly lines or construction crews know more about their jobs than corporate managers. When men don't have input into their jobs, their productivity suffers."

Jason obviously knew how to challenge his staff, for they worked longer hours than any other of Todd Industries's employees and with better results. He was as tough an employer as Winston, although his positive approach with his employees was just the opposite of his grandfather's.

From the airport, they flew by helicopter to the Todd Industries headquarters. Along the way, they both read their own copies of the New York *Times*. Raymond was thumbing through the paper to find the financial section when he let out a low gasp.

On the front page the headline read:

HARRINGTON TODD FOUNDER OF PRESIDENTIAL AWARD
Does He want the Honor of Receiving It, Too?

"All right, Raymond, what do you know about this?"

Raymond cleared his throat. "Well, I . . . I don't know why, but your grandfather asked me to spread that rumor." Then he quickly added, "But I didn't. I swear I didn't. He obviously found someone else." Raymond avoided Jason's eyes, looking at the Manhattan skyline below. "Your grandfather . . ."

The chopper blades drowned out his words. "I can't hear you, Raymond," Jason said irritably.

Raymond spoke his next words in Jason's ear, fearful that the pilot might be Winston's spy. "I don't think he cared if I spread the rumor. He was more interested in your reaction to the news. I don't know why. I'm not the enemy, Jason. I don't approve of whatever he's up to. And, Jason, I suggest you scrutinize your own organization. I don't mean to alarm you, but I'm sure there's a mole there somewhere." When he pulled away, his eyes steadied on Jason's solemn features. He had spoken the truth; Jason knew it.

The chopper sat down on the headquarters' rooftop landing pad. On this very spot, in April, Winston had refused to accept Jason's suggestion to submit sketches of the new Todd Centers to the newspapers.

"I don't let anyone see anything I'm doing until the last nail is in place. Industrial espionage began during the technological revolution. From the start, competitors attempted to obtain trade secrets from untrustworthy employees, or from employees who were plants, or by hiring away a valuable executive who would divulge the secrets of his former employer. Not only do I keep a close watch on all Todd Industries's projects, but on all her employees as well, as I'm sure you can imagine."

"I should have told you sooner about the mole," Raymond said when they were in the elevator.

"How long have you known?"

"Over a year."

The confession accentuated Jason's anger, not at Raymond, but at himself. He had been waiting for Winston to break the pledge. He should have been more alert.

"Yes, that would have been helpful," he said at last.

When Jason returned to his office he found several messages from Marcus and the buzzer sounding on his private phone. He unlocked the drawer in his desk, using a tiny computer, and picked up the receiver.

"We have trouble," Marcus said. "Walter Kent just called your father. I'm sure you saw the morning headlines. Shaun Miller is the one spreading the rumors. Harrington's decided on a press conference in Washington D.C. tomorrow. I'm sending Jack Combs with him. It's the only recourse, except resigning, and Harrington doesn't want to do that. He believes too much in this award."

"He confronts things head-on," Jason said approvingly. "I'm going to do the same."

Jason flew in to Los Angeles late that evening. Before entering the Bel Air home, he told Marcus, "I want Laster to replace Al Smith as Kierston's bodyguard. Put Sy Gottleib on Thomas and Katharine. Thomas might have someone from Garvin Enterprises backing up Sy. We'll ship Al Smith back to New York with us to work with Jack Combs. You can take care of Father. Our team is going more out into the open. I want Jack and Al near me; I think one of them is the mole."

Inside, he told Kierston that the vision of Winston sitting in the drawing room before Diana's portrait, which had always affected him so greatly; no longer affected him the way it used to.

"With what I'm about to do, I know he'll be destructive. If he acts as I'm sure he will, he'll destroy all my feelings and himself in the process."

Up early the following morning, he sat in Thomas

Garvin's office at Garvin Enterprises in Beverly Hills. Marcus
accompanied him to the meeting.

Thomas sat beside them in a chair, not behind his desk as
Winston would.

"I've already talked to Bobby," Jason said. "Lascom's
been in business for over a year, and we planned on a year and
a half before we put out our product. Bobby's placing the
employees on double shifts. Even if it means we'll have
tremendous back orders to fill, I want our computer samples
on the market by February of 1966. That's just five months
from now. If you like what you see, I'm prepared to make
you an offer."

"Make it now."

"Garvin Enterprises stock for the sale of Lascom. Later
on I might ask you about your offer to sell Garvin
Enterprises. Right now, Marcus will be placing a security
team around you and Katharine. I've already warned
Kierston that we're moving more into the open."

"Problems?"

"We think there's a mole in our camp," Marcus
explained. "For once, Raymond and I agreed on something.
He told Jason the same thing yesterday."

"Who is it?"

"Jack Combs, Sy Gottleib, or Al Smith," Jason said.
"And when we find out who he is, I don't want him fired. If
we expose him, Grandfather will find someone else to take his
place. From what I understood from John, Marcus felt the
same way about Vincent Morello long ago."

Marcus cringed at the name, but neither Jason nor
Thomas seemed to notice.

Thomas's admiration for Jason was reconfirmed. He
allowed his approval to show, then a twinkle came into his
eyes. "Garvin Enterprises will be yours, Jason, for a high
price, of course."

"That's fine with me," Jason said smiling. "We both
have our Anaid, remember?"

CHAPTER XXX

"Jason! I haven't seen much of you in months," Winston said in greeting. "Happy New Year! We're going to celebrate tonight. Windsor Royal hasn't had a thousand guests since the Todd Gala! Sit down, sit down."

For over a year, Jason had continued with his whirlwind existence, flying between Los Angeles, Chicago, and New York to check on the Todd Centers' progress. Midway into 1966, he had suggested to the Board that the Centers' opening be reserved. His plan was to have the Chicago Center's opening coincide with the Democratic Convention the summer of 1968, and utilize the 1968 Academy Awards for the Todd Center West opening where those ceremonies could be booked for the Pavilion. Hosting the Convention and the Awards would be the equivalent of millions in advertising. The Board applauded his daring and voted for the change. Winston went along with it, and Jason knew Winston did so because he had something to gain. Who had told Winston about the recent activities of Lascom? Al Smith, Raymond Baren, or both?

Jason closed the door to Winston's office.

"Too bad about your father and the Presidential Award. Is there anything I can do?"

"That was months ago, Grandfather, and old news," Jason said, coming into the room. He hid his anger, although furious. Everyone knew Winston had sabotaged the Presidential Awards. Winston was showing him how he worked all right. His grandfather waved a red flag and just dared him to charge. He had to control himself, for Jason didn't want to charge blindly.

"Yes, I heard it," Winston said, intrigued that Jason refused to acknowledge his involvement in the Award's demise. 'He's becoming more sophisticated,' Winston told himself. Although amused, he shifted ground. "Still, it was a shame that it got postponed until election year. You can't blame the President, though. He'll probably need all the help he can get with the country in its present mood. But enough about that. We have more important matters to discuss."

"You're the one who brought it up, I was just making conversation," Jason said, looking out the window. The tips of a few skyscrapers pierced through the billowing mass of black clouds. The city lay below; he knew it, just as he knew Winston was waiting for him to acknowledge that the pledge had been broken. But Jason would not. A new game had begun. Never let the other guy know what you know.

Desiree Richards, the cunning elderly society matron, and Shaun Miller, her protegee and Winston's mistress, had lobbied for the Award being given during election year. At intimate dinner parties, they had spread the word. The country wasn't in the mood for grandiose awards. Desiree had been loyal to Winston for fifty years, Shaun for the last thirteen. 'Some trick,' Jason thought, especially since Winston despised women. Winston had broken the pledge, and he had to have his wits about him.

"I hear that your friend, Bobby, is a very bright young man. Implementing your ideas in a new computer field should be most lucrative."

'Why's he bringing that up?' Jason wondered. 'He's known about Lascom for two years.' "Computers aren't new. During World War II . . ."

"I don't need a history lesson," Winston said irritably. "Lasers and something to do with silicon chips, isn't it? Laser Computer Corporation?"

"You've done your homework." Jason waited.

And so have you, Winston thought dryly. Al Smith had discovered that Jason planned to make an outlandish proposal to Todd Industries to buy Lascom. Once it was turned down, Thomas Garvin would buy the company.

Lately, Thomas had begun garnering support from many of Todd Industries's largest shareholders, somewhat like an unannounced Presidential candidate who was garnering support. Jason and Garvin wanted Todd Industries. Winston smiled to himself. Wouldn't they be surprised when they both worked for him.

Lascom was turning over a tremendous profit for a two-year-old business. Government contracts gave it an air of stability. Its product paired with competent distribution and creative advertising produced a mass market appeal. With Lascom's addition to its banner, Garvin Enterprises would be considered a corporate trendsetter.

This fact alone would not only impress many financiers along Wall Street but might influence banking and insurance company executives who voted large blocks of Todd Industries's stock for trust and pension funds. Tonight at the New Year's Eve party, Winston intended to watch and listen. Someone might slip and give him a clue to the Lascom proposal, which Jason was bringing him soon. He hoped it was Raymond, but it might even be Mel Christian.

"Well now," Winston said, standing and coming around his desk, "I thought you'd be smart enough to see that I'm upset." He tossed Jason a disparaging look and moved to the high-glossed mahogany table to pour himself a glass of water. "Two years ago, I was confronted with this Lascom popping up in your corporate contract. You placed me in a most difficult position. I've been talking to the board about expanding WJ Electronics into the computer field."

"I've heard nothing about it."

Winston sipped the water from a crystal glass and returned it to the silver tray. He eyed Jason severely and returned to his chair. "As a matter of fact, just a few weeks ago WJ Electronics started to reorganize. Computer technology will be its major thrust from now on."

Jason quickly digested this information. If this future investment were true, the Board of Directors and the shareholders of Todd Industries would be extremely aggressive about getting a sound return on their dollar. His loyalty to Todd Industries could certainly become a conflict with his ownership of Lascom. But was Winston bluffing, putting on a show to warn Jason what he could do if Lascom or Jason became a threat? It would be a moot point soon.

Jason poured himself a glass of water. "You don't have any intention of converting over WJ Electronics to computers," he said, looking at Winston at last. "Why play this game?"

"Are you calling me a liar?"

"Those are your words, not mine."

Winston was too delighted by Jason's new façade to continue with the charade. He chuckled. "I placed a hypothesis before you as a warning. You should consider the consequences of your independence, Jason. Although you're my heir, you do have to be prudent, that is if you wish to gain control of Todd Industries. That is your intention, isn't it?"

Although he maintained his guard, Jason responded to Winston's honesty by relaxing. "Let's get back to the issue, shall we? Suppose your hypothetical situation became a reality, both our reputations would be on the line. I have a signed contract. How would you look, claiming that you hadn't read my disclosure of Lascom, or better yet, that you were bamboozled into signing my contract."

"That's just a mere formality," Winston said, flipping his hand, as if the remark were irrelevant. "Don't take this so personally, Jason. You're right, Todd Industries isn't converting WJ Electronics. I was just raising future possibilities. You agreed I could show you how I work. You have to keep alert."

Jason sighed. "You call this work?"

"Of course. I bring up a probability which men usually think is a reality. Most men run for the hills. You, of course, paused to reflect. I knew you would, but you should take me somewhat seriously. I do have the power to do what I say, if I should so desire. You probably already know what that could do to your position at Todd Industries."

Jason paused a moment to consider his next statement then decided to go ahead. "I was surprised when you signed my contract. Why did you do it?"

"Lascom's your pacifier. I want you somewhat happy with your new job. Without Lascom? Well, I didn't want to spoil our little game."

"You signed the contract before Christmas Eve, but even two years ago you were firmly convinced I wouldn't work for Todd Industries without Lascom?"

Winston wondered where Jason was going with these questions. "I said I'd show you how I worked. I didn't say I'd tell you everything at once. Try and figure it out yourself."

"All right, Grandfather, if you prefer, I'll try and figure out your schemes rather than construct the Centers and . . ."

"You're missing my point, Jason, you have to do both."

Jason rested his hands on the top of a chair. "I'm at a disadvantage, Grandfather. I have two jobs while you have only one."

"It doesn't have to be that way, Jason. If you joined me, truly joined me, then you, too, would have only one job."

"I fell right into the trap."

Winston appreciated his candor, which for the moment represented a time-out. "How do you like the way I work?"

Jason clapped. "I commend you on a brilliant performance."

"This is going to be even more entertaining than I thought," Winston said.

"You've been itching for an audience for years, Grandfather. Maybe that's why you enjoyed having me around."

"That is a point in fact. I've never found anyone to whom I could reveal my secrets without their trying to take advantage of them. You, with all your morals, would never dream of doing things my way, even though that's how you tried to make it appear before you came to work at Todd Industries. That makes it easier for me to be honest, if you understand my meaning."

"I do indeed," Jason said thoughtfully. "But what if I did sway and decided to come over to your side?"

Winston peered out at Jason from beneath his commanding white eyebrows with hooded shrewd eyes. "I'd have to be sure you were an ally, not an adversary, before I let you know everything." He smiled expansively. "Oh, before you leave, Jason, I thought you should know, I never was very good at keeping my word."

Jason laughed. "I've never known you to be so direct. Maybe you're slipping over to my side. See you at the New Year's Eve party."

Kierston looked out the helicopter window as it circled Windsor Royal. She studied the structure, well lit and clearly visible from the air. Bundled up in Katharine's black mink coat with the fur hood buttoned tightly to her neck, Kierston was still cold. She snuggled closer to Marcus sitting beside her and reached for his hand.

Thomas had engaged the helicopter, which flew Harrington, Marisa, and all their friends from LaGuardia Airport to the estate for the New Year's celebration. While the helicopter circled to land, Kierston thought of Jason's words on the phone last night.

"The only positive side to this party is that your father will learn how many people we can count on," Jason told her. "Otherwise, we wouldn't go. I want you to stay close to Marcus. Grandfather's going to try and rattle you, dearest."

"Fancy chance of that, JT," Kierston retorted. "But don't be surprised if he pastes pictures of me in my formal regalia all over the papers. That'll probably make my contemporaries picket the box office. Remember what he did to Marisa and your father? But let him. I'm going to enjoy myself. After what he did to your father, he deserves a little agitation."

"You're going to aggravate him enough with *Your Year With Mine*. Behave. I can't wait to see you!"

The helicopter set down.

Marcus had noticed Kierston squeezing his hand. He looked at her with grave concern. She was approaching her twentieth year, a poised young woman, able to hold her own in most any company. Yet, Marcus didn't like her under Winston's scrutiny.

"I'll be watching you tonight."

"You and Winston," Kierston said, her eyes flashing as she kissed Marcus's cheek.

The whirl of the propeller stopped and the pilot opened the door, jumped down into the snow, unfolded the steps, and helped everyone out of the helicopter. They rushed across the snow.

Winston and Jason stood on the veranda. Winston's hair was now white, and he was wearing an overcoat and muffler. Jason, wearing just a tuxedo, stood beside him.

From above the rose-garden paths, they heard Winston's voice boom out. "Well, Harrington, you've made another grand entrance, I must say." Then aside to Jason he said softly, "I couldn't resist," and chuckled. But when the group joined them on the veranda, Winston spoke to Harrington without a trace of malice, a significant change, which filled Harrington with uneasiness.

"You're looking quite well," Winston told him. "I'm happy to see you. Ah, hello there, Miss Benito. How lovely to see you." Winston shook Marisa's hand warmly and then told the others, "It's brisk out here. Please, follow me into the house."

Marisa wanted to laugh, but Harrington was very serious. He held her arm, lingering behind the others with Jason and Kierston. "Don't do anything foolish because of that Award," Harrington said seriously.

Just seeing his father and Winston together made Jason question his earlier love for Winston. He must have been out of his mind.

Inside the Renaissance Room, the butlers closed the French doors while other servants took coats and boots and mufflers.

"So, this must be Kierston," Winston said, walking over to her. "I haven't seen you for years."

She wore a strapless Dior gown which molded to her figure in soft lines of white crepe de Chine. Much to Winston's surprise, Kierston wore Diana's emerald clustered earrings. The green color somehow seemed to intensify the violet in her eyes. Her black hair, parted on the side, fell naturally down her back. She was breathtaking.

"Yes, I'm Kierston Garvin," she said softly, extending

her hand. "And who are you?"

Winston chuckled, feeling her soft skin. "You have a good sense of humor, Kierston. I like that."

"Thank you, Mr. Todd."

"Call me, Winston. Thomas, I believe you have a daughter very much like yourself."

"But he is not alone," Kierston said, smiling. "My mother should also be included in your compliment."

Winston laughed, viewing her with cold eyes. "As she should be, my dear, as she should."

Guiding Katharine and Thomas ahead of the others, Winston led them into the Grand Reception Room. Kierston and Jason lingered behind.

"You're in rather a feisty mood this evening. Who is he, indeed!"

Kierston threw her arms around Jason's neck and pulled him to her. "And this must be Kierston, indeed!"

Jason laughed heartily.

"Bobby sent the security team to Bel Air," Kierston said.

"You've moved in then?"

"Yes."

"And you have your car . . ."

"Just like yours."

He took her hands into his own and felt a hard object inside her purse. She was carrying a gun.

"You're sure about this, Kierston?"

She nodded.

He kissed her, then gently straightened her hair. When he touched her shoulders to sweep loose strands behind her back, he felt her tremble. So she was apprehensive. It made him the more protective. He held her a moment, then they entered the Grand Reception Room behind the others.

"Jason!" Winston was beckoning to Jason down the hall.

"I have to join him for awhile, Kierston. Father, look after her, will you?"

Kierston laughed. "Afraid I'll get lost?"

Jason kissed her cheek. "No, dearest. I want Father to keep you out of trouble."

Jason stood beside Winston as the guests filed through

he enormous oak doors. The same families that used to attend the magnificent Todd Gala attended the New Year's party tonight. Over the years, Winston had gathered information about each person present. If he had desired, he could have set a wave of fear through any one of them. He observed the crowd with satisfaction.

The Todds had supplanted the Dareels as the wealthiest family in the United States. The captains of industry, the members of the House and Senate, the foreign dignitaries—all owed him favors. Shaun Miller attended without her mentor, Desiree Richards. She was the only person present whom he owed. When Shaun entered Windsor Royal, he kissed her cheek and whispered that he had bought her an estate in Virginia.

She kissed him in return. "I owe you one now. Isn't that the way you like it?"

"Yes, my dear, it is," Winston said, smiling benevolently.

Shaun tried to kiss Jason next, but he held her at arm's length. "You don't owe me a thing," Jason said. "Let's keep it that way."

Winston chuckled. "That wasn't very gracious of you, Jason."

"No? I thought I was rather pleasant under the circumstances."

Once the doors were closed, the servants bustled about the mansion, scurrying from the foyer to the living room to the Grand Reception Room to the Grand Ballroom with silver trays brimming with hot hors d'oeuvres, and crystal glasses filled with drinks for nearly a thousand guests.

Jason left Winston only to bump into Raymond Baren, whom he guided to the side of the crowd.

"Has Grandfather spoken to you?"

"Not yet, but I can feel it coming."

"Remember what I said. If you have a chance, ask him what I intend to do if he doesn't buy Lascom," Jason reminded Raymond. "Don't forget."

"You've told me a hundred times. Don't worry, I won't."

They walked among the guests towards the Grand Ballroom. Nicole was standing in the doorway, and waved.

Her soft lime dress, almost white in its paleness, hugged her bosom and swept to the floor. She wore diamond earrings that sparkled against her red hair and a diamond necklace against her fair skin. Raymond smiled.

"Excuse me, Jason. I want to dance with my daughter."

Harrington and Marisa stood in a corner surrounded by admirers. Kierston was nowhere to be found. Before Jason could break through to ask where she was, a voice spoke up.

"She's dancing with Winston," Marcus told him. "She insisted."

"Terrific," Jason said.

Kierston and Winston made quite an impression on the guests. Winston could be totally disarming and elegant when he wished to be, and tonight he was in his element.

Winston caught sight of Raymond and Nicole twirling close to Jason and Marcus out of the corner of his eye. Tomorrow, Raymond would get a call. His daughter was having too much of an effect on him. Women, he thought contemptuously, then zeroed back in on Kierston.

"Well, my dear, how do you like my grandson?"

"I love your grandson," Kierston said bluntly. She looked around the room as Winston twirled her across the floor. Then her gaze returned to him. "You don't have a very high regard for women, Mr. Todd," she said softly. "But I'm not offended."

Winston chuckled. "Do they teach young girls in school to be disrespectful to their elders?"

"No, they teach young girls to think," Kierston said smiling.

"Beautiful women don't have to think. You should have learned that by now."

Kierston couldn't help herself; she laughed. "If I had 'learned' that, I would have had to think. Then I'd be contradicting your theory."

Winston chuckled. "You are a spirited young girl, aren't you? I see why Jason enjoys your company. By the way, your purse is rather heavy, isn't it? What's inside? You didn't bring a gun with you, or did you?"

She balanced the clutch purse on his shoulder and watched him try to glance at it from the corner of his eye.

Kierston laughed gaily. "What do you take me for, Mr. Todd! That's my bag of lucky silver dollars."

The music stopped.

"Are you two having a good time?" Jason took Kierston's arm and looked at Winston in amusement.

"She's truly a delight," Winston said. "She reminds me of your grandmother when we first met." They were interrupted by a bell. "Save another dance for me later," Winston told Kierston. "Maybe we should try your purse on my other shoulder for the next round." He chuckled at Jason and walked off.

"He was telling the truth just then about my grand-mother," Jason said, walking with Kierston to dinner.

"But he'll forget tomorrow," Kierston said.

Jason nodded. "You're pretty smart, aren't you. What was that about his shoulder?"

Kierston told him.

Jason held her closer. His grandfather's intuitiveness surprised him. That made him more alert. He should never be surprised, he reminded himself, never.

The Garvins approached, accompanied by Ambassador and Mrs. Walter Kent. No mention was made of his violation of Diana's will. Jason had assured Harrington that Darnley Enterprises would be safe under the Todd Banner. Now that Walter was no longer Ambassador to the Court of St. James, he might turn into an ally if he didn't want a lawsuit on his hands. Jason asked that Thomas keep up appearances. All they needed was to know what Winston had on Walter and to ultimately protect him.

Thomas nodded slightly at Jason. Obviously, Walter was a potential "yes." With him, they had three of the twelve board members.

Jason already knew he was more at risk than Thomas. If the future Garvin Enterprises/Todd Industries merger ulti-mately went through, Jason would have to work for Todd Industries for five years before everything reverted to their control. If they lost the Board, Jason would be signing a "slave's contract." Jason was willing to take that risk.

At midnight, there was a fireworks display outside, rockets shooting into the sky. Afterwards, inside, the staff presented gifts to the guests—a perfect one-carat diamond for the women and a uniquely designed sterling silver comb and brush set for the men. Photographers took pictures for the following week's society pages while reporters scribbled down names and questioned guests.

"Remind me never to have Kierston come here again while he lives," Jason told Marcus as they prepared to leave.

"Don't show your discomfort. He'll know."

"If he knows, then he'll also understand what will happen if he touches one strand of hair on her beautiful head."

Kierston was helped into her coat and hastily took Jason outside. "You and I were taught to deal with this life."

He was helpless against her. He held her in his arms. "It's just that I love you so."

Kierston kissed him. "It's only another year . . . 1968 and it will be over."

Although he feigned bewilderment at being summoned on a weekday to the country, Raymond Baren knew he was in trouble. Without a word, he shuffled over to the oval table and sat beside Winston. Winston had given him many hard looks last night, and he was scared.

"What did you want to see me about, Winston? Lascom perhaps?" 'Oh, there you've done it,' he told himself. 'Just hand him the information on a platter. You might as well tell him you've been talking to Jason, you fool!' He sat up, infuriated by his own stupidity. Winston's lips had twisted into a smile, which caught Raymond off guard. "I wouldn't have expected that reaction."

"And why not, Raymond?"

"Lascom's success is a serious matter. I . . ."

The national newspapers reported last February that Lascom was manufacturing "the product of the future." Lascom's business computer stored massive amounts of information. Within the next seven years, Lascom President Bobby Christian predicted that Lascom would produce compact computers.

"I don't want you speaking to Jason anymore. Is that understood?"

Raymond's thoughts were racing. Not only had he told Jason about this very room, but he had detailed many of Winston's illegal operations. How had Winston found out? Raymond had been right to warn Jason. There was a mole in Jason's camp. The thought made him quiver.

"You asked me to speak to Jason . . ."

"I didn't realize I had to specify exactly what you were to say or not say."

Raymond considered his vicarious pleasure upon hearing that Lascom had been granted a government contract to build computers for spacecraft. He had a dim notion that he should protect Jason now, but self-preservation took precedent. He fought against himself in his thoughts. He wasn't going to talk about Jason or Lascom. He wouldn't!

"What is Jason planning to do with Lascom?"

"He's going to offer you a proposal to buy Lascom," Raymond blurted out. How he despised himself!

"My, my, I wonder what's become of you, Raymond?"

"What do you mean?"

Winston didn't bother to answer him. "What are the terms?"

"I have no idea."

"You're a bit confused, Raymond. Take your time. Of course you know."

"I do?"

"You know the terms as well as you know that you never mentioned to anyone in Washington that Harrington wished to receive that award!"

"What?"

"Forget about changing old habits. I'll ruin you and your daughter. Now what are the terms?!"

"All stock . . ." Raymond mumbled.

"What?"

"All stock!"

"No cash?"

Raymond shook his head. "He knows you won't accept it."

The all-stock transaction must mean that Jason would one day try to take over Todd Industries with a Garvin Enterprises/Todd Industries merger, just as Winston had suspected. Winston was delighted. Had Jason wanted him to know? Why? "That's very amusing, don't you think?"

"But I thought you'd be upset."

"Oh, I am, I am," Winston said easily. "I've never been so upset, but not with Jason or with Lascom!"

Raymond's nerves jumped about in his body as if someone had stuck him with a cattle prod. He tried to maintain his calm, but the phone rang, jarring his thin line of composure.

"Yes," Winston said, picking up the phone, his eyes riveted to Raymond's face. "Leave your keys to this room and the elevator and get out of here, Raymond."

"But . . ."

"Don't worry. You'll receive a new set when the locks are changed."

For the first time in his life, Raymond admitted that he hated Winston. To admit this, and then to think of all the years he'd worked for Winston and that he had just exposed Jason's plans, sent a chill through his body.

As he walked over to the elevator, he suddenly remembered Jason's words: "If you ever get the chance, Raymond, and it fits into your conversation, ask Grandfather if he knows what I intend to do after he refuses my proposal. Don't forget, Raymond."

Winston was already talking in hushed tones into the receiver. Raymond was too obsessed with his new mission to wonder to whom Winston was talking.

"Uh, Winston?" he called out, interrupting the phone conversation. "What do you think Jason's going to do if you don't buy Lascom?"

"Sell it to Thomas Garvin of course," Winston said impatiently. "That's old news, Raymond! Good-bye!"

When he was sure Raymond had left, Winston continued talking to Al Smith. Jason was getting too cocky, and it was all because of Kierston. Without her, Jason would have no feelings at all and slip over to his side forever. "This is what I want you to do, Al . . ."

It was the last week in August, 1967, that Jason sent Winston the proposal. An exchange of stock was involved that would make Jason an equal shareholder in Todd Industries with Winston. Jason had sent copies of the proposal to each member of the Board. The offer was high, but the prospects for Lascom's growth were great. Only Winston knew the true meaning of the proposal and the true thrust of Jason's long-range plans.

Just before noon, Jason walked into Winston's office and closed the door. Winston was scanning the Lascom proposal and didn't bother to greet his grandson. Jason sat down.

"I'd like to think this over," Winston said at last.

"I'll give you one month. Then I'll have to open up the bids," Jason said easily.

"What's your hurry?"

"Let's just say I'm an impatient man."

"We Todds never have been patient, but your offer reeks of mutiny," Winston said pleasantly.

Jason stood. "Possibly, if that is the way you wish to look at it. But I would rather say that it places the authority in the hands of two and is better for both. Too much power in the hands of one can be dangerous, don't you agree?"

Winston looked at him from beneath white eyebrows. "Speaking as one who knows, I'd say not, but I'll consider your proposal." Jason headed for the door. "I've come to a decision," Winston called out. "It's no deal."

"I'd like that in writing," Jason answered.

Winston buzzed his secretary. Briskly, he dictated a memo refusing to purchase Lascom. She typed it quickly and returned it for his signature.

"I'll have to send this rejection to the Board Members . . ."

"I would expect it," Winston answered grandly. "We wouldn't want them to think you hadn't given us first offer to bid . . ."

"No, we wouldn't."

When Jason left the office, he had the original of the memo in his hand. The war had begun.

He returned to his Waldorf suite only to find Raymond Baren and Al Smith standing in the hall. What a peculiar combination.

Jason opened the door. "Wait outside, Mr. Smith."

Raymond trembled as he brushed by the balding security man, whom he had never met before, and entered Jason's suite and closed the door. Jason threw his briefcase in the bedroom and stood in the bedroom threshold, his eyes in the shadows, his arms idle at his sides. Raymond stared from Jason to the luggage by the door.

"Are you going somewhere?"

"What do you want, Raymond?"

"I've betrayed you, Jason," he said, caving in at once. "I told Winston that Thomas Garvin was going to buy Lascom, and the specifics of your deal."

"Did you ask him if he knew who I'd sell Lascom to?" Jason asked calmly, much to Raymond's surprise.

"Yes," Raymond said, trying to figure Jason out. "He said Thomas Garvin. Is that true?"

Jason's eyes flickered with undeniable fury. Marcus had given Al Smith that information. Al was the mole and was standing right outside the door.

Raymond mistook Jason's anger to be directed at him. "I know what you're thinking, and you're perfectly justified in never believing me again." Raymond walked tentatively towards Jason. "I'm not a brave man. I'm a coward who has hidden behind the shield of a powerful man and therefore appeared braver than I actually was." He stopped before Jason, searching his face. "I'm an order-taker not an order-giver. I don't hold that against myself. What I can't accept is that I've betrayed you."

Raymond sat down at the table. As if this admission were too much for him, he placed his head in his hands. "I apologize," he mumbled. "I don't know how I'll be able to make it up to you after I promised Nicole I'd change."

"I knew you'd tell Grandfather about Lascom all along."

Raymond lifted his head, his brown eyes moist with tears. "What?"

"In essence, you helped rather than hurt me," Jason said, for Raymond had acted as a double-agent again without even realizing it. And perhaps just as profoundly, Jason believed he was watching Raymond's transformation from being Winston's man to being his own, something which Jason had to remind himself could happen to him in reverse if he wasn't careful.

Raymond peered at him in astonishment.

Jason pulled a chair over beside Raymond's and straddled it, placing his arms over its back. "You were almost trustworthy."

"Winston hinted that he'd hurt Nicole!"

"That isn't the full reason."

"I was afraid," Raymond admitted. "But I could still help you."

"Why should I want your help?"

"If Nicole is safe, I'll give it, no strings attached."

"That doesn't answer my question."

"You probably don't want my help, because you consider me a desperate man."

Jason reflected on the conversation he had had with Marcus. Winston would use violence as a weapon. Jason knew his turn would come. Raymond obviously felt his time was near.

"I'm not sure I'm in imminent danger, but it's not far off." Raymond sighed. "And it's really not me that I'm concerned about, rather it's Nicole. You see, if I should die, everything goes to her. He wouldn't want her voting my stock. Moreover, he would hurt her to get at me." He looked into Jason's eyes so full of strength and said, "He won't come after you, though. I know that. But your father or Kierston, now they're a different story."

"What would happen if Nicole were to die?"

"My entire fortune would go to you."

"What?"

"I changed my will last year. You're more a man at twenty-five than I am at seventy. You don't understand how deeply I feel about you. There are many reasons besides just who you are. You set Nicole straight years ago. You helped to bring my daughter back to me. She's the joy of my life. An inheritance is a small price for such a precious gift."

At this very moment, Jason should have been on his way to the airport. Thomas Garvin and his Board of Directors and largest shareholders were waiting.

'Now what about Raymond's safety?' he asked himself. "Your gesture with the will is very generous, Raymond . . ."

"I'm not trying to buy you."

"What are you trying to do?"

"I'm not sure."

"Until you have the answer, we have nothing to discuss."

"I want your grandfather stopped, and you're the only person who can do it."

'The only person?' Jason thought. 'Don't you know he'll do it to himself?' "I might help you, but only if you take me out of your will."

Raymond bowed his head, choking back his tears.

Jason grabbed his shoulder. "You'll be fine, Raymond. In the beginning you might need me as a shield—and I'll be there. In the end, you'll be able to stand alone."

Raymond lifted his eyes. "The fight has been hard, Jason."

John Stevens had told Jason to surround himself with men such as himself. He reiterated the words to Raymond. "You've never had a chance. Grandfather can do that to people." 'Even to me if I'm not careful,' Jason thought, standing abruptly. "You're a corporate officer at Todd Industries, Raymond. Tomorrow is a working day. You should get home and get some rest."

"All right." He could see that Jason was preoccupied. He felt unsure of just what he should do. "But what about Todd Industries? I know he's making it rough on you."

"Do you think I care?"

"I . . ."

"I don't," Jason said. "If people are stupid enough to believe what Winston Todd says about me, then let them be his bedfellows." He started to tell Raymond about his trip to California, but then thought better of it. He could only hope that one day Nicole's father would gain the courage to be trustworthy. Anyway, Winston would hear soon enough from Al Smith.

'Al Smith,' he thought angrily. They should have known at once Al was their man. John Stevens had warned him. As with Joe Field, Winston had picked a dupe who was a master of disguise.

"Don't ask any questions. Just do as I say, Raymond. I want you to walk to the door. Open it. Then call me a bastard, or anything you wish. Afterwards, storm down the hall like there's no tomorrow. Do you understand, Raymond?"

Raymond sensed the guard had something to do with this, and his safety was at stake, but he didn't comment. "I understand."

Jason had to admire Raymond's performance. His angry outburst was so convincing that Jason almost believed Raymond really was furious.

"Jesus, Jason," Al Smith said, coming into the suite. "What the hell happened in here?"

"You know how loyal Raymond is to my grandfather, Al. Sometimes he just thinks I'm a pain in the ass. Now I have to get going. You can drive me to the airport. In another year, we won't have to worry about Raymond or Grandfather," he said, planting the seed to buy more time. Winston's greed would hopefully preclude his violence for a few months—if not, they would be ready.

Although Jason had left Al Smith back in New York, he still felt his presence when he landed in Los Angeles. How strange it was, Jason thought, having Al work for him, knowing he was the mole. When would Al strike?

Jason was driving to the MicNic Ranch. Although Marcus was following him, he kept looking in his rearview mirror.

Conrad and Harrington had abided by his wishes that *Your Year With Mine* be filmed in secret. What better place to shoot it than Nicole and Michael's ranch. Yet, he was still concerned for Kierston's safety.

They traversed the curving mountain road, shaded with eucalyptus and edged with rock formations, framed with the distant forest of the Santa Monica Mountain Range.

"Have you ever considered, Jason, that you might be one of the most extraordinary young men living?" Winston had asked him a few weeks before. "Why aren't you afraid of me?"

"Who are you flattering, me or yourself?" Jason had

asked.

"Both of us, of course. But I am curious."

"I don't think about fear."

"Haven't you noticed we're on a battlefield?"

"We really aren't at war," Jason had answered. "Our concerns are directed at Todd Industries. We're both interested in her fate, but we disagree about the strategy that should be used to keep her strong and the choice of weapons with which to defend her."

Therein lay the key, Jason thought as he entered MicNic Ranch.

"You think men are immoral and therefore that you are morally justified in being immoral yourself."

"Yes?" Winston had answered.

"I know many men who are immoral, but I don't choose to become one of them in order to accomplish my goals."

"Then you won't deal with anyone whom you feel is dishonest?"

Jason remembered the question had turned his stomach. 'I wouldn't be talking to you if that were the case,' he had thought to himself, but had said, "You misunderstand me. I'd be penalizing myself and limiting my marketplace. I said that to deal with dishonest men one doesn't have to be dishonest, oneself."

"That's the most ridiculous thing I've ever heard!" Winston declared. "You get caught up in the dishonesty whether you like it or not."

Jason had to accept that there was an element of truth in that statement. Hadn't he been dishonest a few years ago with Harrington? What about now? Kierston was his only confidant. Had he allowed Winston's influence to taint his other relationships? If so, there was nothing he could do.

When Harrington rewrote *Your Year With Mine*, with Jason and Kierston in mind, he had added horseback riding, a favorite sport of theirs. Jason had insisted that Jim come out from New York and bring a few of his thoroughbreds. Jim had told Winston he was going on vacation and had refused to divulge his destination.

"How did you sneak in?"

Jason was walking with Jim, leading two thoroughbreds down the corridor towards the open stable door. With the reins in his left hand, Jason placed his right hand around Nicole's shoulder. "Hi, Red. I came straight to the stables. I thought you'd be out at the pond. Hello, Michael!"

"The headlines in yesterday's papers were impressive as hell," Michael said in greeting.

The sale of Lascom headlined the morning financial page.

"Oh, Jason, it's wonderful news!" Nicole said.

'Dangerous news,' Jason thought, yet nodded in agreement.

They rode north as Jason told them about Garvin Enterprises' stock. "By closing, it had jumped five points."

"I don't believe it!" Michael said. "You did it, Jason!"

Jason smiled. "We did it, Michael, you, Bobby, and I. It's been a long time since Harvard."

"It's all been worth it, though," Michael said emotionally.

'It has,' Nicole thought happily, relaxed for the first time in Jason's company. Her love for Michael welled up inside her. "I have more good news. Later this year, when Michael goes to Europe on business, I'm going along, and we're going to get married in Florence."

"Congratulations!" Jason said.

"Oh, and here I thought you'd be offended that we didn't accept your grandfather's offer to have the wedding at Windsor Royal."

"I'm very happy you've decided on Florence," Jason answered firmly. He sensed that they were waiting for him to bring up Raymond, and he came to the point. "Your father and I spoke. It went well. Don't worry, Red."

"O.K.," Nicole sighed. "I'll let you and Michael talk. Jim, why don't you and I ride ahead and let Kierston know Jason's coming."

Michael stared after her affectionately. "She won't be happy until we're all rid of your grandfather. To tell you the truth, I'm tired of hearing his name. Was Raymond really that bad?"

"He's trying hard," Jason said.

"Good. By the way, I called the office this morning. They're hundreds of phone messages and telegrams: congratulatory messages from executives to secretaries at WRIB, WJT Oil, Todd Land Development, and all the subsidiaries. It's unbelievable. Who would have thought any of them would understand?"

"I don't think any of them do."

"Maybe some?"

"Possibly, but only a few. Your father and Raymond Baren, and they don't see the whole picture."

"It's kinda lonely, isn't it?"

"Don't be disappointed, Michael. Motives are conceived by people and each person draws from his own experiences conclusions about another's intent. No matter what I say, people will think I'm only trying to oust Grandfather. Grandfather understands more than any of them."

"What?"

"Why do you think he allowed me to build up Lascom? Why do you think he allowed me to sell it?"

"Allowed?"

"He's never been laughed at in his life. Everyone thinks I'm putting one over on him. They're wrong. He suspects the prospects for the future will make the sacrifice worth it. He allowed this all to happen. It's all premeditated, although he's playing in the highest stakes game of his life." As Jason said the words, he knew he'd said too much. He laughed it off. "Come on, Michael. This is my first day of leisure in many a year and I intend to enjoy it!"

Nicole and Jim were waiting for them just south of the set and gestured for them to be quiet as they approached. "I wasn't able to talk to Kierston," Nicole whispered as they dismounted.

They moved quietly to the set while Jim stayed behind with the horses. Only the essential crew was present. Harrington had not wanted to inhibit Kierston's performance today, but even so there must have been thirty people watching Kierston tumble around in the water with her co-star, William Wall.

When the assistant director yelled "Cut," they moved in

closer. It was then that Jason saw Kierston. Her wet clothes clung to her body. A dresser rushed forward to place a robe around her, as her eyes drifted to Harrington and then directly behind him to Jason. Not only was she startled, but she was virtually frozen to the ground.

"Wonderful," Harrington mumbled under his breath. "Why don't you change, dear? I'll take care of him." She just nodded and left for her trailer.

"I didn't know you were coming, Jason," Harrington said, leading him away from the group. "What're you trying to do, inhibit the girl? Didn't you know she was doing a love scene?"

Jason regarded him with a touch of amusement. "And it's all in the name of art, right?"

Harrington grinned. "You're impossible. And I'm so proud! I read about Lascom. Fine work!"

"That's one reason I'm here, Father. You have to carry that computer with you now. It's time."

The seriousness of the moment was broken by the crew laughing and joking as they closed down the set for the day. Overhead, the sun was drifting closer to the mountain range, and a cool breeze swept over their heads.

"And I thought that Kierston had something to do with your being here," Harrington said, avoiding the computer issue.

"That she does."

"I'm happy to hear it."

Kierston had hastily changed her clothes and stood there with a towel hanging around her neck.

Jason smiled. "You looked pretty good out there. Why'd you change your clothes?"

Her eyes brightened. "I didn't know you liked my attire. But if you want, I'll change back."

He caught her arms, knowing she just might do it. "I have a pool at the house. It'll do the trick if I'm interested later."

A member of the crew had walked up to Nicole. "I hear Harrington's son is here."

Nicole pointed to Jason, who was talking quietly to Kierston.

"That's his son?" the crew member asked, perplexed. "They sure don't look alike. I'd never have guessed."

Harrington's heart sank, but no one noticed that brief instant when the truth was in his eyes; he was remembering just who Jason's father actually was. Although Harrington did not show it, his heart continued to pound heavily.

The crew member introduced himself to Jason, shook his hand, and pointed to other members of the cast and crew who wished to say hello. Jason was polite and cordial to everyone.

"Oh, darn," Kierston said, kissing Jason. "I forgot my pages for tomorrow. I'll be right back."

Jason watched after her closely, then ushered Harrington aside. From his shirt pocket, he took out a miniature computer control device and pressed in the keys to buzz Marcus back at the hacienda.

"I dislike carrying that around," Harrington said. A control identical to Jason's was in his breast pocket. "I know, I know. It's necessary." Jason's expression was so severe that Harrington stopped in mid-sentence. "What is it, Jason?"

"From now on, you'll have to put up with more than the computer. It's begun, Father. Everyone will be heavily guarded."

Jason saw Kierston's Ferrari coming down the road. He looked back to Kierston who was walking towards them. Momentarily, he forgot about Winston. Kierston had that affect on him. He was always surprised she could make him forget.

"Jason!"

He felt a hand grab his arm. He heard a car speed by. He saw Kierston's face registering disbelief. Then he saw the Ferrari heading right at her. Jim Johnson was nearest to Kierston. He lunged at Kierston, pushing her with all his weight, nearly getting hit himself. Kierston tumbled over on the graveled road. The Ferrari sped away.

Those of the cast remaining and all of the crew started running over to Kierston, but Jason got to her first.

Jason placed his jacket around Kierston, and she threw it off. "I'm fine, Jason. Just look at me. Not a scratch!"

Then, Jason's sportscar skidded to a halt and Marcus

and Laster jumped out. Marcus assessed the situation, saw the Ferrari disappearing in the distance and told Laster, "Get him. Don't let the bastard get away!"

Laster jumped back into Jason's car. Once he had maneuvered through the crowd, he floored it.

Harrington had ordered the crew back. The head of transportation and security hurried the crew to complete their task and keep their mouths shut. Harrington thought at any minute Jason would explode.

Kierston was looking over at Jim. "Thank you, Jim. I froze.".

"It was a close call," Jim said, looking from her to Jason.

Kierston followed Jim's eyes. "It's okay, Jason."

"It's not, Kierston. It's not okay at all!"

"I've got Laster on the line, Jason!" Marcus yelled. "He's keeping up with Al!"

Jason took ahold of Kierston's hand and hurried over to Marcus. His voice was heard all over the valley as he grabbed the receiver from Marcus's hand. "You get that bastard, Laster! I want him stopped!"

Harrington strode over to Jason and grabbed him tightly by the shoulder, but Jason shrugged off Harrington's grasp and wouldn't let go of Kierston. Murder was in his eyes.

Kierston knew what he was about to blurt out. She shouldn't be doing that movie! She should be guarded. Placed somewhere in a prison.

"We'll be prepared when he really means it," she said in a low voice. "That was just a test, to see how we would handle it."

Jason knew she spoke the truth. "This isn't a joke, Kierston."

"I'm not laughing, Jason. I'm just letting you know, I'm sticking by your side, no matter what you say."

Laster lost the Ferrari on a back road in the hills of Malibu, only to find it deserted as he spotted a helicopter flying off in the distance. The setup had been perfectly orchestrated, and they had lost Al Smith.

That evening Jason was silent, but his eyes never left

Kierston at their Bel Air home. She had seen glimpses of this behavior whenever they were alone together. It was as though to deal with Winston one had to forget how to feel, how to give. One could only think. Feelings were a luxury Jason could no longer afford.

'I know, after tonight, I might lose him forever,' Kierston thought. 'But he's going to feel—he's going to give —then he can go.'

It occurred to her, then, that by Jason's protecting her and Harrington, he was protecting a part of himself. Was it not her turn to do the same for him?

They dined on the patio and the moon drifted out from behind a cloud. "Your present is finished," Kierston said suddenly. "It'll be perfect in this light. Come back to my workroom in five minutes."

When he built the Bel Air home, he had constructed a special room for Kierston. Unless asked, he never intruded on her privacy. He knew neither what she made nor what the moonlight had to do with her present, only that she had worked on her gift since the new Year's Eve party. He waited a few more minutes and then walked down the hall.

The back of an easel was set up in front of him; the painting was not visible from his viewpoint, but he noted that the moonlight flowed through the open window and haloed the easel.

Kierston was standing in the corner, leaning against the wall, watching his expression as he came around the easel. The painting was of him standing on a hilltop very like the one at Windsor Royal where he, Kierston, and Nicole used to ride. In the moonlight, the colors were brilliant and emphasized the muscles of his body as he stood leaning into the wind. He was fascinated with the style in which she had painted his body. She had captured a quality that he could not define and that he had never considered to be an intrinsic part of him. He could almost feel the glorious freedom of the figure, the strength of his purpose as he stood against the wind. It seemed such a foreign feeling now, that feeling evoked in him by her work.

He made her sit down, and he stood behind her, his hand on her shoulder, his eyes fastened to her creation. For a long while, he stared at it without uttering a sound, too moved to speak. Instead, he finally spoke in a gesture as he took her hand and kissed the palm.

He led her upstairs to the bedroom. There, he helped her out of her clothes. He felt the smoothness of her breasts against his chest and her hand at his back. Her lips met his as he gently wrapped his arms around her. They stood naked, pressed against each other as the moonlight filtered through the window. He cupped her face in his hands, "I love you, Kierston. I'm sorry this happened." He bent and kissed her.

"It wasn't your fault, Jason."

He felt her warmth, consuming him, loving him. He knew he was opening his heart when he could not afford to.

"Just for a few minutes," she said, reading his thoughts. "Just let me know you can. I need to know, Jason."

CHAPTER XXXI

W inston was delighted at the turn of events by the New Year of 1968. Thomas Garvin approached him about the purchase of Garvin Enterprises, which had jumped ten points within the first week of purchasing Lascom. Winston had anticipated his offer and, months before, had instructed his attorneys to draw up the papers.

Now, in late March, just before the Academy Awards, he had called in Al Smith. A door opened at the far side of the Operations Room. Al Smith entered in disguise. His bald head was covered with a brown toupee. His suite coat was padded to make him look overweight. He wore glasses and a beard. He crossed the room and sat down beside Winston. His forehead wrinkled in concern. "Lucky you called me in when you did. Marcus was closing in."

Winston reached for the note pad, which Al had brought into the room. Before going underground, Al had bugged MicNic Ranch, Garvinhouse, and Jason's Waldorf suite. By the length of his notes, the bugs had not yet been detected.

"Raymond'll stick around in New York," Al said, watching Winston thumb through his notes. "So will Mel. Nicole and Michael were married in Europe. They've been staying with Marisa Benito in Florence. Nicole's expecting a kid, due in late August."

"Are they heavily guarded?"

"No. All the rest of Jason's group is set to go to the Academy Awards. Only Marcus, Laster French, and a few security guards are protecting them."

Marcus Mancini was smarter than that. His men were on alert, ready to protect his camp. Winston took this in without comment, then said: "Have you made all the arrangements?"

Al nodded. "Now, about my money, sir?"

"I told you. When the merger is finalized, you will have your money. You already have your airplane ticket and freighter pass. You know how to get in touch with my contacts after the Academy Awards. You've money enough to sustain you until you resurface again in August. If you fail, there won't be any more cash. If you succeed, you know about the bonus. You'd better not disappointment me!"

"I won't."

"Good, then you have nothing to worry about." Winston stood slowly, but with authority. "If you get my call to proceed, I'll see you a month from September 2nd, Mr. Smith, and not before . . ."

"I know, I know, Mr. Todd, unless something goes wrong, which it won't. And I'm supposed to use that private number."

Three days before the Academy Awards, Winston made an appearance at the Todd Center and summoned Jason to the penthouse suite.

Diana Darnley Todd was credited that morning in the New York *Times* with having built the New York Cultural Center. The article's headline read: **TODD CENTER WEST DARNLEY PAVILION: Credit Given to Original Founder and Owner of the Todd Cultural Center in New York.**

As soon as Jason walked into his office, Winston saw

Jason's change. Cool, shrewd, and emotionless, just the way he wanted him, for Winston was furious about the Darnley Pavilion. His grandson had gone too far.

"Congratulations," Winston said dryly, uncorking a bottle of Dom Perignon. He poured champagne into two crystal glasses and handed one to Jason. "You move quickly. I admire that." He held up his glass and clicked Jason's. "To the future."

Jason sipped the champagne.

Winston gulped it down, raised his arm, and threw the glass at the wall. It shattered to pieces. Abruptly, he turned and walked around to sit down at his desk. "You'd better deliver, Jason," he said, taking his chair. "You've done everything your own way."

Jason set down the glass. "And you've allowed me to do so."

Winston raised a white eyebrow. "Very good. You figured that out all by yourself." He paused. "And consider this, I alone know how far you've gone. Be careful. You're playing my game now. And as a little inducement, I've already gotten approval from the Board to make you CEO of Todd Industries. I've always thought it was important that when one fails, one does it with style. So congratulations, Mr. CEO, enjoy your position as long as you can.

"Don't get too comfortable," Winston continued. An abrupt expression of revulsion spread over his face. "From this moment forward, you'd better protect yourself. No more concessions. No more privileges. You're on your own." He stood. "Don't forget to look over your shoulder. Beware at all times. I'm going to strike where it will hurt you most, and at a time when you least expect it. You'd better watch your step when you walk out the front door."

The coldness in Jason's eyes matched Winston's, although he smiled and his voice sounded perfectly natural. "Don't take it so personally, Grandfather. This is business. I just wanted to show you how *I* worked, too." He started for the door.

"Just a moment," Winston called out.

Jason had already opened the door. Marcus was waiting or him right outside. As Jason turned, Marcus unshielded is gun to protect Jason without his knowledge. Jason only aw Winston aiming a gun directly at his chest.

"I told you to look over your shoulder."

Jason strode back across the room and grabbed the gun rom Winston's hand. "The next time you point a gun at me, oe prepared to use it. The safety is on." He unfastened the afety and handed it back to Winston.

"You're fighting for the wrong side," Winston said, rate at Marcus's presence inside his office. "Ask Harrington bout Vincent Morello, Jason. He's your real father. He aped your mother and Harrington married her. Why, hasn't Harrington told you? You're a bastard!"

Jason started to laugh. "From where you stand, Grandfather, I probably do look like a bastard. But as I told you, it's only business."

When Jason was gone, Winston picked up a private line and dialed. "It's a go. Shoot to kill!"

Marcus stepped out onto the Todd Center West Business Complex rooftop on Academy Awards night, and the door banged shut behind him. Security guards pivoted, rifles aimed, as they scrutinized the area to see who had invaded their turf.

At five o'clock, the sun looked like a giant gold pocket watch dangling over the horizon. Its light hit Marcus square in the eyes, and he took his sunglasses out of his tuxedo breast pocket. Against the glare, the men looked like massive black outlines, targets on a shooting range who could fire back.

Laster French joined Marcus at the door and spoke to him quietly as the other guards respectfully nodded and resumed their positions around the roof. "The celebrities are pouring in, but we haven't seen anything unusual. Not even Vietnam War protestors."

"Let's take a look," Marcus said.

The Awards had been delayed by two days because of Martin Luther King, Jr.'s, assassination. Delays always made

Marcus nervous no matter how many times they went ove
their plans.

They crossed the helicopter landing pad to the roof
ledge. A cool breeze tickled Marcus's nostrils as he peere
into the abyss below.

Hundreds of people crowded into the bleachers an
gathered behind barricades guarded by the Los Angele
Police. Movie stars paraded up the red carpet that serpen
tined down the five-hundred-foot promenade between mas
sive buildings of slate and glass. Fans waved homemade sign
bearing endearing messages to their favorite stars as Matt
Mann, the emcee at the podium, announced the stars
arrivals.

"This is a helluva place for an assassination attempt,"
Laster grumbled.

"But Jason's right. This is one place Al might strike. I
he doesn't, we'll cover Van Nuys Airport and Air Researc
and use alternative plans for everyone's departure."

Marcus picked up a pair of binoculars to get a bette
look at the crowd.

Starting in the west, he viewed the fifteen-acre Tod
Center West complex with all of its buildings. Hooded guard
were positioned like ornaments scattered around the classi
slate thirty-story business center. In between the buildings
the Pacific Ocean etched itself along the horizon in a thin blu
line. To the north, sharpshooters dotted the business annex
and the smog partially covered the top of the massive Ediso
Building. To the east, the Modern Arts Museum, with it
geometric design, seemed to pierce the sky, leaving a blue tin
to spill over the museum walls. In between the triangula
domed shields masking the roof, Marcus spotted additiona
men, rifles drawn, viewing the crowd below with thei
telescopic lenses.

He shifted his sight back down to the promenade where
a special television crew filmed the crowd and beamed it
picture directly into a police van. He observed the ushers, als
armed beneath their tuxedos. Marcus carried his .45 in a
shoulder holster, now a familiar part of his attire, having

worn it since he left that special division of Army Intelligence after World War II.

Then he saw Todd Industries's limousine approaching the entrance. The Garvins and Conrad were inside with Marisa, Nicole and Michael Christian, and Bobby.

When Michael and Nicole heard that Bobby was taking this chance by riding in the limousine that Al thought Jason, Kierston, and Harrington would arrive in, they returned on an overnight flight from Florence with Marisa. Everyone wanted to participate and create a united front. It caused more problems with security. Marcus didn't want Al so furious that he took out his vengeance on those inside the limousine. However, his additional men, down below, were prepared for anything.

Marcus looked at his wristwatch. It was 5:10 P.M. The limousine stopped at the entrance, just as Marcus heard an approaching helicopter.

"Call the copter in, Laster. They've got to land now."

From the copter, Jason saw the crowd below and the security lining the rooftops. He couldn't hear the pilot trying to speak to Marcus and Laster on the rooftop, but he did get the high sign from the pilot.

"We're going to land," he told Kierston and Harrington. "Get ready. Everyone below is safely inside."

Before the pilot cut off the motor, Jason bolted out of the helicopter. The chopper's blades still clipped the air, mussing his long, but styled, coal-black hair and flapping his tuxedo jacket away from his chest.

Into full view, Kierston emerged. Her gold beaded dress, held up over her full bosom by thin straps, shimmered in the retreating sunlight like a twinkling galaxy. Her jet black curls were intertwined with golden beads, and fell behind her shoulders to her waist.

Harrington was next, also dressed in formal black. His brownish blond hair was backlit by the blazing sun and a few single strands fell over his startlingly blue eyes as he hopped out of the copter.

Surrounded by security guards, father and son escorted

Kierston towards Marcus and Laster.

"You're edgy. Is everything all right?" Jason asked Marcus when they finally joined him.

In answer, Marcus took Jason in his arms and hugged him. Then he knew, as he'd always known since Jason was a little boy, that Jason was destined to survive. Marcus could almost feel Jason's nerves beneath his muscular frame. Holding him was like getting an electrical charge. Jason was like a cat, just as agile, and Marcus hoped, with just as many lives.

They were guided inside and down the stairs, passing security guards along the way. They headed to the underground tunnel joining the Business Center with the Cultural Center's elevator. Kierston sensed the tension in the air and tightened her grip around her evening bag and felt her gun inside. Jason and Harrington wore their weapons in shoulder holsters beneath their tuxedos.

As they approached the open door of the waiting elevator, the tunnel exploded with gunfire. Shots thundered like an angry god shouting out in a fury as Marcus shoved the trio into the elevator and Laster closed the door.

Jason banged on the door as the elevator quickly ascended to the lobby of the Darnley Pavilion. "Marcus! Goddamnit, Laster, we should have waited for Marcus!"

They were all standing in the security room where the L.A.P.D. had set up their headquarters in the Darnley Pavilion. Jason was on the telephone, trying to find out what had happened in the tunnel. All of Marcus's security below refused to answer their walkie-talkies.

An announcement had been made in the Pavilion to all the guests and at the same time had been put on television that an attempt had been made on their lives. The Award's telecast was delayed for fifteen minutes, and then the network proceeded. Neither Harrington nor Jason wanted to join the festivities until they were sure Marcus was alive.

"He's over here, on this line," a police sergeant called out to Jason.

Jason allowed Harrington to take the call while he and Kierston tried to listen in.

Marcus was happy and breathless. "The FBI agents think they have Al Smith out front. We only have a few wounded men. They'll be all right. I'm going over to the Business Center now. They're holding Al in the penthouse suite away from everyone. If there's any problem, I'll signal you in the Pavilion. Go have fun!"

When Harrington, Jason, and Kierston walked into the Pavilion during an intermission, the crowd roared their approval and stood to applaud. There wasn't much time for fanfare, however, as the national telecast resumed and everyone directed their attention to the stage.

The Awards began. Best Supporting Actor: George Kennedy in *Cool Hand Luke*. Best Supporting Actress: Estelle Parson in *Bonnie and Clyde* had already been presented.

Jason held Kierston's hand, looking outwardly calm while he seethed inside. During each break, he looked for Marcus while Nicole and Michael, Bobby, and the Garvins whispered with Kierston and Harrington.

Jason was on edge. Was Al in custody or not?

Cinematography: *Bonnie and Clyde*; Tatira-Hiller, Warner Bros. Best Actor: Rod Steiger in *The Heat of the Night*, Mirisch, UA.

The best actress nominees began. Jason was suddenly jarred back to reality when Kierston's name was mentioned. He squeezed her hand as the winner was announced. Best Actress: Katherine Hepburn in *Guess Who's Coming to Dinner*.

"You're a winner forever with me," Jason said, kissing her.

"We both are," Kierston said, holding his hand tightly. "We're alive."

"Conrad and I have got to get backstage," Harrington said during the next intermission. "Neither of you move until we get back. You see to it, Thomas."

"Don't worry, Harrington," Thomas said.

Jason smiled. "We're not that adventurous."

Katharine placed a hand on his shoulder. "I'm very glad to hear that."

Laster French escorted Harrington and Conrad to a side door. The auditorium crowd buzzed. Kierston and Jason avoided peoples' glances. They weren't interested in answering any questions.

"If it weren't for Conrad, I'd walk out of here now," Kierston whispered nervously.

The break ended, and Bob Hope walked to the podium. "This man needs no introduction," Hope said. Then, in an aside: "What did you say your name was?" The audience laughed as Harrington walked onto the stage. "Ladies and gentlemen, Harrington Todd."

Everyone in the pavilion stood. The ovation lasted three minutes. It looked like the Awards were going to run overtime as Harrington tried to calm the audience to no avail. They continued to applaud in spite of his pleas. He stood there taking it in, unable to do anything else. He was a star . . . glistening golden-brown hair, startling blue eyes, rugged yet elegant. Handsome and powerful, he stood for excellence, and his appearance, his presence, and his manner mirrored his beliefs.

"Thank you," he said loudly over the crowd. "Thank you." He smiled his half-cocked grin. "I've waited many years for this evening, and I am most proud that my son, Jason Todd, was able to build a humble, but appropriate, pavilion for this gathering."

A roar of laughter went through the crowd. Although blinded by the stage lights, he stared in Jason's direction, and the television cameras zeroed in on Jason's face.

"Seldom does one have the honor of paying tribute in front of the world to a man who has been such a profound influence in one's life," Harrington continued from the podium. "Without Conrad Coleman's guidance and friendship, without his gifts as a remarkable writer and director, I would not be standing here tonight. He created words; he created images—of which I have been a part. As an actor, I found no finer creative force with whom to work.

"Conrad has been challenged as a man and as a creator by the enormous pressures in our history. He's been a participant in the motion-picture industry for sixty-five years. He is more than a man for all seasons. He is more than a gifted director, writer, producer, and creator. He is a man whose soul has touched the heart of man. His influence will live on for posterity. There is no better way to show testimony than through the film clips of his most masterful motion pictures."

The theater lights dimmed and the film started to roll. Conrad's films spanned the period from the silent movie era to the present. During the five minutes of clips, the movies familiar to millions brought back a taste of nostalgia.

The Triumphant Few was highlighted, which had so deeply affected Cara that she had written to Conrad Coleman in 1929. *The Rich in Spirit* brought back memories of the Depression years and Sterling Darnley. *My Immigrant Father*, one of Cara's scripts, described an immigrant's respect for America and his loyalty to America while he fought his homeland during World War II. *The Hero* stirred up recollections of the Second World War, and the men coming home. So did *The Restless*. Cara's script, *My Sister, Kierston*, depicted the ironies of a universal theme: that death, through war or natural circumstances, was tragic— sometimes the more tragic without war. *Your Year With Mine*, another of Cara's scripts, with the pairing of Harrington and Marisa Benito, was slotted into the McCarthy Era as a message that people had to love themselves and one another to combat fear in a fearful world. *Tomorrow My Love*, another love story with Harrington and Marisa, carried a similar theme. No one had listened, however, and it was then that Conrad had created *The Invisible Power*, which had a message that was heard around the world. *Breeze*, the script Harrington wrote about Winston Jason, Jr., again, a depiction of troubled youth in a troubled time—the early 1960's. *The Accused*, again with Kierston, portrayed the stirring plight of a young white woman helping a black man in American society. *Your Year With Mine II*, was Conrad's message to America's young, through a love story, that they should work within the society and not tear it apart. And then there was *The Flowerchild*, with a similar theme told through the eyes of a liberal woman. A similar point was made with a different solution. These, plus scenes from some thirty other motion pictures, showed the life and times of a man who had been a historian of the times through his art.

When the lights came up, Conrad was standing beside Harrington. The entire audience rose to its feet, generating crashing applause.

Harrington stood aside to allow Conrad to bask in the honor he deserved. Conrad's eyes shone with emotion as the applause continued on and on until he took the podium to relay his thanks. He would have savored this moment if he weren't so worried about Jason and Kierston. 'Well, old friends,' he thought of Diana and John, 'watch over us all tonight.' Then he began.

"I'm deeply touched, thank you." His lips curved in a slight smile. His eyes scanned the audience, although he could see none of them because of the stage lights. He requested that the house lights be turned up. "I like to see to whom I'm talking," he said.

The audience laughed, having heard for years how Conrad inevitably talked face to face with an actor, never talking through an assistant.

"There you are," he said at last, scanning the crowd. Then he began: "With my successes and failures, I have had gifted artists to sustain me. Young men and women have grasped my ideas and cultivated new frontiers. They had the advantage of unfulfilled dreams to spur them on, while sometimes I felt I had none left. These young artists, like Harrington Todd, Marisa Benito, Kierston Garvin, and Burt Small have kindly stirred in me that which at times I had thought I'd lost—the ability to reach for the ideals that clarify the common denominator among us all—to communicate through our art our perceptions of human frailties and triumphs.

"Since I am more a visual than a vocal man, I thought it only appropriate that my thanks to all of you be placed on film, for this industry indeed is based on collaborative efforts . . ."

Again the lights dimmed. Conrad had worked day and night editing thousands of feet of film into three minutes. The film showed men's accomplishments as interpreted by the greatest filmmakers of all time. It was a most unusual gesture from a recipient.

Harrington returned to the stage. Unable to stop the ovation and to confer the award, he finally handed Conrad the statue without the proper presentation.

The Best Picture Award was presented: *Oliver!*, Romulus, Columbia. John Woolf. When the program ended, the television cameras closed in on Kierston and Jason, and then picked up the picture of Conrad and Harrington holding up Conrad's award in triumph.

Then Jason saw Marcus. He stood anxiously at the side door of the Pavilion auditorium below the stage with a group of plainclothesmen. Although the Awards had ended, the audience continued with the ovation. Marcus was gesturing at Jason and Kierston.

"Thank you," Conrad boomed over the audience. He and Harrington left the stage and the applause slowly died.

The audience began to talk among themselves, gathering their coats and walking into the aisles. Kierston and Jason hurried through the crowd to Marcus.

Their group hurried after them.

"We've found our answer," Marcus said succinctly as they joined him. "A helicopter is waiting on the roof's landing pad. I'm sorry Thomas, Katharine. They got the wrong man. Al Smith is still at large. We've got to get them on that copter and back to New York. We've got to hurry. Thomas, we'll be using your jet."

Katharine and Thomas kissed and hugged the young couple, as did Nicole and Michael and Bobby, and then they were escorted out.

A cool night breeze whistled around them as Jason and Kierston followed Marcus across the Todd Center West roof. Kierston's gold, beaded evening gown glistened in the dark.

Marcus spoke to them softly, away from the guards who surrounded the landing pad. "They did round up a group out at L.A. Air Research. Cubans. The L.A.P.D. has an interpreter with them now." Marcus was frustrated and furious. "I know Al's still got gunmen around. I wish I knew where. I want you in New York until this is all cleared up. Since Van Nuys Airport has been quiet, we're going to leave your plane there and put you on a copter for L.A. Air Research. The Garvin Enterprises jet is standing by.

"You two will take the first copter. Harrington and I will follow in the second. Once we're in the air, we'll decide where we're going to land in the East. It might be New Jersey."

Immediately, he helped Kierston up the stairs into the copter. Jason lingered.

"You and Father will be right behind us?"

Marcus nodded. They heard the whirling, clipping sounds of a second helicopter overhead. "Get going. That copter has to land. Laster's getting your father. We'll be right behind you. Get the jet ready for take-off." He watched Jason climb inside, then uttered the words, "Be safe," and slammed the door.

Jason and Kierston talked while the copter swung southwest.

"I was going to give you this after the party tonight," Jason said, taking out a tiny velvet box, "but now seems an appropriate time." He glanced at the stone-faced security guards, who were trying to avert their eyes. Kierston took the box and opened it. Inside was a glittering band of diamonds and emeralds. "My father gave it to my mother twenty-eight years ago." He slipped it onto Kierston's finger.

Kierston boldly kissed him on the lips, then settled in his arms. The guards nodded in approval.

Jason laughed. "I guess that means you'll marry me."

The pilot began talking into his headset as they approached Air Research, just southwest of the Los Angeles

International Airport. "Yes, Mr. Mancini, everything's in order."

The co-pilot turned and winked at Kierston and Jason. Then the pilot turned. "They lifted off five minutes ago."

Jason looked at his watch. Ten minutes had passed.

Air Research came into view below, and with it, the dim outline of the Garvin Enterprises private jet. The pilot and co-pilot of the craft were standing in the doorway of the lighted cabin. An entrance staircase was rolled up to the plane.

There was one building at the private airport, and it was dark. A gate surrounded the field. Four security guards were posted, with rifles ready, on the landing strip near where the helicopter would set down. Jason smiled to himself. Marcus was taking no chances.

The pilot circled the area once at a low altitude, using the landing lights to scan the area as a precautionary measure. A public parking lot in front of the darkened terminal building was illuminated by the glare. About twenty cars were parked for the night. All were empty. Before setting down, the pilot radioed Marcus, verifying that everything was in order and that they were ready to land.

Once on the ground, all the guards surrounded Jason and Kierston and headed towards Thomas's jet. The helicopter lifted off to make way for Harrington's copter, which was approaching momentarily.

The lone light in the aircraft directed Kierston, Jason, and the guards along the darkened field towards the jet. The pilot and co-pilot were silhouetted in the doorway of the plane.

"Everything's ready," the pilot called out. He looked up at the helicopter, a hundred feet overhead, and suddenly screamed, "My God! Watch out! Watch out!!!"

Before anyone could react, an explosion shook the ground, deafening their ears: the departing helicopter exploded in flames in mid-air, scattering metal all over the field. Gunfire rang out and tore into the security guards, wounded the pilot and co-pilot, who crumpled above them, rolling head over heels down the stairs.

Jason hurled himself on top of Kierston, knocking her to the ground. Guards around them screamed out as the unexpected bullets riddled their bodies. The chief guard fell face down beside them.

Kierston's head hit the pavement and her breath was jarred from her. A trickle of blood ran down her hair. She had just found her purse when Jason grabbed her hand, and together they crawled beneath the stairs of the jet. Gunfire flew around them, flashing into the night like deadly streams of lightening. Jason was hit in the shoulder and leg.

"Jason, you're wounded!" she whispered, then frantically ripped open her purse, took out the computer, punched a red-alert, and took out her gun.

"Lie still!" he whispered angrily.

As Jason pulled his own gun out from his shoulder holster, pain shot through his wounded shoulder. The gun dropped from his hand, clattering to the pavement. When he reached to pick it up with his left hand, the gunfire began again from behind them. He was hit a third time in the side. It ripped through his body, stunning him. He fell onto Kierston, the gun gripped in his fingers.

"We can't shoot until they're upon us," Jason whispered through his pain. "Keep down!" he told her.

Kierston felt the warmth of his blood flowing onto her body. The gun was still in her hand. Ever so gradually, he rolled off of her and landed on his stomach with a groan. She cursed the gold beaded dress, which shimmered in the night and made them an easy target. She raised her head an inch and saw two figures coming towards them. Jason saw them, too. Out of the corner of her eye, she watched him unsteadily aim his gun.

A calm spread through her body. There were footsteps behind them, too. She listened intently. There was no more gunfire, just footsteps. All their guards were wounded or dead. The figures coming towards them from the front were closer than the figures approaching from behind.

She focused on the gun in her hand and how Marcus had

taught her to use it. She didn't think of the figures coming towards her as men. They were the enemy. Something clicked in her mind. Something happened inside her body. Her hand steadied as she raised her gun and without hesitation fired at first one figure and then another. She didn't see whether they fell and didn't hear Jason's gun firing. She rolled over and fired at the two figures coming from the other direction.

Then she heard footsteps and wounded men crying out in Spanish. Wildly, Kierston maneuvered her body around. Jason lay nearly unconscious beside her. She stared in the direction of the footsteps. A figure was running towards them, his gun poised. She lifted her .45, aimed, and shot him in the chest at twenty yards.

She was holding Jason in her arms when Harrington's chopper set down. Her jaw tightened; her eyes glazed over wildly. It wasn't over. There were more! All she thought about was saving Jason. She picked up her gun and aimed.

"No!" someone cried out.

"Kierston! No! It's Father!" Jason moaned.

But it was too late. At Jason's warning, Harrington and Marcus had hit the ground. She fired just as Jason reached up with his last ounce of strength and grabbed her arm. The bullets ricocheted off the belly of the aircraft, deafening everyone.

The helicopter light settled on the jet and lit up Jason and Kierston covered with blood. She could now see Jason, and in shock, she mumbled, desperately trying to figure out where to touch, to comfort. "Look what he's done to Jason!" she screamed. "Look what he's done!!"

"No, dearest, look what he's done to you. Look what that bastard did to you!" Jason whispered, and then he lapsed into unconsciousness.

CHAPTER XXXII

"Hold those reporters back!" a burly police sergeant shouted from the emergency room door at the U.C.L.A. Medical Center. "How'd the students find out about this so quickly! Get them back!" He cursed under his breath.

Dr. Koblin rushed down the ramp to the well-lit parking lot. The copter was setting down. Marcus left the chopper first. Harrington was next. They both helped Kierston out. The crowd gasped.

"She's wounded!" a girl cried.

"Look at that blood," another screamed.

Jason was lowered onto the stretcher, an oxygen mask covering his face and an oxygen cylinder carried alongside him. On television, viewers watched Kierston Garvin, who less than an hour before had been dressed exquisitely in a gold gown, transformed into a wild woman, wearing the shreds of a blood-drenched dress.

As the stretcher disappeared inside the Medical Center, the crowd's voices soared in anger. A reporter from a local news station shoved a microphone in front of a group of male students. "Gentlemen, do any of you know Kierston Garvin?"

"Everyone knows Kierston Garvin," one of them exclaimed, angrily poking his finger at the camera. "And if anything happens to her or Jason Todd, we're going to find the people responsible and kick the shit out of 'em!" The footage was shown on the late evening news with the obscenity bleeped out.

At the Todd Center West, the guests of the Academy Awards were finally leaving backstage after press interviews and photo sessions. Conrad Coleman was among them. A reporter asked for his reaction to the Air Research shooting.

"They just left—" he stared at his watch "—why, no more than forty minutes ago! Where did you say they were being taken? U.C.L.A. Medical Center?" Conrad pushed his way through the reporters.

At seven A.M. the following morning, Kierston sat in the intensive care waiting room. She looked like a forgotten manikin in a surgeon's shirt and pants, sitting between Thomas and Katharine. Across from her sat Harrington and Marcus with Conrad. Michael and Bobby paced the room.

By the time Jason had been wheeled into surgery, he had lost a tremendous amount of blood. The doctors agreed that, until they had him on the operating table, they could not assess the extent of damage left by the bullet that had entered his side. It had shot through his chest cavity and had ripped a hole in his upper back.

Kierston refused to speak to the restless press who were set up downstairs. She had succinctly explained to the police and to the FBI agents what had happened to them at Air Research just a short eight hours earlier. She hadn't noticed the astonishment on the men's faces when she told them she had shot six men. Her thoughts were with Jason.

Harrington's eyes were fixed on Kierston. He noticed

Diana's ring, Cara's ring, on her finger and the sight nearly broke his heart. The future Kierston Garvin Todd had saved the life of Cara Franco Todd's son. He could not dismiss the thought as he studied her stoic expression.

"Miss Garvin, please follow me."

Kierston was out the door after the nurse. Jason was in a private room in ICU, with a window looking out to a nurses' station. Several rooms composed the restricted area. She walked through the door.

Jason was there, alive and breathing. He had a feeding tube into his stomach and an IV in his arm. His black hair fell against the pillow. The doctors were questioning him. She could barely hear him talk. She walked right up to the bed, ignoring Dr. Koblin. Jason stopped in mid-sentence and stared at her. His blue eyes were alert. A smile passed over his lips.

"Kierston." His eyes indicated a rollaway bed across the room. "That's for you. Sleep."

Dr. Koblin placed an arm around her. "He won't sleep until you do. He's going to be fine, Kierston." He inspected the bandages on her forehead. "How do you feel?"

Kierston said she was all right. Her eyes never left Jason's.

"He has to rest, Kierston," James Koblin said gently, beseechingly. "Please, lie down."

She could not. The doctors had to move out of the way as she bent over Jason and kissed him.

He blinked his eyes. "I love you, Kierston. Rest now."

She sat on the bed, her face rigid. Suddenly her lips began to tremble. She fought to control herself, tensing her body. James Koblin slowly pushed her back against the pillow. Only then did Jason allow his eyes to close. The doctors left them. Outside, the nurses continually monitored Jason's condition.

Kierston stared at the ceiling, a tear beaded on the side of her right eye and dropped down into her hair. Then another. She rose, pulled a chair up to the bed, and sat beside him. Curling in the chair, her hand on the bed, she felt the weight of her body overpower her will to remain awake. She was asleep instantly.

Jason's eyes opened. He nodded to Dr. Koblin, who was staring at him from the doorway. The doctor went to find Harrington and Marcus.

The two men entered the private room and walked quietly past Kierston, curled up asleep. Without a sound, they pulled two chairs up to the other side of the bed.

"Al Smith?" Jason whispered at once.

Harrington bent over to whisper in Jason's ear and explained that Al had not been found, nor was he at Air Research among the casualties.

Marcus was damned angry, without an outlet for his rage. Al Smith had fooled him and the authorities, and the results lay before him.

Jason closed his eyes momentarily, digesting the information. Then he forced them open. "Has Kierston talked about it?"

"Just to the police," he whispered. "Only the facts."

Jason blinked. "She saved my life." His hand twitched and Harrington grabbed it. "Stay put," Jason said firmly. Then he smiled. "Wait until tomorrow, we'll talk together, just you and me . . ." he glanced at Marcus, "and you . . ." His eyes fluttered shut under the influence of the medication. "Has Grandfather called?"

Harrington told him. "Yes, and he's talked to the press already. He's made it seem as though he's in danger, too, and that's why he can't come to see you. He's sending Todd Industries security out from New York right now."

"Keep them away, Marcus. I have plans, the rest of my plans. I'll tell you tomorrow." Jason was asleep.

Harrington gently placed Jason's hand on the bed. He stared at his face and then at Kierston's. Visions of last night at Air Research forced their way into his mind. The blood, the horror of it, and Kierston's words: "Look what he's done to Jason! Look what he's done!" Harrington's eyes drifted down Jason's body, which was bandaged from his shoulders to his legs.

His neck tensed, and his head began to shake in rage. Tears gathered behind his eyes and choked down in his throat. He stood abruptly, his hands shaking. Softly, he bent to kiss Jason's cheek. He knew what Jason had done and had fought to preserve. "I love you. Oh, how I love you," he whispered.

"We have to get into that 'Operations Room,'" Harrington told Marcus outside, alone in the hospital corridor.

"We need all our men here. I'll find a way to get into the Operations Room, but not now."

The following morning, Jason refused any more pain killers. Although the pain was severe, he wished to think clearly. The omnipresent bodyguards were posted outside the unit.

"Come here, bright eyes, and sit beside me."

Kierston's eyes lit up. She joined him in a chair beside the bed and kissed his hand. "You looked so angry while you were sleeping."

"Do you blame me?"

Her eyes drifted to his body and the tubes and bandages. Her exquisite face tightened in frustration and pain. It jarred him out of his own thoughts and forced him to think of her.

Although the IV inhibited him, he touched her hair at her shoulder and then covered her hand with his, feeling the engagement ring beneath his palm. "You saved my life. My wounds will heal," he said softly. "What about yours? Talk to me, Kierston. Please."

Although tears beaded her eyes, her gaze was direct and unwavering. "In the night, I did wake up with the vision before me of all those men dead on the airfield. And I thought about myself, and that I actually killed another human being. I will never regret that I did it. I only mourn that I had to." She held his hand more tightly, without realizing it. "For awhile, I'll remember that night whenever I hear the sounds of a helicopter; whenever you and I are alone on an airfield. Yet, Jason, with all that and more as a part of me now, I would do it over again."

Jason fought back a desire to destroy the world that had hurt her. "Come closer. Closer still. No, lie beside me. I don't give a damn about these tubes . . ."

Kierston's cheek was hot against his, but she did not lie on the bed. "But I do. I want you well."

His hand tightened over hers as he whispered angrily, "Goddamnit! Why did it have to be you?"

She straightened. Her heart was heavy, but her voice was firm. "You were protecting me on the airfield. In essence, you saved my life so I could save yours. You have protected me all these years. Why would you expect any less from me?"

He blinked his eyes, taking in a deep breath. His face, though edged with pain, shone with respect. "I shouldn't."

"Here they come! Here they come!"

Kierston and Harrington walked beside the wheelchair in which Jason reluctantly sat. Marcus maneuvered the chair out of the hospital doors. The Garvins, Conrad, Michael, and Bobby followed. On her doctor's orders, Nicole had returned to MicNic Ranch. She was in the middle of her pregnancy and quite upset about Kierston and Jason.

There was a long overhang outside the medical center. A driveway straight ahead was full of reporters. Thousands of spectators and fans crowded behind barricades. Three microphones were set up on a table in front of the reporters. Jason was leaving the hospital two weeks ahead of schedule. The press had questions. He and Kierston would only answer a few.

The press had been instructed to restrict their questions to the incident at Air Research, for it was feared that Jason and Kierston might still be in danger.

"How are you feeling, Mr. Todd?" a reporter from CBS national news asked.

Jason didn't hesitate. "Angry."

Reporters glanced at one another and then eagerly looked back at Jason. They anticipated the press conference would be explosive.

"Would you tell us exactly what happened on the night

of the Academy Awards just eight days ago?" Harrington's friend, Jay Gansberg from the Los Angeles *Times* called out.

The cameras zoomed in on Jason as he related the facts from the time he and Kierston left the Center to the time Kierston saved his life. The television cameras closed in on Kierston's face. Stoically, she kept her eyes riveted to Jason.

Another reporter asked, "And why did these Cuban terrorists try to kill you?"

"I can't answer that at this time," Jason said.

"You recently became CEO of Todd Industries," a reporter from the Boston *Globe* called out. "Does that position place you in potential danger?"

Jason's eyes momentarily steadied on the reporter. He was tempted to say "you're goddamn right it does," but instead, in good humor, he said: "I'm running a company, not an army."

This brought a cheer from the college students.

As a reporter called out Kierston's name, a hush came over the crowd. "Miss Garvin," the reporter shouted, "did you have to kill all those men?"

Jason's face turned rigid, but Kierston sat straight and spoke without hesitation. "No, I didn't. I could have let them murder us, instead."

A murmur went through the crowd. Students began to boo the reporters. The television cameras scanned the crowd and then returned to the table.

"It's difficult to understand, Miss Garvin," Jay Gansberg called out up front, his eyes gentle, "why anyone would wish to murder you."

Kierston's eyes flickered momentarily in sadness. "I assure you, I find it as perplexing as you do."

Aside, Jason said, "Let's go, KT."

Kierston stood and reached for Jason's crutch. They left the table. Jason had his arm around Kierston and the crutch under his right arm.

The reporters followed, baraging them with questions. They kept walking towards the Garvin Enterprises limousine.

In Jason's mind, he was thinking, 'Ladies and gentlemen

of the press, I'd like to add that there are a few men in our society, and I literally mean a few, who believe that they rule our country and have the right to control Americans by instilling fear in their minds. That fear—I am referring to that apprehension about employment, integrity in government, war, social and economic unrest—that fear confuses and frustrates the population. That is exactly the way these men wish the public to feel in order for it to remain weak. Those are the men who placed Kierston and me in jeopardy. When we could not be controlled by fear, violence was used. But we will never submit to the tactics of terrorists, whether they carry guns or wear blue business suits.' But what the hell. Who would have believed him?

The press conference was over.

Once Jason and Kierston were back in New York, Jason shifted his world into combat zones. Marcus ordered security guards already stationed in Los Angeles, San Francisco, San Jose, and New York to get into position.

The thirty-eighth and thirty-ninth floors of the Waldorf Towers, where the Garvins and Jason had their suites, became an impregnable fortress. Jason was obsessed with Kierston's safety. Harrington tried to argue against restrictions on his movements, but Jason lost control and angrily told him never to leave the thirty-eighth floor. Harrington obeyed his son's wishes.

Marcus placed Jack Combs and extra security around MicNic Ranch. Lascom literally became a *fortress*. Sy Gottleib, who had taken Al's place, oversaw Lascom security. Even Marcus was careful never to leave the Waldorf without security. Only Thomas could roam freely now. Winston needed him alive until the merger was over.

On June 5, 1968, the plan of merger was set to be voted upon by Todd Industries' and Garvin Enterprises' Boards. On the eve of the vote, after the California primary victory celebration at the Ambassador Hotel in Los Angeles, Robert F. Kennedy was mortally wounded. National businesses closed for four days as the country mourned yet another leader's death.

Winston thought back over the years to London in 1951 when Jason had spoken to Thomas Garvin. Jason had been right about television. Watching the Vietnam War on the nightly news had caused the peasants to rebel against the war. The peasants would never learn.

The Todd/Garvin Boards finally passed the merger, subject to the approval of their respective shareholders. By the first week in July, shareholders of Garvin Enterprises and Todd Industries were being mailed the Notice of Shareholders Meeting, which included a summary of the Plan of Merger, the Annual Reports of their companies, and a Management Solicitation of Proxies. In addition, biographies of Thomas and three potential directors were included. The shareholders would be voting on September 2nd at the special Todd Industries Shareholders Meeting.

The points to which Thomas and Jason paid most attention were the issues of payment and the expansion of Todd Industries's Board. The structure of the merger created an interesting future for Thomas. Within five years, with the maturity of the first series of convertible debentures, he and Jason would have control of Todd Industries. Until that five-year period expired, it was Jason's future that was on the line. Jason was gambling everything, not Thomas, because Jason would still be working at Todd Industries—if he could stay alive.

The additional proposal to expand the Board was the key to the Garvin/Todd strategy. Although they would not control Todd Industries with majority stock for five years, they hoped to control Todd Industries through the Board. If the Board was expanded to include men picked by Thomas and Jason, they would in essence have control without the shares.

During the negotiations, it was agreed that the issue of an expansion of Todd Industries's Board of Directors would be placed before Todd Industries's shareholders at the time they voted on the merger. In return, Winston had a clause inserted stating that Thomas would waive his right to veto the merger, if the merger were approved by both corporations' shareholders, but the expansion of the Board was not.

The second week in August, Thomas and Katharine flew back to California to prepare for the Garvin Enterprises Shareholders Meeting. They were heavily guarded.

Winston was gratified by all that had transpired, but lonely for Jason and furious at Al Smith. How could the idiot have almost murdered Jason?! Al knew better than to make that mistake again. If Jason died, so would Al!

It was mid-August. Winston was down in the Operations Room waiting for his final phone call from Al, who was out of the country now, in Cuba. He read the New York *Times*.

The Democrats were getting ready to descend on Chicago for the Democratic National Convention.

When the phone rang, Winston answered it swiftly. His expression was severe. "Get it right this time, Al."

"There won't be any more mistakes, I promise," Al said, his voice crackling over the wire. "I'll see you on September 3."

On Monday, August 26, the Democratic National Convention and the Todd Center in Chicago opened simultaneously. Raymond Baren and Mel Christian attended the ceremonies and returned to New York promptly afterwards.

The following day, Walter Kent walked into Jason's office escorted by Marcus. Michael excused himself and Marcus closed the door. Jason immediately offered the elderly statesman a chair.

"I'm happy to see you looking so well, Jason. Are you fully recovered?"

"Yes," Jason said, refusing to admit his shoulder still pained him. He was more interested in the meaning of Walter's presence here.

"I'm sorry, Jason," Walter said, "I can't stay. I just came from seeing your grandfather upstairs. I won't be able to vote for your side."

Jason remained standing. Everything had already been set in motion. "But two days ago you called and said you would. We'll protect you, Walter. Whatever Grandfather has on you, we'll take care of it."

Walter Kent looked grave. "I'm sorry, Jason, especially with all you've been through."

Although Walter had tried to stymie Winston, Jason's grandfather had gotten to him. When Walter left, Marcus entered.

"We knew it was coming, Jason. It's only the beginning."

Laster had been appraised by contacts at the FBI that Winston had sent agitators to the Democratic Convention in Chicago. Students gathered in Chicago to support their candidate, Eugene McCarthy, with hopes that he would be nominated as the Democratic candidate to run against Richard M. Nixon. Their enthusiasm turned to frustration when they were restricted to designated areas such as Grant and Lincoln Parks, well away from the Convention Center, and tension mounted between the press and the police.

That afternoon, millions of television viewers were watching the Democratic Convention when network coverage abruptly shifted to Grant Park. Hundreds of demonstrators, who had tried to march towards the Convention Center four miles away, were being attacked by police with rifle butts and clubs.

That evening, in Jason's suite, Kierston watched the Convention on television. The television showed one scuffle after another throughout the night, and the newly opened Todd Center was often shown.

This was not the picture that Jason had anticipated when he had convinced the Board of Directors that the opening in Chicago would be the equivalent of a multi-million dollar ad campaign.

The following morning in Malibu, Nicole, Michael, and Marisa walked slowly through the courtyard at MicNic Ranch. It was a glorious clear day. They had been discussing

Nicole's future plans. Once the baby was born, she planned to return to New York to visit Raymond and all their friends.

"Thank goodness everything will be over then," Nicole said wearily.

She wore a light, cotton, flower-print dress. In her ninth month of pregnancy, she looked more beautiful to Michael that the day they married. Hand in hand they strolled through the garden, up a hill overlooking the Pacific Ocean, and continued talking about New York.

"It isn't that I don't like it here," she said, shielding her eyes against the sun. "Marisa would like to see Harrington . . ."

"I would indeed," Marisa said, winking at Michael. "But I don't go until you do."

Michael playfully tipped the floppy hat Nicole wore to guard her white skin, which in spite of her efforts, had grown pink from the sun.

"I know, I know, you both want to be near everyone, but we'll have our time, Nicole. I promise."

She grabbed onto his arm. "Michael!"

"What!" he choked, holding her up.

Nicole was laughing. "My water broke!"

Marisa ordered the car brought around. They had practiced this procedure hundreds of times. Michael helped Nicole to the front of the Villa. Marisa was already in the back of the limousine with the guards.

Jack Combs yelled from the balcony. "Michael! Marcus is on the phone. It's important!"

Michael looked from Nicole to Jack.

"Go on, darling," Nicole urged. "You and Jack can follow right after us. I have to go!"

Michael ducked into the limousine, kissed her happily, and took off for the steps, yelling to Jack to bring around the Mercedes sedan so they could follow the women.

The moment he received Marcus's message, Michael ran frantically out into the driveway. "Jack!" he called out.

Jack skidded the car in front of the steps. Michael jumped in. "It's Al. The Malibu police stopped him on

Sunset!"

Jack skidded around the courtyard, yelled at a guard to
follow, then raced down the mountain. They traversed the
curves, skidding around the mountain's edge, and finally
spotted the limousine. It was speeding wildly around the
curves as if it had lost its brakes.

"Get in front of it!" Michael yelled.

Jack daringly took a curve on the wrong side of the road
and sped ahead, just missing an oncoming car. As they passed
the limo, Michael saw Nicole screaming in the back seat.
Marisa was trying desperately to comfort her, although she
looked scared to death. Chills ran down Michael's spine.
"Get over, Jack!" he yelled. He motioned to Nicole's driver to
try and bump into their car. Maybe they could slow down the
limo.

Below them, over the mountain ledge, the drop was two
hundred feet. Michael glanced quickly at the speedometer. It
read 50 miles an hour. The limousine bumped their car and
Jack applied the brakes as they rounded curve after curve.
Perspiration dripped from his forehead.

"I don't know if we can hold them, Michael."

They were jarred over and over but Jack kept his head
forward and his eyes intently on the road. In spite of his own
warning, Jack could feel that the cars were reducing speed.

"Keep it up!" Michael yelled.

He turned around, jarred with every bump, and had to
brace himself as he felt the car slow down. He threw a high
sign to Nicole. Marisa waved, and Nicole struggled to sit up.
They never saw the automobile coming around the curve
until it was upon them. Al Smith was driving.

"It's Al, Jack," Michael yelled. "Watch out! He's
coming right at us!" Al was obviously surprised to see their
car stopping the limo. He had been interested only in
challenging the limo in the curve to have it swerve and leap
over the edge. When he realized Jack was in front of the limo,
it was too late. His car swerved and skidded into a spin,
crashing his left bumper on the limousine, jolting it out of
control. The limo swerved, smashed against the barrier, and

sailed over the edge to the rocks below. Jack swerved out of the way just in time to keep from being hit and also sent over the cliff. Al Smith was not so fortunate.

Three hours later, in New York, Raymond Baren was ushered up to the thirty-ninth floor at the Waldorf, where he and Jason met alone. Kierston waited outside, staring at the city lights in virtual darkness, numb and disbelieving. She jumped up when Raymond entered the study. Jason stood in the doorway watching Raymond stumble into Kierston's arms.

"He murdered Nicole!"

"Oh, Raymond!" Kierston said, unable to contain her emotions. "I wish I knew how to help you!" She started crying, too, as Raymond sobbed against her chest, a broken man, just as Winston had wanted.

"I'll never see my grandchild, Kierston, never. And Michael, that poor man. . . . Excuse me, Kierston. I have to be alone."

They heard him sobbing behind the closed bedroom door.

Kierston stared at Jason in silence, tears running down her face. 'He told me this would happen. He told me what Winston could do. I've got to hold on. I must! Who would have ever believed this? We're at war within the boundaries of a civilized society. I can walk out on the street and say hello to a stranger, and that stranger can take my life. Not now,' she thought as she remembered how she had demanded to be a participant and not an observer, and then had retreated to safety. 'You can't break now,' she thought as Jason came towards her with cold eyes. 'Not now,' she thought as the ring of Nicole's laughter rang in her ears. 'You can't cry now,' she thought, seeing Marisa's smiling face and missing them so much her heart was breaking.

Jason handed her the newspaper. It was 10 P.M. on Sunday evening, the night before the Shareholders' Meeting. An exclusive interview with Winston headlined the New York *Times*. His photograph was placed above the article.

"I am deeply grieved," he was quoted as saying, "that my grandson, who is such a brilliant young executive, should be faced with the catastrophic events of the last forty-eight hours. After all his efforts, the Chicago Todd Center is standing in the midst of shambles . . ."

"Kierston?"

The newspaper fell to her side, dangling in her hand like a dead weight. She looked into the eyes of a stranger.

"I tried to build, to show the executives through my accomplishments what could be done despite Grandfather's tactics. They couldn't see it. They're scared. They have a right to be. I can't stop him—not the way he fights. I still don't know what happened to Nicole's car. Most of our strongest allies have left our side. Mel is frantic about Michael and Bobby. Raymond is broken. Walter Kent is being blackmailed and so is every other member of the Todd Industries Board. I have no choice but to go."

Kierston's heart cried out with a piercing agony and a warning which she refused to hear. "What if something happens to you?"

"Than you will be in charge."

She thought she was being strong. She held her head up. She looked at him with determination, and he stared back at her with that cruel look in his eyes. She denied herself the luxury of throwing her arms around his neck and dragging him away from all that had happened and might happen to him.

"How can you talk of your own life so casually?" she asked quietly. "Have we come so far that murder is just another word?"

"I have to go," Jason said simply.

"I want to go with you."

And he wanted to hold her, to love her, wishing that he could give her comfort. But in his mind something had clicked. If he began to look at the situation as he used to,

Winston would win; for in Winston's arena, men such as Jason had never prevailed.

Despite his thoughts, he reached out with a gentle hand and lifted the tears from her cheeks. "This is why you can't go, Kierston." He turned on his heel and walked out the door. Thomas and Harrington were waiting for him outside.

It was past midnight, just nine and a half hours before the Shareholders Meeting. From the end of Mayfair Road, in a van, in the driver's seat, Marcus watched the guard booth at the entrance to Windsor Royal. Two guards sat at a desk, clearly seen in the glow of a single lamp. Another was patrolling the entrance. Jason and Bobby watched the mansion and the grounds, by television screens hooked up inside the van, along with Thomas and Harrington.

"I can jam the alarm system any time you wish," Bobby said abruptly to Jason.

Jason picked up a microphone, which was hooked up by earphone to Laster, Jack, and Sy. "We're ready."

He counted down from ten and a blue Chevrolet rolled past the van up Mayfair Road in the dark, without showing its lights.

From the side road, two other cars met the Chevrolet at the entrance. "Now!" Jason commanded.

Bobby jammed the system at the same time Marcus's men spilled out of the cars. Using high-powered electric stun-guns, they instantaneously paralyzed all three guards. The drug would not wear off for two hours.

"Let's go!" Jason ordered from the van.

Jack and two guards took over posts at the gate while Laster and Sy drove into the estate. At a designated one-mile point, they would park their cars in a secluded area off the drive and walk to the mansion on foot with their teams.

Marcus guided the van up Mayfair Road and turned left along the side street that led around the east side of the estate. Meanwhile in the back, Bobby reactivated the alarm system.

Using the map, which hung on the van wall, Jason said, "Remember, Bobby, if anything happens to me, you enter, here." He pointed to the estate grounds, where the Barens' old cottage was located. "You have the coordinates to re-jam the system. At 1:00 A.M. sharp, turn the switch."

Bobby choked back his emotion. He still couldn't get Nicole out of his mind, nor Michael's breakdown. "Get the bastard, Jason!"

Harrington, Marcus, and Thomas had left the van and helped Jason on with his knapsack. Then Thomas handed him a rifle. They closed the van door, and Bobby fastened it from the inside.

They were outside the inner sanctum wall. Winston had obviously thought no one would wish to traverse the hilly terrain to gain entry to the inner sanctum by way of the cottages near the creek. It would take them forty minutes on foot, but it was the safest route with the fewest guards posted. Guard dogs also patrolled the area. Jason kept in contact with Laster and a third party coming in from the north by the general store and the Baren home.

Quietly, they approached the southern grounds. A soft breeze swayed the trees, rustling the branches and drowning out their footsteps.

"Did you hear something?" they heard someone ask.

Jason froze. Marcus and Thomas aimed their rifles in the direction of the voice. Harrington, who was closer to Jason, raised his rifle. They stooped down silently among the bushes near the creek.

"Wake up! Hey, old man Todd's going to be furious. You aren't supposed to be sleeping on the job!"

"He's a fool, if you ask me," they heard a guard reply. "We've been patrolling this area for months and we haven't seen a soul."

"Get on your feet!" the first man ordered.

They heard a groan and then footsteps.

"Get back over to your post. I'm going to make sure the alarm is on," the first guard said.

Jason looked at his watch. It was 1:00. He gestured to Marcus that they should try to proceed forward. Thomas shook his head vehemently and cautioned Jason to keep quiet. Almost as though his warning were an omen, they heard a guard shout: "The alarm's off. Warn the mansion!"

CHAPTER XXXIII

On September 2nd at 10:00 A.M., Conrad guided Katharine and Kierston into the Todd Center Convention Hall in Manhattan. The lobby circled around an auditorium. Marble edged up to the thick red carpet. Chandeliers glistened overhead. Groups of shareholders gathered together in small clusters.

"They're ready to begin, ladies and gentlemen. This way please," an usher at the door called out, urging everyone into the auditorium.

Kierston was dressed in a black business suit with a white blouse. Her hair, combed back, fell down to her waist, thick and straight. Her expression was professional and calm, while inside her heart was filled with sorrow for the loss of their friends, and anguish, for she had neither seen nor heard from Jason, Harrington, Thomas, Marcus or Laster.

As they walked across the marble to the carpet, the murmuring in the lobby grew louder. People stared and stepped aside in order for them to enter the auditorium where approximately a thousand shareholders were gathering.

Besides the men who had accompanied Jason to

Windsor Royal, only Kierston knew what Jason had planned. Instead of looking at the crowd, she focused on the stage. Sitting at the podium were the Chairman of the Board of Todd Industries, Winston Todd; ex Chief Executive Officer and now President, Mel Christian, Jr.; Board Secretary, former Ambassador Kent; and three other members of the Board. Raymond Baren, corporate Treasurer and Board member, and Jason Todd, Board member and CEO, were noticeably absent. Kierston thought her legs were going to give out, but the moment she felt Winston's eyes, she straightened and slowly took her seat.

Mel Christian, Jr., sounded the gavel to bring the meeting to order, but the crowd only murmured louder. Harrington and Thomas suddenly came down the center aisle and took their seats on either side of Kierston and Katharine. Jason and Raymond were crossing the stage to the podium. Winston glanced down the table towards his grandson, who seemed to ignore Winston's polite bow.

From behind, Kierston heard a man whisper that Jason had botched the opening of the Todd Center in Chicago. "And now look at him," the man whispered. "The young punk is being disrespectful to his grandfather who's done everything for him."

"Shhh!"

"I won't shhh! I'm sick and tired of these young rebels! I don't care if he has been shot. They should shoot them all."

Mel Christian, Jr., finally quieted the crowd and welcomed the shareholders to this special session. Then he introduced Winston.

Winston slouched a bit as he stood. Then he straightened, truly looking like a leader of men. His eightieth birthday was approaching. The glint in his eyes made him look much younger. Only the lines in his face, carved deep into the sides of his mouth and around his eyes, gave any indication of the traits most predominant in his personality. Today, he appeared to be in his glory. White hair and white brows against the charcoal gray suit created a stunningly masculine, commanding impression.

With unusual grace and charm, he began. "Today is a momentous occasion. Before I expound on what I consider to be one of the wisest business ventures in our company's history, I would like to break with protocol and introduce

Thomas Garvin and his family." Winston gestured in their direction. "Thomas, Katharine, Kierston . . . please stand."

Thomas helped Katharine and Kierston up, and they bowed slightly with a smile and sat down.

Winston remained poised, his eyes watchful, his lips curved into a smile as he viewed the gathering once again. "There are times in a man's life when he has the fortune of working with men of value, men of vision. The executives at Todd Industries are such men." He preceeded to introduce each member of the Board and Todd Industries' highest officials, who were sitting on the stage and at the podium.

As he continued, Thomas Garvin was calculating the number of shareholders they had lost. He had received many calls. Each director of a bank, each individual with large blocks of Todd Industries' stock who was present today had made a comment about Jason's bad luck. Some had still agreed to side with him; however, the vote would be very close. Very close indeed.

Winston finally sat down, and Mel Christian, Jr., returned to the podium. He spoke briefly about the merger. Then he asked that the shareholders hand their marked ballots to the center aisle.

Kierston had placed her name on the ballot and X'd in "yes" to the "issues of the merger" and the "expansion of the Board."

The mailed proxies had already been counted, and according to Mel Christian, Jr., favored the merger, but were running a few votes short of favoring the enlarged Board. That vote either meant a Thomas Garvin/Jason Todd takeover, or a reaffirmation of Winston Todd's supremacy.

The ballots were gathered quickly, and Ambassador Kent stood at a door to the room alongside the stage where they were to be counted, behind closed doors. Part of the Plan of the Merger established an impartial panel to handle the votes, overseen by the Todd Industries Secretary.

Mel Christian, Jr., who was devastated by Nicole's death, put up a good front as he announced that the shareholders were invited to partake in a luncheon at the headquarters' restaurant.

Winston gathered his Board members around him to speak quietly on the stage, while shareholders closest to the lobby began to file out of the auditorium. Those nearest the front began to filter down the aisle to say hello to Harrington and Kierston.

Kierston noticed that Jason had led Raymond backstage and that Mel Christian disappeared after them moments later. Then she was distracted, for the shareholders were no longer acting like shareholders but rather like movie fans.

At 1:15, the shareholders returned from lunch and again filtered into the auditorium. Mel Christian, Jr., pounded the gavel to bring order to the seated crowd. Finally silence engulfed the room. Everyone, except Raymond Baren, was on the podium now. His seat, next to Jason's, had been removed. Mel Christian made no mention of this as he began.

"Mr. Todd, Mr. Winston Todd, that is," Mel said graciously, smiling down the row of men to Jason, "has requested," he said, returning his eyes to the audience, "that we proceed with the order of business concerning the vote as quickly as possible, because, hereafter, a special Board meeting will convene." He gestured to Mr. Kent. "Ambassador Kent, would you please read the results of the vote."

Mel left the podium, and Ambassador Kent stood before the crowd. "The vote of merger has been passed." He allowed the crowd's enthusiasm to die down. "The vote for an expansion of the Board has been defeated." A low murmur was heard in the group. Jason took the news stoically. Winston rose to his feet. Ambassador Kent sat down.

At the podium, Winston smiled out at the shareholders, a happy dictator benevolent to his subjects. "I, and the members of the Board of Todd Industries, thank you for coming today. You will hear from Mr. Garvin at our next shareholders meeting in March. Unfortunately, our time is limited. As Mr. Christian said, we do have a Board meeting scheduled, where we will discuss your interests. Thank you and good day."

Without warning, reporters entered from a side door and photographers began to take pictures of those on the podium and in the front row. Thomas and Katharine stood up. Conrad and Kierston followed. All eyes turned to the stage where the Board members were heartily shaking Winston's hand. When it came to Jason's turn, he too shook Winston's hand, and the photographers snapped their pictures.

The crowd lingered, but Winston had arranged for the Board members to be ushered from the stage through a private corridor. He didn't gloat, but the light in his usually guarded eyes was triumphant. Winston was in the lead, but he turned around at the private elevators, which would take the Board members upstairs.

"Thomas, please bring your family along . . . Harrington . . . Conrad, please also join us. My assistant will show you the penthouse suites while our Board meeting is in session. It shouldn't take but a few minutes." Winston glanced at Mel Christian, Jr. "Isn't that right, Mel?"

Mel could only nod now. He was seething.

Thomas and Jason followed the others into the boardroom. As they entered, they heard Winston speaking.

"Why, Raymond, I didn't expect to see you. I certainly didn't. I'm terrible sorry about Nicole. Such a tragedy. If there's anything I can do . . ."

Jason was the last to enter. He closed the door.

Raymond's eyes were rimmed in red. He looked as though he could barely hold himself up, but managed to do so when he saw Jason.

Winston sat down in the chairman's seat. Jason sat opposite him with, Raymond to his right and Thomas Garvin to his left. The others sat according to years of habit.

"Are you sure you're quite up to this, Raymond?" Winston asked, feigning concern.

This time, Raymond stared down the table. "I'm up to it."

Thomas's respect for Raymond increased. It was an unusual gesture for a tragic man.

"To expedite matters," Walter Kent said, "I'd like to make this an oral vote on the new Chairman of the Board of Todd Industries. Are there any objections?" He looked at each member in turn. Then his eyes fell on Winston. "Do you object?" Winston shook his head no.

"In that case . . ."

Raymond Baren stood. "I'd like to case my vote first, if you don't mind."

"Of course, Raymond," Winston said, speaking over Walter. He leaned back in his chair, for he knew Raymond's vote would go to Jason. But it didn't matter now.

"Did you have a good night's rest in Manhattan?"

Raymond asked him, suddenly enraged.

"Yes, Raymond, a very good night's sleep in my Fifth Avenue apartment. Now, would you please cast your vote."

Jason eyed Raymond severely. Raymond held his emotions in check. "I cast my vote to Jason Sterling Todd."

Winston fastened his eyes on Raymond with a coolness that had once made Raymond flinch.

"Raymond Baren casts his vote for Jason Sterling Todd as Chairman of the Board," Walter Kent repeated. "Shall I now proceed with the roll call vote, Mr. Todd?" he asked Winston.

Winston nodded curtly.

"Mr. Garvin, for whom are you voting for Chairman of the Board?"

"For Jason Sterling Todd."

Mr. Kent repeated Thomas's vote, his mind on the phone call he had received early this morning from Jason.

"Mr. Kent," Winston demanded, "please proceed."

"Mr. Howard," Mr. Kent said, looking across the oval table to the middle-aged director. "For whom do you cast your vote for Chairman of the Board?"

"For Jason Sterling Todd."

Winston leaned forward. "Repeat please."

"For Jason Sterling Todd."

Winston stared at the Board member in cold contempt as Mr. Kent bypassed his own name and called out the next Board member.

"Ambassador Kent," Winston interrupted. "You forgot yourself."

'I forgot myself? Indeed I have, Winston! All these years!' He had been shocked when Marcus Mancini appeared on his doorstep in the early morning hours this morning. Then Jason's call came through to his Manhattan apartment. He was flown by helicopter to Windsor Royal. Drugged guard-dogs were being carried to kennels, drugged guards were awakening to find themselves handcuffed. It seemed like years ago that he had talked to Jason, yet it was only hours. In the interim, a lifetime of fear had been lifted off his shoulders.

"Mr. Kent!" Winston stormed. "Your vote, please!"

"I cast my vote for Jason Sterling Todd," Walter declared.

"Repeat!" Winston demanded.

Ambassador Kent stared contemptuously back at Winston. "You heard me, Winston. Jason Sterling Todd! Mr. Kelly . . . Mr. Christian . . ."

Mel had an edge to his voice as he said, "I vote for Jason Sterling Todd."

Winston didn't bother to hide his feelings. He was being betrayed, and he intended to do something about it. He allowed the meeting to continue until it came to his own vote.

"This meeting is our of order."

"You're out of order, sir!" Ambassador Kent declared. "How do you vote?"

"For myself, of course!"

"Another vote for Jason Sterling Todd," Ambassador Kent said, ignoring him.

"I said, I vote for myself!" Winston stormed.

"I have marked it that you've cast your vote for Jason Sterling Todd. That makes it unanimous. The Board has voted its new Chairman. Congratulations, Mr. Todd," Ambassador Kent said, smiling at Jason.

Winston turned vivid red and started to stand, but Jason was quicker. "I think you'd better stay where you are."

The words hung in the air.

Jason finally turned to Ambassador Kent. "Is there any further order of business that can't wait until next week?" he asked, rounding the table.

"No, I move that this meeting be adjourned until 10:00 next Monday morning," Ambassador Kent said.

"I second the motion," Raymond quipped. He rose and spit out words at Winston with quiet hatred. "You're a murderer. I have enough evidence to . . ."

"Raymond?"

Raymond looked into Jason's eyes and turned quiet. Jason would take care of everything. Jason would see to it that the bastard never hurt another living soul. Unashamedly, Raymond threw his arms around Jason, sobbing against his chest. Thomas and Mel had to lead him from the room to where Michael was awaiting them.

"I'll tell you, Thomas," Raymond cried. "You future son-in-law is quite a man."

As the Board members filtered out, they passed by Marcus and Laster French. All Winston's security was gone.

Marcus stepped inside to make Winston aware of his presence. Then he stepped outside and closed the door.

Winston sat back in his chair. "You'll never get away with this, Jason."

The remark led Jason to think about the early morning hours he had worked with Bobby.

It had taken them longer than they planned to gain entry to the Operations Room. The files had to remain in the basement, but he never wanted Winston to know that they were still at the mansion. A computer system was set up that had a scanning device and a self-destruct mechanism. After the computer was hooked to all possible accesses to the room, Jason was left alone. He devised his own combination, punched it into the main computer, and placed his hand on a designated spot to register only his fingerprints, pulse, and blood pressure. The data locked into the computer's memory bank. All the doors immediately latched shut.

From that moment, he became the only person allowed by the computer to open the Operations Room. If anyone else tried, the computer alarm would sound. If he didn't activate the safety switch within thirty seconds, the room would self-destruct.

Jason had stayed in the room for over an hour, alone with the heart of Winston's power. Winston's extensive personal espionage system was mind-boggling, even to Jason. He photocopied files pertaining to Ambassador Kent and extracted material from Diana Darnley Todd's files. Afterwards he met with Walter Kent, whom Marcus had awakened from a sound sleep and had flown to the mansion.

By the time he and Walter left the operation's room, Walter was reeling. For all those years, Walter had lived in fear of Winston having proof that he was a homosexual. Jason had read the first page of Walter's file and then closed his mind to it. He didn't need a file to know Walter Kent. Walter, Raymond, and Mel Christian received their files back immediately. The remaining Board members did not. Whether or not they received their files would depend on them.

Jason now looked down at Winston's contemptuous gaze. He turned away and walked back towards his chair.

"The press release will state that your Board remained intact, and that I was voted its Chairman and CEO with your full endorsement and blessing. It will also state that you have decided to retire to the country. On Sunday, everyone in the United Stated will read about your accomplishments through the years. In that article, you are going to give due credit to every man you bought, cheated, or blackmailed. Gradually, throughout the following months, I'm going to discredit politicians, world leaders, and businessmen who have plundered and corrupted at your order. Your name will be linked subtly to that information so that your cohorts will come to believe that you are out to destroy their power."

"I won't allow it!"

Jason ignored him and proceeded. "Through your efforts, a number of dangerous men will either come to trial or will be hunted down. Because these men will think that you have betrayed them, you will be placed in extreme danger. Your first article uncovering corporate corruption will appear in a syndicated column a week from today. From that moment on, you will be a hunted man. The members of the Board will deny any knowledge of your articles. Each article will place you in greater danger."

Winston seemed amused. "I would like to know how you swayed the Board members. I'll have them tossed out in the streets before the night is out, but I am curious."

"I'm sure it won't be long before you find out," Jason said. "Just know, it's over, Grandfather. You're very lucky that I decided what I would do when I was in a rational frame of mind. Otherwise, I'd have shot you like a common criminal! Now if you'll excuse me I have funerals to attend."

Jason started to leave, then he turned around.

"When you die, I intend to have your body cremated and sprinkled before the gates of hell. Until that time, your former cohorts will make your life so miserable you're going to wish you were already there!"

Winston met his driver outside of Todd Industries' headquarters, feeling strangely out of sorts. All his security guards were gone. Only his limousine driver remained. Once on his way out to Windsor Royal, Winston questioned the chauffeur. The driver seemed ill informed about any of the other employees. Winston was infuriated, forgetting that he had insisted over thirty years ago that Raymond Baren hire him a chauffeur who didn't think, just drove.

Minute by minute on the road out to Windsor, Winston

grew more agitated. What had happened to Al Smith? Why
did Winston feel vulnerable? He rejected the idea that Jason
had somehow gotten into his Operations Room. It was out of
the question. Still, he commanded his driver to speed up. He
had to get out to Windsor Royal.

When they reached Mayfair Road, Winston leaned
forward in the seat. The gates were open to the inner
sanctum. The guard waved to him as usual. His heart beat
unmercifully as he urged the chauffeur once again to speed
up the drive.

He almost ran down the Grand Reception Hall to the
library. Once inside, he locked the door. He breathed heavily
and had to stop and catch his breath. More slowly now, he
edged over to the secret wood-paneled door. He opened it
triumphantly and started to walk in. He almost smashed into
a solid metal door.

Jason and Kierston had arrived with Marcus by
helicopter twenty minutes before Winston. They watched
Winston on a television screen, one of many, from the control
room off the library.

Jason and Bobby and a Lascom team had set up this
system the night before. Each room on the mansion's first
floor was monitored by its own television camera, and a
monitor had been built into the control room where Jason
sat. Upstairs, Jason had placed cameras in Winston's
bedroom and two other suites including his own. He stared at
the library monitor, watching Winston panic.

Jason knew what he was thinking. The heart of his
power was down in that room, out of his reach. All the
business files, all his contacts' numbers and code names.
Everything that had kept Winston in power all these years
was stored below him in a room to which he couldn't gain
entry.

Winston stumbled out of the library. They followed his
progress on the different monitors as Winston staggered
down the corridor through the Grand Reception Hall to the
staircase. His bedroom monitor lit up. On the monitor, Jason
saw him frantically pulling open a closet that they had
overlooked. He watched Winston bend over and pull out a
file, then another and another.

"Come on!" he said to Kierston.

Marcus was beside himself. So Winston had all his

business files in the Operation's Room and had hidden the personal files in his bedroom. How in the hell could he protect Harrington from those files getting into Kierston and Jason's hands? He'd have to improvise.

They were outside Winston's room within seconds. Jason pulled out his gun and entered first. Winston had placed all the files in his fireplace and was about to burn them up.

"I wouldn't do that, Grandfather."

Winston spun around. Jason rushed into the bedroom and stood between him and the files. A match burned in Winston's hand. Marcus wished he'd throw the damn match and burn up the evidence.

"Marcus!" Jason ordered impatiently. "Would you please take Grandfather to Newport."

Marcus moved, but slowly. Jason looked at him in astonishment, then he nodded sadly to Kierston. Kierston called out.

"Laster! We need you up here."

Marcus whitened, and then he noticed Jason's eyes. They were directed at him coldly.

Kierston touched his arm as Laster led Winston out of the room. "It's O.K. Marcus . . . whatever we find."

"It's not O.K.," Jason said darkly. "Everyone out! KT, you stay." Jason sat down. He opened the first file— Harrington Todd.

Just before dawn the following morning, Jason, Kierston, and Laster took off in a helicopter from the great lawn.

Winston had refused to let Marcus and Laster take him to Newport. As per Jason's instructions, they had allowed Winston to pick his own destination—anything away from Windsor Royal.

On the ride into Manhattan, Winston had asked about Al Smith. When he found out Al was dead, Winston suffered a heart attack. He had been flown to the Todd Medical Center in Virginia where he was under a doctor's supervision. Jason refused to post guards by his door.

On the flight to the Todd Medical Center, Jason still was unable to believe how he'd been played for a fool all these years. Kierston sat silently. What could she say? When they set down on the rooftop of the Medical Center, Jason squeezed her hand, left the copter, and disappeared into the Medical Center.

Laster had found out the night shift's hours. Few doctors and nurses were on duty at 4 A.M.. Winston was monitored, but unattended.

Jason was stoic as he stood at the foot of Winston's bed. Winston looked peaceful, his large frame relaxed. Someone had combed his hair and even his commanding eyebrows. His fingernails were manicured. He wore navy blue silk pajamas with his initials, WJT.

He sensed Jason's presence in the room and his eyes fluttered open, at first curious . . . then his expression turned to fear. He tried to move his lips, then he beseeched Jason to come forward. Jason did so. "He's not the man you thought he was."

Jason straightened, his eyes blazing. "But you are."

Without another word, Jason left the room, unaware that Winston was trying to get up.

When the buzzers started blaring, Jason opened the door to the stairwell. Before it closed behind him, he heard a nurse scream. "Get the doctor! He's having cardiac arrest!"

Three hours later, Jason stood in the doorway of Windsor Royal as Harrington and Marcus drove up into the courtyard. Jason began to remember all the times Harrington had appeared uneasy: Harrington's shock at the scrapbook clipping of Vincent Morello's death; Harrington and Marcus's reaction after Sue Ann Baren's funeral, when he mentioned Vincent Morello's name; Harrington's pale expression when a crew member had said he didn't look like Harrington's son. Then there was Winston's pledge and conditions if Jason found Harrington to be a man other than who he seemed. And most of all, he had found it mystifying that he had not found these personal files in the Operations Room the night of the Windsor Royal raid. Now he knew why.

Harrington had told himself he must face Jason as he always had. Whatever Jason had found in the files, it didn't change Harrington's feelings for Jason. Somehow he would convince Jason of this—if Jason didn't hate him now.

Harrington wore jeans and cowboy boots and an open-collared white shirt. His blue eyes were filled with frank

affection as he took in Jason's figure on the front steps.
Marcus lumbered after Harrington to greet Jason, his brown
eyes steady, and a rare smile on his face.

"You're looking healthy!" Harrington said, coming up
the stairs.

"I'm feeling fine," Jason said. "I thought you might
want to spend a few hours alone."

Although he noticed that Jason's mood was unlike his
own, Harrington nodded enthusiastically. "Where is Kierston?" he asked as Jason led them into the mansion.

"She's on the veranda outside the library." Jason glanced
at Marcus. "Why don't you join her? She's been looking
forward to seeing you."

Although the words sounded genuine, the tone of
Jason's voice was shaded with a roughness. Harrington and
Marcus exchanged quick glances, and then Marcus said,
"Are you sure you are well?"

Jason was dressed in black jodhpurs, with a black shirt
and riding boots. His face showed a tension, not in the
clearness of his deep blue eyes, but in the tautness of his skin.

Jason just nodded. "Come on," he said to Harrington.
"I'm a man of leisure for a few days. Let's go riding."

"Jim!" Jason called out as he and Harrington entered
the stables. Jason walked down the corridor between the
stalls as Jim came out of his office. "Saddle up Sable Lady IV
and another horse. We're going riding."

Jim didn't budge until Jason stood before him. Then,
instead of saddling the horses, he walked around Jason,
eyeing him severely. "You can't ride in your condition." He
came back around in front of Jason and softly touched his
shoulder. Although Jason didn't flinch, Jim detected immediately that the shoulder was tender. Although this was the
most severe of his wounds, Jason's leg had also been
bothering him.

"I've tried to convince him," Harrington answered,
"but he doesn't seem to wish to listen to reason for the first
time in his life."

Jim tossed Harrington a knowing look then said to
Jason, "I'm not saddling the horses . . . you look sickly to
me." Jim glanced at Harrington. "He does look strange,
doesn't he?"

Keeping his eyes on Jason, Harrington nodded, then he noticed a photograph sticking out of Jason's pocket. "What's the picture of?"

"I'll show you later. Saddle up the horses, Jim. I've hiked over the estate in the last few weeks. A horse ride won't hurt me at all."

Jim wondered why Jason was acting so strangely, but he was more preoccupied with Jason's present expression. Jim was drawn back to when Jason was a child and in need of a man-to-man talk. There was also a coolness in Jason's eyes, and Jim decided he'd better do as Jason asked.

"All right," he conceded.

Jason noticed that Harrington was uncomfortable about the ride. "Don't you want to ride?"

Harrington's eyes flickered in concern. "Not if it causes you pain."

Jason laughed, suddenly his old self. "You and I . . . we've seen a lot of that in our lives. It has not stopped us before."

"Jason . . ."

He turned to Harrington. His expression was one of sadness and love. "Come on."

As they left the stables, and Jason settled into his saddle, he said, "A beautiful day, isn't it? Let me show you a favorite spot of mine."

They walked their horses over the great emerald lawn to the creek. They came to the clearing below the hill and rounded the huge boulder.

Jason's eyes looked upward as they ascended the mountain. He was thinking of his conversation with Kierston after reading the files.

"What is love to you, KT?"

She was surprised by his question.

"Freedom."

"Freedom?" he repeated, curious.

"Freedom to be who I am, for the one who loves me to allow me to be who I am. Freedom from the one I love, to allow me to choose what I wish to bring to a relationship; and the freedom that the one I love knows I will place restrictions on myself of my own choosing, which naturally will be compatible with his wishes. Freedom, Jason." She had taken his hand and kissed it. "Freedom, which you must give to

Harrington Todd. You love him."

"Love?" Jason asked, his eyes dark. "He lied to me, KT."

When they reached the hilltop, they dismounted. Harrington walked beside Jason, who limped along, to the cliff's edge. The entire estate was laid out at their feet.

"From here, the view places everything into perspective, don't you think? How do you feel in retrospect about all the events surrounding your life?"

Harrington turned to him. There they were on the cliff, two proud men. Harrington remembered the day he had first seen Jason. It seemed an eternity ago. He felt the weight of it, the burden of it. Instead of answering Jason's question, he asked: "Did it hurt you too much that I never visited you?"

"Only in that I missed you. But it was my decision. And each time we did see one another it was quality time. Isn't that what's important?"

"Yes." Harrington said, trying to control his emotions. "What is that picture in your pocket, Jason? Does it relate to the personal files?"

"Yes. It's a copy of a photograph of you and I and Mother."

Harrington stared at the print and almost lost his balance. He tried to speak, but the words stuck in his throat. There was Cara, his beautiful Cara, with the shiny blonde hair, the deep blue eyes so like Jason's. Her delicately chiseled face was lit up, her head tilted to one side. Harrington could almost hear her saying: "You can do it, Todd. You can do it!"

"Oh God," Harrington said, backing up and balancing himself against a boulder. His eyes filled with tears. "Jason . . ." His pain crashed around him. "I can't lose you. I can't bear to lose you now!"

Jason's voice was gentle. "What do you want to tell me?"

Harrington swallowed hard. Jason's eyes bore into him, searching his face. He had to tell Jason the truth. But when he started to speak, he could barely get out his words, "I didn't tell you, Jason . . . because . . ." Harrington stood up and grabbed Jason by the shoulders, his eyes filled with such agony that Jason could not tell Harrington he was pressing the shoulder with the wound. "I left you with him. I blamed him. I blamed the world that your mother died. She and I had something that comes along only once in a lifetime . . . but when I saw you, oh, what a magnificent child you were!" Harrington's eyes filled with brightness at the recollection. "Jason, you almost broke my heart." He shook his head. "I tried to live according to my beliefs, to be true to myself . . . but I lied to you, Jason. . . . I should have told you, but I couldn't . . ."

"What is it that you haven't told me?" Jason asked softly.

Harrington forced himself to let Jason go. He wished only to surrender to his hurt and pain, opening his heart to the man whom he had long considered his son. He stood apart. He stood proudly without even realizing it. He placed his hand to his chest, as if the words he was about to speak would mortally wound him. But he had no choice. The truth had to be told. "I am not your father, Jason. Of course you already know that after reading the files."

Jason took hold of Harrington's arm. "Come over here and sit down. I know what I've read, but I want you to tell me about it in your own words."

Harrington was surprised by Jason's reaction. He watched as Jason leaned up against the boulder. He was waiting for an explanation. What could he say? The breeze whipped around them in a sudden gush, and a chill shot down Harrington's spine. "Your mother . . ."

"Yes?"

Harrington swallowed hard, forcing himself to remember. He told Jason about Vincent Morello, the rape, his suspicions of Dr. Smith, and his opinion of foul play, although Marcus had never been able to prove it. Jason could prove it now.

"So," Jason said gently. "What did you suspect? That Winston Todd knew all along that I wasn't his grandson, but he wished an heir so badly that he took me anyway?"

Harrington considered the question and found himself confused. "Now let me think about that . . ." he said, groping. He took a few steps, pondering the question, trying to remember back to 1946 and his thoughts at that time. Suddenly he looked at Jason. "When I left you with him, I didn't think he knew. Marcus even assured me he didn't. Recently, I'd forgotten . . ."

Jason let this pass for a moment and said, "I can

understand why you didn't tell me about Vincent Morello when I was a child, and even into my teens, but when you became aware that Winston Todd knew, you should have come to me, no matter what the consequences! Didn't you know he would use that information as a weapon to destroy us if Al Smith were unsuccessful?"

"I've made mistakes, Jason. I didn't want to take the chance of losing you." Jason turned pale, and Harrington was at once at his side. "Jason? What is it, Jason? Why are you looking at me so?"

They were face to face. Jason could not speak.

Tears appeared in Harrington's eyes. "I love you, Jason. I can't allow you to carry the burden alone. No matter what I believe, nor what I would have done, things are as they stand. It doesn't matter to me whether you're my own flesh and blood.

"I feel what you feel. I believe what you believe. We are one in spirit. If part of yours dies then mine will die. If it happens, then it is right that we should be together . . . Jason, let me help you. Please, Jason, you don't look well at all."

"It was a game," Jason said so quietly that Harrington didn't hear him.

"What?"

Jason grabbed his arms. "It was a game! Mother wasn't pregnant when you married. Winston blackmailed Dr. Smith to say so. Then, when I was born, he murdered Smith to keep the secret safe and stole Smith's files. He had the hospital records altered within minutes of my birth. I was born prematurely—one month premature. He counted on the fact that you were in love, and that love would lead you to consummate your marriage. He instigated, then capitalized, on your tragedy to muddle up your minds, to dim your wits, to make you believe Mother was carrying Vincent Morello's child. He couldn't be sure it would work, but when he found it had, he was ecstatic. You misjudged him. Winston Todd would never raise a child who wasn't a Todd. It's all in his files! It is you who have been tricked. If I hadn't stumbled onto the truth, you would have gone to your grave thinking I wasn't your son, no matter what I said!"

"What? What are you saying?"

"You are my father. I am your son."

Jason raised his eyes to the sky, tears dripping down his cheeks. "He almost won! He almost took my own father from me!" He grabbed Harrington's arm and pulled himself up. "I've never suffered like you. You gave to me, thinking I was Vincent Morello's child! You loved me," Jason said, touching Harrington's shoulder. "You supported me. You even signed over the Cultural Center, when the Cultural Center was your only weapon against him. You are the most remarkable man I've ever known. I wasn't wrong about you. He was."

Harrington blinked in open astonishment at Jason's tears and the meaning of his words. Tears gushed forward, swelling behind his eyes then onto his cheeks, but he was smiling.

"You really are my son!"

Jason laughed. "Yes!"

Harrington was so stunned and so happy, he wondered what in the hell he was going to do with himself. He looked at Jason, then he glanced at the photo of Cara, Jason, and himself. Jason did have his eyes, the deep blue irises, and they did dance when he talked. People said his did, too. And there was the outline of his frame—that too was his. Hell the boy looked at lot like him. Was everyone blind? He laughed to himself. He shook his head, baffled that he hadn't seen it before. It was all so new to him. He took a couple of steps and looked down at Windsor Royal. This is where it had all begun. Now there were new beginnings. Drawn back to Jason, Harrington stared deep into his eyes.

"You know what your mother would have done?"

Jason searched his face. He had been worried about his father's reaction to the news. Now he was totally amused. Harrington would never let him down. His father's resilience was unbelievable. "No," he said at last, "what would Mother have done?"

Harrington broke into a brilliant smile. "Cara would have headed right for the typewriter and . . ."

Jason laughed. "Come on, Father, stop joking."

They walked back to their horses, Harrington with his arm around his son's shoulder.

"I mean it, Jason. You'll get script approval, of course."

"Of course," Jason said, humorously. "And we'll call it **Inherit the Storm**, right?"

Harrington threw back his head and laughed. "How did you guess!"

You, too can
INHERIT THE STORM

OFFICIAL ENTRY FORM

Last Will and Testament

I, WINSTON TODD, being of sound mind and body, hereby bequeath my mansion,

_____

(enter correct name here)

and my entire estate, to: my wife,

_____

(enter correct name here)

my son,

_____

(enter correct name here)

and my grandson.

_____

(enter correct name here)

In addition, I bequeath $5000.00 to

_____

(print your name here)

as an act of goodwill towards humanity.

To claim inheritance, fill in the information above,
or write it on a 3" x 5" piece of paper.
See other side for contest rules and mailing address.

INHERIT THE STORM
Tudor Publishing, Dept. E
255 East 49th Street
New York, N.Y. 10017

No purchase necessary.
Void where prohibited.

NAME _____

ADDRESS _____

CITY/STATE _____ ZIP _____

PHONE _____

All entries must be postmarked by
October 15, 1988.

CONTEST RULES

1. On an official entry form or a plain 3″ x 5″ piece of paper, print your name, address and telephone number and mail your entry to INHERIT THE STORM, Tudor Publishing, Dept. E, 255 East 49th Street, N.Y., N.Y. 10017. No mechanical reproduction of entries permitted.

2. Entries must be postmarked no later than October 15, 1988. Not responsible for misdirected or lost mail.

3. The winner will be determined on November 1, 1988 in a random drawing from among all entries. The winner will be notified by mail.

4. This contest is open to all U.S. and Canadian residents 18 years of age or older. Void where prohibited by law.

Employees and their families of Tudor Publishing, their respective affiliates, distributors, advertising, promotion, and production agencies are not eligible.

5. Taxes on all prizes are the sole responsibilities of the prize-winners.

6. No substitution of prizes is permitted.

7. Information necessary to fill in the blanks is available by writing to the publisher.